What people are saying about

Unexpected Dismounts

"Nancy Rue has once more proven that Christianity doesn't necessarily arrive in a double-breasted suit or wearing pearls. Sometimes it roars in on a Harley, packing more punch than a three-part sermon."

DiAnn Mills, author of *Under a Desert Sky*

Praise for ...

The Reluctant Prophet

"I love this book! Hop on and ride with this 'reluctant prophet'— but hold on tight, because the call of God not only takes Allison the Tour Guide out of her comfort zone, but the reader as well. An important novel about the awesome, quirky, breathtaking adventure of obeying God's Nudge."

Neta Jackson, author of The Yada Yada Prayer Group novels and The Yada Yada House of Hope series

"In Allison Chamberlain, Nancy Rue has created a fresh and unique protagonist to challenge all who follow Christ. How will we change the world? By being willing to leave our comfortable pews and habitual routines to truly *listen* to the voice of the Spirit ... and show the world that Jesus called us to love. Not to take care of ourselves, but to take risks in loving others. *The Reluctant Prophet* is a wonderful book with the power to changes hearts and lives."

Angela Hunt, author of *The Debt*

"In her latest novel, *The Reluctant Prophet*, Nancy Rue asks this question: What can God do with broken people? The answer Rue comes up with is humorous, hopeful, and challenging. A story to remind us that God is involved in the everyday, and in love with everyone. You'll cheer this motley band of people who decide love is more important than living a safe, easy life."

Bonnie Grove, award-winning author of *Talking to the Dead*

"If you believe following Jesus can be an exciting adventure that is baffling at times and even a little messy, with zero tolerance for self-righteous complacency, then *The Reluctant Prophet* is a book for you."

Bill Myers, author of *The God Hater*

"*The Reluctant Prophet* is a bold, wonderful novel. If you have ever felt a Nudge and thought it might be God trying to get your attention, read this book. It might just give you the courage to follow that Nudge and see where it leads. Nancy Rue writes about the tough issues of life and faith with grace, love, and daring. I am so glad God Nudged Nancy to write and so glad that she followed, Harley and all!"

Joyce Magnin, author of *The Prayers of Agnes Sparrow* and *Charlotte Figg Takes Over Paradise*

UNEXPECTED DISMOUNTS

A NOVEL

NANCY RUE

David C Cook®

transforming lives together

UNEXPECTED DISMOUNTS
Published by David C Cook
4050 Lee Vance View
Colorado Springs, CO 80918 U.S.A.

David C Cook Distribution Canada
55 Woodslee Avenue, Paris, Ontario, Canada N3L 3E5

David C Cook U.K., Kingsway Communications
Eastbourne, East Sussex BN23 6NT, England

David C Cook and the graphic circle C logo
are registered trademarks of Cook Communications Ministries.

The website addresses recommended throughout this book are offered as a
resource to you. These websites are not intended in any way to be or imply an
endorsement on the part of David C Cook, nor do we vouch for their content.

This story is a work of fiction. All characters and events are the product of the author's
imagination. Any resemblance to any person, living or dead, is coincidental.

John 13:14–15 quote taken from the Holy Bible, New International Version®,
NIV®. Copyright © 1973, 1978, 1984 by Biblica, Inc™. Used by permission
of Zondervan. All rights reserved worldwide. www.zondervan.com.
Matthew 7:15 quote taken from *The Holy Bible, English Standard
Version*. Copyright © 2000; 2001 by Crossway Bibles, a division of
Good News Publishers. Used by permission. All rights reserved.

LCCN 2011934564
ISBN 978-1-4347-6492-8
eISBN 978-1-4347-0459-7

© 2011 Nancy Rue
Published in association with the literary agency of Alive Communications,
Inc., 7680 Goddard St., Suite 200, Colorado Springs, CO 80920

C. S. Lewis quote in chapter fourteen paraphrased from *Surprised by Joy*, published
by Harcourt in 1955 © C. S. Lewis PTE Limited, ISBN 978-0-15-100185-9

William Sloane Coffin quote in chapter sixteen paraphrased from
Protestantism in America by Randall Balmer and Lauren F. Winner
© Columbia University Press, ISBN 978-0-231-11131-7

The Team: Don Pape, Jamie Chavez, Amy Konyndyk,
Nick Lee, Renada Arens, and Karen Athen
Cover Design: DogEared Design, Kirk DouPonce
Cover Photos: iStock

Printed in the United States of America
First Edition 2011

1 2 3 4 5 6 7 8 9 10

073111

*For my fellow pilgrims at Academy 31,
who have shared their Nudges, and their
Whispers, and their Unexpected Dismounts*

Acknowledgments

There are two kinds of readers—those who skip the acknowledgments and those who see them as peeks at what breathed real life into a book. If you fall into the latter category, enjoy a glimpse at the people I counted on unashamedly.

- **Rich Petrina,** who introduced me to the term "unexpected dismounts." I made several in my vain attempt to learn to ride a Harley.

- The staff at **Bumpus Harley-Davidson** in Murfreesboro, Tennessee, who provide an endless supply of information (including how to lift a fallen motorcycle *after* an unexpected dismount) and wonderful Harley-isms, and who are always willing to assist me with my Harley wardrobe. It's all about looking cute on the passenger seat.

- **Pamela Talley,** whose research assistance kept me from making up adoption details as I went along.

- **John Painter,** RNC, MSN, FNP, whose expertise kept all the medical scenes from looking as if I obtained them from an episode of *House.*

- **Jackie Colburn,** prophet and friend. It's hard to tell where one ends and the other begins.

- My Tea and Talk friends, whose input got this second book in the Reluctant Prophet trilogy under way: **Gail Seavey, Wesley Paine, Margot Baeder, Margery Mayer, Carolyn Oehler, Judy Chambers, Lisa Ellis, Kendall Hinote, Karen Dahlinger, Nancy Lown,** and **Kacky Fell.** Bright, eloquent women all.

- **The Reverend J. Mark Forrester, MDiv,** Vanderbilt University Methodist chaplain and director of the Wesley Foundation, whose sermons and spiritual direction have kept me on course, and who introduced me to the work of his mentor, **William Sloane Coffin.**

¤ **St. Augustine's Chapel, Vanderbilt University, Nashville, Tennessee,** where my feet have been washed and anointed with oil many times. Jesus was always there.

¤ The works of **Abraham Heschel,** 1907–1972, and **Rami Shapiro**, whose understanding of prophets both biblical and contemporary opened the strange new world for Allison.

¤ The entire editorial and marketing staff at **David C Cook. Don Pape,** who took a leap of faith for this trilogy. **Ingrid Beck,** whose patience with me is angelic. **Karen Stoller,** who believes enough to keep on marketing Allison et al., and **Renada Arens,** who has the thankless task of keeping me on track with details.

¤ **Jeane Wynn of Wynn-Wynn Media,** who may be personally responsible for your knowing about this book.

¤ My editor, **Jamie Chavez (www.jamiechavez.com),** who truly is one of the best in the business, and who has cared for Allison and her crew like friends.

¤ My agent, **Lee Hough,** without whom the last eight years of my career would have paled. I am blessed to have such a godly man representing me.

¤ My husband, **Jim Rue,** who takes me anywhere I want to go on his Harley. We have yet to make an unexpected dismount together.

¤ **The Academy for Spiritual Formation,** Academy 31 class, to whom this book is dedicated. I am a different kind of Christian because of them. And so is Allison.

Now that I, your Lord and Teacher, have washed your feet, you also should wash one another's feet. I have set you an example that you should do as I have done for you.

—John 13:14–15

Every time I think I'm lost, that this world's nothin' but luck God always sends someone down, just to stir things up.

—Radney Foster, "A Little Revival"

CHAPTER ONE

You'd think I would know what my next move was supposed to be.

Seriously. I found Jesus seven years ago. Two months ago I'd finally discovered what to do with him. But now, as I squinted through eyelids that were supposed to be closed in contemplation and peeked at the five women kneeling around the trunk-turned-coffee-table, I had no idea what *Jesus* was doing with *me*. For somebody who's supposed to be a prophet, that would be an important thing to know.

Hank opened her eyes and reached for the soup bowl we were using for the ashes. She *always* seemed sure of her next move, which made me wonder why she wasn't the one God picked out for the whole prophecy thing. If God had asked me, I'd have said Henrietta D'Angelo was infinitely more qualified than Allison Chamberlain. But then, I hadn't been consulted.

"My Sisters," Hank said.

The other four heads came up. Hank spread her fingers just above the fine black dust, and Mercedes eyed it suspiciously, pursing the voluptuous lips that let no mess go unscolded-at. She had scrubbed the trunk top within an inch of its gone-shabby life before we started the service, and I'd have bet money she had a sponge at the ready in her lap right now so she could wipe off any escaping specks. Mercedes could not be convinced that "Cleanliness be right next to godly-ness" wasn't a verse in the Bible.

"It was the custom among the early Christians," Hank said, "to

11

use this season of Lent to prepare new believers for holy baptism."
She swept the group with a warm gaze. "That would be you."

Jasmine's big liquid eyes, of course, spilled over. Mercedes
handed her a Kleenex.

"And it's a time for anyone who's turned away from God to
change direction and—"

"I ain't no Catholic."

We all looked at Zelda. Her face was pinched, though, granted,
some of that was due to the way she had punished her drug-broken
hair into a pitiful ponytail. But her eyes slit down even farther as she
pointed her chin at Hank like an accusing finger.

"Lent isn't just for Catholics," Hank said, with vintage patience.
That particular Jobesque quality was the reason *I* wasn't answering
the questions.

Zelda sniffed. "My granddaddy was a Mefodis' preacher and he
never did no Lent."

Sherry leaned into a shaft of noon light shooting across the tiny
living room. "Maybe he should have."

"I ain't the only one need to 'change my direction,'" Zelda
snapped back at her.

Hank folded her compact hands, my cue to take over. I did
know the answer to this one.

"Exactly," I said. "You notice that I'm kneeling right here beside
you with my own pile of stuff."

"We don't got to say it out loud, do we?" Zelda chopped her
arms into a fold across her chest. "I ain't doin' that."

Mercedes mumbled something—I thought it was "Well, you got
to do it sometime ..."—but I shook my head at Zelda. "This can be

between you and God. It's about feeling the separation and wanting to close it up."

Jasmine let a small sob escape. Zelda pulled her glasses down her nose and peered at her. "I don't got to cry, do I?"

"What you got to do is hush up so we can concentrate," Mercedes said.

I put my hand on Mercedes's arm and nodded Hank on. A smile played at Hank's lips. She probably hadn't run into this kind of discussion at Ash Wednesday services when she was an army chaplain. There wasn't a lot of saluting and accepting without question around here.

"Ladies," Hank said, "this is an invitation to continue looking at yourself and going to God with the things that are getting between you and him."

Jasmine sniffled. Zelda snorted. I squeezed the lifeblood out of Mercedes's arm.

"We'll all have the opportunity to pray and fast and think about God's Word," Hank went on. "And if we want to deny ourselves something to bring this time into deeper focus, we'll support each other in that."

"I don't got to deny my*self* nothin'." Zelda's voice was like a tight rubber band. "Y'all have done enough denyin' *for* me."

Jasmine burst completely into tears. "Miss Angel, can't you stop her?" she said to me. "She ruinin' everything."

Mercedes gave her signature mmm-*mmm,* followed by, "Somebody got to, and I know you don't want me doin' it."

Yeah, see, this was where it was blatantly obvious to me that I was not cut out to be the prophetic spiritual leader of this little band. I did okay when I actually got the Nudge from God on how to proceed in these kinds of situations. But recently God hadn't been so much with the Nudges or the shoves or, for that matter, the slightest hints.

I surveyed the full gamut of expressions in front of me: Jasmine's puffy-eyed pleading, Zelda's adolescent resentment in a thirty-year-old face, Sherry's pale but powerful I'm-about-to-smack-somebody, and Mercedes's dark, smoldering I'm-about-to-smack-*every*body. I'd have taken an out-and-out punch in the face from God right now. Since I wasn't getting that, I had to go with what I already had in the bag.

"All right, here's the deal," I said. "Every one of us is in a different place, so every one of us is going to approach this differently."

"Or not at all," Zelda said.

"Or not at all."

Sherry raised an almost-transparent white hand. "But if somebody doesn't even try, does she still get to stay? I mean, I could have this all messed up in my head, but isn't Sacrament House about wanting to get healed from all your junk?"

Zelda's face nearly came to a point. "You sayin' I ain't already workin' my steps?"

"Okay, look," I said. "We're here to go from wherever we are … to where God wants to take us. There are ways to open up to God doing God's thing in us, and that's what this is about. So, what do you say we just listen to Hank and take it from there?"

Mercedes devoured Zelda with her eyes. "In other words—"

"I don't think we need any other words on that at the moment," I said. "Hank, let's go for it."

Zelda sat back on her heels. Hank waited until Mercedes stopped breathing like a freight train and then held her square hands out, palms up, over the bowl. All the straight-up Boston smoothed from her face as she tilted her dark head back and spoke.

"Father, you have made us from the dust of the earth. Please let these ashes be a sign of our human failing and our desire to be reconciled to you. Help us to remember that it is by you that we are forever forgiven."

Finally, Sacrament House was wrapped in the cotton silence I loved. With Zelda hardening like a corpse beside me, I knew it wouldn't last long, but I settled into the moment. I hadn't done that much settling in the past few weeks. Maybe that was why it felt like God had given my assignment to somebody else, somewhere else, and I was left alone to deal with four recovering drug-addict-former-prostitutes in a thousand-square-foot house.

Just a little poke, God. It doesn't have to be Allison, go buy a Harley. *Although, if you will recall, I did that, along with everything else you've pushed me to do ...*

"You're free to just stay in this quiet space," Hank said.

I sneaked a glance at her to make sure she hadn't telepathically heard my thoughts, as, personally, I believed she did half the time. But her gaze was once more sweeping over the Sacrament Sisters.

"If you'd like to have a cross in ashes on your forehead, just nod as I touch your hand."

Jasmine was already bobbing her head and soundlessly weeping. God love her. She cried every time Mercedes smashed a cockroach in the kitchen. This was sending her right over the top. She had about thirty years of held-back tears to shed, and she'd cried only fifteen years' worth since she came off the street.

Hank dipped her thumb into the ashes and placed it against Jasmine's bronze forehead. "Remember that you are dust," she said, "and to dust you shall return."

Beside me, Zelda went so stiff I was convinced rigor mortis had set in. Hank turned to Sherry, who nodded and seemed to turn another shade of pallid as Hank pressed a cross just beneath her thin hairline. The starkness of it made her look even younger than her twenty-three years.

Mercedes didn't have to nod. She closed her eyes and lifted her face to Hank like she was waiting for a kiss. The cross nearly disappeared against her earthy skin, but I had a feeling it burned on the inside. Among the four of them, no one worked harder to own her stuff. I was convinced all Mercedes's oven scrubbing and toilet disinfecting was a reflection of the scouring going on in her soul. I felt like a slacker next to her on a daily basis.

Hank looked at me, thumb blackened and poised, and I offered her my head. I wasn't sure which was more velvety—Hank's touch or the puff of ashes themselves. "Remember that you are dust," she said.

There was no doubt about that. It struck me that maybe God had decided I was more dust than anything else, that I needed more work before I was going to be of further use.

And then it struck me that Zelda's glasses were flying across the trunk. That was how violently she was shaking her head.

"You ain't puttin' that stuff on me." She gritted what was left of her meth-rotted teeth. "I ain't no piece of dirt. I am clean and sober."

I put my hand up before Mercedes and Sherry could jump into the fray or Jasmine could go straight into hyperventilation.

"Let's go out on the porch," I said to Zelda.

Mercedes got in a "Yes, do that thing." Everyone else just breathed audible sighs as I steered the scrawny Zelda out the front door, grabbing both our jackets from their hooks on the way. It's a myth that Florida is warm year-round, at least north Florida. February in St. Augustine can get your attention, which was what I was banking on.

I drew my arms through my leather sleeves and tossed Zelda the donated denim jacket Sherry had decorated for her with fabric markers, but she flung it to the porch deck and wrapped herself into a bare-armed fold. I picked it up pointedly and wrapped it around her bony shoulders. She squinted at the floorboards.

"Do you want me to go in and get your glasses?" I said.

She gave me a lip curl, once again revealing her lack of dental work. We'd gotten her to the optometrist. The dentist was on the agenda for tomorrow. If she made it that far.

I sat on the first of the three steps and smacked the place beside me. Zelda dropped to the step below, flanked by one of Jasmine's struggling camellia bushes on each side. Even she didn't hesitate when I went into what Mercedes called my Miss-Angel-ain't-playin' mode. She had her back to me, but I let that pass.

"So what's the problem?" I said.

"I need me some space," she said. "It's too crammed-in here. I feel like I'm livin' in a can of Vienna sausages."

Now there was an image I hadn't heard before. The message, though—that I'd heard over and over from this woman.

"Sorry, Zelda," I said. "I'm only hearing new business today."

She gave me a sharp profile.

"You have a clean bed to sleep in every night. Three meals a day. Someone always available to talk you through—"

"See, that is *it,* right there."

I got a full frontal, which I stared at blankly. "That's what?" I said.

"People always in my face, wantin' me to talk." She jabbed a thumb toward the front door. "Just like that in there, tryin' to make me go on about how bad I am. I ain't no piece a dirt, just like you ain't no angel, Miss *Angel.*"

She waggled her head. I didn't bother to remind her that I hadn't given myself that name. We'd been over the fact that she was free to call me Allison. Or Wicked Witch of the West, for that matter.

"So the lack of space isn't really the problem," I said. "It's the fact that now that you aren't using, you think you're done and you don't want to work on what got you addicted to drugs in the first place."

The scowl I received was something you wouldn't want to confront in a dark alley.

I shrugged. "This isn't my first rodeo, Zelda. It's the truth, and you know it."

She squirmed inside the jacket caped around her—as much as a piece of wire can squirm—and glowered in the direction of the one forlorn palm tree stuck in the ten bedraggled feet between the house and San Luis Street.

"You used to talk nicer to me," she said.

"Back when you'd have cracked like an egg if we looked at you wrong."

"Maybe I'm still fra-gile," she said, emphasis on the *gile.*

"No, maybe you just like everybody taking care of you all the time, which is not the point of being here. We'll give you all the help you need to start walking, but we aren't going to carry you anymore." I nodded at her feet. "Where'd you get those Nikes?"

"You *know* you give 'em to me yesterday."

"*I* didn't. One of my HOG friends did, after he drove all over St. John's County collecting stuff for you ladies."

"I said thank you."

"Fabulous. Now it's time for you to get off your butt and use those shoes."

Her whole face writhed into something out of an Edvard Munch painting. "That's what I'm sayin'. You too … blunt."

"Just because Miss Angel say it like it is don't mean there ain't no love in it."

We both twisted to look up at Mercedes, who was closing the front door behind her. The fact that the Sacrament House sign on the door didn't swing reassured me that Mercedes had gotten past wanting to slap Zelda up the side of the head. The ashes must be doing their job.

"She tellin' you she loves you right now," Mercedes said to Zelda. "She just don't care if everybody don't like how she say it."

"I sure don't," Zelda said.

Her face closed off, and she got to her feet.

"Going somewhere?" I said.

"To my room. The one I got to share with somebody."

"Good choice," I said.

I waited for the door to slam, and for Mercedes to put the sign back on its nail, before I pulled my legs against my chest and sighed.

Some of the women I "got" right away. Geneveve had been like that. Jasmine and Mercedes and Sherry had taken longer, but I'd figured them out eventually, once I learned that they were more than their current issues, and that whatever operated beneath their addiction constituted their real journey. But even after two months, I didn't have a clue where Zelda was going, except maybe out the door.

Mercedes was already sitting next to me, big warm hand rubbing my leather-clad knee. "You think she gonna stay?"

"I don't know. Maybe not. Which is a horrible thought. I don't want to see her going back to West King." I ran my thumb across her knuckles. "You're officially the house Big Sister now. Tell me what you think. What does she need?"

Mercedes grunted. "She need somebody in her face twenty-four-seven. I can do a lot, but I also got my own stuff to work on. Not to sound all selfish or nothin'."

"If you don't take care of yourself, you can't take care of anybody else." I didn't add that Mercedes had been clean and in Sacrament House for only four months herself. Saying it out loud would strip my whole vision naked: that we could somehow save every woman working West King Street.

I wasn't sure we were any closer to that than we were Christmas night when Zelda had found her way to my door to join the others. Yeah, we had nonprofit status now. We had a board of people who actually gave a rip. We had my Harley-riding friends gathering clothes and food and a vast assortment of toiletries, which they delivered to the doorstep almost weekly.

But a woman I'd had so much hope for was practically out the backdoor, where it was only a three-block crawl through the gap in the fence back to the pit we were trying to keep her out of. That alone made it feel like we were going backward.

"I hate to break this up," Hank said from the door. The thing was starting to resemble a turnstile. "But you and I have a meeting, Al."

She handed me my helmet and slipped her own on.

I gave Mercedes's hand a final squeeze and stood up.

"So, whatchoo want me to do 'bout Zelda, Miss Angel?" Mercedes turned a creamy palm to me. "And don't worry, I promise I won't tie her to the bed or nothin'."

That was at least progress.

"Just love her and call her on her stuff and pray for her," I said. "That's all you can do."

When the door closed behind Mercedes, Hank pushed her visor to the top of her helmet. "You're sagging," she said.

"Is it that obvious?"

"Only to me. So what's the deal?"

"What isn't? We need more space. We need more money. We need more volunteers. We may be about to lose Zelda, and I don't feel like there's anything I can do about it."

"Which is why we're having this meeting. India says she thinks this donor she has lined up may give us enough to buy that place."

She nodded toward the house across the street.

"Are you serious?" I said.

The structure had more once-mint-green paint hanging precariously in peeled-off chips than was still attached to its cinder block walls. The roof shingles curled like a blown-dry hairdo, and the broken window sealed off with a black garbage bag gave it the appearance of a pirate who should have gone into retirement long ago. Somewhere in its history, a resident had tried to turn it into a home, as evidenced by the concrete porch lions minus their facial features and the stagnant fishpond in the middle of the front yard.

I dropped even lower.

"I know it's a fixer-upper," Hank said.

"It makes this place look like the White House."

"Nah, I think this one was worse, and you've got more people on board now to help get it into shape."

"We've got carpenters and plumbers. What we need are more people around to prevent this Zelda kind of thing from happening."

Hank poked her fingers into her glove. "Leighanne and Nita—everybody at NA—has told you we're not going to have a hundred-percent success rate."

"I hate numbers."

"I know. Which is why India is the one setting up these donor meetings, and why Bonner and Chief are there to do the talking."

"In other words, I should keep my mouth shut."

Hank's lips twitched. "Actually, India says this old lady we're seeing today is just as feisty as you are. Maybe you'll speak the same language."

"Is she old money?"

Hank nodded.

"Then she might as well be speaking Swahili."

She donned her other glove and took me by both shoulders, no easy task since she was half a foot shorter than my five-nine. "For once you might want to recall some of that old-money breeding you got in there someplace."

It was my turn to grunt as I followed her out to our bikes. "Recalling" wouldn't even begin to get me there. "Digging out with a backhoe" might come closer to doing the job.

I fastened my helmet and flung my leg over the seat of my Harley, and the bike let me hunker down on her. I settled in the minute her engine growled itself to life. Now, that was a sound like no other. The closest I could come by comparison was a powerfully attractive male calling my name. It eased me into sorting-out mode. That was what happened most times when I got ready to ride, which was why I was convinced that my Heritage Softail Classic had a soul. I never said that to anybody. A lot of people thought I was weird enough as it was.

When I got her up to second and made the first leaning turn, that was when the Pathetic Pleading Prayer kicked in: *So, God ... a Nudge? A whisper? A nod in the right direction?*

Something?

I followed Hank's lead out onto vacuous West King Street and across the dividing line that was Ponce de Leon Boulevard. The line between all the people we had yet to touch—the drug dealers and the drug users and the prostitutes who qualified as both—and the seekers of the past and the refrigerator magnet collectors on ancient St. George Street who weren't even aware that six blocks away there were people who sought only to *forget* the past, and didn't want a souvenir to remind them.

Of course, I still wasn't the steadiest rider ever to mount a motorcycle, which meant I also had to concentrate on things like squeezing the brake so I didn't mow down a coed jaywalking her way to Flagler College. That was probably why God sometimes chose those times to speak to me: because they were the few occasions when I actually shut up long enough to listen. Besides, God was the one who had put me on this thing in the first place and steered me from there to where I was going now.

And that was where exactly? India had said we were meeting at this woman's residence, which was apparently tucked into the capillaries of the historic district. Since St. George was closed to vehicles, to allow the tourists the freedom to wander from the Oldest This to the Oldest That without fearing for their pedestrian lives, Hank led me along the east side of Flagler College and up Cordova past the funky restaurants and shops travelers could come upon by surprise and think they'd discovered secret treasures. From there she took me across St. George on Treasury Street to Charlotte, with the brooding Cathedral Basilica whipping by on one side and a row of resale boutiques passing in a campy blur on the other. By the time we careened into Toques Place off Hypolita, my prayers had morphed into *please-please-please-don't-let-me-be-killed*. As for hearing God, forget about it.

Toques was little more than an alley whose drippy walls bounced our engines' roars back into my face and revved me into a near panic. I missed taking out a row of trash cans by a hair and was just about convinced that Old Lady Whoever must be a figment of everybody's imagination when Hank finally stopped. My heart was beating like a jackhammer, and I was in absolutely no shape to meet anybody with any breeding whatsoever.

"Seriously?" I whispered to God. "Ya got nothin' for me?"

The words whispered inside my helmet.

I'm giving you this: Wash their feet.

Oh.

Now, that cleared everything up.

Wash their feet? *After weeks of nothing, you're giving me 'wash their feet'?*

"You waiting for an escort, Classic?"

I jerked the wheel and started to go sideways. A long-legged man with a narrow brown-eyed gaze pushed me back to a vertical position. If an eagle had a smile, it would look like his: wise and infuriating.

"You might want to set that kickstand," Chief said.

"I *know*," I said, voice rising like it belonged to an adolescent girl who, in truth, knows nothing. "Just give me a second."

I tried to look like I was going through my mental shutdown checklist. In the first place, I hated looking like a motorcycle moron in front of Chief, a look you'd think I'd be used to achieving by now. And in the second place, I was trying to decide whether I'd heard the instruction to bathe somebody's heels or just imagined it. Though why I would have conjured up that image on my own was beyond me. I'd done a stint as a pedicurist twenty years ago and had had an aversion to feet ever since. Although, truth be told, God seldom made much sense to me at the front end of these commands.

I glanced at Chief, who was still giving me the half smile. One thing was for sure, I wasn't going to share this particular message with him until I had a handle on it. He did get me better than most people, but even he might actually move his face enough to raise an eyebrow at this one.

"They're waiting for us, Classic," he said.

He took my elbow as I climbed off the bike and steered me toward the end of the alley. I got the usual was-that-an-electric-shock?

sizzle at his touch. That, and the way he parted his lips only enough be heard by the people who were really paying attention, always sent a bit of a current through me. Curse the man.

"Where are we going?" I said.

"Around the corner. Cuna Street."

"Then this lady *must* have money."

"Oodles of it."

I smirked up at the raptor profile. "You did not just say *oodles.*"

"I'm quoting India. Where were you?"

"I had to deal with a Zelda issue," I said. "Where did Hank go?"

"Still back there combing her hair."

I noted that he'd obviously already combed his, a graying pony-tail that hung in dignified fashion between his squared-off shoulders. He'd already shed his leathers and was looking lawyerly in a crisp white shirt and red tie.

"I guess I should take off my chaps," I said, although the Target jeans I had on underneath weren't a whole lot more businesslike. India tried to dress me in outfits from her boutique, Secrets of India, but I still didn't own anything appropriate for begging money from women whose wardrobes alone were worth more than I was.

"You might want to wipe off your forehead," he said.

"It's ashes. For Ash Wednesday."

"You don't have time anyway. India's probably recycling her small talk."

"Hard to believe."

"Bonner's already oohed and ahed over every figurine in the Lladró collection."

"What in the world is Lladró?"

"Yeah, we're in trouble." Chief stopped me at the bottom of a set of much-painted wooden steps that led up to a wide, very white veranda. "You might want to let us do the talking. Unless you get one of your Nudges. Then I know there's no stopping you."

I didn't remind him that they weren't *my* Nudges. The fact that he even accepted them as somehow real and not something I pulled out of my imagination was huge for a man who consistently stiff-armed the Divine. On his best day, Chief viewed God as a worthy opponent.

"You might take off your helmet, though," he said.

I obeyed and shook my hair out and unzipped my jacket and zipped it back up again.

"Oh, let's just go in," I said. "I'm a lost cause."

Though three stories high and venerable, on the outside the house was as plain and white and gray-trimmed as a Southern gentleman. However, one step inside the massive wood-and-glass door, which a grave-looking Hispanic woman opened for us, and the effect was something out of a Victorian novel full of eccentric heiress aunts. The walls were papered in gold brocade, the ceiling hung with lead-crystal chandeliers that hungrily picked up what little light sneaked in past the layers of silk festooning the windows. If Jane Eyre had floated down the red-carpeted steps, I wouldn't have batted an eye.

The woman led us into what could only be called a parlor, complete with velvet camel-backed sofas and the scent of lavender valiantly trying to overpower the Florida mildew. Bonner Bailey, who looked starched beyond his usual real-estate-broker attire, stood before an open china cabinet cluttered with porcelain clowns and angels and horses in impossible positions. He wasn't quite tapping the toes of his loafers, but the small red smear at the top of each cheekbone spoke volumes about my tardiness.

India sat in the center of a couch, whose two ends faced each other as if to force a conversation. With luscious hair just brushing her rose pashmina shawl, she poured tea from a silver pot I was surprised she could lift and chatted away like Amanda Wingfield in *The Glass Menagerie*. There was no Allison-where-the-devil-have-you-been evident in her deep, dark eyes, but then, India had way too much class to mix irritation with china cups.

For Hank, on the other hand, "bull in a china shop" could be taken literally. She jockeyed from behind me and nearly knocked over a marble bust of some composer or other as she offered her hand to the figure ensconced in a green velvet high-backed chair.

At least, I thought there was someone there. The woman was so small I had to look twice to be sure she wasn't just a large housecat with blue-tinted fur. The cobalt frock with its ham-shaped sleeves could have just as easily been wearing *her*.

"Allison, honey," India said, voice like refined maple syrup, "I'd like for you to meet Ms. Willa Livengood." She pronounced it *liven*, though *livin'* would have fit the old lady's lifestyle better. She apparently had everything but a butler, and I wouldn't have been surprised if one had appeared, heeding the call of a bell.

"Ms. Willa, this is our Allison," India said.

"Does she have a last name?"

I stopped midway to her and stared. There was nothing frail—or syrupy—about her voice. It sounded so like a terrier barking out of its nose, I had to practically swallow my tonsils to keep from laughing.

"Chamberlain," Bonner said for me. "Allison Chamberlain."

I finally found the woman's face tucked in the middle of the mane of blueish whiteness, and I knew immediately that face wasn't happy. I didn't get the impression it always looked like it was on the edge of a snarl. This was a little something special just for me. And I hadn't even opened my mouth yet.

"Chamberlain," she said. "Any relation to Alistair Chamberlain? Of Chamberlain Enterprises?" She spat it out like it was a taste she had to get rid of.

"Alistair Chamberlain was my father," I said. "But I haven't been connected with the family or Chamberlain Enterprises for twenty-five years."

Her small dark eyes sparked at me like angry suns. The rays of wrinkles deepened. Her voice didn't.

"If you're a Chamberlain, what do you need *my* money for?"

My neck stiffened. "As I *said*, I am completely disconnected from all things Chamberlain."

"What did they do, disown you?"

"Yes," I said. "Right after I disowned them."

Her mouth went into a startled pucker, which gave me a moment to try to get my bearings. Bonner was already pinching the bridge of his nose with his fingers, and India was pushing a steaming cup toward Ms. Willa. What happened to everybody else doing the talking?

The old lady waved the teacup off with a hand so veined she seemed to have teal yarn running beneath her skin. I was actually surprised she could move it at all. There must have been fifteen carats worth of diamonds weighing down her skeletal fingers. We could slide those babies off and probably pay for *two* more houses.

"Is she telling the truth?" Ms. Willa said to Bonner.

He cleared his throat, rendering him apparently not quick enough, because she turned to Chief. "What do you know about it?"

"I'm privy to her financials, Ms. Livengood," Chief said. "She is, essentially, devoid of significant cash flow."

The shriveled thing settled back into her chair and poked a finger toward the ottoman located nearby. "Sit," she said to me.

"Don't mind if I do," I said.

I could hear Bonner clearing his throat even more emphatically, and I imagined Hank and Chief exchanging significant glances behind me. India gave up on the tea service and bit into one of the petit fours.

"Talk," the old lady barked.

India moved the cake away from her mouth, but Ms. Willa pointed at me. The stifling of moans was thunderous. None was harder to smother than the one in my own head.

But I said, "I'm sure my board members have already explained our ministry."

"This is your board?"

"Yes, ma'am."

"What kind of board rides around on motorcycles?" She eyed me shrewdly. "Don't think I didn't notice half of you came in here dressed like the Heck's Angels. And what's that dirt on your forehead?"

I didn't dare look at Chief. A guffaw at this point would not be a good idea.

"Don't let that fool you, Ms. Willa," India purred. "Miss Allison has a heart as—"

"She has a *bleeding* heart, far as I can tell." Ms. Willa waved the bejeweled hand at India without taking her eyes from me. The old lady's talons were polished to a crimson sheen.

"These women," Ms. Willa said, "don't they have food stamps and Medicaid and everything else my tax dollars are paying for?"

"Yes, ma'am, they do," I said. "We use every service available to them."

"Then again I ask: What do you need my money for?"

Bonner purged his throat yet again. I was beginning to suspect he had a hairball. "Ms. Livengood, what we're most in need of is an additional residence so we can house more women and provide them with the kind of personal assistance—"

"You want me to buy them a house."

I thumped the ottoman. "There you go. That would be fabulous."

The old lady leaned forward in her chair, leaving an indentation in the cushions just big enough for a five-year-old. "Can you prove to me that these ho-ahs aren't going to turn the building named after me into a drug den?"

It took me a few seconds to realize "ho-ahs" was Southern for "whores." India leaped into the stunned silence.

"That's the beauty of it, Ms. Willa. Once they come into the Sacrament House ministry, they can leave their old lives behind. They don't need drugs anymore."

"Nobody 'needs' drugs in the first place," Ms. Willa said. "They choose to take them, and the minute you give them everything else they want, they'll just go out and do it again. They'll be coming around here robbing our homes. I've taken to keeping a gun in the house because I *know* how these people are."

"Really," I said. "You have some drug-addicted friends, then?"

Ms. Willa drew herself up to her full sitting height, all of about four foot ten. "I most certainly do not!"

"Then how do you know 'how they are'?"

"I think what Ms. Willa is trying to say—"

Ms. Willa chopped India off with the diamonds yet again. "Don't tell me what I'm trying to say."

"Then *you* tell me, lady," I said. "Because I'm not getting how you can sit there and tell me you know all about something you haven't been within a hundred feet of."

"I read."

"Can I read a book about you and know Willa Livengood?"

"No one has written a book about me."

India tittered an octave out of her range. "I wish they would, Ms. Willa. That would be a best seller, now, wouldn't it?"

Ms. Willa ignored her this time and craned her neck at me like a ticked-off turkey. "All I know is that you *might* be able to rehabilitate a person who has turned herself over to drugs, but you cannot keep her rehabilitated. People don't change."

She sat back and pursed her lips like she was pulling a drawstring. At first all I could do was blink at her—and listen to the nervous shuffling around the room, which was enough to rattle the Lladró in its cabinet. I'd have cheerfully yanked open the glass door and let every china-faced angel jitter itself out. Until I heard it again: *Allison, wash their feet.*

Yeah. Somebody get a bucket so I can soap up this lady's gnarly old dogs. I wasn't appreciating God's sense of humor at that point.

"Maybe we should regroup here," Bonner said.

"Would some figures help?" Chief said.

"I think we all just need to take a little break and sweeten our palates," India said.

Or let's all take off our shoes. *Really? 'Wash their feet? That's all you have for me in this situation?*

"Well?" Ms. Willa was watching me, a victorious glint in her eyes.

"Well," I said. "If people don't change, then I guess we're done, because evidently I have a bleeding heart. And yours is completely anemic."

Ms. Willa gasped. Or maybe that was India. Actually it could've been anybody in the room, except Hank, who didn't appear to be breathing at all.

I wasn't sure how we got out of there. The next thing I knew we were all back in the alley with the three bikes. Hank leaned over her silver blue Sportster and laughed until I thought she was going to throw up.

"I just do not see what is so funny," India said. She tossed one end of the pashmina shawl over her shoulder and planted her hands on her hips. "You just completely blew it with a woman who probably has more money squirreled away than Bill Gates spends in a year. I don't see the humor in that."

Chief evidently did, because his eyes sparkled at me. "You sure have a way with people, Classic."

"Just people like her," I said. "I grew up with that crowd."

"You couldn't prove it by your manners." Bonner's reddish hair picked up the shaft of sunlight in the alley as he shook his head. "Seriously, Allison, did you have to tell her she was bloodless?"

"I said she was anemic."

"Oh, that's so much better. I'm surprised she didn't pull her gun on you."

"All right, listen, y'all." India swept the other end of her shawl over her arm and shifted her face from Appalled Bystander to Madam Chairperson. "This was our first try with a wealthy potential donor, and I think we learned something."

"Definitely," I said. "That I shouldn't be within a hundred yards of any of them."

"You have to be," Bonner said. "You're the heart and soul of this ministry."

"Just not the mouth," I said.

"I can help with that." India's voice had recovered its honey smoothness. "I'll coach you, Allison."

"This I have to see." Those were basically the first words Hank had spoken since we walked in Willa Livengood's door, and they were probably the most accurate. She dabbed at the laugh-tears in the corners of her eyes and supported herself on Chief's arm. Her shoulders were still shaking.

"No, really now." India's eyes begged Bonner. "Don't you think with a different kind of venue, where Allison can speak from a podium instead of—"

"Getting into discussions with anybody east of King Street?" Chief said.

"There you go." I ran my hand down my neck to smooth the quills I was sure were standing straight up.

India tucked my other hand between hers. "I've seen you be positively eloquent, Allison. You don't whine like you have a personal ax to grind. You speak for God, and that is the whole reason I came over to your side."

"We're not choosing sides," I said. "I want to get rid of the sides."

Bonner pulled off his glasses and replaced them with his Ray-Bans. The black Croakies dipped toward his shoulders. "You're going to need a nylon strap to pull Ms. Willa over."

"You can't pull a fat lady out of a doughnut store with a nylon strap," India said. "We've got to get us a chain." She finally flashed her handsome smile at me. "I'll work on that."

Chief glanced at his watch. "Look, I have to go. I've got a meeting with a judge." He backed toward the Road King. "Tell Desmond I'm sorry I couldn't come to his show, but we'll make it up tonight."

"What time is it?" I asked.

"Almost two," Bonner said. "I have to get going too."

He took India's arm, and as Chief roared out of one end of the alley, I watched the two of them stride toward the street at the other end like the pair of polished entrepreneurs they were. Surely one of them should be the spokesperson for Sacrament House. They could probably make even "Wash their feet" sound sane.

"You out of here?" Hank said, helmet under her arm.

"Yeah. Desmond's getting an art award. I promised him I'd be there."

"You okay, Al?"

I shook my head. "You keep calling me a prophet, so why don't I know how all of this is supposed to pan out?"

"Because you're a not a 'foreteller'—you're a 'forthteller.' Think in the present, not the future."

Hank watched me for a moment longer before she climbed on her bike and eased it down the alley.

The present. Did she mean the present where wealthy blue-veined women heard two words from my mouth and tucked their checkbooks back into their purses? That present?

I mounted my own bike and flipped down my visor.

"God?" I whispered. "You're going to have to be a whole lot clearer."

Then I remembered my long-ago breeding and added, "Please?"

CHAPTER TWO

I barely made it to the gym at Muldoon Middle School before the presentation started. Between having to climb over several rows of parents to find a seat on the aging bleachers, and the fact that I was still in chaps and bandanna and had an ashen cross smudged on my forehead, it was hard not to gather stares.

The only pair of eyes I cared about, though, was Desmond's. It wasn't hard to locate the big ol' head perched atop the skinny body with enough arms and legs for an octopus. Before I started having his ginger-colored Brillo pad cut every other week, Chief used to say the kid looked like a mulatto Q-tip.

He was sitting on the speakers' platform, already sending me a "Where you been, Big Al?" look and pointing at the Harley watch dangling from his bony wrist. I'd let him wear it to school only for this special occasion, since it usually provided too much of a distraction in the classroom. Although, what about Desmond *wasn't* a distraction in a seventh-grade classroom?

I grinned and motioned for him to pay attention to the fluffy woman approaching the microphone. Desmond always referred to her as Vice Principal Foo-Foo. She did sort of have the air of a Pekingese show dog, but I'd threatened Desmond with permanent loss of his motorcycle helmet if he ever called her that to her face.

While she thanked everybody and their mother for attending and sang the praises of the two art teachers, I shifted into mother mode. That was still a grinding move sometimes, since I'd only been at it for a few months. At age forty-two, it was hard to take home a twelve-year-old baby whose previous home life had consisted of abandoned storerooms and whatever food he could rip off without getting caught. The only thing harder to believe than the fact that I was this kid's current mom was the fact that he was stepping up to the microphone to receive an award for something besides the ability to charm the change out of just about anybody's pocket.

"Our first award," V.P. Foo-Foo was saying—what *was* her real name, anyway?—"goes to a young man whose artistic talent just amazes us."

"Ain't nothin' amazing about it," Desmond's voice shrilled through the mike. "It's just what I do."

The audience laughed, and Foo-Foo shuffled her notes. Desmond grabbed that opportunity to take over the sound system. "And I couldna done it without Big Al," he said. "That's my mama. Well, she almost my mama. And Mr. Schatzie. Where you at, Mr. Schatzie? Stand up and take you a bow. You, too, Big Al. Come on, both of y'all."

Down on the bottom row of bleachers, my next-door neighbor Owen Schatz rose and doffed his golfing cap, revealing a sun-leathered scalp. His dentures gleamed at the crowd like he'd coached Picasso. I only let my backside come a few inches from the bench and sank back down.

"You've got yourself a character," said the father next to me. His eyes glanced over my forehead and looked away as if he'd just noticed I had an extra nose growing there.

The woman in front of me was less appreciative. "There *are* other kids getting awards," she said, sotto voce, to her husband.

Desmond waved his blue ribbon at his adoring fans and did

some kind of hip-hop move back to his seat. I smothered my mouth with my hand and shook my head at him. He pumped the ribbon up in the air until I finally acknowledged with a large nod that he was, indeed, cooler than cool itself.

If, as the miffed mother had pointed out, there *were* other kids getting art prizes, I barely noticed. I kept my focus glued to Desmond, vigilant for signs that he might be planning to leave the platform and work the crowd like David Letterman. As soon as the other eight students, none of whom gave an acceptance speech, were in possession of their ribbons and we were free to browse through the "gallery" set up on the gym floor, I made a beeline for the kid. But by the time I reached him, he was surrounded by what he called his "women," a bevy of pubescent girls who followed him around like he was Edward Cullen. So I made instead for the aisle of portable walls where his work was displayed.

Some of it I'd seen in progress, since at home, when he wasn't wheedling for a ride with me on the Harley or finding ways to empty the snack drawer, he was drawing. Pen and ink was his current medium and caricature his style. I chortled at the faces that blossomed like comic strips on steroids from the wall before me.

He had informed me back in January, when he'd started this series, that as "a artist," he knew what features of a person's face to "blow up all big." When I'd asked if he meant "exaggerate," he'd said, yeah, that was the word, adding, "You got you a kick-butt vocabulary, Big Al."

We were still working on his.

His drawings, however, said far more than verbiage could, in my view. He had a gift for overstating the right facial features until the final portrait was fully loaded with the person's essence. At least as he saw it. Gazing at the drawings was like climbing right into Desmond's head.

Each of the Sacrament Sisters had her own piece in a four-paned panel. He'd managed to capture the sarcastic twist in Sherry's mouth and the constant pout in Zelda's. Jasmine's eyes took up most of her face and drooled oversize tears. Mercedes was all lips and in-charge eyes and held a gigantic sponge in her hand. I loved that there wasn't a trace of their pasts in sight.

When Owen caught up with me, I'd just moved on to a squatty likeness of Hank, on which everything about her, including her shiny bob of hair, was square except her mouth. Desmond had caught it midway into an overblown twitch that made me want to twitch back.

"I'm s'proud of our boy I'm about to pop my buttons," Owen said at my elbow. "I'm like a peacock strutting through here. I mean, didn't he just hang the moon?"

I didn't even try to sort through Owen's usual mishmash of metaphors. I got his drift, which essentially matched mine.

"This is pretty incredible," I said.

"It's pure genius." He waved an age-spotted hand toward a like-ness of a wizened man with a toothy grin the size of a watermelon slice. "Now, this one's new to me. I know I've seen this character, though."

"You have, Owen," I said. "In the mirror."

"Well, I'll be."

"Okay, check this out." I pointed to one of an ancient woman engulfed in her own wrinkles, with one huge ear straining for the side of the page. There was no mistaking my neighbor on the other side, whose current career was making sure I didn't turn our tiny Palm Row street into a red-light district.

"That's Miz Vernell all over, isn't it?" Owen said. "He's got her looking like an old crow. Exactly like the biddy she is."

Crow. Biddy. Next she'd be a—

"Looks like she's going to fly right out of there like a honkin' goose."

At least this time he'd kept all the similes in the same genus. Or was it class?

Owen turned to a parent who had the misfortune to stroll down our aisle and began to extol the virtues of Desmond's undeniable brilliance. I continued to soak in the drawings. One depicted Bonner in swollen sunglasses that made him cute in that preppy kind of way. Another grouped some of the members of our Harley Owners Group, each HOG resplendent with gigantic leather shoulders or a Darth Vader–sized helmet. "Mr. Chief," of course, had his own piece, bigger than most of the others because Desmond had portrayed him as larger than life. While I personally would have chosen his broad chest to exaggerate, or the crinkles of sixty-two years around his be-still-my-heart eyes, Desmond had selected the high cheekbones and the ponytail. The difference in our views of Chief was startling. To Desmond he was the bad Harley-ridin' daddy who didn't take nothin' offa nobody. To me, he was the most provocative human being who ever climbed on a motorcycle—

Okay. Don't go there.

I put both hands to my cheeks and commenced convincing myself I was just having a hot flash. It was time to locate Desmond, and I was about to turn away from the wall of drawings when one more caught my eye. The contrast between it and the rest of them was so jarring, I actually caught my breath.

It was a more distorted figure than the others and was drawn from the shoulders up. Desmond had hyperbolized a black patch over one of his subject's eyes; the other seethed. A shudder ran through me, and I wanted to turn away, but the longer I looked at it, the more it forced me to stay. Was that half of the man's head missing, or just the shadows Desmond had uncharacteristically shaded in behind him? He didn't appear to be of any race at all. He was at once wild beast and cunning human, and the only thing I was certain of was that this person wasn't anyone I knew.

But Desmond must know him, and that was more disturbing than the drawing itself.

"Owen," I said, eyes still locked on the piece. "Did Desmond tell you who this is?"

Owen turned to me, and the father he'd been holding hostage bolted for the next aisle. Owen shook his head as he scrutinized the drawing. "That's not one of his."

I stuck a finger toward the signature at the bottom—Desmond Sanborn—curled around an unmistakable Harley-Davidson logo. "He signed it," I said.

But Owen was still wagging his head. "I helped him with his whole portfolio, and this wasn't in it, unless all the icing has slipped off my cupcakes, but last time I checked, I still had all my marbles."

"Mr. Schat-*zee*."

We both turned to Desmond, who'd managed to slip up behind us despite the gargantuan proportions of his motorcycle boots. His feet were growing so fast, he was already on his second pair since Christmas.

He and Owen did their private hand-slapping combination before Desmond turned to me, grinning lobe to lobe. I did not, of course, try to hug him. We had an understanding that I didn't act like a mother in front of "other women."

"You ain't seen the one I done of you yet, Big Al," he said. He squinted at my forehead, but he didn't ask. I'd explained it to him beforehand, which apparently I should have done to the entire community.

Owen was pointing at the dark drawing, but I shook my head at him.

"Where *is* mine?" I said to Desmond.

He reached inside his sweatshirt and wafted out a page that flapped the blue ribbon attached to it.

"This what won me the prize," he said. "I call it 'Classic Mama.'"

I choked down a sudden lump and studied the drawing he presented to me. I had to admit he'd drawn me to a T. Light hair to my shoulders, about six weeks past the due date for a trim. Long face, eyebrows raised halfway up my skull, mouth in midword. He was right there: I was pretty much always telling him something, whether it was, "Keep your pickin' fingers off my Oreos," or "This is not West King Street, Clarence. We don't pee off the back stoop." He usually straightened himself out when I called him Clarence.

But what kept me staring at Desmond's caricature of me was the look in my eyes. The gaze he'd penned stared back more through me than at me, and for a very strange moment I hoped this two-dimensional figure could tell me what I was thinking.

"Looks like I got you right here," Desmond said. He tapped his palm with the index finger of his other hand.

"Dream on, kid," I said. "I am not one of your women."

His eyebrows drew in over his nose. "You dig it, though, right?"

"I definitely dig it," I said. "Is my face really that bony?"

"Them's muscles, Big Al." He cupped his hands to his own cheeks. "You got, like, somethin' strong going on here, you know what I'm sayin'?"

"Strong enough to keep you in line." I didn't actually believe that, but I figured as long as I had him fooled, he might survive on my watch until he was eighteen.

"Desmond," Owen said, "your mother and I are wondering about this particular piece."

He nodded toward the eye-patch drawing. The sheen evaporated from Desmond's eyes.

"That ain't s'posed to be here," he said. "I don't know who put it up there."

"I did."

I turned to the very round woman with the cascade of mahogany-tinted hair who was all scarflike skirts and clay bead bracelets up to her dimpled elbows. Although I remembered the clothing that looked too rich for an educator's salary, I almost didn't recognize her as Erin O'Hare, Desmond's history teacher. At our last parent conference she'd been a blonde. It must take several bottles of dye to color that mane; it was almost as long as she was tall.

Although Desmond had reported to me on more than one occasion that "Miss All-Hair'" rocked, he was now giving her the same look he gave me when I told him he couldn't watch Lady Gaga videos. It didn't seem to faze her.

"I found it under your desk when you left one day, and I asked Mrs. Pratt if she wanted to enter it." She turned to me, head first, hair following. "It shows his range, don't you think?"

"Oh, absolutely," Owen said. "This young man has more depth than the St. John's River. We're talking the Grand Canyon here. I've seen shallower wells."

Miss O'Hare only stared at him for a fraction of a second. I guessed if you taught middle schoolers all day, you heard pretty much everything.

"I'd say it was one of your best pieces," she said to Desmond, "if I had the actual subject to compare it to."

"There ain't no actual subject," Desmond said. I was glad this wasn't his English teacher we were talking to. "It's just somethin' I made up."

That may have been more disconcerting than the idea that Desmond might actually know somebody that creepy.

"Then as I understand it, we can't really consider it a caricature," Miss O'Hare said, gesturing toward it with a drapey sleeve. "Not if you don't have an objective set of physiognomic features to draw upon for reference."

Desmond's brows shot up to his mini-'fro. "You still talkin' American, Miss All-Hair?"

She wrinkled her nose at him. "That'll keep you quiet for a while."

"Good luck with that," I said.

Desmond reached for the drawing, eyes still scowling. "Imma take this down—"

"Step away from the display," Miss O'Hare said. "You'll get it back when the show's over."

He opened his mouth, obviously to protest, but I said quickly, "You better go get your stuff together. We've got to get home so you can finish your homework before we head out with Chief."

The smile sprang back to his face and he raised a hand to high-five Miss O'Hare.

"Right back at ya," she said, but he was already on his way down the aisle, one of his "women" Velcroed to each side. Maybe the momentary storm on his face had just been my imagination.

Owen also took his leave, still remarking to everyone along the way at the fathoms which Desmond's artistic talent reached. Whether they were interested or not.

"So, Miss Chamberlain."

I turned back to Miss O'Hare. "Please—it's Allison."

"Hence the 'Big Al' nickname," she said.

"I'm just grateful it isn't anything worse."

"Are you serious? He loves you. But, listen, while I have you alone …"

My antennae sprang up. "This can't be good."

"It isn't 'bad.'" She grimaced slightly. "I just wish he were doing as well in my class as he is in art."

"Is he still drawing pictures when he's supposed to be reading?" I said. "We've talked about that. Well, *I've* talked."

"No, we're okay there."

"Look, I know he thinks he can charm his way out of anything, so if that's it, I can …"

She was shaking her head, no easy task with fifteen pounds of tresses to drag along. "Desmond and I have an understanding about that. Don't tell him, but I sort of like it when he tries to butter me up. Trust me, in this job, his are some of the kindest words I hear all day. I take what I can get."

"Then what's the problem?"

"Two things actually." She held up a Sharpie-stained index finger. "One, he's at a disadvantage because he doesn't have the history background most of the other kids have just by virtue of growing up here. Somehow he missed out on all the field trips in elementary school, and he says his biological mother never took him to the Oldest School House or even the fort."

"She never took him out of West King Street," I said. "And it's been all I can do to get him to the dentist and the barber and the pediatrician."

She was nodding. "You're obviously doing a wonderful job with him."

"Just not good enough."

I started to rake my hand through my hair and realized too late that I was still wearing my bandanna as a do-rag. I knocked it off the back of my head, spastically tried to catch it, and bumped the heel of my hand against my forehead. I had an immediate visual of a three-inch smear of black ash collecting in the folds of my brow. Erin O'Hare had the good grace to act like she didn't notice.

"If you have a chance, just hit a few of the historical high spots with him," she said.

"I can do that. I actually used to be a carriage-tour guide."

"Then you could probably teach *me* a few things."

I stopped short of telling her there was a fat chance of that, since

I had neither a college degree nor her command of the English language. I was still wondering what *physiognomic* meant.

She was holding up a second finger. "The other thing is Desmond sometimes seems distracted, not by the other kids, but by whatever's going on inside his head." She gave a frustrated shrug. "I don't know exactly how to describe it, but he'll just seem especially anxious and then he'll withdraw. It's only started happening recently, and then other days, he's his usual outrageous self. Have you seen that at home at all?"

I tilted my head in thought. The only thing similar I'd seen was just a few minutes before, when he saw the drawing of Mr. Eye Patch on the wall.

"Well, in any case," she said, "it's something to think about. I only mention it because I know you're going through the adoption process, and I would hate to see bad grades go against you."

Speaking of anxious. "Do they look at that?" I said.

"I don't know, but just in case."

"I'm on it," I said.

"If you need anything, anything at all, you know where to find me." She patted my arm. "But I think you know him better than anybody."

Was that true, I wondered as I went off to pry Desmond away from his female devotees. Because at the moment, in terms of his bottomless depth, I wasn't sure I'd plumbed more than a couple of inches.

I planned to run that by Chief, the way I did most things Desmond. I thought that evening's ride out to the beach—Chief's way of making up for missing Desmond's art show—might be the perfect opportunity.

Silly woman.

In the first place, whenever Chief was around, Desmond never let more than a few inches of space exist between them. The minute Chief turned into Palm Row, Desmond was out the side door, over the porch rail, and across the lane to Chief's parking spot in front of the garage before the man pulled into it. Granted, the street was only four houses long, but Desmond did have getting to the garage in seven seconds down to a science. Or, in his case, an art form.

I joined them at a more sedate pace, carrying Desmond's gloves, scarf, and toboggan cap.

"I don't need all that, Big Al," he said, predictably. "I got my leathers."

"They aren't going to keep your fingers from freezing off," I said, and pressed his gloves into his hand.

He looked at Chief, who was wearing not only gloves but a turtleneck that nearly reached the bottom of his helmet.

"I ain't no wimp," Desmond said. "I'm only doin' this 'cause you won't let me ride 'less I do."

"That is absolutely correct," I said. "You'll thank me when that ocean air starts biting your face."

He whipped his head, which now looked three times smaller with the cap pulled over his hair, toward Chief. "You ain't playin' with me now, Mr. Chief. We for real ridin' all the way to the beach."

"All the way. We can't ride on the sand tonight because it's high tide, but we'll take A1A to Marineland and back."

"Sa-weet," Desmond whispered. It was the kind of awe a person usually reserved for rock stars and mountain ranges, neither of which

Desmond had ever seen in person. Erin O'Hare was right: He did need to get out more.

Desmond climbed on with Chief and leaned back on the "sissy bar" Chief had recently installed so the kid wouldn't drop off the back. I had to admit, as I followed them on the Classic out of Palm Row and onto Artillery Lane, that Desmond appeared to be in perfect sync with Chief. He leaned only when Chief and the Road King did, anticipating nothing, and kept his hands clamped to the sides of Chief's jacket. When they eased over the far side of the Bridge of Lions and into the relative darkness of Anastasia Island, it would have been easy to mistake them for one rider.

Anastasia was a barrier island, shielding the mainland from the brunt of the ocean's force. As the long curve onto State Road A1A brought the crests of the Atlantic into view, I started to feel a little protected myself, at least from the brunt of the day behind me. Both the beam from the St. Augustine Lighthouse and the glow of the silver-coin moon sparkled on the water, rendering its inky blackness friendly. And I could smell the brine and the fish and the sea grass. One of the things I loved most about riding a motorcycle was breathing in the life scents that were hidden like secrets from people closed up in cars.

It was easy at times like that to feel like I might get this Harley-riding thing down. It hadn't come naturally to me, the way it had to Chief and Hank and Leighanne and Nita and just about everybody else I knew who'd ever fired up a hog. But tonight I felt confident on the Classic, floating over the causeway south of Pellicer Creek with the Atlantic roiling on one side and the Intracoastal Waterway rippling in relative calm on the other. For a moment I felt more like still water than a restless sea.

Yeah. Until I followed Chief and Desmond into a now-deserted parking area at the Fort Matanzas Monument, rounded the curve, and felt the bike slide. There was no changing her mind. Even as I was going down, thigh meeting the pavement, I wondered crazily what a mini–sand dune was doing this far back from the beach.

Chief squatted beside me. "You all right?"

I had no idea, unless *mortified* was the same as *not all right,* in which case I was half-dead.

"Hey—I said, are you all right?"

"Yes," I said. "Just help me up."

"Right after I get this bike off you."

Well, yes, my 760-pound motorcycle *was* halfway on top of me. There was that.

Chief squatted with his back toward the seat, gripped the back fender and the lower handlebar, and raised the whole thing with his butt, at least as far as I could tell, without so much as bulging a vein. That probably took all of about twenty seconds, but by then I'd determined that the only thing hurt was my riding esteem.

"You done took a dive, Big Al," Desmond said.

"Ya think?" I said.

Chief let down the kickstand and squatted again to look over the bike. "Tell him what happened, Classic."

I folded my arms so Desmond couldn't see them shaking. "I used the front brake and not the rear."

"Kinda weird, huh, how you know what you doin' wrong but you do it anyway." Desmond gave a sage, helmet-clad nod. "That happen to me *all* the time."

Chief stood up and dusted the sand from his gloves. "You bent your back rest, but other than that—"

"My what?" I said.

Chief slanted his eyes briefly toward Desmond and back to me. "Your sissy bar," he said between his teeth.

"Hey," Desmond said. "Don't be callin' it that, Mr. Chief, sir. I ain't no sissy. Matter of fact, I could ride without that thing, 'cause I got me some serious balance. Sissies don't got no balance."

"Thanks," Chief said to me.

I needed to brush up on my Harley-equipment terminology.

"Can we just walk down to the beach?" I said.

"She tryin' to get outta that lecture you 'bout to give her, Mr. Chief," Desmond said.

He took off ahead of us, bouncing back and forth between the railings on the wooden walk that wended its long way down to the dunes. Chief folded his fingers around my upper arm and pulled me along beside him.

"I'm going to get one anyway, aren't I?" I said.

"One what?"

"Lecture."

"Yep."

"I *know* what I did wrong."

Chief slanted a glance at me. Another one of those mannerisms I could have recharged my phone with. "You don't want to know what you did right?"

"That would be a first."

"Once you go into a slide like that, you can't stop it. So you let it go and go down with it."

"That's what I did, all right," I said. "Will you be less impressed if I tell you I didn't do it on purpose?"

"Basically, you have to feel the bike, sense what it's going to do."

"Feel it," I said. Wonderful, seeing how my feelings had always been the last thing I could trust.

We reached the first landing on the walkway, just before it turned and buried its last steps in the dune. Below us, Desmond chased the ocean back from the sand and then turned and ran like a spindly-legged fawn to keep it from nipping at his heels. Fortunately, he'd already parked the boots up near the grass and stripped out of his leather pants, but his jeans were water-darkened from the knee down. I could hear his shrieks over the surf.

"I bet you've never dumped a bike in your life," I said, still watching Desmond cavort.

"I've had my share of unexpected dismounts."

I grinned at Chief. "How is it that a lawyer can make the lamest thing sound acceptable?"

"It came in handy when I was a public defender," he said.

He didn't grin back. Chief seldom parted with a smile. But the mirth was in his eyes as he gave my face a perusal.

"There are two kinds of riders, Classic," he said. "Those who *have* dumped a bike, and those who *will*. Now you know which category you fall into."

Yeah. I'd heard that before.

"So does this mean I've reached my quota and I'm good to go?" I said.

"It means you need to stick with me and I'll teach you everything you need to know."

Yes. Please.

We now had very little moonlight between us, just enough for me to see that Chief was looking at my lips. Close enough to make it safe for me to close my eyes—

"Hey, Big Al! I just seen a shark!"

"Really?" I could feel Chief's breath on my mouth. "*Really?*"

I backed away to lean over the railing. Desmond was flailing an arm toward the black horizon and dancing in the shallows like a marionette with a couple of strings missing.

"How could you see a shark?" I yelled to him. "It's dark as pitch out there."

"I seen it! It had a—"

The rest was lost in the crash of a wave that took him down and washed him, sputtering, up onto the beach. Chief emitted a rare guffaw.

"He can't swim," I said, and made a move toward the steps, but Chief caught my sleeve. "He's fine. He's too ornery to drown."

Desmond was indeed back on his feet and again gesticulating at imaginary fins. I looked up at Chief, but the moment had passed. It had a way of doing that. One kiss on Christmas Eve was the extent of our physical relationship so far. The way my neck was burning under my scarf … maybe that was a good thing.

"Let's walk," I said.

Chief let go of my sleeve and followed me down to the beach, though he might as well have thrown me over his shoulder. Just being on the same planet with the man made me positive he could hear me thinking, *Come over here and—do—something*. His face that near me, his eyes seeing into me that way—it was a miracle I hadn't crawled inside his jacket, Desmond or no Desmond.

Or not. Because in all truth, I couldn't. Not with the risk of Chief backing up and saying, "Are you serious? Is that what you thought this was?"

I stumbled into the sand and almost had an—what did he call them?—unexpected dismount right there. We were in serious need of a topic change.

"Desmond!" I called over the wave smashing. "We're *walk*ing, we're *walk*ing."

"Once a tour guide, always a tour guide," Chief said, eyes twinkling at me. Curse the man. He knew exactly what I was doing.

"I'm going to have to brush up on my spiel," I said, and launched too fast into a rendition of my conversation with Erin O'Hare while Desmond loped ahead of us, shaking moonlit droplets from his hair. When I included the dark drawing Desmond had wanted to rip off the display, the sparkle in Chief's eyes disappeared.

"That's not like him," he said.

"Can we even say that? I mean, seriously, do you realize how little we really know about what happened to him before he came to us—me?"

Nice. Talk about your unexpected dismounts.

"You know what Geneveve told us—you," he said.

Did he miss nothing, this guy?

"But how much time did I actually have with her once she got sober?" I said. "A month? The Sisters have told me some, mostly Mercedes. I sure don't get much out of Desmond."

"Oh, you get a lot out of him, just not about his past." Chief did grin then. "One thing you have to say about the kid: He lives in the moment."

As was currently being proven by the amount of wet sand that bagged down the seat of Desmond's jeans. The fact that the child had no hips didn't help.

"Should I tell him to pull his pants up?" I said.

"Nah," Chief said. "He'll figure it out."

"Hopefully before he steps out of them. Did his grandfather ever tell you anything about him?"

"All old Edwin ever said was that he was a good kid inside, but he couldn't take care of him anymore."

"That whole family had so much potential," I said. I had to fight down the thickness that always set in when I talked about Geneveve. "Except Geneveve's sister who took off and left her in the street with her kid. What's her name?"

"I don't think I ever heard it."

"Something pretentious sounding—like Daphne or—was it Millicent?"

"Moving on," Chief said.

"Yeah, well, she did, to Africa or someplace. Anyway, it's just hard with nobody to ask about what all he's been through."

Chief stopped and nodded my gaze to the wiry half child, half adolescent who was currently on all fours, digging in the sand like a dog.

"I don't know, Classic," he said. "Maybe his past is better left right where it is. It's his future we've got to focus on now. You remember we have a meeting with the adoption people tomorrow. Liz Doyle and Vickie—"

"Rodriguez. It's on my calendar."

One side of his mouth went up. "I hope you handle them better than you did Willa Livengood."

"Have I mentioned that you are slime?"

"Not so far tonight."

I actually opened my mouth to do it, but Chief put his fingers in his mouth and gave the Desmond whistle. Desmond turned like a drill bit in the sand and lunged toward us. I should *have* that kind of influence on the boy.

Or the man.

I managed to stay vertical all the way home, and then spent the first ten minutes after Chief left getting the sand out of Desmond's and my leathers, although Desmond had enough in the rolled-up cuffs of his jeans to make the whole kitchen floor look like Crescent Beach itself. That was helped along by the fact that he was all over the room. I hadn't seen him that agitated since the last time I took away his helmet.

"What's going on?" I said.

"Nothin'," he said.

And then proceeded to open the snack drawer, paw through the options, and shut it—which made me want to check him for fever. He went from there to the phone I'd had disconnected months before, listened like he was expecting a dial tone, and abandoned it for the basket of apples on the bistro table, fruit being a food group he'd never shown the slightest interest in, and didn't now either. The whole time, his long fingers traveled arachnid-like across the counters, and his eyes glanced off of everything and landed on none of it.

I considered telling him to light someplace, but wedging a word in was impossible, the way he was muttering under his breath. I folded my arms and leaned against the counter until he finally hiked himself up on one of the stools, lanky legs dangling, and said, "Here's the deal, Al. I keep gettin' this thing in here." He jabbed at his temple. "It's tellin' me this ain't gon' work out, you adoptin' me."

"Des—"

"It makes me wanna use the D-word and the S-word, which I ain't gonna do 'cause I done give that up. Also the B-word—"

"Got it—"

"But I got to just chill, 'cause it is gon' happen. I got you and Mr. Chief." He stopped again to flash me a grin and tapped his palm, "and I think I got that Liz lady right here."

I opened my mouth to say, "Undoubtedly," but I wasn't quick enough.

"I gotta tell you somethin', Big Al," Desmond went on, eyes wise.

"What?" I said.

"You a real good listener."

He held out his fist to bump mine and then crossed the kitchen with a new lease on the snack drawer.

For a good listener, I didn't feel all that relieved at what he'd just talked himself into.

CHAPTER THREE

When Desmond was in bed, I retreated to my second-best place to let God in. The red chair-and-a-half in the living room had been the site of Nudges and whispers in the past, so I curled up there with my Bible and an afghan and tried to close the gap that seemed to be widening between God and my growing list of questions. Zelda. All of Sacrament House, for that matter. Chief. Now Desmond, who apparently had a gap of his own that he was trying to fill by drawing threatening creatures with eye patches and ramming around the kitchen having conversations with himself.

But at first, I just stared at the wall of Desmond art that now hung above the couch. The house on Palm Row was in its third evolution of decor, at least in my lifetime. Who knew what had hung on these walls from the 1800s until my parents bought it before I was born? Since then, it had gone from my mother's dreadful reproduction of a golden age that never existed, to the bright, overstuffed comfort zone Sylvia had transformed it into when they left it to her. Its current look was Essential Big Al and Desmond.

His drawings in the bright-colored frames that HOG friend Stan had made for us. My favorite, the one that sort of looked like Chief but was Desmond's vision of God.

A red and black Harley-Davidson throw Chief had given Desmond, which the boy insisted needed to be spread on the green striped chair.

Plants Jasmine was growing for me, in pots Sherry made in the class her NA sponsor took her to weekly, placed in front of the long windows facing Palm Row and the side of Owen's place.

My life had become the people who reached out to me in this house.

The people you virtually dropped one by one on my doorstep, I said to God. *So—is it too much to ask for a little help with what to do for them now that I've let them in?*

I shifted uneasily in the chair, feeling like I was in Vice Principal Foo-Foo's office. I didn't expect ask-the-question-get-an-answer-move-on. God may have worked that way with some people, but clearly not with me. I'd learned to search the Nudges and whispers given to prophets long before me, guys who were clearly better choices for the job than I was. And I knew to center myself and leave space where I could be moved. I had even figured out that some healthy venting about the situation God had plopped me into could leave me more willing to hear his side.

I did all of it that and still nothing. Nada. I remained Nudge-less. Which usually meant to keep going with the last Nudge. But wasn't I doing that? Wasn't I helping the Sisters move toward their baptisms? And Desmond toward his, though he was admittedly several miles behind them, due to the side trips he made along the way. That was the last thing I'd clearly heard from God.

Unless you counted *Wash their feet.*

I didn't. That one had to be the result of sleep deprivation. Maybe early menopause. Or the insanity I always suspected was lurking just around the next bend.

Yeah. I woke up Thursday morning, an hour late, with a crick in my neck.

I'd left the van with Mercedes so she could take Zelda to the dentist, which meant I had to cart Desmond to school on the Harley, not the most comfortable ride with a behind bruised by last night's dismount. I made Desmond cling to me like a koala bear because Chief had removed the bent sissy bar. Another thing I had to take care of in an already crowded day.

I checked for voice mail as I watched Desmond stroll toward the school building. Our one-sided talk the night before seemed to have soothed his fears about the adoption. I could have sworn I heard him cry out once in his sleep, but when I'd peeked in on him in his room off the kitchen, he was in hibernation. Maybe it was just the Oreos he ate before I discovered he'd consumed half the package.

There was a message from India: "Honey, call me as soon as you get this," which I did before I pulled away from the school. She picked up with "Darlin', you are not gon' believe this."

"There's not much I wouldn't believe," I said. "Try me."

"Willa Livengood wants to meet with you again."

"That I don't believe."

"She called me yesterday evening, and now, I'm not saying she *wasn't* on her second glass of sherry, but she was lucid."

"How lucid?"

"Enough to say she liked your spunk."

"Then she must have been on her *third* glass. Last time I saw her she was about to throw a piece of Yardbird at me."

"Yardbird?"

"Whatever that stuff is in the china cabinet."

"My *soul,* we have a lot of work to do." I could picture India re-arranging her expression. "Now, listen. Ms. Willa told me she started thinking about it and she decided that you couldn't possibly be that much like your parents, and maybe she ought to give you another chance."

I shifted my helmet to my other hip. "What does that mean?"

"I guess we'll find out. But we definitely gon' find a different venue for it. We've got to get her off her throne. So, what if I set up a luncheon-slash-fund-raiser and have her as the guest of honor?"

"Tell me some more," I said. Any time lunch became a luncheon, I immediately had visions of my late mother serving up crustless cucumber sandwiches in the dining room on Palm Row. Not my favorite memory. Or menu.

"We'll need a program to draw people in," India said. "I could do a fashion show, maybe find us a nice string quartet."

What about a footwashing?

The Harley wobbled on its stand, and for a second I thought I'd said it out loud, but India went brightly on. Even though she was now my staunchest supporter, she was still adjusting to God telling me to buy a motorcycle. This *last* message, if it even came from God, was going to require some serious leading up to.

"What do you think?" India said.

"I'll tell you what I don't think," I said. "I don't think a fashion show and chamber music are going to get rich women to fork over cash for the Sisters of Sacrament House."

"Honey, it's what they're used to."

"Isn't the point to take them *out* of what they're used to? Seriously, what does Mozart have to do with women sleeping in gutters and eating out of Dumpsters?"

"Did you have another plan?" She still sounded India-cordial, bless her heart, but I pictured her rearranging her whole body at that point.

"Let me think about it," I said. "I've got a meeting to get to."

"Then how about this? I'll just send out a save-the-date announcement and leave the rest mysterious." She gave a ladylike harrumph. "Maybe you're right. These women could use a little mystery in their lives."

"Go for it," I said, hung up, and glanced at my watch. I needed to be at the FIP—Family Integrity Program—office in thirty minutes. Their building was only three blocks south of Sacrament House so I had time to swing by there first and see how Zelda was doing.

When I pulled up, the front door was open and I could see through the screen that Mercedes was bustling around the living room with her usual vigor amped up several notches. Not a good sign. She had either just busted somebody's chops or was about to.

But it was Jasmine who pushed the screen door open before I even reached the bottom step. I could tell she'd been crying. No surprise there.

"I heard you at the corner," she said. "We was gon' call you after you had your meetin'."

"Call me about what?" I said.

At which point she burst into tears.

"You ain't no good to nobody that way, Jasmine," Mercedes said. "Go get you a Kleenex."

"What's going on, Merce?" I said.

"Zelda."

"Is she locked in her room again?"

"No. She gone."

"Gone where?"

"Just gone. For good probably."

"How do you know that?"

"We was tellin' her las' night that she needed to get her a NA sponsor if she want to make any progress, and she just had one a her fits 'bout how we tryin' to run her life and get in her business. We tol' her she need to go deeper and she says 'I ain't deep. I'm so shallow, you couldn't go swimmin' in me.' Then Sherry start yellin' and Jasmine start cryin'. It was a mess."

"You, of course, completely kept your cool," I said.

"I almos' did, till she start talkin' trash 'bout you. Then I lost it." Mercedes went back to dusting the trunk coffee table with the vengeance of Attila the Hun. "She went all huffy to her room, and when we get up this mornin', she gone."

Jasmine emerged from the dining nook, blowing her nose. "Did you tell her what else?"

"What else?" I said.

Mercedes wouldn't meet my gaze.

"What else?" I said to Jasmine.

"She done took the money in the jar."

"That money you give me for when stuff come up, like we need a lightbulb or somethin'," Mercedes said.

"I don't know why you tol' her where it was," Jasmine said.

Mercedes gave her a black look. "What do I look like? I never tol' her. She just a drug addict thief. They can smell money inside of a steel vault."

"You think she's going to use it to buy?" I said.

"There wasn't enough in there for a fix. Besides, I don' know and I don' much care, which is why I'm cleanin' this room. I got to do some kinda penance or somethin'."

I didn't even know where to start telling her what was wrong with that theology. I had to get to the meeting or Chief was going to make *me* do penance.

"This is nobody's responsibility but Zelda's," I said. "Everyone who comes here has the choice to leave whenever she wants. Just— pray for her and I'll see if I can find her. But don't either of you go looking, are we clear?"

"Yes, ma'am," they said in unison.

"And tell Sherry that too, would you?"

"Sherry done gone to work at her daddy's," Mercedes said. "You go on now. We be fine."

I fished in my pocket and pulled out two crumpled-up twenty-dollar bills. "Put this in the jar and I'll bring you more later."

Where I was going to get more, and how I was going to locate Zelda and talk her back into Sacrament House, I had no idea. Nor did I recognize the sinking sensation that settled over me even after I was on the Harley and headed for Old Moultrie Street. It might have been a sense of failure, but who knew? I'd never cared about a job enough to give a rip whether I failed at it or not.

I leaned into the parking lot and came headlight-to-face with a startled elderly man in a business suit who was heading toward the building. He held up his briefcase like a shield and jumped out of my way, and, I was sure, staggered inside to have his coronary.

Enough, Allison. Get your mind lined up with a solution or stick it all somewhere for the moment before you mow somebody down.

Or blow this meeting.

I pulled up to the curb and hauled in a deep breath. That wasn't an option. Not this time.

Chief was already seated at the conference table in Vickie Rodriguez's office when a harried administrative aide showed me in. I could tell from the way the paperwork was lined up on the tabletop in precise piles that the aide was suffering from Boss Intimidation. When I got my first glimpse at the back of Vickie Rodriguez at the coffeepot, I saw why.

Either the woman was a former ballerina or she was wearing a steel back brace. I'd never seen a spine that straight. Atop it was a longish head on which dark straight hair had been disciplined into a French braid that dared not allow a strand to come loose. I glanced at Chief, who motioned for me to take off my bandanna. *A stop at the ladies' room would've been a nice touch,* his eyes said.

But it was too late now. The Rodriguez woman turned, stainless steel mug in hand, and looked at me and the wall clock in almost the same instant.

"Am I late?" I said. "I had to take Desmond to school and—"

"You're not any later than I am!" a voice sang out behind me.

I could have hugged Liz Doyle at that moment. She, of course, flung an arm around me and murmured, "Don't let her get to you," before she dumped her purse, tote bag, and the stack of papers that apparently fit into neither, onto the table, sending one of Vickie's neat stacks over the side.

"Oh! Sorry!" she said.

Liz's eyes, made greener by the jade jacket now pushed to a rak-ish angle, blinked at überspeed. I could never decide whether that was from stress or just a bad pair of contact lenses. She was clearly not the picture of efficiency, but somehow she managed to run the FIP's foster-care program, for which I loved her. She was responsible for getting Desmond into my home and getting this particular ball rolling as well.

Unless Stick Woman stuck her foot out and stopped it. I couldn't get rid of the image of an uptight soccer goalie as Vickie Rodriguez somehow made her way around Liz and offered me her hand.

"Miss Chamberlain?" she said.

"Yes—ma'am," I said.

Her hand was cool. Mine was invitingly clammy, I was sure.

"You can call her Allison. She's good people." Liz beamed at me and, of course, blinked. "She and I go all the way back to high school."

"Is that right?" Vickie said. I couldn't detect a trace of interest.

"She kept the bullies from making my life miserable," Liz said. "I'll never forget that."

Obviously Vickie already had because without comment she motioned me to a chair and slipped into hers while simultane-ously pulling on a pair of rectangular reading glasses and pushing the retrieved stack toward me with white-tipped nails. Was I the only woman in the city of St. Augustine who didn't get a weekly manicure?

"Let's get started," she said and flicked a glance at Chief with gray eyes that would have been pretty if she weren't using them like a laser pointer. "Mr. Ellington, I assume you have been through the forms with your client."

I did my usual double take when someone referred to Chief by his real name. He was, thankfully, in Mr. Ellington mode, and assured her that he had assisted me in filling out the forms, and that as far as he was concerned everything was in order.

"Good on my end too," Liz said. "Let me just see …"

She dug into her tote bag, and Vickie Rodriguez all but rolled her eyes.

"So, we're all set then?" I said to Ms. Rodriguez.

But Vickie only watched Liz until she produced the set of papers she was evidently waiting for. I was in agony as Vickie swept her eyes down the pages. It was all I could do not to grab Chief by the lapels and scream, "What is going *on?*"

When I couldn't hold it in any longer I said, "Excuse me. Is there a problem?"

Vickie shook her head, eyes still on the page in front of her. "No, I just didn't receive these beforehand so I need to read through." She snapped that stack to the table, picked up another, and finally said, "There are just a few potential red flags."

Chief squeezed my knee under the table. "And those would be …?" he said.

Vickie scooped up yet another set of papers and scanned the top one. It occurred to me that if in that moment she were blindfolded and asked to describe my face, she wouldn't be able to. Now, her paperwork—*that* she could have probably recited without missing a syllable.

"Your job description indicates that you work with recovering prostitutes." Vickie's eyes flashed at me and down again. "You don't have any currently living in your home, do you?"

"No, ma'am," I said. "They have their own residence."

"But you had them residing with you at your address on Palm Row at one time."

I looked at Chief, who nodded.

"I did," I said, "before the Sacrament House Ministry was formed and they moved over there."

"And you do have another form of transportation besides your motorcycle?"

"Uh, yeah—yes, ma'am."

I was back in Vice Principal Foo-Foo's office.

Vickie finally looked at me over the top of her glasses, gaze resting somewhere around my upper lip.

"I have a van," I said. "Well, the ministry has a van that I owned and then donated. I have access to it."

An eyebrow went up.

"All the time," I said.

Chief squeezed my leg again, which I was sure meant, *Do not tell her Mercedes has had it for a week.*

"Now in terms of financial support."

Vickie fanned through the pages she was holding, gave her brow permission to furrow only slightly, and picked up the final stack. I resisted the urge to wipe off the beads of sweat she had stared out of my upper lip.

"You are the founder and director of Sacrament House."

"Yes, ma'am."

"That sounds impressive, but I don't see a salary listed here."

"I don't draw one. Yet."

"Miss Chamberlain is currently working pro bono," Chief said. "As more funding is acquired for the nonprofit, she'll be a paid employee."

He sounded so sure. Vickie Rodriguez, not so much.

"And in the meantime?" she said.

"In the meantime, Miss Chamberlain's inheritance from Sylvia Mancini is sufficient to support her and Desmond."

"That isn't going to last forever."

"Nor does it need to."

"Health insurance? Oh, I see that you have the adoptee on your policy."

The back of my neck bristled. "The 'adoptee'?" I said.

I could almost hear Chief groaning, but honestly—

"I apologize," Vickie said, with no audible signs of remorse. "Desmond. He's referred to here as 'the adoptee,' so I—"

"Then might I suggest that you get your nose out of your paperwork and look at me so you can tell what kind of mother I'm going to be?"

Chief sat back in his chair. Liz came forward in hers.

"She doesn't mean to be impersonal, Allison," she said. "It's just that—"

"I can answer for myself." Vickie Rodriguez lowered the forms to the tabletop and set her glasses on top of them. "I don't have to look at you to know what kind of mother you're going to be, Miss Chamberlain. Anyone who would voluntarily take on a twelve-year-old mixed-race boy with the kind of background he has is already mother of the year, as far as I personally am concerned."

I felt my lower jaw drop.

"The judge, on the other hand, is going to want every *i* dotted and every *t* crossed before he'll grant the adoption."

"The judge?" I said.

"I told you—" Liz started to say.

"It will merely be a formality if he feels that everything is in perfect order. So, if we could continue?"

"Absolutely," Chief said.

He didn't have to torture my leg again. I was still sitting there with my mouth hanging open.

The glasses went back on. "You own a home free and clear, in a decent neighborhood."

"It's a little more than decent," Liz put in. Was that a pout I saw?

"The biological mother, Geneveve Sanborn, is deceased."

"Before her death she stated in a legal document that she wanted Desmond put in Miss Chamberlain's care," Chief said.

"I see that the father is 'unknown.'"

"That is what his mother indicated," Chief said. "You'll see that in the document as well."

If Vickie Rodriguez picked up on the fact that Chief sounded like he was measuring his words out with a teaspoon, she didn't show it. I myself was barely able to keep from blurting out more than anybody needed to know on that subject.

"I'd like to have that spelled out," was all she said.

"I'll get on that," Chief said. He wiggled my leg. "I'm going to have to hire a paralegal just to handle *your* stuff."

In other words, *Lighten up, Classic.*

"What?" I said. "You mean I'm not your only client?"

He rewarded me with a smile.

"You won't need a paralegal for this case, I don't think," Vickie said. "I never make promises, but I honestly don't see anything standing in your way."

"Okay, I just want to make sure," I said.

"We're making sure, Allison," Chief said.

"No, I have one more question."

Vickie nodded at me.

"Does the fact that he's still struggling in school—is that going to go against us?"

"The fact that he's even in school is a hundred percent improvement," Liz said. She tilted her chin up at Vickie until Ms. Rodriguez gave her a grudging nod.

"That's right," she said crisply. "Nobody expects him, or you, to be perfect."

Well, then, there was that at least.

Vickie flipped open a large calendar book and ran her nail down the side, turned the page, trailed it down some more. What was she scheduling, the Louisiana Purchase?

"I'm going to request a court date of April fifth," she said. "Does that work for you?"

Chief had his hand around my arm before he and I even got to the elevator. I was sure he'd have put the other one over my mouth if the bunny rabbit of an admin aide hadn't been scampering past us on her way down the hall.

"Tell me you didn't expect to walk out of there with the signed adoption papers in your hand," he said.

"No. But I didn't think we'd have to wait until April."

Chief steered me into the elevator and mashed a button. "Do

you think something's going to happen between now and then to stop it?"

"Do you?"

The elevator reached the first floor, but Chief pushed the CLOSE DOOR button. He turned his face down to me, eyes going right into mine.

"You're worried about Desmond's father."

"That wasn't what you'd call full disclosure in there," I said.

"Geneveve stated it in the guardianship document: 'Father unknown.'"

"We both know she lied. Sultan is his father."

"Was. You were there when he died."

"I wasn't there when somebody made off with his body. We don't even know if there's a death certificate."

"All the more reason to let Geneveve's document do the talking for us."

I pushed both hands through my hair. Chief caught my wrists in his and held them together at his chest.

"I'm asking you to trust me, Classic. Can you do that?"

"I'm sorry. I'm just freaking out."

"Does Desmond know you're freaking out?"

"No. But I think *he* is."

I filled him in on Desmond's debate with himself in the kitchen the night before. I could see Chief's mouth resisting a smile.

"What?" I said.

"Desmond thinks you're a good listener." He pressed the OPEN DOOR button. "I'd like to see him tell that to Vickie Rodriguez."

"Yeah, what is with that woman?" I said as I walked with him across the lobby. "Does she have, like, ice tea in her veins?"

"Too bad you didn't rescue *her* from bullies in high school."

"First of all, she wasn't even born yet when I was in high school, and second of all, I bet she *was* a bully."

Chief stopped to let me pass through the door and into a drizzly rain. "You think she's that bad?"

"I think I'm just intimidated by anybody who could possibly take Desmond away from me."

The tears in my eyes surprised me. I yanked the sunglasses I didn't need out of my bag and fumbled them onto my face. The rain misted them at once.

"I hear ya, Classic," Chief said. "I hear ya."

I had paperwork to take care of for Jasmine's insurance, but I didn't head home to do it. I was going to need some distance from my Vickie Rodriguez experience before I felt anything close to competent about forms again. Besides, I had the undeniable urge to make a pass down West King to see if Zelda was hanging around. It wasn't likely. The street was usually all but deserted until sundown, but I had to start somewhere.

True to form, there wasn't a soul in sight. Not even the homeless guy who usually slept with his dog in front of the Dumpster no matter what the weather. As I pulled my Classic into the parking lot at Sherry's dad's auto repair shop and looked across the street, I saw why.

A large SALE PENDING sign hung on the door of the tattoo parlor, which until last week had been one of the few going concerns on the block. The real estate agency had obviously cleaned up the place. There was no garbage regurgitating over the side of the Dumpster, and no Dog Man curled up to his canine friend below.

That wasn't the only FOR SALE or SOLD or PENDING sign I saw. The entire other side of the street was a veritable gallery of the things. The representing agencies were all different, but the force behind them was as obvious to me as the beer-and-cigarette stench belching from the Magic Moment Bar. It had Troy Irwin and the Chamberlain Enterprises written all over it. Who would give this barely human block a second glance if Troy hadn't sold his gentrification project to every investor he could lure to his Learjet? He'd warned me in December that it was "on" between us. So far, it looked like he was winning. The people I had hope for were being sold to the highest bidder.

"You don't have sense enough to come in out of the rain?" said a voice behind me.

I turned, already grinning at Maharry Nelson, who stood wheezing in the doorway of his beloved Choice Auto Repair Service with an open umbrella. I met him halfway, dodging pothole puddles as I went. The storm had picked up and water was already running down my neck when I got to him, but I ducked under the umbrella anyway. There was still something of the gentleman left in Maharry, and since he didn't have a whole lot else going for him, I couldn't deprive him. Or point out that the holes in the nylon rendered it pretty much useless.

"You better shake like a dog before you come any farther, Miss Angel," Sherry said from behind the counter. "I just mopped in here."

I had to admit the place had improved since Sherry started clerking for her dad again a month before. She'd been in his employ some before she got clean, though the word *worked* had been used loosely back then. But now the piles of tires were straight and dusted, and I could actually tell what color the floor was still trying to be. Beyond the counter, through the now-clear glass window, I could see a land yacht primed for a paint job. That alone made me coax out a smile.

"Business is picking up, I see."

"That's your friend Stan's car," Sherry said.

"Very cool. He sold me my motorcycle."

"He tried to sell Daddy one."

"I'd pay a great deal of money to see that, actually," I said to Maharry.

He squinted his already minuscule eyes behind thick, smeary spectacles. "He's not the only one trying to sell me things I don't want."

"Who else?" I said.

"You don't want to know," Sherry said.

The grit of her teeth told me I did. "Who?" I said again.

"Some fella come in here wantin' me to invest my money in the ..." Maharry ran a hand over his slicked iron hair. "What did he call it, Sherry Lynn?"

"Save the City Project," Sherry said.

"'Save'?" I said. "That's just another word for running people out of their own neighborhood so money can be made off of it. You know that, don't you?"

The tiny veins in Maharry's old cheeks seemed to rise to the surface. "You think I was born yesterday? I told him not to let the door hit him in the backside when he got the Sam Hill outa my store."

"Good for you."

I tried to catch Sherry's eye, but she was crouched behind the counter, muttering something about twenty years' worth of receipts stuffed under there. I turned back to Maharry, who was shuffling once more toward Stan's waiting car.

"You know they'll be back to try to get you to sell, don't you?" I said.

"They already were."

I held my breath. Even though business had grown from none at all to a car a week, I didn't see how much longer Maharry could keep C.A.R.S. open. Sherry had said he had no retirement funds set aside, that he wanted to just breathe his last with his head under somebody's hood. But the way he was breathing right now, he would spend time in a nursing home before that. A good offer had to be tempting.

"What was the deal?" I said.

"Too good to turn down." Maharry turned and creased his wrinkles. I swore some dust puffed out, which allowed me to see the small twinkle. "But I did."

He resumed his shuffle through the glass door. I went to the counter and leaned over to look at the top of Sherry's head. She was on the floor, surrounded by piles of yellowed slips of paper.

"Do you believe this?" she said. "Who keeps receipts from nineteen seventy-two?"

"You got me. I can barely find mine from last year." Much to Chief's chagrin. "Can I ask you something, Sher?"

She looked up at me, and I had to smile into her eyes, eyes I'd first seen dulled by addiction and hopelessness, now alive with irritation and importance and all the things that make up a normal human being.

"Is it about Zelda?" she said.

"Yeah, that's one thing."

"I haven't seen her."

"You'll let me know if you do."

"Of course." Sherry shrugged. "She gets on my last nerve, but she's my Sister."

I nodded and watched her dip into the mass of receipts again. I might have let it go, not stirred her out of the peace she'd been able to find, if it hadn't been about Desmond.

"I also wanted to ask you about Sultan," I said.

The light left her eyes. "What about him?"

I tried to use Chief's teaspoon approach. "I just wondered if you'd heard any scuttlebutt on what happened to his body?"

"No," Sherry said. "And if I did, I wouldn't pay any attention to it. He's dead, and that's all I need to know."

Her voice was as thin as the ubiquitous siren that wailed somewhere in the bowels of the West King neighborhood. I needed to back off, and I would—as soon as I was sure.

"I know he's dead too," I said. "At least he was last time I saw him."

Nothing.

"But if anybody knows where his body is, you—"

"Look, I don't. I just want to put that part of my life behind me."

"Okay," I said. "I'm sorry. It has to do with Desmond's adoption, but don't worry about it."

Sherry leaned against the set of shelves inside the counter and closed her eyes. As the siren wailed its way toward King, I gave her a moment to compose her face. That was something she couldn't have pulled off six weeks ago.

"Is that why he was asking me about him?" she said.

"Who?"

"Desmond."

I felt my eyes widen. "When was that?"

"The other day, I guess. I told him the same thing I'm telling you, Miss Angel. That sorry piece of filth is dead, and we all just need to leave it alone. Just let it be."

It took every fiber of my being not to pin her down on when and why and where Desmond was asking about his biological father. Any time I had ever spoken the man's name in his presence, Desmond had flown into a riot of panic I was hard put to quell.

But as Sherry feigned studying an ancient receipt, I saw her hand trembling. Right after the shooting, she'd said those exact words to me: *Let it be.* If I didn't want her to lose six weeks' worth of ground, I had to take that advice.

I couldn't have pursued it if I'd wanted to. The angry siren whooped in front of the shop, followed by a glass-breaking crash that simultaneously shot out all the lights and shook Maharry from the back.

"Did they run into my building?" he cried.

"No." I peered out the front window through the downpour.

All I could make out were two police cars across the street, lights flashing indignantly, and an already beaten-up sedan smashed into the utility pole.

"I didn't even hear any tires squealing," Sherry said as she let herself out from behind the counter.

"I don't think whoever it was even tried to stop."

"Drunk," Maharray said in disgust.

I didn't point out that it was only eleven a.m. Most people just *stayed* drunk or loaded around here.

Beside me, Sherry swore and pressed her hands to the glass.

"What?" I said.

"Zelda! That's her getting out of the car!"

Not getting out, falling out. Her body tumbled from the now-open driver's-side door and splashed into the gutter.

"Stay here!" I said to Sherry.

Before I could get out the door and across Maharry's parking area, Zelda tried to get up and only tottered for a few seconds before she dropped again, this time face-first into the murky water racing down the curb.

A beefy-looking officer reached for her, and I shouted as I ran, "Wait! I can handle her! Let me handle her!"

Either he didn't hear me or he thought I, too, was a lunatic, though I suspected the latter because he didn't even glance at me as he pinned her arms behind her back and pulled her up. When I got to him, she was shrieking, "I ain't no ho no more!"

"I don't care what your job description is, girl," the officer said to her. "You're under arrest."

"I'm responsible for her," I yelled at him over Zelda.

He looked at his bejowled partner. "I'd say she's doing a heck of a job, wouldn't you?"

"Oh, and you've got a total handle on it," I said. "Just let me take her home."

When I put my hand out to grab Zelda's, the jowly officer was suddenly between us, hand on his holster.

"Ma'am, I'm going to have to ask you to step back."

"You don't get it. She knows me. She'll respond to me."

The bulky officer who had a hold on Zelda pulled up her lolling head to face me.

"You recognize this lady?" he said to her.

Zelda's eyes rolled back into her head.

"I'm going to take that as a no." The officer went for his handcuffs, but Zelda lurched to life and stuck her arms straight in front of her. One icy hand caught my face and clawed at it before her limbs, all four of them, sprung out as if they were trying to escape from her body. I pulled my own hand to my cheek and drew back a palm smeared with blood.

"She's bleeding!" I said.

"No, that's yours," Officer Jowls said. "I'd get to the ER and get a tetanus shot if I were you."

He, too, had to shout to be heard over Zelda's screams, which were now one long unintelligible slur. It took both officers to keep her from lunging at me or them or whoever she thought we all were. Then, just as suddenly, she deflated and slumped over the officer's beefy shoulder. White vomit trailed from her mouth and dropped into a crack in the sidewalk below. The rain worked at it until it disappeared.

"What did you do to her?" I said.

"Didn't do anything," one of them said. "She's labile."

"*What?*"

"She has flipped her, uh, stuff, all the way out."

The handcuffs were on Zelda by this time, even though I was sure she'd never move again. And then she did. One bare foot kicked out and banged into the side of the cruiser they were dragging her to. The other jerked back and caught Officer Jowls squarely in the shin. She spat out expletives like so many gobs of phlegm, something about somebody stealing her shoes, but I ran to her as if she were calling my name. She clearly wasn't. Her eyes were scarlet and so dilated they looked ready to blow. They weren't sending a message to her brain about me, or anyone else for that matter.

And yet I still wedged myself between the struggling trio and the car. "Please," I said, "just take her to the ER, and I'll take responsibility for her from there."

Officer Jowls opened his mouth, undoubtedly to threaten *me* with handcuffs if I didn't move, but the heavyset one looked back over his shoulder and said, "Kent, you wanna deal with this, please?"

He was talking to a third officer who must have just joined the scene, seeing how he wasn't soaked to the skin like the rest of us. I recognized him as young Officer Kent, a red-haired rookie I'd had dealings with more than once. Why did they hire fourteen-year-olds as police officers?

"Come on, Miss Chamberlain," he said. "Let these officers do their job."

He didn't take me by the arm, but I knew that was next. Or Jowls and Beef Face were going to throw me in the back with Zelda, who once again looked like a ragdoll in a coma.

"Ma'am, please, for the last time."

I glared at Jowls and let Officer Kent nudge me away from their police cruiser and toward his own.

"Let's get out of the rain," he said.

"I'll go on my bike," I said.

"Where are you going?"

"To the hospital. With them."

"They aren't taking her to the hospital."

"She needs help!"

"Come on. We'll talk."

It struck me as he ushered me into the front seat that Officer Kent had done some growing up in the few months since I'd last had a brush with him. Maybe he was even shaving now.

I didn't realize I was shivering until he joined me in the car and turned the heater to full on. He produced a blanket and politely handed it over. I stuffed my face into it for a few seconds so I wouldn't scream, *What is the matter with you people?* A Nudge would have been wonderful about then. And not *wash their feet*. Mine, and Officer Kent's, were already sopping wet.

When I brought my face up, he said, "They'll see to her medical needs. You might want to see about yours." He pulled the visor down so I could look in the mirror. There were four unmistakable claw marks down my left cheek, although I was sure that the blood-mixed-with-rain made it look worse than it was.

"I'm fine," I said, but he handed me a wet-wipe anyway, and I dabbed halfheartedly at my face. What I really needed was oxygen; I was clearly about to go into cardiac arrest.

"You're not familiar with somebody flipping out," Officer Kent said.

"The women who come to me are usually half out of it, but not like that."

"You've seen people on downers," Kent said. "I think we're talking speedball in this case."

"Speedball," I said.

"They mix heroin and cocaine on aluminum foil, put a straw in their mouth, and then light it from underneath."

I didn't know how Zelda could have afforded heroin and cocaine. There wasn't that much in the petty-cash jar.

"How long before I can bring her home?" I said.

Officer Kent looked at me as if I were the one who was fourteen. "We're not just dealing with a drug offense," he said. "She led us on a five-block chase before she crashed her car into the pole."

"It's not her car," I said, and then wanted to rip my tongue out.

"Correction. A stolen car."

"We have a good lawyer," I said.

"Would you mind some advice, Miss Chamberlain?"

I would mind, but I nodded anyway.

"It isn't worth it for you to get yourself hauled in for interfering with an arrest. You're already getting a little bit of a reputation—"

"What isn't worth it?" I said. "That woman? That human being whose father gave her methadone when she was ten years old doesn't deserve my help?"

Splotches of color bigger than his freckles blotched Kent's face.

He studied the steering wheel. "How much help are you going to be if you're in the cell with her?"

"Then you tell me, Officer Kent," I said. "You tell me what I'm supposed to do."

"Let us—"

"Let you do what? Haul her in, dry her out, slap a fine or a jail sentence on her, and then turn her loose with the same shame and hopelessness running through her veins until she has to replace it with something she can tolerate and then the whole thing starts over again? Is that what I'm supposed to let you do?"

"I'm just saying."

"I know what you're saying. I've heard it before," I said. "And I'm sure it won't make any more sense to me now than it did the last twenty times. Thanks for the blanket."

I chucked it into his lap and exited the cruiser. Then I stood on the sidewalk, arms folded, until he eased the car away from the curb and followed the other cruiser down the street.

When they were all out of sight, I got on the Classic, but I couldn't start it up yet. *Don't ride when you want to smack somebody,* Chief always told me. And there was definitely nothing I wanted to do more just then than knock those cops' heads through the window of the Magic Moment, or find Zelda's supplier, or any supplier, and strip his veins with my teeth.

So I sat there astride my bike and let the anger circle the drain. When it didn't find its way down, I wanted to claw my helmet off and collapse in the King Street gutter.

I clutched the handgrips, but my palms sweated inside my gloves, so I ripped them off and flung them and hugged myself hard to keep my heart from slamming its way through my jacket. Utter hopelessness chained me, paralyzed, at the curb, until I could convince myself that what had just happened to Zelda wasn't happening to me.

Just days before, I was so sure I had ministry to drug-addicted prostitutes down to a science. You did what you could for them and let God fill the gap between that and anything else they needed. It was working. Now I was a quivering mess, as if the whole thing, not just Zelda's thing, was taking place inside my soul.

When my pulse stopped hurting, the rain, too, showed signs of slacking off, and I started the bike. I made a U-turn in the middle of King and looked toward C.A.R.S. Sherry was still standing in the window. I should go in and reassure her, but I wasn't sure I could. I gave her a thumbs-up and rode east toward town.

Think, Allison. Think it through.

This wasn't about me and what I felt. This was about Zelda right now. I had to find a solution, and I would. Like India said the day before, I didn't have a personal ax to grind.

Huh, I thought as I rode through the drizzle. This felt pretty personal to me.

CHAPTER FOUR

I forced myself to wait until midafternoon before I went to the police station. It would take that long for them to book Zelda, especially in the shape she was in. I hoped she spent more time on the spaced-out side of labile than the volatile side during that process. I didn't have a lot of faith in the way Officers Jowls and Beef Face would handle it if she didn't.

Besides, I knew I should take Chief with me. But I couldn't get in touch with him. His overworked secretary said he'd be in court all day, and then accidentally hung up on me. I left him a message on his cell phone, but when I didn't hear from him by two, I had to go on alone. If I waited too much longer, I would be late picking Desmond up from school. Chief was probably going to stop speaking to me altogether.

The St. Augustine Police Department building was the last nod to genteel history before West King Street wagged its head at the dissipated present. Right on the line between decency and decadence, the marble-look structure invited its citizens up wide, sun-washed steps and between not only two Grecian urns overflowing with lavender but a pair of Corinthian columns, which stubbornly promised that justice and fair treatment could be found within.

Of course, once you passed through the double doors, all bets were off. We're talking bulletproof glass separating those who were in uniform from those who weren't, and about thirty signs saying what wasn't allowed there.

I ignored them all and went to the window, where a weary woman with an outdated perm looked from her computer screen to me with no visible change in expression. I might as well have been an icon she could click. Until recognition registered in her eyes. This wasn't my first trip to the police department.

"One of your women get busted?" she said.

Dear God, thank you for this glass, or I would gladly rip this person's nosehairs out.

"One of the Sisters is in trouble, yes," I said. "I need to see her."

"Name."

"Allison Chamberlain." As if she didn't know.

"The perp's name," she said.

The perp. Yes, thank you for the glass. I was thinking red-hot tweezers.

"Her name is Zelda—"

"I'll buzz you back. Sign in."

Okay, so maybe there was something to be said for being a regular around here.

Still, I thought as I went through the lockdown door and followed a wide, spikey-haired female officer down the hall, I never got used to the place. The naked floors and stark cinder block walls, the metal-and-plastic chairs strewn where their last inhabitants had left them in haste or anger or despair. Nothing—nothing—in these all-too-familiar halls held any hope. I never wanted to get used to hopeless.

Officer Spikey stopped outside a windowed door. "You're her attorney, right?" she said to me.

"No, I'm—"

"You're her attorney, *right?*" She raised her eyebrows, plucked to within an inch of their lives.

"Something like that," I said.

"That's what Jack Ellington says." The brows went down and she unlocked the door.

"Has he been here?" I said. I sure hoped not, or he was going to be ticked off that I was doing this without him.

"Nope," she said. "We just have an understanding."

She surprised me with a smile. A he's-hot-isn't-he? smile.

I had to smile back.

Until I saw Zelda.

There was a lone table in the airless room. The top half of Zelda's body was draped over it, arms sprawled, head turned to the side so that the tabletop smashed her cheek into her eye. This should be an effective meeting. Unless she suddenly rose up and came at me with her teeth bared.

I turned to the officer, who was just closing the door behind her.

"You going to be outside?" I said.

"Don't worry. She probably won't even wake up." And then she added, "Ten minutes."

The door clicked shut with finality and I turned back to Zelda.

"Did you hear that?" I said. "Ten minutes between this or a future."

"I ain't got no future."

She drooled more than spoke the words. Saliva leaking from the corner of her mouth, Zelda sat up and blinked at me with the only eye that was still working. The other was swollen shut.

"They hit you," I said.

She put her hand up to her face as if that hadn't occurred to her before.

"Who did this?" I said. "The officers who arrested you?"

"I don't *know,*" she said, as if I were asking a ridiculous question.

Maybe I was. The now eight minutes and thirty seconds we had left wasn't enough to deal with this and the ninety-seven other issues that sat before me. I lowered myself to the chair across from her and took a breath as she followed me with her head. I watched her mind catch up like a foot dragged sluggishly through the mud. I needed to get to the point before she sank down into it.

"You know who I am, right?" I said.

"Miss *Angel,*" she said. She wasn't too loaded to sneer.

"Then you know I want you out of here and back to Sacrament House. But you're going to have to—"

"Who says I want to go back?"

"It's there or this." I looked around at the bare room I could hardly breathe in. "This can't be what you want."

"All I want is for you to leave me alone," Zelda said. "Just lemme be."

She dropped her torso onto the table again, and then jerked her head up. I forced myself not to bolt for the door.

"No, wait," she said. "Don't leave yet."

"Wasn't planning to," I said.

She tried to lick her lips, though she'd have gotten more moisture out of a piece of sandpaper.

"Have they given you any water?" I said.

"They ain't given me nothin' but a bad time." Zelda gave me a misshapen smile. "See how far I come? I was gonna say they ain't given me nothin' but—"

"Great," I said. "You can go further. Chief and I will go to the judge, ask him to release you to Sacrament House."

I waited for her thoughts to slog forward.

"God gonna be waitin' for me there?" she said.

"God's waiting for you *here*."

Zelda slitted her functional eye and looked around the room. If the Almighty did make an appearance, he could expect a spit in the face.

"I'll go back to Sacrament House," she said, more to the wall above my head than to me.

I waited. Something made me wait, and I waited. Nothing filled the silence but the heaviness. Even God seemed to be holding his breath.

"I'll go," Zelda said again.

"You know it isn't going to be easy," I said. "We'll love you, but you have to do the work. You and God."

"See, that's where ... that's where, no."

"No what?" I said.

"No God. I'll go back, but I don't want to hear about no God."

She tried to raise her chin at me, and though her head wobbled, she was a picture of defiance even Desmond couldn't have drawn.

"That would be like pretending Mercedes wasn't there," I said. "Or ignoring Jasmine like she was invisible. You know that's not going to happen, Zelda."

"Then what I always knew is right."

"And that is?"

"You don't care nothin' 'bout me. You just one more person tryin' to shove their religion down my throat."

I leaned across the table. "Is that the same throat that I spooned water into the night you came to me with no place else to go?"

An expletive exploded from that throat. Before I could recoil from it, Zelda's claw hands snatched at the hair on both sides of my face and yanked me into her forehead. I heard our skulls slam together before I felt a blinding pain.

Another expletive burst from the doorway, this one out of Officer Spikey, who had Zelda pinned against the wall by the time I could see again.

"You okay?" she said to me.

"Fine," I lied.

"She assaulted you. You can press charges. "

I looked at Zelda, but her good eye was closed. And so was her face.

"No charges," I said. "I'll be back, Zelda."

I started for the door, and stopped.

"Just one thing," I said. "Who gave you the drugs today? And don't try to tell me you bought them. Who gave them to you?"

I didn't really expect an answer, but if I didn't ask, I was going to be in more trouble with Chief than I already was. Zelda writhed against Officer Spikey's hold and got nowhere.

"You gonna answer the lady or what?" the officer said. "You got ten seconds."

"Satan," Zelda said. "Satan give 'em to me."

"Yeah, well, I already knew that," I said. "Like I said, I'll be back."

I turned toward the door. Behind me, a wet sound spewed and hit the table.

I was right. She did spit at God.

As I stepped into the hall, I felt it running down my soul.

A restroom. That was what I needed, and then some ice.

Before I could get the WOMEN sign into focus, someone's strong fingers curled around my arm.

"You just need to wear a helmet all the time, Classic," Chief said in my ear.

"Yeah, right?" I said.

I gave up trying to tell him I just needed a restroom. He was pulling me down the hall at his top long-legged rate.

"We running from somebody?" I said through my teeth.

"Yeah," he said. "But not fast enough."

A door opened several feet ahead of us, and a familiar form crossed its arms in our path.

"Detective Kylie," Chief said with a nod.

He didn't slow his pace, but the detective stayed planted in the hallway. Chief's idea of just passing through was squelched.

The instant we got close enough, however, the detective gave a low whistle. "You filing charges for that?" he said, pointing to my face. "That why you're here?"

"We were just consulting with a client," Chief said.

"Actually," I said, "I'll tell you exactly why I'm here."

I felt Chief moan.

"One of the Sisters in my program was given a speedball on West King. Can you tell me how much that was probably worth? Just a ballpark figure."

Detective Kylie's arms tightened across his chest. "Somewhere around a grand. I guarantee you nobody just gave it to her."

"Well, she sure didn't pay for it."

Chief's fingers squeezed around my arm. If this day didn't end, I was going to have more bruises than Mike Tyson.

"Let me get clear," Kylie said. "This was one of your hookers?"

I glared, but I nodded.

"It's not typical, I'll give you that."

"So who do we know that would have access to high-end drugs like that? Nobody on West King, surely."

Kylie looked at Chief. "She's getting streetwise, this girl."

"Hello. Right here," I said. "Who has that kind of thing going on? And why would they offer it to a woman who would have taken a joint and been happy with it? Doesn't that seem like a waste to you?"

"It all seems like a waste to me," Kylie said.

He let one arm loose long enough to rub absently at the back of his head.

"So … does anybody come to mind?" I said.

"What did your client say?" Kylie looked again at Chief.

"She said it was Satan," I said. "But that was just to spite me."

I expected a nod, or at the very least an eye roll. What Kylie gave me was a double take.

"What?" I said.

"You think that could be an alias?" Chief said.

"I've heard worse." The look had passed from Kylie's face. He was back to scrutinizing the two of us.

"So, you going to try to get your latest off with rehab?" he said.

Chief nearly squeezed my arm off. "She hasn't seen the judge yet. We don't even know what bail's going to be."

"Yeah, well, talk about your waste, huh?"

Kylie delivered the nod I knew Chief was waiting for and went off down the hall.

"Let's at least get outside before you blow," Chief breathed into my ear.

"I'm past blowing," I said.

"Well, I'm not," Chief said.

Yeah. That was what I was afraid of.

By that night, Zelda's scratch marks were no more than faded stripes on my face, and I managed to cover the bulge on my forehead with my hair. But India still had her fingers pressed to her mouth in horror ten minutes into our board meeting in my living room.. There was almost no convincing her I didn't need plastic surgery.

"If we do decide to bail her out," Bonner said from his usual corner of the couch, "I suggest we wait until we're sure she's completely detoxed."

"And declawed," Hank said drily. From the other end of the sofa she pushed the impressive antipasto tray toward me, a little something she'd whipped up.

"I don't think there's any 'if' about it," I said. "The longer Zelda stays in there, the harder it's going to be to bring her back. She's gone way further down than any of us thought. "

"Honey, what are you planning to do with her when you get her released?" India said.

Chief elbowed me from the arm of the red chair. "She can't stay here."

Before I could open my mouth, he said, "Do the words *Vickie Rodriguez* mean anything to you?"

I nodded. He was, indeed, still speaking to me, even after the lecture I'd received outside the police station. I didn't want to push him.

"I don't see us putting her back in the house with the other Sisters," Hank said. "You know what my suggestion is." She popped a Greek olive into her mouth and waited while she chewed. Nobody could wait like Hank.

"You talking about the house on San Luis?" India hitched her silk turtleneck up under the matching rods of jet dangling from her lobes. "That would be perfect if it wasn't going to take us a month to get it through escrow and probably another two to make it livable. We don't even know if it's for sale."

We all looked at Bonner, who was already making a note in his iPhone.

"Funds?" Chief said.

India's face brightened. "Allison didn't tell you about Ms. Willa having a change of heart?"

I had, in fact, completely forgotten about that. Too much head banging, maybe?

"How much change?" Bonner said.

"We don't know yet. One of the things I wanted to talk about at this meeting is the fund-raiser." India looked at me. "I'm getting RSVPs by the boatload, so keeping the format mysterious just might be the ticket. But you *are* gon' have to tell *me* eventually."

As soon as God tells me, I thought grimly.

"It wouldn't hurt to ask the owner what he plans to do with the place, would it?" Hank said.

India smiled at Bonner. I often wondered, with a smile like that, what in the world was wrong with her ex-husband, a man she coldly referred to as Michael Morehead. You'd practically have to be a granite countertop to resist her. "Maybe he'll just want to donate it like you did the first one, Bonner," she said.

He actually blushed.

"Yeah, well, if you're going there," I said. "Take India with you. I'm obviously a liability in those conversations."

Chief looked up from the spreadsheet lying across his thighs like a lap blanket. "Getting back to Zelda ... We can't afford to post bond for her." He lowered a look at me that clearly said, *And don't even think about taking it out of your own pocket.*

"Somehow she managed to come up with the bucks for cocaine and heroin," I said. "Where are those resources when it's time to get her out of jail?"

"Have you asked the Sisters who might have supplied her?" Bonner said.

I shook my head.

Hank looked at me, this time with a slice of prosciutto between her thumb and index finger, the way only a true foodie can hold an hors d'oeuvre. "Maybe the judge will order rehab, which gives us a little more time."

"Rehab is a joke for somebody like Zelda," I said.

"But it'll keep her from killing herself with another overdose."

I shivered, but I nodded.

"I'll stay on it and keep you posted," Chief said. "What else do we have on the agenda?"

"Brain food," Hank said. She tapped the edge of the tray. "Anchovies are proven to be good for thought processing."

"That must be why I am clueless about half the time," India said. "But do let me taste that cheese. Now that looks like it could put a few more dimples on my thighs." She smiled again. "Which means it is absolutely scrumptious."

Chief was looking at me.

"I got nothin'," I said.

Actually, that wasn't true. I had plenty of God-work to keep me busy over the next several days. There was the usual counseling of Sister meltdowns and backslides, as well as the chauffeuring of everybody to NA meetings and the never-ending dental appointments to repair meth damage. Plus the hauling of Desmond to the Harley store for yet another pair of boots.

Still, Zelda crammed herself into my thoughts. I was talking up C.A.R.S. to HOG friend Rex, whose Toyota needed a paint job, and suddenly there she was in my head, ramming somebody's vehicle into a utility pole. Who did it belong to? The same guy who gave her a cocktail she couldn't handle?

Anything could trigger the questions. I walked past the front door on Palm Row where she had first come to me and found myself aching. What happened? Why was she so anxious then to do any-thing to change, and so angry now at the God who tried to change her into herself? I spit in the sink while brushing my teeth and felt the pain all over again, the pain that asked, Why did she so easily take drugs from Satan, when we were offering her Jesus?

I tried to see her, despite Chief's protest. I say protest. It was actually just a look that said, *You'll regret it. Just sayin'.*

And of course, I did. Evidently Chief's being hot was no match for Detective Kylie's new edict that only attorneys were allowed to see their clients during anything but visiting hours. Those were held on Sunday, which by that time I'd already missed. I told myself that maybe that was a God thing. Maybe I needed that time to figure out how to get Zelda back to God. Because if she wasn't willing to do that … Yeah, maybe I needed time.

Meanwhile, there were the Sisters' baptisms to prepare them for. And Desmond's. With the women, it was a delicate dance, trying to balance their enthusiasm for denying themselves everything and their deeper need to go within. Desmond just wanted to give up homework for Lent.

We had a rousing discussion in the living room at Sacrament House the Wednesday after Ash Wednesday. Jasmine and Mercedes and Sherry and Hank and Desmond set about discussing their respective "stuff." If left to their own devices, the Sisters would have referred to their struggles as their—well—some form of excrement. Stuff, though somewhat euphemistic, served us well. At least the three Sisters, and even Hank, were able to put words to their confusion and begin to untangle it. Desmond was less forthcoming, although he did begrudgingly admit that he still had a snack-hoarding habit— shocking—but he was working on it.

"I'll get that beat 'fore I get baptized," he told us.

As for me, I played moderator. Fortunately nobody called me on my lack of transparency about my own where-is-God-what-am-I-doing "stuff." But I couldn't avoid it in the silence we observed before the communion.

As we stood around the table in the dining alcove, chins to our chests, eyes fluttered closed, Sacrament House settled into a quiet so still I was afraid the rumblings in my head would rattle the Sisters out of their private conversations with God. All conditions were right for hearing the Divine Voice—the just-cleaned smell of Mercedes's relentless scrubbing discipline, the singe of the candle curling heavenward, the peace so thick it even settled over the furniture and made it seem less shabby. It should have been easy to hear God, detect a Nudge. And in fact, I almost felt one.

Almost.

"Almost," my father used to say, "is just another word for not good enough." The veins in his neck would bulge when my ninety-two average was almost an A, or the tennis ball I hit nearly cleared the net, or the job I took came close to what a Chamberlain ought to earn. It infuriated him so much that by age fifteen, I deliberately did almost enough in everything, just to see his jaw muscles twitch. In my mind, if he didn't like it, it must be good. *Almost* became a habit for me.

It never bothered me before God started forcing me to reach past almost. But now, being so close to whatever was niggling at the edge of my brain was like Chinese water torture. Hearing *wash their feet* yet again, without knowing what it meant, was palpably painful.

Wasn't I doing that already? Hadn't I washed enough blood and vomit and sweat from these women to show I got it?

You've got it, Allison. But do they?

I opened my eyes. The rest of the heads were still bowed. Desmond's was wagging back and forth like an imitation of Stevie Wonder, but he clearly hadn't heard what I'd heard. I closed myself into darkness again. All right. If this was where we were going ...

Who? Who doesn't have it? I cried out in my head.

Wash their feet. All of you—wash their feet.

It came like an unwelcome emotion this time, like anger you can't express without committing a Class B felony, like frustration you can't take out—on anybody.

"Dang it—*whose* feet?"

My eyes came open. Jasmine stopped moaning, and Mercedes scowled like she was about to belt somebody before she realized I was the one who had broken the silence.

"It ain't my feet smellin'," Desmond said.

Mercedes did start to whack him, but I put my hand up and turned to Hank.

"Let me say this before I talk myself out of it," I said.

"Go for it," she said.

I closed my eyes. "We need to tell India that the fund-raiser is going to be at my house—on Palm Row. And we're not going to bring in caterers and servers and all that. We'll prepare the meal ourselves, like the kind of feasts Jesus used to go to. All of us are going to prepare it, and we're going to serve the people we're asking to serve us. That's all I know."

I let my eyes come open. They didn't look convinced, necessarily, or inspired, but nobody was looking at me as if medication were the next logical step.

"I don't mean to be dense," Sherry said, "but I don't see what this has to do with feet."

"Forget that," I said. "It's just an image that—never mind, that part's complicated."

"I trust you want me to head up the cooking end of this," Hank said, mouth twitching.

"Oh, Lawd, don't you let Miss Angel do it," Mercedes said. "Nothin' against you, Miss A, but girl, you the only person I know can ruin a baked potato."

"I don't want to do no cookin'," Desmond said.

"That's good news too," Hank said.

"But I could be like the Mother D."

"Mother D?" Jasmine said. "Whatchoo talkin' 'bout, boy?"

I tried to keep the chortle out of my voice. "Do you mean maître d'? Like the head waiter?"

"The one gets dressed up real sharp and lead the ladies to their table," Desmond said. "I seen it in a movie."

"That would be so you, Desmond," Hank said. "But I don't know if that's what your mother has in mind."

I didn't really know what God had in my mind. We were clearly talking metaphor here, and I didn't have the whole meaning yet.

But at least it was closer than almost.

Chief's Road King was still in its parking place on Palm Row when Desmond and I got home.

"Mr. Chief gonna spend the night?" Desmond said as we hung our helmets in the garage.

"*No!*" I said.

"You don't need to get all up in my dental work, Big Al," he said. "I was jus' wonderin'."

I didn't even know what to say to that. Maybe I could put Chief on it. I did manage, "Okay, no hanging out with Mr. Chief tonight. You need to finish your history homework before bed. You remember what he said about if you try to bring your grade up, he'll take you riding *on* the beach."

Desmond danced backward in front of me as we crossed the lane. "Try? Ain't no tryin' about it. Imma get a A-plus on my next test. Mr. Chief gonna have to take me all the way to Daytona."

"You can never tell," I said.

He stopped at the bottom of the side porch steps. "You serious?"

"Only one way to find out."

Chief looked understandably surprised when he opened the kitchen door and Desmond swept past him with a perfunctory, "Hey, Mr. Chief. I gotta study."

"Did you check his pulse?" Chief said when Desmond had disappeared into his room.

"That's your doing," I said. "He thinks if he aces the test you're taking him on a road trip."

I waited for at least a half smile from Chief, but he barely seemed to have heard me. He glanced at Desmond's closed door and nodded me toward the living room. My heart began a slow descent.

"What?" I said.

But he waited until I was perched on the edge of the chair-and-a-half. He sat on the ottoman facing me.

"This can't be good," I said. "What's going on?"

"I didn't have a chance to tell you this after the board meeting."

"Tell me what?"

"I finally found the right person to talk to."

"About?"

"Jude Lowery. Sultan." Chief winced. "He hasn't been declared legally dead, and he won't be until either they find his body or seven years have passed."

"No! He dead! That man *dead!*"

My head jerked so hard toward the figure in the dining room doorway, I could feel the tendons in my neck wrench. Desmond's normally creamy face was bleached, and his mouth couldn't seem to hold itself still. The newly prominent Adam's apple worked painfully up and down his neck.

"He *is* dead," I said.

"Then why you sayin' he ain't?"

"Come here, buddy," Chief said.

Chief held his arm out and waited until Desmond crossed to us. I moved over to make room for him in the chair with me, but he just stood there.

"I know he's dead too," I said. "I was there, remember?"

"Then how come they sayin' he might not be?"

"Because somebody took the body," I said. "But don't worry about it, okay?"

I was apparently completely unconvincing because he swallowed hard again and turned doubtful eyes to Chief. "How come somebody took him?" he said.

"Because they're cowards," Chief said.

I sat up straighter in the chair. Chief's voice had an edge I hadn't heard before.

"Sultan had a bunch of losers working for him. They knew as soon as Sultan was gone somebody else would take over their territory because they don't have the goods to protect it. You see what I'm saying?"

"Maybe."

"If they made it look like Sultan was still alive, somebody else, somebody stronger, wouldn't be so likely to try a takeover." Chief nodded at Desmond as if they were both man enough to get this. "Sultan was a bad dude. Nobody's going to try anything like that until they're sure he can't come back and mess them up. That make sense?"

Desmond pressed his lips together. The color still hadn't returned to his face. I'd seldom seen him take this long to snap his coping mechanism back into place.

"What about Zelda?" Desmond said, to me this time.

"I told you she left."

"You didn't tell me she flip out in the street and got busted. I hadda hear you talkin' about it when Barnum and Bailey and them was here."

"What are you, half bat?"

"What kinda drugs make her lose her stuff like that?"

I looked at Chief, and he nodded.

"It was a speedball," I said. "That's—"

"I know what it is," Desmond said. "And ain't nobody can get that on King Street 'cept Sultan."

"Or one of his lackeys now that he's gone," Chief said. "Look, I'll tell you what. I'll do some investigating and see if I can find out what's going down on West King right now—who's controlling what, who's getting what, all that. Then you can let your mind rest. Sound good?"

"How long you think thatta take?"

The waver in his voice caught in my own throat. The kid was genuinely scared, and even Chief wasn't able to chase that fear away.

"Give me a week," Chief said. "Meanwhile, just so you know, nothing is going to stop the adoption. You're going to be stuck with Big Al no matter what."

"Bummer," I said.

Desmond finally made an attempt at a smile, and his Adam's apple stopped bobbing. It would only be a matter of time now before he'd be suggesting that a package of Peanut M&M's would set the whole matter to rest. I beat him to it and told him to grab something from the drawer before he went back to studying.

"Imma ace the test," was his parting shot. "Then we goin' all the way to Miami."

"I hope that test happens soon," Chief said when Desmond was as safely out of earshot as he was ever going to get. "Or we're going to wind up in Key West."

"Chief."

He sat back down on the ottoman and parked his forearms on his knees.

"You're still not okay with this," he said.

"No, and neither is he." I lowered my voice to a whisper. "You have to tell me if you really believe this is just Sultan's people protecting their turf."

"I've got my eye on it, Classic," he said. "I have ever since the night he was shot."

It was almost as good as the kiss I wanted. Another almost.

Bonner had yet another almost for me when he called Friday morning, just as I was heading out the door.

"I'm going to walk while you talk," I said into my cell. "I'm already late meeting Hank at the Galleon."

"She gets you every Friday," Bonner said. "She can spare me five minutes. Besides, you want to hear this."

I hoped he was sure about that. People were telling me a lot of things lately that I didn't want to hear.

"I talked to Dexter Taylor."

"Who's that?"

"He owns the place across from Sacrament House."

I stopped at the corner of Palm Row and Cordova and sat on the low wall that ran along the sidewalk. The palm trees along the side of the Lightner Museum slapped their fronds together in the March wind. "Talk to me," I said.

"He said his original plan was to rent it out again, but somebody told him the house across the street—ours—had a bunch of hookers living in it, so he decided to sell."

"I hope you set him straight."

"I did."

"And unlike me, you did it without making him want to press charges." I let a half-empty sightseeing trolley pass and crossed Cordova.

"He said he's definitely selling, and … are you close to anything breakable?"

"Why? Am I going to want to throw something?"

"You might."

"This has something to do with Troy Irwin, doesn't it?"

"Taylor told me that the Chamberlain Foundation just bought another house down the street and he was hoping maybe they'd make a bid on his once he put it up for sale."

"He can't."

"There's nothing stopping him, Allison. I couldn't even ask Taylor to hold this house because we don't know if we're going to have the funds to make an offer. He did say he wasn't going to list it until he fixed it up some. Evidently the last tenants were pretty rough on it."

"How much time does that give us?" I said.

"Not much. When's the fund-raiser?"

"The seventeenth—two weeks."

"Then let's just do what we can with that window, okay? Don't hurl any projectiles yet. Are you at the Galleon now?"

"Yeah."

"Good. Hank'll keep you in line."

As I hung up and shoved through the door into the coffee shop, I wasn't sure even Hank could keep me from erupting. She took me in with a glance from our usual table and called over her shoulder,

"Patrice, we need an emergency chamomile tea out here. Make it a double."

"It's a personal vendetta now, Hank."

"You talked to Bonner."

"You know."

"Sit."

I wanted to pace around and throw random pieces of reproduction armor, but I punched myself down onto the chair and proceeded to shred a carrot raisin muffin.

"It's not enough to redline all of West King. He's got to take our street. He doesn't need it. He's not going to get investors to open restaurants and bed and breakfasts back there. This is just to get to me."

"We *are* talking about Troy Irwin."

The lion-haired woman who owned the Galleon placed a cup of tea at my elbow. "You sure you don't need something stronger than that?"

"Am I making too much noise?" I said.

She looked around at the empty tables. "Yeah. You're disturbing all the other customers."

"Business not good?" Hank said.

Patrice shook her head. "We're closing the fifteenth of this month."

"Tell me she isn't selling to Chamberlain too," I said when Patrice returned to the kitchen with the decimated muffin.

"What are you going to do, Al?" Hank said.

"Not what I want to do."

"Which is?

"Blow into his office and tell him what a heinous pile of garbage he is."

"You tried that before."

"I did."

"And how far did it get you?"

"It sent me backward."

"Then there you go." Hank folded her hands neatly on the map-of—St. Augustine placemat. "So what else you got?"

"I don't know, Hank. I don't know anything anymore, seriously. And this feeling." I plastered my hand to my chest. "This is creeping me out."

"Tell me some more."

"I've never felt hate like this before, and that's what it is, just pure hate."

"Of course it is. Not to beat a dead dog, Al, but you *are* a prophet. Prophets hate injustice, and they feel it a hundred times more deeply than the rest of us."

"Willa Livengood is just as callous as Troy Irwin. So's the Reverend Garry Howard, for that matter. But I don't hate them, not this way."

"You don't have the history with them that you do with Troy."

"I'm over that, though."

"Really." Hank's bob of dark hair splashed across her cheek as she tilted her head at me. "Let me ask you this: If Troy Irwin completely backed out of West King Street and left the whole thing alone, would you still want to spit every time you heard his name?"

"Yes," I said.

Her mouth did its twitchy thing. "You don't even have to think about it for a second?"

"No, and I don't even know why." I shoved a hand through my hair. "I told you, I don't know anything for sure anymore."

"What don't you know about this?"

"I don't know why, after God has completely turned my life around, and I feel like I might be actually living the way I'm supposed to—why I'm still hung up on something that happened twenty-five years ago. My head has let it go. Troy Irwin, high-school lover, hurt me, blah, blah, blah—done—over it. But it's still on me like some kind of oozing … thing."

"It's not just on you," Hank said, "it's in you. And you're not used to things being in you."

"What things?"

"Whatever it was you were experiencing Wednesday night when you blurted something out about feet and then covered it up with some fund-raising idea."

"You don't like the Feast idea?" I said. "India does."

"I like it fine, but that isn't what you had going on inside you. Am I right?"

"Yes." I shook my head at her. "Do you lie awake at night thinking of things I don't want to look at so you can put them in my face?"

"Pretty much."

Patrice produced another muffin.

"Eat this one," Hank said to me, and waited until I'd chewed and swallowed a bite that went down like a wad of sawdust.

"So, Wednesday night," I said. "It was all these emotions, and it was the same way when I saw Zelda all wigged out—feelings that don't have any connection to anything. And that's like with Troy. I have all this hate, and it makes me wonder if that clouds my judgment. I don't know. I'm not used to this."

"Not used to feeling?"

"I have always *felt,* but …"

"But not like you wanted to throw body armor or pull some police officer's larynx out." Her mouth gave its signature twitch. "Or jump a man's bones, so to speak."

"Tell me we're not still talking about Troy. That just makes me want to barf." I looked distastefully at the muffin and pushed the plate away.

"No, it wasn't Troy's bones I was referring to."

"You're talking Chief."

"Oh, yeah."

"I don't want to jump Chief's bones."

Hank chewed.

"Okay, I do, but I can't."

"Because of Troy Irwin."

"*What?* No, not because of him!"

Hank considered the whipped cream on her Belgian waffle. "Who was the last man you trusted before Chief?"

"We were eighteen."

"That's a long time not to be able to enjoy a relationship. I'd hate a man too, if he was responsible for me living half a life for twenty-five years."

The muffin blurred in front of me. I swallowed so hard I reminded myself of Desmond, choking down his fear.

"How is it that you know more about me than I do?" I said.

"I don't think I do. I just yank the covers off of you so you have to look at yourself."

"No, really, Hank, you're the prophet."

"And you?"

"Let me get back to you on that," I said.

I was only half-joking. The other half was still having an identity crisis when Chief, Bonner, and I went to dinner at O. C. White's that night. Desmond was hanging out over at Owen's, which gave me a chance to discuss the Troy Irwin house situation outside of his bat-radar range.

"The more I think about it," I said over our order of oysters on the half shell, "the more I think I *should* just storm his office and tell him that I know this isn't just about money, that it's all about power and his ego and him wanting everybody to think he's this Henry Flagler benevolent benefactor."

"And that is going to accomplish what?" Chief said.

He had that edge in his voice again, and I could see that Bonner heard it too. Either that or he always stabbed his oysters twelve times with a fork before he ate them.

"It'll make me feel better, maybe," I said.

"It'll get you thrown out on your ear," Chief said.

Bonner dabbed his mouth with the black napkin. "We need publicity, Allison, but not that kind. Something positive would be good."

"You mean like in the news? Going all political? No. I hate that."

I didn't mean for my voice to rise, but it obviously did because Bonner began to torture yet another oyster. Chief's voice, on the other hand, dropped lower, which irritated the hairs straight up on the back of my neck.

"This is not a fight *against* Troy Irwin," he said. "It's a fight *for* the Sacrament Sisters. At least, that's what you've always told me."

"I hate it when you do that."

"What?"

"Throw my own words back in my face."

"I'm not throwing anything."

His voice was so low now I had to lean toward him to hear it. We were almost nose to nose. In my peripheral view, Bonner just kept stabbing.

"What if I did go talk to Troy again?" I said.

"What would make it different from any other time?"

"I'd have more information. I'd be calmer."

Bonner must have finally gotten the oyster into his mouth because he choked on it.

"I'm not going to let you do this, Classic," Chief said.

I didn't ask him how he was going to stop me because he just had.

Bonner not so subtly skipped dessert and left us a couple of twenties for his entrée before he begged off for the rest of the evening. I hoped Chief would have dessert. He needed something to sweeten the glower he was still delivering in my direction.

"Their key lime pie is to die for," I said.

"I'm testy," he said.

"That would describe it, yes."

"You won't like this. Well, you will and you won't."

As long as it wasn't *I'm sick of you and I'm out of here,* I thought I could handle it.

"What else is new?" I said. "Bring it."

"I kept my promise to Desmond and checked around about Sultan's people. It wasn't much of a promise. I was doing it anyway."

"What did you find out?"

"Good news for you: There's no Sultan-style action going down on West King. Not since he was shot, actually."

"Who is that bad news for?"

"Desmond. I can't tell him Sultan's people are still down there handing out speedballs." Chief grunted. "Not that they ever were. I never heard of anything like what happened to Zelda, not down there."

"So what does that mean?" I said.

"It means I can't try to make Desmond believe the story I told him. It also means there has to be another explanation, and I don't know what it is."

"Depends how you spin it."

"I can't believe you just said that."

"I know, right? But it's true, Chief. There's no more Sultan business, so Sultan must be dead. Whatever that other explanation is, Desmond doesn't need to worry about it."

"You think he won't?"

"No."

"Nether do I." The tiny lines around his eyes deepened. "I love that kid."

"I know," I said.

There was a lot of love going on at that table.

CHAPTER FIVE

On Sunday afternoon, while Chief and Desmond were out on their usual ride with the HOGs and I was trying to get ready to go see Zelda, India came over with a quiche from Bistro de Leon and the current guest list for the Feast. She also brought some news.

"Ms. Willa's a 'maybe,'" she said while I pulled out the only china plates Sylvia and I had saved for special-occasions-for-two. The rest of my parents' dishes we'd sold to fund a trip to the Caribbean. I preferred those memories over the finger sandwiches.

"I thought she was supposed to be the guest of honor," I said.

"She probably will be, depending on how things go at lunch tomorrow."

"Lunch tomorrow." I stopped pawing through the disheveled silverware drawer. Desmond had obviously been the last one to empty the dishwasher. "What lunch?"

"I hope you're free. Ms. Willa wants to treat you at 95 Cordova, just to get clear on a few things."

"What things?"

"Honey, I don't know specifically, but you'll do fine now that you know what she's like. Just focus on the real thing and let the bigotry nonsense just roll off your back. I think half the time she goes on like that just to see what you'll do. "

I abandoned the fork situation altogether. "Tell me you'll be there too."

"Actually, I can't. I have a vendor coming in with a whole new line."

"What about Bonner?"

"Darlin', what is the problem?"

"I'm going to blow it, that's the problem. What have I not blown in the past two weeks? Willa. Zelda. The cops. Chief."

"Chief?" India's eyes drooped at the corners, not difficult considering the amount of eye shadow she wore. I always marveled that she could keep them open under the best of circumstances. "Y'all haven't broken up, have you?" she said.

"No. There's nothing to break up."

"Now, honey, I don't believe that. The man is completely smitten with you."

"I just don't think I can handle Ms. Willa alone, and get a donation out of her."

"That's not what this is about." India picked up the pie knife I had managed to uncover and cut two triangles of quiche with the elegant precision of a hand model. Another reason she was the one who should be lunching with Ms. Willa.

"What *is* it about, then?" I said.

She opened the dishwasher and selected two forks, which she laid delicately on our plates. "Personally, I think it's you she's curious about. I think she was taken with you."

"She was taken with the fact that I disowned myself from my parents. That's a great foundation for a relationship."

"Does it matter, if it's a foot in the door?"

"I just smell disaster. What if she doesn't come to the fund-raiser because I tick her off again?"

"Then we don't need her ol' money, do we?" India tore off two paper towels and folded them into napkins resembling origami. "But

I really don't think that's going to happen. You just talk about the Sisters and your love for them and your passion for what God is telling you to do, and she will be at your feet. Just like everybody is when you forget yourself and just let go and let God."

As much as I hated churchy clichés, I let that one slide. "We do need her money," I said. "But I won't take it if it's not given in the right spirit, you know what I mean?"

India set the plates on the bistro table and turned to me, sleeves flowing over her hands as she folded them at her waist.

"Ms. Willa may be cantankerous, Allison, but she is not Troy Irwin. In fact, nobody but Troy Irwin is Troy Irwin, and I think it's time you trusted some people. Cut them a little slack. I told you this once before: Not everybody can bring home a hooker, but most of us can do a little something. You can't be putting all those little somethings under a microscope."

I sighed. "What time tomorrow?"

"Eleven forty-five. I brought a couple of things for you to try on, just in case you want to dress up a little."

I didn't tell her I was planning to go to lunch on the Harley.

Or that I was taking somebody with me.

Mercedes was so dolled up when I went by to get her the next day, I decided to leave the bike parked at C.A.R.S. where Sherry could keep an eye on it. I didn't have the heart to crush her carefully straightened do under Desmond's helmet or ruin the look with a bulky jacket. In a swollen-houndstooth plaid pencil skirt and black blouse engulfed in ruffles, Mercedes wouldn't have met India's approval, but she was so completely herself—and so completely not the woman I'd first met hawking her wares in front of the tattoo shop—that she definitely met mine.

I, on the other hand, was in leathers and a cobalt silk scarf, my only concession to the two-hour makeover India did on me. The makeover that made me too late to see Zelda. Chief had assured me it was okay. She wouldn't even see him, said she "didn't need no lawyer." It wasn't okay. She was showing up almost hourly in my thoughts, and it clearly wasn't okay.

But there was today, and Mercedes and I linked arms as we crossed Ponce de Leon Boulevard and strolled the remaining four blocks down King to Cordova. That day, the March breeze had the quality of a warm caress, one of the reasons for living in Florida. Ask me in wilting July, and I wouldn't be able to remember that, but in early spring, with the freesia stretching their hopeful necks from the pots along the sidewalk and the sun splashing its sparkle onto last night's puddles, it felt like home. I chose to take that as a God sign, and I smiled at Mercedes when the doorman rushed to greet us.

Her brow lowered all the way down to her eyelids.

"What?" I said.

"You not gon' give me any instructions, Miss Angel?"

"Why would I? You know how to conduct yourself in a restaurant."

Okay, so, granted, our fine-dining training had been at the Waffle House out on US 1, but I refused to stress her out with a lecture on what utensils to use in what order. I wasn't sure I even remembered that myself.

"You're delightful, my friend," I said. "If this lady can't see that, we'll move on."

"Like Jesus said 'bout brushing the dirt off your sandals when people blows you off."

God love Hank and her Bible study.

"That's it," I said. "And thank you, sir."

The ancient doorman had been patiently waiting, door open, for us to clear all that up. He was in fact so old, I looked twice to make sure he hadn't just fallen asleep, or worse.

Once inside the 95, the fashionable darkness elicited mumbles from Mercedes about needin' a flashlight in there. But my eyes grew accustomed to it by the time the "Mother D" led us to Ms. Willa's table. It was all the way in the back, sheltered by a pair of potted orange trees. Even as miniscule as the woman was, she and her mane of hair presided as if she owned all she could see. And there was definitely nothing wrong with her eyesight.

"Who's that you have with you?" she barked to me before I was even halfway to the table.

"See?" I said to Mercedes out of the side of my mouth. "You don't have to worry about your manners."

"Mmm-*mmm*," Mercedes said.

"Nice to see you too, Ms. Willa," I said when we'd arrived at the table, and the other diners' heads had stopped turning. "This is my friend Mercedes Phillips. She's involved in the Sacrament House ministry, and I thought she could answer any questions that I might not be able to."

"Aren't you the head of it?" Ms. Willa said.

"Actually, God is the head. I guess you could say I'm second in command, but there are probably things that go on that I'm not privy to."

It didn't occur to me until Ms. Willa blinked her too-bright eyes several times that I was waxing far more eloquent than I had at our previous meeting. Of course, a chimpanzee would be an improvement over that.

"I've already ordered," Ms. Willa said as we took our seats. "The turkey croquettes are good here."

Yum.

"Sherry?" she said.

"She couldn't come, ma'am," Mercedes said. "She have to work."

Ms. Willa looked at me. "What's she talking about?"

"Another woman in our ministry is named Sherry," I said.

"I'm not talking about her. I'm talking about this." She tapped one of her scarlet nails against a bottle. "Do you want a glass of sherry?"

"Is it got alcohol in it?" Mercedes said.

"Well, of course it has alcohol in it. I don't think they make it without."

"Then no thank you," Mercedes said.

"I'll pass too," I said. "But you go ahead, please."

"I will." Ms. Willa appeared to be trying to snap her fingers, but they weren't cooperating. She waved a hand instead, and the server scurried over and filled her glass.

"We're ready to get started now, Bruce," she said to him.

He actually bowed before he once again scurried. Ms. Willa leaned in, which wasn't easy, since her shoulders barely cleared the table. I leaned in, too, and Mercedes followed my example. Our heads were all so close, I caught the scent of lavender in Ms. Willa's white mane. Come to think of it, her hair had more of a purple tint today, as did her entire outfit, fingerless mitts included. Violet feathers trimmed her sweater, making her look more like a small bird than ever.

"Do you know how old I am?" she said.

"I'd guess between eighty and eighty-five," I said.

Ms. Willa pulled in her negligible chin. "Well, at least you didn't try to flatter me. I'm eighty-four. But nobody can say I haven't changed with the times."

I wanted to say that, yes, I was sure her hair hadn't always been the color of a petunia, but I just nodded. Mercedes did too.

"Today, we have a white waiter," she went on. "Used to be they were all black as the ace of spades."

Oh, dear God, hold me back.

"But today I'm having lunch with a colored woman, instead of having one serve me, and I'm not even batting an eye." She gave the table a resounding smack that jittered the glass and sent the sherry splashing dangerously close to the rim. "So don't let my age fool you. I can be very broad-minded. Very."

I didn't notice any change in Mercedes's breathing, but I still stole a glance at her. She was nodding, lips pressed together. Bless her heart. She was trying not to laugh.

"Oh, here are our salads," Ms. Willa said.

I looked doubtfully at the anthill-sized pile of lettuce he set in front of me. It appeared that someone had weeded a garden and dumped everything on the plate with a curl of carrot and a drizzle of watered-down raspberry jam.

"You know just how I like it, Bruce," Ms. Willa said.

Double yum. I felt Mercedes watching me as I selected the fork farthest from my plate. I hoped that was the right one, although Ms. Willa was too busy noisily sipping to notice if we ate it with our fingers.

"Now, then," she said. "About this ministry of yours."

"Miss Angel," Mercedes whispered, as much as a cigarette alto like Mercedes can whisper. "We gonna pray first?"

"Absolutely," I said. "The Lord be with you."

"And also witchoo."

"Let us pray."

I blessed the food, and Mercedes punctuated the prayer with an enthusiastic *amen*. I raised my head to catch Ms. Willa staring at us over the top of her glass. I couldn't tell if she was uncomfortable or just flabbergasted.

But she recovered quickly and talked as she cut her salad into confetti-sized pieces with a knife and fork.

"I've been thinking about it," she said, "because I told you I can be broad-minded. I've decided I like the idea of getting those women off the streets and into some kind of program. You said you had a way of keeping them from going back to the drugs and the men, and I want to believe that. Like I said—"

"You're very broad-minded," I said. I was still bristling at "those women." Mercedes was focusing on getting the carrot curl onto her fork, so I let it pass for now.

"But what I want to know is, do you just give them everything, or do you teach them how to help themselves? I've seen those television shows where they mollycoddle people that're on drugs and treat them like we're being served here. I don't believe in that, now."

"This is what I was trying to get across to you the other day," I said. "If you could see how hard the women in the program work, not only to take care of themselves, but to help each other. I would be willing to take you over to Sacrament House right after lunch."

Ms. Willa waved her fork. A tiny piece of lettuce took timid flight and landed on the saucer of butter slices.

"I'm not interested in rubbing shoulders with them," she said. "Giving money is as far as I go. I just want to know exactly how it's going to be used. And I think you're the kind of person who will give me a straight answer."

She was right about that. The straight answer I had in mind was something along the lines of "People spelunk in caves broader than your mind." But I could hear Chief saying, "You certainly have a way with people, Classic." And India saying, "Just let all that bigotry nonsense roll off your back."

And God saying, *These are the feet I want you to wash.*

He couldn't be serious. Wait. Metaphor. Think metaphor.

"All right, I'll be straight with you," I said. "You are already rubbing shoulders with one of 'those women.'"

I could have sworn Ms. Willa's hair stood completely on end.

"Mercedes is a former prostitute and recovering drug addict. How long have you been clean, Merce?"

"One hundred and twenty-five days."

"She's the Big Sister in our House," I said, "which means she's responsible for supervising two other women who are on the same journey."

Ms. Willa sipped.

"She's learning job skills," I said. "She is a contributing member of society."

"Huh. Oh, no, Bruce, we're not ready for our entrée."

Bruce backed away with the tray of turkey croquettes, directly into a man approaching our table. It would have been comical, if the man hadn't been Troy Irwin.

There was no mistaking him. The studied business-casual way he dressed, his hair obviously mussed by a stylist on a daily basis, and never any grayer in one newspaper photo than in the one before it. But his facial expression seemed different today. This wasn't his typical, *I don't need your admiration, but I appreciate it anyway.* The whimsy around his mouth, the amusement in his too-blue eyes clearly said, *This is going to be too easy.*

My insides lurched so hard, I was certain I'd throw up in the salad greens. The prayers kicked in with the stomach acid. *Please, God, don't let me rip his tongue out right here. Please.*

"It is good to see *you* out and about," he schmoozed to Ms. Willa.

"Why wouldn't I be out and about?" she said. "I'm not an invalid."

"Exactly the opposite. I was about to ask you to dance."

"There's no music." She waved him off and licked her lips as if she'd just tasted the croquettes and found them wanting. The sour look she gave me the first time I met her? Multiply that by about fifty and you had the expression Ms. Willa now wore. Interesting. That might keep me under control for a minute, anyway.

And I had Mercedes with me. To my knowledge she had no idea who Troy Irwin was, and I wanted to keep it that way. As it was, she was surveying him the way she did every newcomer: eyes astute, jaw clenched. And India thought *I* had trust issues.

"I didn't realize you knew Allison Chamberlain," Troy said to Ms. Willa, his gaze still on me. "I can't imagine how your paths would've crossed." He feigned an epiphany. "Wait, she's hitting you up for a donation, isn't she?"

I started to come up out of the chair, but Ms. Willa beat me to it. She didn't stand up, but she did put one of her gnarly hands right in his face.

"She wasn't hitting me up for anything, whatever that means. I was offering. Matter of fact, hand me my purse, Mercy. I'm going to get my checkbook out right now."

I wondered vaguely if she was also packing heat in there. Her terrier voice was reaching a pitch only other terriers could hear, and once again, heads turned in the dining room. Mercedes handed over her purse, and Ms. Willa began to claw through it, hands shaking furiously. I was too astonished to move.

"One thing you should know," Troy went on, as if he hadn't just been swatted away like a mosquito. "Allison is very picky about who she accepts money from. You probably don't know this, or maybe you do: She and I were childhood sweethearts."

Ms. Willa stopped pawing in her bag and shot me a look. "I hope you came to your senses."

Troy didn't give me a chance to answer. "I've tried every way I know to help her with her little program, and she just cannot seem to let the past go and accept what I have to offer."

I couldn't have spoken if he'd let me. My mouth was paralyzed in a furious *O*.

"Now, she does have passion for the things she believes in, I know that from experience."

He winked at Ms. Willa, who recoiled as if he'd spat venom at her. Only that kept me from spitting some myself.

"And she's stubborn as a pit bull, which could work in her favor. But, and here's where you're going to have to do some serious thinking: She didn't stay around her father long enough to learn lessons in reality. Not like I did." He nodded at the leather checkbook Ms. Willa now had clutched in her claws. "So you go on and write a check. I don't blame you. I've always had trouble resisting her myself. But I just thought I'd give you a heads-up …"

He reached past Ms. Willa, and before I could wrench myself away, he cupped his hand around my shoulder. His fingers sent a chill through my skin. I delivered what I knew was a death stare at his knuckles, but he squeezed tighter.

"Remove your hand, please," I said.

"You see," he said to Ms. Willa, "I told you she was—"

"I think you better get your hands off Miss Angel right now."

Mercedes's chair scraped the floor and fell backward behind her. Her eyes flashed as she curved toward Troy like a condor.

"It's okay, Mercedes," I said.

"No it ain't! You said to get off you, and he still holdin' on. You turn loose of her now!"

"Ah, now here's a program that's obviously working," Troy said, smirking at Ms. Willa.

And then he made the fatal mistake. He tossed his head back and laughed, hard and cold and loud.

I had to throw my arms around Mercedes to keep her from

diving across the table and taking him down. It was all I could do not to let her go for it.

"He isn't worth it," I said into her ear. My teeth were gritted so hard, pain shot through my ears. "Don't throw it all away for this piece of slime."

"He was dissin' you, Miss Angel," she cried out, turning heads in the restaurant across the street, I was sure. "I can't have that."

Troy was still laughing in short, harsh bursts.

"Get away from me," I said over the top of Mercedes's head.

"Or?" he said.

Again, I didn't have an opportunity to answer. Below us, Ms. Willa's eyes popped from her tiny face, and she wheezed into a fit of coughing that brought not only Bruce but the entire serving staff.

I flattened myself between Mercedes and Troy and tried to reach for the old lady at the same time.

"Call nine-one-one!" I said.

Ms. Willa glared at me and shook her head and continued to wheeze herself blue. Troy formed a synthetic smile.

"She has the same effect on me," he said to her.

Mercedes tried to lunge at him again. This time he had the good sense to turn and weave his way through the small crowd that had gathered, but I was still hard put to keep her from leaping tabletop to tabletop to bring him to justice.

"Let's just get outside," I said. I sounded like I was coaching a losing basketball team. "Just maintain until we get outside."

I checked with Bruce once more to make sure Ms. Willa wasn't about to expire before I tucked Mercedes's arm into mine and steered us both toward the front door amid faces that ranged from outraged to delighted to be rescued from boredom. I didn't know whether to pray that we wouldn't run into Troy Irwin outside or that we would.

Mercedes was starting to breathe like something smaller than a locomotive by the time we reached the maître d's stand. And then someone—I couldn't even tell if it was male or female—stepped out of the darkness and flashed a camera in our faces. Mercedes flung out a hand to grab it, and only by the grace of God and adrenaline was I able to shove her out the door before she could commit assault and battery.

Once outside, she ripped away from me and flattened against the wall beside the glass doors. I peeled her away and guided her a few yards down. I didn't want the doorman to have the stroke he seemed to be leaning toward. I already had Ms. Willa's asthma attack on my head.

No. It was on Troy Irwin's head. The man was a jackal. The hate I told Hank I wasn't supposed to feel was burning a hole through my soul.

"Okay, I just got to breathe, Miss Angel," Mercedes said. "I'm sorry. I done messed things up bad. I know I did."

"It's all right," I said. "You just did what I wanted to do."

"I couldn't stand seein' that—"

She swore, and then punched her hand to her mouth.

"I give that up," she said. "I done give that up for the Lent, and here I am cussin' right out here on the street."

"Not only did you do what I wanted to do, you said what I wanted to say." I put my hands on her shoulders. "What do you need, Mercedes? How can I help?"

"I think I need to talk to Leighanne. She always be able to talk me down."

That was what NA sponsors were for, and I was glad to let Leighanne take over. I was in need of a sponsor myself about then.

"You take my cell phone," I said. "Her number's in there. Go into the gallery, see? Just next door? Go in there and call her and if she wants to come get you, that's fine."

The hand that took my cell was trembling. It looked the way I felt in the pit of my gut.

When she'd slipped into the art gallery, I turned back toward the restaurant, fully intending to find the person with the camera and take all my frustrations out on him. I almost plowed into a twenty-something guy wearing a necktie and a Bluetooth.

I tried to maneuver around him and tripped over something, probably my own feet. He steadied me with both hands, not something I'd have expected from a kid in his generation.

"You okay?" he said.

"I'm fine," I said.

"I don't see how you could be. That was a pretty hinky scene in there."

I narrowed my eyes until he was a mere blur in my gaze. "Are you a reporter? Was that you who just stuck a camera in my face?"

"No, see, I'm unarmed." He opened his jacket and smiled a rather charming smile at me. "Actually, I'm an attorney. My name's Kade Capelli."

The kid sure wasn't Italian. New England, definitely, judging from the accent. I'd worked in Massachusetts as a taxicab dispatcher for a while in my own twenties, and I could pick up those wide vowels from a hundred yards. But he must have taken after his mother because he was fair-skinned and sandy blond and had blue eyes that were still youth clear. No self-respecting full-blooded Italian looked like a California surfer.

"Capelli?" I said. "Seriously?"

"Seriously." He produced a business card from his shirt pocket. There it was all right: *Kade Capelli, Attorney at Law*, followed by a phone number with an 857 area code.

"Nice to meet you," I said. "Now I really need to go."

"And you are?"

"Allison," I said, and made the decision to get Chief started on legally changing my last name. It was becoming a worse liability than a rap sheet.

"Listen, I couldn't help overhearing what went down in there." Kade gave a soft shrug. "Who could?"

"Nice."

"It looks like you might need some legal representation."

"Are you an ambulance chaser?" I said.

The shiny face fell, and I was immediately sorry. He seemed like a nice enough kid. It wasn't his fault he'd caught me post–Troy Irwin.

"Sorry," I said. "This hasn't been my best day."

"No doubt."

"I already have a lawyer, and you're right. I'm probably going to need him."

"Okay, well, just thought I'd offer."

He stuck out an eager hand for me to shake and I took it. I expected a sweaty palm, but his skin was cool and dry. Somehow that impressed me.

"So, you still have a Massachusetts area code," I said. "You're obviously new in town."

"Been here about a week." His consonants were hard and heavy, not matching the boyish grin at all.

"If you're looking for work, I know an attorney who might be hiring a paralegal. Could be good for starters. It can be hard to break into a small town like this."

"Tell me about it."

"If you have a pen."

I took the slim ballpoint he handed me and wrote Chief's name and number on the back of his card. I wasn't sure why I was doing it, except that he seemed so—what? So free of the stuff that everybody else I'd had contact with today was trying to operate under? Was that it?

"I really appreciate this," he said.

"I hope it helps," I said. "I'll call Chief, Mr. Ellington, and let him know to possibly expect a call from you."

"I'll definitely be in touch with him, yeah. And good luck with ..." He nodded his blond head toward the restaurant.

"I don't believe in luck," I said. "But thanks."

He looked like he was about to ask something. I might even have answered, but Mercedes reappeared and handed me my phone. It was ringing. I mouthed an apology to Kade and picked up.

"Allison?" a female voice said.

"Yes, is this—"

"Yeah, it's Erin O'Hare."

I forgot Kade Capelli, Willa Livengood, even Troy Irwin. "What's wrong?" I said. "Is Desmond okay?"

"I'm not sure, actually," she said. "He's fine physically. He doesn't even know I'm calling you."

"Why are you?" I didn't mean to sound testy, but really, I was coming to the end of today's rope.

"I thought he was studying for today's test."

"He was. We went over the material last night. He knew it all cold." I didn't mention that I hadn't had time to take him on the historical tour we'd talked about. I was already feeling guilty enough and I didn't even know where the conversation was going.

"Something happened, then, because he got to class late, and he was in one of those places again, like I told you about. Very distracted and anxious. I gave him a minute before I started him on the test, but he just sat there and stared at it all period. When he turned it in, he hadn't even written his name on the paper."

"I don't understand."

"Neither do I. I kept him after class and asked him about it, but all he said was … Here, I wrote it down." I heard the rustle of paper. "He said, 'History don't mean nothin' anyway. It's all about now and tomorrow. That's all.'" The paper crackled again. "Does that mean anything to you?"

"Not at the moment," I said. "But I'll talk to him."

"I hope you can, because, really? I've never seen him like this. It's like he's completely shut down."

Right now, that sounded like a decent option.

CHAPTER SIX

God apparently had other plans because I didn't shut down. My angst and fear were so large and close, I'd have had better luck dodging a team of bouncers down at Scarlett O'Hara's.

It didn't seem that Desmond had closed down either. At least that was what he tried to make me believe when I picked him up after school. He was wearing the curled-lip expression of disdain he always put on when I showed up with the van.

"Why we got to ride in this tired ol' thing?" he said as he climbed in.

"Because I haven't had a chance to get the si—the backrest fixed on the bike."

"I don't need no stinkin' bar. I know how to hold on."

"Forget it. I don't want to have to buy one of those T-shirts."

"What T-shirts?"

"The ones that say, 'If you can read this, the kid fell off.'"

Desmond's eyes went into slits. "They don't make no T-shirt like that, Big Al."

"Then I guess you don't ride with me until I get it fixed."

"When's that gonna be?"

It occurred to me to say, *When you tell me what's going on with you.* But something about the exaggeration in every mouth twist and eyebrow lift cautioned me to hold back. The Adam's apple action alone was enough to make me hold my tongue, at least for now. The discussion we had ahead of us seemed like something Chief should be involved in. I pulled out of the school driveway and drummed my fingers on the steering wheel.

"You ain't gon' ask me about the history test?" Desmond said.

I almost ran the van over the curb.

"You drive the bike way better'n you drive this," he said.

"Okay," I said. "How did the test go?"

"It didn't."

"What does that mean?" I felt a little bad pretending I didn't already know, but if he was going to lie, we might have to have the discussion right here.

"Means I froze up." He squirmed in the seat belt to face me. "It came on me when I was havin' lunch, like this ice ball just hit me in the face and froze my brain. I had to go in the bathroom and try to thaw out."

He waited, eyebrows expectant.

"Very poetic," I said. "So then what happened?"

"I got to the class late and I thought Miss All-Hair wasn't gon' let me take the test, but then she did."

So far his story matched hers, but for some reason it sounded like a well-constructed alibi. It was probably the relative correctness of the grammar.

"Give me more," I said.

"I guess I didn't thaw out enough 'cause when I looked at that paper, my brain cells was like ice cubes in there, you know what I'm sayin'?"

I hadn't had that exact experience, but I nodded.

"And then all the sudden, the bell was ringin' and I hadn't written nothin' down. I probably flunked it."

"Uh, probably. And what did Miss O'Hare say?"

He paused for the first time. I could almost hear him flipping through his options like he was going to perform a card trick.

"I tol' her, I said, 'Miss All-Hair, history don't mean nothin' anyway. It's all 'bout now and maybe tomorrow. That's what I care about.'"

It was so close to what Erin quoted to me, I glanced over to see if he, too, had written it down.

"Is that what you really think?" I said.

He didn't even hesitate. "That's what I thought right then 'cause I felt like some kinda loser. But now that I had time to melt them ice cubes in there"—he tapped his bushy cap of hair—"I'm thinkin' I better ask for some extra credit."

"Or we can ask Miss O'Hare if you can retake the test. Only …"

"Only what?" Desmond scrunched up his eyes. "Aw, Big Al, you ain't gon' take away my Harley privilege 'cause I froze up. I couldn't help that, now."

"Relax. I wasn't even thinking that."

He didn't relax, not with his knees rocking the way they were. Yeah, that whole story had taken him most of the afternoon to create.

"I'm thinking we need to find out *why* you froze up," I said.

"I just did."

"So what's to prevent it from happening when you take the test over?"

Everything on him stopped moving. I pulled the van up to the garage and took my time turning off the engine. He still sat motionless.

"I don't expect you to know the answer to that," I said. "It's my job to help you find out. That's why I'm the mother."

His eyes finally moved to look out the side window. The Adam's apple, too, was once again fully operational. He was going to learn to hate that telltale thing.

"I think Miss O'Hare is right," I said. "She told me that day at the art show that you need to experience some of the history and maybe it'll stick with you better."

"How I'm s'posed to do that?" he said to the window.

"Tomorrow, right after school, you and I are going on a personally guided tour of all the old stuff in town."

He turned just enough to slit his eyes toward me. "We ain't takin' one of them trolley things, are we? I heard them guys on them intercoms they got, tryin' to make jokes. Big Al, they ain't even funny."

"Do you seriously think I would subject you to that? I'm your personal tour guide, Clarence. You've forgotten that I used to drive a carriage and show people the sights?" I wiggled my eyebrows. "I know the good stuff they don't tell you in the history books."

"That good stuff gon' be on the test?"

He had me there, but his eyes showed enough of the faint glimmer of his infuriating self to make me grin at him.

"I don't know," I said. "But at least you won't be bored."

"Can we go on the Harley?"

"Are you serious? Desmond, we live right in the middle of all of it. No, we're not going on the Harley. We're going to walk."

He surveyed the windshield for a moment. He was obviously questioning the wisdom of pushing that further because he looked at me and gave a long-suffering sigh.

"I guess thatta be a'ight," he said.

He got out of the van. As I watched him pull up the garage door that was so old it didn't have an automatic opener, I knew I'd won that round too easily. Way too easily.

❧

The next morning I was trying once again to cull something, anything, from Isaiah or Jeremiah or Joel—anybody with prophetic credentials—when I got a call from Bonner.

"Have you seen today's paper?" he said.

The clip in his words made me set my tea down on the bistro table.

"Do I want to?" I said.

"What in the world happened at the 95 yesterday?"

"That made the *paper?*"

"Front page of the *Record.*"

"Are we hard up for news around here?"

"You going to tell me what went down, or should I believe what I read?"

"What's their rendition?"

I could almost see him propping his reading glasses on his nose. "This is what's under the photo."

"The *photo!*"

My voice went so high I sounded like Ms. Willa.

"'Former heiress Allison Chamberlain leaving the 95 Cordova after an altercation with Troy Irwin, CEO of Chamberlain Enterprises.'" Bonner cleared that hairball he always seemed to have in his throat at times like this. "Didn't you promise Chief you weren't going to confront Irwin?"

"I didn't confront him. He just showed up at the restaurant when I was having lunch with Ms. Willa, which, if you'll recall, all of you practically forced me to do."

"She made the news too. Here it is, 'Mrs. Willa Livengood, widow of the late Quincy Livengood, was treated by paramedics at the scene but refused to be taken to the hospital. Witnesses say she'—and I quote—'was so upset by the confrontation between Chamberlain and Irwin she was unable to breathe and nearly lost consciousness.'"

"She didn't 'nearly lose' anything," I said. "Except maybe her lunch. What about Troy Irwin *doesn't* make people want to hurl? Bonner, why did you even tell me about this? That article is so skewed, I don't even know where to start straightening it out."

"How about here? 'Chamberlain was accompanied by an African American woman who allegedly threatened Troy Irwin, claiming he assaulted Chamberlain.'"

"Oh, for Pete's *sake!*"

"Is any of that true?" Bonner said.

"No." I put my fingers to my right temple, which was already throbbing. "Okay, Mercedes—"

"You took Mercedes with you?"

"Are you going to let me finish or what?"

"Sorry."

"Troy put his hand on my shoulder and I told him to let go and he, of course, didn't, so Mercedes made it a little clearer."

"How much clearer?"

I told him the story, as much as I could remember it. Right now it was hard to differentiate between the facts and the turmoil taking shape in my chest. I longed for Desmond's talent for turning every disaster into a stand-up routine.

I managed to come up with, "You said we needed publicity."

"Not this kind!"

"What do you want me to do about it, Bonner? Tell me and I'll do it. Maybe."

There was a short silence, during which I was certain he was rolling up the sleeves of his Oxford shirt.

"I don't know," he said finally. "Maybe I'll write a letter to the editor that sets the story straight."

"Do you actually think the *Record* is going to print it? Doesn't Troy Irwin own it, too?"

"Not officially. Just politically."

"Then don't waste your time," I said. "Let's just leave this one to God. The more we fiddle with it, the worse we're going to make it."

He let out a long sigh that sounded strangely like relief.

"What?" I said.

"I'm just glad to hear you putting this in God's hands again. I mean, I know you probably always do, but the rest of us like to hear it."

"How long has it been since I've mentioned it?" I said.

The hairball was still giving him trouble. "A couple of weeks? Maybe I'm wrong. It could just be my insecurity."

"What insecurity?"

He grunted softly. "How much time you got?"

He sounded genuinely wistful. Bonner and I used to spend a lot of time together. Our friendship was actually stronger, more honest now than it was back when he thought of me as dating material. But the opportunities to just share an order of fried shrimp at the Santa Maria and talk about our "stuff" were practically nonexistent, now that our focus was on the Sisters.

I closed the Bible and picked up my tea mug for a sip.

"You're not wrong," I said. "I'm not talking about God as much because I don't think I'm hearing from God as much. Not like I was for a while. I just keep getting this one—I guess you could call it a message."

"One of your Nudges?" he said.

"No. I mean it's like a Nudge, but I can feel it inside, too. Sort of like you feel nauseous when you eat bad crab."

"I'd question whether that was God too."

He didn't ask me what the message was, which suddenly made me want to tell him. He was the first person I'd confided in about God's command that I go buy a Harley, and although he'd been dubious then, here he was, giving me his trust and his time and his ear.

"All I keep hearing is, *Allison, wash their feet.*" I said. "I know it has to be a metaphor, which is why we're doing the Feast and all of us are serving instead of asking to *be* served."

"So it's our potential donors' feet that we're washing," he said.

There was so little disbelief in his voice, I would have hugged him if he hadn't been across town.

"That's what I'm getting," I said. "What do you think?"

"I think you better have the buckets ready."

"It's not meant to be taken literally."

"Oh," Bonner said. "Well, you're the prophet."

Yeah. That's what they kept telling me.

Desmond and I set off on foot down St. George Street after school that day. I had a cheat sheet tucked into the pocket of my denim jacket in case I suffered a memory lapse. Keeping him from sidetracking me into gift shops and eating establishments was going to take my total concentration.

"You gonna make me take notes, Big Al?" he said as he loped beside me across the intersection of St. George and East King.

"You don't need to take notes. You're like a sponge."

"You mean like I'm all the time scrubbin' things?"

"Um, no, that would definitely not be your MO. I mean you absorb everything you see and hear." I gave him a sideways look. "Which sometimes serves you well and sometimes doesn't."

"Like when I listen in on what you and Mr. Chief sayin' about me when I ain't s'posed to be listenin'."

"Exactly. Matter of fact, today, just pretend you aren't supposed to be hearing what I'm saying and you'll be fine."

"Unh-uh," Desmond said. "You gon' be impressed with how good Imma listen to you."

He was actually true to his word. During his first foray through Castillo de San Marcos, the enormous seventeenth-century Spanish bastion that still guarded Matanzas Bay as if an attack by a band of marauding Englishmen was imminent, Desmond watched my lips as I regaled him with tales of pirates hunting the treasure fleets and of the intrigue of three hundred years of back-to-back colonial wars, in which the fort was never defeated.

But I was more impressed with the way he climbed on the

bronze cannons and pressed his ear to the wall to try and hear the screams and fighting in the *coquina,* just as the legend had it. He gazed from the always-burning watchtower light to the bay beyond, as if he, too, were watching for his comrades coming from Spain. And he shivered in the dungeon where even after at least a hundred visits, I also felt the death and dread and victory that seemed to ooze from its weeping walls. It was late afternoon and the busloads of school kids had already left for the day, so there was no one to pretend to be cool for. He was finally the child he'd never gotten to be, and I no longer cared whether he passed history or not. This was the test *I* couldn't fail.

The Oldest Wooden Schoolhouse near the City Gates on St. George Street was about to close when we got there, but I knew Cricket, the current guide, so she let us slide in, pointing out the button for the self-guided tour. I nixed that. Desmond would have a field day with the robot professor. He actually took one look at the tiny ramshackle bald-cypress-and-cedar room and decided this was far superior to the school he was currently attending.

"I don't think so, dude," I said. "They wouldn't let you chase girls here like you get to do at Muldoon Middle."

He smiled slyly. "I could chase women anywhere."

Yeah, I definitely needed to get Chief to have the talk with him. Again.

The sun was sinking beneath the tops of the palm trees when we emerged from the school's outhouse, clearly Desmond's favorite part of the school experience, which meant all the other historical sites were closed. I decided to just take him for a stroll down carless St. George Street and fill him in on some of the lesser-known stories along the way. I was just getting into the Dragon of St. George Street when a voice called out,

"Now there's a lady who looks like she could use a nice aperitif to finish off the day. Don't you think, Lewis?"

"If 'aperteeth' mean food, I am there," Desmond said, and bolted for the Monk's Vineyard, where two old guys sat on the front porch sipping the fruits of their own vines.

"It doesn't mean food," I said, on Desmond's heels, since he was already going up the two small steps.

"It *can* mean food," said the one who'd been referred to as Lewis. He had a ridiculous mustache that looked like he'd stolen it off the figure of Yosemite Sam in the wax museum on the Plaza. "We serve appetizers now."

The other man rocked his chair onto its back legs and waved in the direction of the chalkboard hanging behind him. His mop of gray curls brushed against it and erased half the items on the menu. Was that hairdo a perm? A *perm?*

Desmond gazed at the board and pointed toward the smeared version of "Wings Hotter than the Surface of the Sun."

"I'll have me a order of them," he said.

"Coming up," Moustache said. "And you, pretty lady?'"

"Flattery will get you nowhere," I said. "Except to a Diet Coke if you've got one."

"You want it with lemon, lime, or cherry? It's all fresh."

They were trying so hard I felt a stab of pity. Five years ago, when the Monk's Vineyard had opened here in the heart of the historic district, they'd served only wine, and the best of it. At first it had taken off, attracting the more trendy locals as well as their traveling counterparts. I used to recommend it to some of my carriage tour customers, the ones who tipped generously and weren't carrying shopping bags full of cheap souvenirs.

But like most specialty businesses, the owners of the Vineyard— two older men whose names I'd never caught—had been slammed by the recession. From the looks of the menu, they'd gone from exclusively selling fine wines to serving up Mrs. Paul's and calling it hors d'oeuvres. It didn't seem to be working. The FOR SALE sign they'd had hanging on the front railing for a year was still there.

"Make that two orders of wings," I said. "The kid has a hollow leg."

Just the thought of eating them nearly gave me the heaves, but the smile it brought to Moustache's face might make it worth a little indigestion. I'd never met these two before and might not again if the place ever sold, so what was the harm? Besides, Desmond was settled in at a table, legs propped on the railing, chewing the proverbial fat with Curly. I hoped he'd find out if that was a perm or natural. I was trying not to imagine the old gentleman under a dryer with rods in his hair.

"You going to give me a hand, George?" Lewis said from the doorway.

"I've got to entertain the guests," George said.

"I could give you a hand," Desmond said.

"No, you couldn't," I said.

"What will you have to drink, son?" Lewis said.

"Whatever'll make my moustache grow like yours. That thing is *cool.*"

"Nothing with alcohol, caffeine, or sugar for him," I said.

George chuckled, a sound seldom heard in anyone but an old man with time on his hands. "That just about rules out everything, doesn't it?"

"Why don't you let him come in and pick something out?" Lewis said.

I sighed and gave Desmond the nod. He was through the door before I could take my next breath. Give it fifteen minutes and he'd be filling orders himself, guaranteed.

"He's a pistol," George said. "Reminds me of myself at that age."

I had to agree in terms of the hairstyle. I forced myself not to ask him for the name of his salon.

"I see you made the papers."

I almost overshot the chair I was just lowering myself onto.

George chuckled again. "Front page too. Now, Lewis, he's an old journalist from way back—used to run the night desk. He wasn't that impressed with the article—said it was slanted—but I got the gist of it, and I have to say, I knew it was only a matter of time before you started to stir things up around here."

"I'm sorry," I said. "Do we know each other?"

"I used to hear you giving your carriage tour spiel. Liked your spirit."

"The owners didn't call it 'spirit,'" I said. "They called it 'sarcasm.'" And worse, but I didn't think it was worth mentioning.

The way George was nodding, I didn't have to. "I've been following your work the last several months," he said.

"And?" I said.

He waited while Desmond presented me with a Diet Coke, festooned with a lime wedge, a lemon slice, *and* a maraschino cherry, and disappeared back into the innards of the Vineyard, though not before calling over his shoulder that those wings would be up in just a minute. I'd once worked in a short-order restaurant, and it was a week before I got that lingo down. He was obviously a natural for the food-service industry.

When Desmond was gone, George leaned forward in conspiratorial fashion. "It's quite the coincidence that you walked by today because I was thinking about trying to contact you."

"I'm not sure there are any coincidences," I said.

He looked up at the porch ceiling, and brought his substantial gray eyebrows into a scowl.

"Would you know anything about a brothel upstairs there?"

I gagged on the cherry.

"You work with the ladies of the night," he said. "I thought you might have heard about these two."

"What two?" I said.

"I don't know for sure. Lewis thinks I'm going senile, which is why I'm mentioning it to you while he can't hear. But ever since we rented that apartment up there to those two women, there's been a lot of foot traffic between the hours of dark and who knows when. When we come in to open up in the morning, their shades go down and it seems like they sleep all day. The next night when the sun sets, it starts all over again, and not always the same guys." He shook his curly head ruefully. "Seems like they're doing a better business than we are."

"Here's your hot wings."

Desmond approached with two steaming plates. He'd donned an apron with a silk-screened figure of a Friar-Tuckish monk holding an impossibly large bunch of grapes on the front of it. Lewis watched fondly from the doorway, wearing its twin.

"What else can I get you?" Desmond said as he set the platters on the table. "Another Diet?"

"Aren't you going to eat?" I said.

"I ain't got time for that. We just had a order called in."

George raised his copious eyebrows at Lewis. "Called in? From where?"

"From above."

"Upstairs above?"

"That's the one."

"No."

"It's for two pastrami on rye and an order of baked beans, George."

"We don't make pastrami on rye."

"We do now." He nodded at Desmond, who was whipping off his apron. "Desi's making a deli run."

"No, really," I said—but I couldn't get more than two words in between George and Gracie.

"We're not taking food up there," George said. "Not until Ms. Chamberlain checks it out for us."

"What?" I said.

"I told her about my suspicions." He nodded significantly toward Desmond. "I'm having her go up and see if we're right. She knows how to handle these things."

"You got you some bad women up there, Mr. Georgio?" Desmond said.

Both men looked at me, hearts probably beating faster than they had in years. Either that, or they were about to stop altogether.

George regained his composure first. "I see the boy is aware of the kind of work you do."

"My bio mom was a—"

"I'm appropriately honest with him," I said.

"You better go check it out, Big Al," Desmond said. "I can hang here with Mr. Georgio and my man Lewie. We got plenty to do."

"Sit down and eat these wings," I said. "I'll be right back." I directed a stony gaze at George. "You'll keep an eye on him."

"I won't let him out of my sight."

I turned to Lewis. "How do I get up there?"

"There's an elevator in the hall," he said. "I'll show you."

I was still gritting my teeth as he led me briefly into the dark interior of the Vineyard and then to an even darker hallway that ran to another door onto the street.

"Thank you for doing this," Lewis said. He pulled at his moustache with nervous-looking fingers. "I keep telling myself George is wrong, but if he isn't, we don't want any trouble with the police."

"I'm just going to look it over and tell you what I see, and that's all," I said.

But "Lewie" was already on his way back to the kitchen.

I decided I must be crazy as I bypassed the deathtrap of an elevator and went for the stairs. Who knocks on a door and says, "Excuse me, but are you turning tricks up here?" What was I, the moral police for the entire town now? Only because I didn't want Desmond to think I was a slacker did I keep going up to the first landing. Okay, that was a lie. I reached the second floor, crossed the hall, and banged on the door only because I knew Lewis and Clark weren't going to let me go until I finished the expedition.

I half-hoped nobody would respond, but my fist hammering was rewarded by "Hang on—I'm coming," followed by a jerking open of the door. A woman blinked at me in the semidarkness. Dressed in cleavage-to-thigh spandex, she was only slightly more classy than the women who still walked West King Street.

Doggone it. George and Lewis were right.

"What is it?" the woman said.

Make that "girl." Even through the smoky air, I could see that the half-inch layer of makeup she was wearing added five or six years to her face. She couldn't have been more than twenty or twenty-one.

"So who are you?" she said. One side of her goopy lip headed toward her nostril, where a tiny gold ring resided.

"I'm looking for a job."

No. I did not just say that. Who was going to believe—

But the girl stepped back briskly and nodded me into the room with a snap of her head. The moment I stepped into the light from the lava lamp on the table, of course, she apparently realized her mistake.

"I don't think you're qualified for the work we do here," she said, words jammed together like a runaway train.

Her polyurethane smile was so condescending, I wanted to shake her. Maybe the girls on West King *were* classier than she was. At least they weren't proud of their profession.

"Sorry." She pointed her breasts toward the door. "We're a modeling agency and quite frankly, you're a little old."

"Get off it, honey," I said. "I know what you're doing up here."

She jerked her arms into a fold across said breasts. "And what would that be?"

As if on cue, a seductive giggle rippled from behind the closed door off the room we were standing in. A muffled male voice responded, followed by another throaty laugh. I watched Chesty swallow. Desmond's Adam's apple had nothing on hers.

"If you're a cop, you better show me a badge," she said.

"Look, I'm not here to bust you," I said. "I'm not even a cop."

A light dawned in her eyes, which were so dilated I wondered she didn't pull a pair of shades out of that cleavage. "If you're looking for your husband," she said, "that isn't him in there. Not unless you robbed a cradle."

I must be having a bad hair day. That was the second slur about my age in the last two minutes.

"I don't have a husband," I said.

"Shocking."

"A, I'm here to warn you that your landlords are on to you, and they *are* going to call the police if you don't either cease and desist or clear out."

At least, that was what I thought they had in mind. We hadn't gotten that far.

"And B." I hesitated because I wasn't sure what "B" was, until it tumbled from my mouth. "B, this is a dead-end deal you've got going on up here, and I can help you turn it around."

"Into what?" The upper lip almost disappeared up her nose, where it would undoubtedly be met by the trail of moisture coming out.

"Into a way of life where you don't have to get high to tolerate your occupation. Or sell your body to *get* high. Whichever way you look at it, you're going nowhere fast. Like I said, I can help you. It's what I do."

And I sure hoped God had a plan for that because none of this was coming from *my* brain. Now was a nice time for God to start speaking through me again. Judging from the way this girl's eyes were bulleting into me, I was sure any minute she was going to produce a handgun.

Instead, she laughed, the second ugly sound to fill the room. The other was the shrill voice from behind the door. It had morphed from a giggle to a torrent of words only half of which I could make out.

"What'd you come here for? You still got to pay! Just get out!"

The last two were accompanied by the flinging open of the door. The man on the receiving end of the tirade had no choice but to get out because a willowy Hispanic girl gave him a shove that landed him on his back on the floor, right at my feet.

Kade Capelli looked up at me.

It didn't matter that he was fully clothed. The ire still marched right up my backbone, and out my mouth.

"Getting to know St. Augustine?" I said. "You should've said something. I'd have gotten you a better tour guide."

"He needs to get out!" the slender girl said to Chesty. Her voice bore the faint trace of Hispanic beginnings.

"What did he do?"

"It's what he didn't do."

"Hey, listen, I'm gone." Kade got to his feet and dug into his pocket, producing a wad of bills that he pushed toward the Hispanic girl. Chesty intercepted the money and pointed haughtily to the door. He backed toward it and at least had the grace to look sheepishly at me.

"I didn't mean to tick her off," he said.

"Why are you telling me that?" I said. "Tell her."

"I don't wanna hear nothin' from you," the girl cried. "Just—"

"I know. I'm getting out."

"You, too, lady," Chesty said.

"Who's she?" the other girl said.

"Don't know—don't care. Both of you, out."

Kade had already beaten a hasty retreat. I could hear him bursting through the door to the street below.

"Did I not just tell you to leave?" Chesty said.

"I'm going," I said. But I still stood in the middle of the garish room.

"That doesn't look like 'going' to me."

"Listen, if you ladies aren't busy on the seventeenth—that's a Saturday, lunchtime—come to Number Two Palm Row. Around noon."

"Why?" Chesty said. "Wait, don't tell me. You're having a revival and we can come be saved."

"No," I said. "We're having a Feast. And I don't know what will happen to you. You'll have to come and find out."

Then I beat it out of there before I was forced to blurt out something else I never meant to say.

When I reached the porch of Monk's Vineyard again, where Desmond was sipping what I hoped was sparkling cider out of a champagne glass, I was barely coherent. All I could get out was, "You were right, fellas. I don't know what you want to do about it." I took the glass out of Desmond's hand and set it on the table. "But we've got to get home."

"We heard the yelling," George said. "Already called the police."

Lewis nodded toward the figure approaching the porch. Wonderful. It was young Officer Kent. Was there some kind of plot afoot that I hadn't been made aware of? First Kade. Now him.

At any rate, I was so not in the mood for any more males of their generation. I hadn't had time yet to figure out why I was this livid about Kade Capelli. I'd be incensed at any guy who exploited women, even higher-end hookers like those two. But I couldn't explain the burning knot in my stomach over this particular one. Maybe it was because I hadn't seen this in him when I met him. I felt like a dope.

Or maybe it was because I'd given him Chief's number and told him to apply for a job as his assistant. Note to self: Contact Chief the minute you can get out of Desmond's hearing range.

"You called the police, gentlemen?" Officer Kent said.

He stood now on the bottom step, just below me and Desmond, who was trying to wriggle from the grip I had on the back of his jacket.

"I did," George said. "But this is the lady you want to talk to. She went up to investigate."

Kent looked like I was the last person he wanted to talk to. The freckles around his eyes folded.

"I guess it won't do me any good to say I wish you'd called us first before you went up there," he said to me.

"None." I looked at Desmond. "I want you to stay right here with George and Lewis. Do not step off this porch or I will take away your helmet. Permanently. I need to talk to this officer."

"We'll keep him busy," Lewis said.

That was what I was afraid of, but I had no choice. I nodded for Kent to follow me and led him all the way across the street to the now closed gate to the Spanish Quarter. If Desmond could hear us over here, he was the bionic boy.

"Did the women admit to you they were soliciting?" Kent said when I stopped on the sidewalk.

"No. If you went up there and asked them now, they'd deny it, and you'd be hard put to find any evidence."

"Then how do you know?"

"It's my job to know. Look, arresting them isn't going to solve anything. We both know that."

He looked at me, the proper words already forming on his freckled lips. And then he let his shoulders drop, until he looked for all the world like a boy who had failed at his post on the safety patrol and had come to turn in his badge.

"I do know that," he said. "And I wish I could do what you do."

"Which is what?"

"Take them in and try to turn them around. I can't do that. If I pick one up, I have to arrest her and from there it's out of my hands."

"So, what if you don't pick her up?"

"I get busted for not doing my job."

"What's your job description exactly?"

He shifted his weight uneasily. "I'm not sure what you mean."

"Isn't it to 'serve and protect'?"

"Supposedly."

He was letting his guard down enough to make this worth a shot. I lowered my voice.

"If you were to call me if you suspected a woman of prostitution, instead of picking her up, wouldn't you still be serving and protecting?"

"I'd be protecting a criminal."

"They're not serial killers, Officer Kent."

"Nicholas."

"I'm sorry?"

"My name's Nicholas."

"Okay—Nicholas. I don't see how tossing them into the same tank as the drunks and the armed robbers and the pedophiles is protecting them. I can protect them, though. Or we can, at Sacrament House. It would be just like you were dropping them off at rehab."

Nicholas hung his thumbs on his belt and studied the sidewalk now splashed with the light from the lamps winking on along St. George.

"The circumstances would have to be exactly right," he said finally. "If somebody's flipping out the way that woman was the other day—"

"Zelda," I said. "Her name is Zelda."

He grimaced.

"Yeah," I said. "It makes a difference when you know their names, doesn't it?"

"But if she's a danger to somebody, I can't just get you on the phone."

"Okay. But if she's merely out there trying to make it through the day the only way she knows how …"

He turned his young, pale blue eyes full on me. "Give me your cell number. If I can do it in good conscience, I'll call you. But you have to do the same in return."

"How so?"

"If you get yourself in a situation with one of the, well, with a Zelda, you call me personally, not the department. And you have to promise to give me any and all information that could lead to the arrest of any perpetrator."

He stuck his fingers into his shirt pocket and drew out a card. When he handed it to me, I curled my fingers around his.

"Thank you, Nicholas," I said.

"Don't mention it," he said, and added, "to anybody."

I hurried back across the street, where Desmond was now astride the porch railing, leaning precariously from side to side.

"Desmond, *what* are you doing?" I said.

"Showin' Mr. Georgio and Lewie how you and me ride our Harley."

"Sounds like you're quite the Motorcycle Mama," George said with a grin.

I didn't tell him that was totally under God's orders. But for the first time in weeks, I felt again what I now knew was coming straight from God. You didn't invite hookers to fund-raisers and set up liaisons with police officers unless you felt the urge deep in the folds of your soul. Unless the yearning was pulling you the way it finally did me.

Maybe now I could get all the stirred-up stuff settled down and get something done. Maybe now.

CHAPTER SEVEN

Officer Nicholas Kent and I had no need of each other in the days of relative peace that followed the incident at Monk's Vineyard.

Emphasis on "relative."

On the home front, Owen was pleased because he finally "got a bead" on a vehicle that he said had been driving up and down Palm Row on a regular basis.

"Beige, late-model Mercury Sable with Florida tags," he told me on Wednesday afternoon when I was outside washing off the Harley. He sounded like he was auditioning for *Without a Trace*. "I couldn't get the license number. I'm getting blind as a bat when it comes to distance. Now, close up, I've got eyes like a cat in the dark. Anything farther than ten feet, you're better off with a mole."

"Thanks, Owen," I said before he could go any deeper into the animal kingdom.

He stepped out of the path of the hose spray. "I hope this doesn't spell some kind of trouble for you."

"It's just somebody eyeballing the houses, I'm sure. People are always looking for property in this part of town. They think they can basically steal something because the economy has tanked."

Owen adjusted the brim of his golf hat. "It's yours they're looking at. The car stops right in front of your house. But the minute I go out to ask questions, whoever it is moves on." He shook his head until I realized he wanted me to shake mine, too. "You aren't thinking about selling, are you? Miz Vernell's worried about undesirables moving in here."

I didn't remind him that not long ago Miz Vernell thought I was one of the undesirables. Me and anybody else on a Harley, who were half the people I associated with.

"I'm not going anywhere," I said. "I couldn't drag Desmond away from you."

He gave me a denture-bright grin. "You're right there."

"Besides, Sylvia would rise up from her grave and set me straight if I even thought about it. I made a promise to her."

That seemed to reassure Owen for the time being. Meanwhile, Erin O'Hare let Desmond retake his history test before school Thursday. His brain cells evidently didn't turn into ice chips, because he scored a B-minus. Erin admitted to me that she gave him a few extra points for the caricature of Pedro Menéndez de Avilés he drew on the back. Desmond was less impressed by his grade than he was that Chief promised him that the day after the Feast he'd get his reward ride on the beach. Desmond immediately started to mark the days off on the Harley calendar on the refrigerator.

On Friday morning, India joined Hank and me for our last breakfast at the Spanish Galleon before it closed. Between commiserating with Patrice and eating one of everything on the breakfast menu, I told India and Hank that I'd invited the two entrepreneurial prostitutes to the Feast. Hank chewed her Walk the Plank omelet and looked at India, who just looked confused. It was as foreign a look on India's face as a cubic zirconium would have been on her finger.

"Are they part of the program now?" she said.

"Not at this point," I said.

"So they're not coming to serve."

"No. If they show up at all, which I seriously doubt, we're going to serve them."

India tapped her lip with her index finger. "Right alongside the Junior League and the DAR."

Hank put her napkin to her lips, but she couldn't hide the fact that she was enjoying this. India held up both hands like she was surrendering at Appomattox.

"I'm not trying to be facetious. I'm just having trouble imagining what this is going to look like. I mean, honey, do you know?"

"I guess it'll look like what it looks like," I said. "Like I said, they probably won't even come. We didn't exactly hit it off."

"Do we want to know what that means?" Hank said from behind the napkin.

"I called them on their stuff. They showed me to the door. And on the way I had this compulsion to invite them."

"God," Hank said.

"That's what I think, yeah."

India merely picked up her Café Olé and sipped.

I let it go. If she wanted to say something she would. I'd created a ripple in her vision, but if I knew India, she would smooth it out with her usual poise. I made a mental note to get me some of that.

🏍

A few of the HOGs put together a sunset ride and supper at the A1A Crab Shack that evening. Chief said I needed a night out and even made arrangements with Owen to have Desmond hang with him. Things had been a few degrees chillier than usual between us since the night at O. C. White's, so I was happy for a chance to warm it up. Just a few degrees.

Chief convinced me to ride with him so I could relax, not exactly a hard sell. Once I was behind him on the Road King, however, his shoulders seemed bastion broad, and the V they formed with his waist pretty much made "relaxing" an impossibility. I wasn't sure where to put my hands until he took both of them and pressed them into his sides, where they at once oozed a less-than-romantic sweat.

"You ready?" he said.

Was he serious?

All the way over the Bridge of Lions to the island, along the watercolor ocean and through the air made of spun silver, I had to be one with Chief, leaning with his leans, stilling myself at his stops, absorbing his confidence as my hands sensed the muscles in his back.

You're not used to feeling? Hank had asked me.

Not like this. Never like this. Never as if breaking away from this oneness would be like splitting myself in half.

By the time we got to the Crab Shack at Crescent Beach, I was a veritable puddle, and I escaped straight to the ladies' room to drain the flush out of my cheeks. And neck. And scalp. I was going to have to do something about this Chief situation before I lost what little of my mind was left, but all I could think of to do at that point was lock myself in one of the stalls and wait for—something. All I knew was if God told me to *wash his feet, Allison,* we were going to have a serious conversation.

But I felt nothing except an increasingly delicious ache in my chest. Maybe Chief was right. Maybe I just needed to relax.

Uh-huh.

I finally stepped out into the "dining room"—a dubious description for a hall of chipped red wooden benches and a deserted purple bar bearing a sign saying DIAGONAL PARKING ONLY. Nita, Leighanne, and Hank, all still in bandannas and chaps like peasants-turned-biker-chicks, were already carrying surfboard-sized platters of steamed shrimp and stone crab claws to the bilious yellow tables with buckets for shells hanging from nails on the ends of them. I didn't offer to help. My former stint as a waitress had only lasted for two weeks for a reason. But I did grab a pile of napkins and follow them.

The guys—Chief, Ulysses, Stan, Rex, and Hank's husband, Joe—were all seated facing us on one side of the two tables they'd pushed together to make a single long one. Rex, the HOG chapter president, was pouring sodas from a pitcher, his oversized-toddler face, as always, an interesting study with the graying temples and mushy middle-aged paunch. Ulysses, who'd unsuccessfully attempted to teach me to ride before Hank stepped in, raised his plastic tumbler, which meant he had one of his infamous toasts at the ready.

"To HOGs," he proclaimed, "who know how to pig out."

An appreciative moan went up.

"A sumptuous repast," Joe said. He wasn't your typical HOG. Actually, he wasn't a HOG at all. It almost took an act of Congress to get him to ride with Hank. That or the promise of stone crab claws.

"I don't know about that," Stan said, blue eyes grinning. "But would you look at all this?"

I was looking. And what I saw caught at my breath and held it in my chest.

This was a gathering of disciples, as blundering and faithful and hungry as any in a long-ago upper room. Leonardo da Vinci it was not, but it had to be a portrait painted by God because something contracted inside me like a squeeze toward birth. It was as real as the words that came out of my mouth.

"I love you," I said.

Ulysses turned to me, curly black bun at the nape of his neck in tow. "Right back at ya, babe."

"I love you *all*," I said. "And what you've done for Sacrament House and the Sisters."

"Aw shucks," Stan said. Leighanne punched him in the stomach.

"We do for you because we also love," Rex said, his shy French accent peeking out between the words.

"You set the tone, though, Allison," Nita said. "You know you do."

"Whatever, but, listen." I took another breath. The squeeze was still there. "We're having a Feast at my place a week from tomorrow. It's a fund-raiser but it's also a footwashing."

"Say again?" Stan said, hand cupped around his ear.

"Don't you want your piggies washed?" Leighanne said to him.

"Harley Riders do not have 'piggies.'"

Leighanne curved her tall body over him, the usual tank-top spillage hidden by a turtleneck sweater. "I've seen yours, Stan. You could use a good pedicure."

"It's not a literal footwashing," I said. "It's like a metaphor. You know, we're serving the people we're asking to serve us."

"Serve you with donations," Stan put in.

"Right, but we want to do for the people who already *have* donated—donated themselves." I opened my arms to them. "Like you. So will you come? Let us feed you and pamper you?"

"But, really, no spa?" Stan said.

"No," I said, laughing. And then I caught Hank's eye. Her left cheek protruded, as if she had her tongue secured there so it wouldn't escape.

"I'll talk to India," I said to her.

She just nodded and took the pair of crab crackers Joe handed her.

As the banter continued over the shellfish, Chief tugged me into the chair next to his at the end and scraped closer. His shoulders shut out the rest of the party as he leaned in.

"I can only assume that was spontaneous," he said, lips barely moving.

"As in it just came out of my mouth?" I said. "Yeah. All of a sudden, this just looked like a picture of—never mind. I can't describe it. It just was there."

"I never question what you hear," he said.

"There's a 'but' in there though."

Chief gave a half shrug. "I'm merely ... inquiring ... whether you're trying to make money, or spend it."

"Neither."

"You're scarin' me, Classic."

I tried to shape it with my hands. "Okay, I know it's supposed to be about getting the funds to do what we have to do, but that's not what's going on inside me. It feels like there's something more. I just can't get a handle on it."

"So, Allison."

I turned to Nita, whose Spanish eyes were earnest.

"Are we the only Harley people invited?" she said. "I mean, because there are some other people who've helped."

"Absolutely. Whoever you think of, please, tell them to come. And—"

I glanced at Chief and at Hank. They were both watching me, their expressions cryptic as text messages: Hank's saying, *I can't wait to hear how you break this to India;* Chief's telling me he could hear the bank account draining. They made sense, and the contraction in my soul made none. But wasn't it the very thing I'd been waiting for? Didn't it get to the root of *Wash their feet?*

I looked back at Nita, still waiting, all short and golden. "Invite anybody else who just needs to be served."

Chief smeared his entire face with one big hand. Hank drowned a hunk of crabmeat in the drawn butter without taking her eyes off of me.

"You want me to do a little Evite maybe?" Nita said.

Leighanne tapped my hand. "Have Desmond do a drawing. We can scan it and put it on there."

"That would be fabulous," I said.

"What are we calling it?"

"The Feeding of the Five Thousand," Hank said, voice dry.

"Just call it 'Community Feast,'" I said. "And then put, 'For Anyone Needing a Holy Meal.'" My eyes locked with Chief's. "And 'Donations appreciated from those who are able.'"

You sure about this, Classic? his eyes said.

No, mine said back.

But God seemed to be, because at last my soul relaxed. I grabbed for a crab claw.

Chief's hesitation notwithstanding, he supported the effort. He went out for forgotten items when Hank and the Sisters were cooking in my kitchen almost every evening. Monday he delivered Desmond's caricature—a line of servers who looked like all of us, carrying streaming trays and sporting oversized bare feet. He came back with fliers to put in, as Desmond phrased it, "places where people needs somebody bein' they Mother D."

"I'm surprised you didn't put *that* on the flier," India said. "Of course, the fliers themselves are a surprise." She composed a patient smile and turned to Chief. "Honey, we are definitely going to need more food."

On Thursday, Chief's job, and Bonner's, was to carry in the carload of imported bowls and platters and Reed & Barton sterling ware and Irish lace tablecloths that India brought over.

"I think these are probably a little more high end than what Jesus used at the Last Supper," Hank told her.

"We don't know that," India said. "And it is gon' be hard enough to get some of the women on the guest list to pass the crab puff to a man with tattoo sleeves as it is." She headed to the dining room with the cherry silver chest, still muttering, "I'm just sayin'."

"Speaking of invited guests," Bonner called to her, "have you heard from Ms. Willa?"

"Not yet," she called back.

"Don't count on Ms. Willa," I said. "If you'll recall, when last she and I spoke, she was in the process of hyperventilating. I'm pretty sure she's changed her mind about that check she was about to write."

"It'll be all right if she doesn't come." India stopped in the doorway. The look she gave me could only be described as ironic. "If half the town is going to be there now, you can probably pass the hat and make up the difference."

"The helmet," said Desmond, who had joined us out of nowhere. "We gon' pass the helmet."

"Oh," India said. "I didn't know there was protocol for community feasts." I started to say something—anything—but she turned to Mercedes. "Darlin', why don't you help me polish the serving pieces? You have such a nice touch."

I occurred to me that India hadn't called *me* "Honey" or "Darlin'" for three days.

Hank brushed past me on her way to the sink with a pot of red sauce. "Later," she said out of the side of her mouth.

"Later" meant when the Sisters had gone to their NA meeting and Chief was in the living room helping Desmond with his math facts and India had agreed to let Bonner take her down to O. C.'s for an espresso. Hank told them all that she and I would muck out the kitchen, but I was certain I was the one who was about to be mucked out.

I opted to cut to the chase. The minute we were alone at the sink, I said, "India still has reservations about the way this is shaping up, doesn't she?"

"I never knew you to be one to understate the case, Al." Hank chopped her hands to her hips. "She's freaking out about it."

"Why doesn't she just say something to me?"

"Would it make any difference? Would you call this off and go back to pasta salad and a jazz quintet?"

"No," I said. "I can't. And it isn't just what I'm getting from God. Or maybe it is." I went after a skillet with a piece of steel wool. "I can't see myself serving finger sandwiches to a bunch of women who can eat at the 95 anytime they want, and letting a whole community go without."

"I applaud your compassion. We all do. But if you alienate the people who are trying to help you serve that community, you're no good to anybody."

I scrubbed harder. "What am I supposed to do, Hank? I'm finally getting something from God after weeks of feeling like he'd reassigned my job to somebody else. Now you want me to ignore it?"

"No." Hank took the steel-wool pad from me and tossed it in the other sink. "But you're going at this the way you're scouring that pan. Of course, if God is telling you to disregard people's feelings, then by all means, blunder on."

I dug my hands into my hair, realizing too late that they were covered in oily suds. "What are you saying? Just come out with it."

She handed me a towel. "India has vision too, and it comes from a place just as deep as the one you're operating from. But you superimposed yours on hers with no regard to how that was going to make her feel."

Hank pressed her lips together, but I knew she wasn't done.

"Don't stop now," I said. "Let's get this out."

"India made a huge sacrifice leaving the church to be part of this cause."

"She didn't have to do that."

"You had to. Bonner had to. How is she any different?"

I looked at the towel, now gray with grease. "I've made a hopeless mess of this, haven't I?"

"It'll wash out."

"I mean with India."

"A mess, yes. Hopeless, no. I think Bonner will be able to get her to understand. None of us has ever done this before. We're all feeling our way." She took the towel from me and wiped at my forehead. "Do what you have to do, but if I were you, I wouldn't make any more changes at this point." She looked me dead in the eye. "That Southern-lady thing does have its limits."

By Friday night, everything was in place for Saturday except the last-minute details. The sauces were at the ready in the refrigerator. The breads were lined up on the dining room table, and Desmond was under the threat of house arrest if he touched any of the biscotti or *panforte* or cannoli that had turned my pantry into a *pasticceria*.

"The only thing missing is a final guest list," India said.

She avoided my eyes, but I tugged her by the silken sleeve out onto the side porch. Bonner and the espresso obviously hadn't been enough to clean up my mess.

The wind was gusting off the bay and bringing in whiffs of washed-up fish and boat oil. India sniffed at it.

"That is nasty," she said. "I hope this dies down by tomorrow."

"You couldn't arrange for that?" I said. I tried a smile. She wasn't having it.

"What's that supposed to mean?" she said.

"It means I appreciate everything you've done to make this the amazing thing it's going to be. But it's basically out of our hands now, and I just want you to enjoy whatever happens."

India wrapped her hand around the porch railing so hard I expected it to scream. "I have invited the wealthiest, most influential women in this city, Allison. People who have the means to allow us to minister to *every* woman who wants our help. I am *not* going to 'enjoy' myself if they are so uncomfortable they leave here not just without writing us generous checks, but without understanding what we're about. They have the power to pinch off donations from now till doomsday."

"And how are they going to understand it if they don't see it?"

A gust picked up a panel of her hair and thrust it in her face. When she pushed it away, her deep eyes had gone deeper. "So help me, Allison," she said, "if you are planning a field trip down to West King Street tomorrow, you better tell me now."

"What would you do?" I said.

"You're not, are you?"

I took her by the shoulders. "No, I'm not. Look, India, I should have discussed all the changes with you. I've been a complete oaf about it. Can we at least agree on that?"

She studied her manicure.

"We're being honest here," I said. "No 'bless your hearts' or any of that."

India gave my face a full examination before she said, "You haven't been as sensitive as I would've liked."

"Is that India for 'I wanted to punch you in the face'?"

"Pretty much."

"Then I'll try. I will. And if I fail, forget you have a pedigree and go for it." I tightened my hands on her shoulders. "But I need for you to get this: We haven't been inviting people to a big enough story."

"Is it going to get any bigger tomorrow?" she said. "All I ask is that you tell me before we run out of cannoli."

I let my hands drop. "I don't think so."

India shook her head. "I want something more definite than that."

"I can't give it to you," I said.

"This isn't fair, Allison," she said.

She swept past me into the kitchen. I stood there smelling the fish and knowing the Southern lady might have reached her limit.

CHAPTER EIGHT

By midmorning Saturday, India and Bonner had the yard and the front porch looking like Scarlett O'Hara herself could sit down any time and entertain her beaus. Pots of jasmine and day lilies and geraniums overflowed on every step, spilling their blossoms one on top of the next, and white wicker chairs and love seats were gathered in chatty groups under the dogwoods, punctuated with coral and aqua and foam-green pillows. India must have transplanted her entire patio to my front yard, and ordered my usually sad azaleas to get happy for the day.

In the kitchen, Hank was running an impressive operation of pots simmering on the stove and aromas seeping from the oven and trays of puffed and golden appetizers covering every horizontal plane. Joe wore a chef's hat, and crisp aprons awaited Jasmine and Mercedes and Sherry and me. I was already close to crying, but when Desmond's bedroom door opened and he promenaded into the kitchen, I gave in to the tears I'd been choking back all morning.

The kid was dressed in a tuxedo. All starched collar and shiny cuff links and pants pressed into a crease like the sharp edge of a knife. Where it had come from, I had no idea, but a tailor was definitely involved. The coat cinched in precisely at his waspish waist and the sleeves melted over those adolescent-ape arms as if someone had fussed over them with a tape measure for hours.

Desmond was finally a Mother D.

"I look so good I made you cry, Big Al," he said.

"Brought me straight to tears, Clarence," I said.

India was tying my apron, the bow I made having fallen short of Morehead standards, when the first Lexus nosed its way onto Palm Row. Owen was out there to direct parking, and Desmond was at the top of the steps with a towel over his arm, practically salivating to say, "My name is Desmond and I'll be taking care of you today," just as India had coached him. I held my breath inside the open front door, praying that his innocent speech wouldn't come out as something that would short out the pacemaker in this Daughter of the Confederacy. But it emerged smooth and sweet, which meant Desmond was a far better student under India's tutelage than I had been. The well-coiffed octogenarian patted Desmond's hand and said, "Now aren't you just the most precious thing?"

Desmond agreed heartily that he was.

Within thirty minutes, the lawn and porch were filled with a veritable sorority of graduates from Southern women's colleges, including Miz Vernell from next door. Granted, she probably hadn't attended college at all, since sixty years ago most females didn't, but she joined her cobwebby voice with the rest as they made known their appreciation for the lunch plated in the kitchen—embellished like pieces of fine art and presented to them by the trained and slightly shaky hands of Mercedes and Jasmine and Sherry and me. Bonner passed among them with pitchers of sweet tea and lemonade, chatting like it was Homecoming Weekend, probably because most of them had bought second and third homes through him as their husbands' fortunes had risen. If Ms. Willa and I hadn't gotten off to two starts that resembled gravel pits, I'd have wondered if it was the lack of cream sherry that kept her away. An hour into the Feast, the supposed guest of honor hadn't arrived.

"She's probably waiting for a limo to pick her up," I said to India.

She didn't answer. A second wave of guests was arriving, on Harleys that rattled the silverware on the china plates.

"Are they coming here?" asked one obvious alumna of Randolph-Macon.

"Surely not," her classmate replied.

Desmond stopped before them, a tray full of sherbets balanced precariously on one hand. "Yes, ma'am, they are," he said proudly. "Those are the HOGs."

Another woman, who was a decade younger and thus had not steeped as long in the waters of propriety, looked at me and said, "And they're here because …?"

"Because they're the ones who've set the bar," I said. "They've already given more than any human being should be expected to and will probably give more." I directed a wide-eyed look at a Junior Leaguer. "Go figure, huh?"

The laughter on the lawn tittered out as Ulysses and Stan and Rex and three quarters of the St. Augustine Harley Owners Group made their way up the lane, their leather clean and soft, their boots shined, their do-rags doffed respectfully. Almost as one, female heads turned to the porch, where India stood with her hands folded at her waist, silk spilling over them.

"How come it got so quiet?" Desmond whispered to me. "Somebody choke or somethin'?"

"I think they all did," I whispered back, and then placed my arm casually around his neck to prevent any more too-astute observations.

India was still watching the HOGs come up the walk. She waited so long I was about to say something myself, but she finally smiled that smile that made bankers lower their interest rates and said, "Welcome! There are still plenty of chairs on the lawn and we're bringing out more."

God love her.

Mercedes was already in the doorway with a tray full of lunches, and I let Desmond go so he could usher them to their seats. Rex tried to take the tray from Mercedes as she came down the steps, but she shook her head firmly.

"We here to serve you, now, Mr. Rex," she said.

Rex's face blotched. Stan hitched his shoulders as Desmond brushed invisible dust from his chair. Even Ulysses seemed to have a hard time sitting down as long as Mercedes was standing.

I went to Nita, who Jasmine had finally convinced to take a seat and a plate, and pushed my voice above the unanimous thought I could almost hear: *Write that check right quick so we can go. The next tier down is here.*

"Y'all need to relax and let us pamper you," I said. I bit into my cheek and let my "breeding" resurrect itself. "And please, introduce yourselves to some of our other guests. Ulysses, have you met Mrs. Kathryn Pendleton-Price?"

Ulysses took off his riding glove and extended his hand to the crepe-bosomed woman sitting behind him. The look she gave it before coming through with a finishing-school handshake was an instant too long. At least, as far as I was concerned.

The breeding bristled right out of me and I moved on, pairing the Randolph-Macon sisters with Nita and Leighanne, encouraging Stan to enlighten a knot of forty-something Junior Leaguers on the refurbishing of Sacrament House, complete with the tale of the devil of a time they'd had replacing the toilet the former tenants had filled with concrete.

India, I observed, was still smiling, still wafting her silk among the guests. Still schmoozing as only she could do.

"We have so much, don't we?" she said to them. "It's time we shared some of that, now, don't you think?"

To me she whispered, "It's only going to take one to get it started. We need Ms. Willa."

She craned her neck to look down Palm Row, and I watched her neck tighten. A round figure with a trail of mahogany hair was virtually waddling up the lane, carrying a heap of clothing. I could barely see Erin O'Hare's face above the pile.

Rex was up from his seat before she could get to the gate and relieved her of the burden. Her cheeks glowed like a pair of ripe tomatoes.

"I thought you could use these for the women," she said in the same volume she undoubtedly used in the classroom. "I don't have cash, but I'm a consignment store junkie and I do have clothes, in every size, depending on what diet I'm on, or not on!"

She laughed and then turned appropriately solemn as Desmond approached.

"I'll be takin' care of you today, Miss All Hair," he said.

Jasmine materialized with a plate and Erin was escorted to a seat among the Junior Leaguers. I winced. It was like watching a scene from a teenybopper film where the clique is forced to sit with the wannabes. Liz Doyle arrived to complete that picture, eyes blinking and straw spring purse spilling out stuff. She tried to get Sherry to sit down with them and let *her* fetch *Sherry* a glass of sweet tea, but

Sherry was firm. I'd seen her grow so weary at times of waiting on people at C.A.R.S., her martyred sighs could be heard all the way to St. George Street; today, she couldn't seem to get enough of refilling glasses that had barely been sipped from and rewarding an unspoken longing for just one more cannoli with said cannoli suddenly there on a china saucer with a tasteful sprinkling of powdered sugar.

"Allison," someone said.

A woman two facelifts into her seventies beckoned me to sit beside her.

"You don't remember me, do you?" she said. Her voice reminded me of a kitten, And not in a good way.

"Give me a hint," I said.

"I'm Trish Todd. Your mother and I were real close friends."

I didn't remember my mother having any close friends, real or otherwise, but the fact that they'd even been acquainted would account for my not being able to recall this woman. I'd made it a point to forget anyone my parents had associated with.

Trish teased my hand out of my apron pocket and tucked it into hers. "Your mama would be so proud of you today. You know, she always hoped you'd come around from being such a little rebel. And now, look at this. You've spared no expense, not for anybody, no matter what their walk of life."

God—tell me she did not just say that. Please tell me.

I don't know what I would have said if a commotion hadn't arisen at the front gate and India hadn't sung out, "Allison! Our guest of honor has arrived!"

A polite smattering of applause rose and fell across the lawn. That woman on the porch said again, "Surely not!"

But Ms. Willa Livengood had indeed made her entrance and was being escorted up the front path by Desmond, who gazed in open astonishment at the old lady's hair. Her colorist was clearly in her teal period this week. If Desmond didn't come out with, "How come your hair's blue?" I would be flabbergasted.

Fortunately, India took over, leading Ms. Willa to a padded love seat on the porch where she could look down on the party. That was, if she could see over the rose-colored collar that fanned up almost to her cheeks. Matching flowered pants completed the day's ensemble and made her look like a tiny teddy bear dressed for Easter.

You'd have thought the Queen Mother had arrived. Every woman over fifty, and that was most of them, approached her in turn to pay homage. The few fortyish guests plastered on polyurethane smiles and pulled out their cell phones.

"Tell me they aren't texting each other about Ms. Willa," I said to Chief.

"One generation younger and it'd be on YouTube."

"That's not the kind of PR we're looking for," Bonner muttered at my other elbow.

"Ladies," India sang out, "and gentlemen."

"And others," I said under my breath because a number of late-comers had by now collected outside the fence. A few more HOGs. Two of Desmond's other teachers. Nicholas Kent. I felt my chin drop when I saw the Reverend Garry Howard among them.

I folded my fingers around Bonner's wrist. "What's he doing here?" I said between my teeth.

"I invited him," Bonner said. "We're never going to win him over if we don't show him what we're doing."

I bit back, *Who said we wanted to win him over?* and said instead, "Let's get those people in here."

Bonner and Chief went to the fence and urged them all through, creating a hubbub that unsettled the texters and jostled those going to kiss Ms. Willa's rings or whatever it was they were doing. I was so busy locating chairs and dispatching the Sisters to the kitchen for more food, I almost missed the figure who trailed in behind Desmond's art teacher.

A Hispanic girl of about twenty-two, she slunk forward, looking over her slight shoulder as if she'd gotten past the bouncer without paying the cover charge. She looked familiar, but I had to blink twice to realize she was the prostitute from the Monk's Vineyard, the one who kicked Kade Capelli out of her room.

Bonner put out his arm to gather me into the fold he'd now formed with Garry Howard, but I maneuvered past them and went straight to the girl. She was obviously having second thoughts about being there because her almost almond-shaped dark eyes darted from face to face and she was already twisting at her willowy waist, back toward the gate. I wasn't too subtle about planting myself between her and the exit.

"You came!" I said.

Her eyes swam across my face like she was trying to place me. One sniff and I knew why. The girl was hungover at best. The brass she'd shown in George and Lewis's upstairs apartment hadn't returned after last night's binge; the whites of her eyes were sallow, and even as I watched she licked her full lips like she was lapping at cotton.

"I don't guess you're interested in anything to eat," I said.

She visibly shuddered and shook her head.

I nodded mine. "We'll fix you right up."

Desmond appeared and bowed to the young woman, a recent addition to his presentation.

"I'll be taking care of this guest," I told him. "Will you tell Hank we need a serving of bread and a cup of tea?"

"You want cream in that?" he said to her.

I thought I saw her face go a little green.

"No, thanks," I said. "We'll be on the porch."

"Up there?" the girl said when Desmond was gone.

"Best seat in the place," I said.

She shrank back. "I'm not dressed right."

I'd been so focused on the vulnerability of her face, I hadn't noticed what she had on. Okay, so leopard leggings and a rib-high black satin jacket that did a poor job of covering her bosom weren't necessarily appropriate for an afternoon lawn party. I pulled off the pale pink scarf India had so skillfully draped around my neck and draped it with a whole lot less skill around hers. The bosom disappeared under it.

"Feel better?" I said.

"I guess," she said.

I took her hand and tried to make our approach to the porch inconspicuous. But as soon as I tucked the young prostitute in beside Ms. Willa, nobody looked at anything else.

Ms. Willa took no notice. She was busy squinting up at Mercedes, who was about to hand her a plate.

"I know you," she said.

"I know you, too, ma'am," Mercedes said.

"I liked your spirit the other day at 95."

Mercedes's eyes sought out mine, already halfway to deer-in-the-headlights.

I pulled a Bonner and cleared my throat. "We haven't had a chance to apologize to you for that, Ms. Willa," I said.

"Apologize?" The old lady looked offended. "Anybody who can go after Troy Irwin like that doesn't need to apologize. You ought to receive a medal."

"Now, Ms. Livengood," one of the women said. She sounded like she was scolding a four-year-old. "I was just about to ask Allison if she'd gone to him for donations. He's very generous. I won't tell you how much he's given to the Heart Association because he's so modest he'd die if you knew, but—"

"If you take a penny from that criminal, you'll get nothing from me." Ms. Willa was looking straight at me. "He took everything that was ever decent about old St. Augustine money and soaked it in his poison. I'm the only woman of substance left in this town who hasn't been poisoned right along with him."

I expected some show of indignation, but everyone within earshot just shook their heads or clicked their tongues or otherwise indicated that Ms. Willa was to be placated because she was richer than any of them. As for agreement, she got none.

Which cramped my innards like a clenching fist.

"Not to worry, Ms. Willa," I said. "I won't be asking Troy Irwin for money. He's offered on a number of occasions but, quite frankly …" I brought my face close to hers. "I'd rather be shot."

I didn't get any agreement from the crowd either.

But Ms. Willa gave a satisfied nod and turned back to Mercedes, who presented her with her lunch, complete with linen napkin spread across her lap.

"You're doing a fine job, Mercy," Ms. Willa said.

"Yes, she is," Surely Not said, as if I hadn't just practically insulted her to her face. "Now, I have to know, what agency are you using for these servers? India said the food was all prepared here, but these girls you have waiting on us, they're some of the best I've seen." She leaned in as if she were about to impart a state secret. "I just have to have them for the fund-raiser I'm hosting for the Lightner next month."

Ms. Willa turned to her, face puckered in disbelief. "Don't you know who she is?" she said, flinging a hand back toward Mercedes.

"No."

"She's a prostitute, for heaven's sake."

Someone gasped.

"*Was* a prostitute," I said.

"Her, too, I assume," Ms. Willa said, pointing to Jasmine on the lawn below and then at Sherry. "And her, even though she's white."

Ms. Willa raised an eyebrow at me.

"No, that's one sin I haven't been guilty of," I said. "But I have my own, just as bad."

Surely Not's sorority sister took hold of her arm as she honed in on me. "I thought they just had problems with drugs."

"How do you think they got the money for the drugs?" Ms. Willa said. "You bunch of turtles need to pull your heads out of your shells."

India swooped in on the wings of her caftan. "Ms. Virginia, honey," she said to Surely Not, "we were just about to start our presentation that will clear all of that up." She shaded her eyes with an elegant hand as she looked out over the yard. "Chief, where are you? Would you get everyone's attention for us?"

There was no need. All eyes were on the porch, accusing eyes that shifted from India to me and back again. Eyes that clearly said, *We have been duped.* But India prayed her hands under her chin and swept her gaze over them.

"If I had told you I wanted you to support a group of former prostitutes, would you have come?" she said.

No one answered. Except Ms. Willa, who barked, "They most certainly would not."

"It was not my intention to mislead you," India said. "I only wanted you to see what's happening at Sacrament House before you had a chance to form a wrong opinion. *This* is what's happening."

She put her arm around Mercedes.

"When Mercedes came to Sacrament House four months ago, you would never have believed she could have become the beautiful young woman that she is today. Is she not exquisite?"

There were murmurs of assent. Mercedes looked as if she would prefer to be enduring a beheading.

"We wanted you to have a chance to discover that she is just as exquisite on the inside," India went on. "The same is true for Jasmine. Where are you, honey?"

Jasmine waved weakly.

"Ask her to tell you her story," India said. "And if you are anything like me, you will pull that checkbook out of your purse and you will say, 'How much is enough?' and then you'll give a little more." She looked around. "Sherry? She must have gone inside."

Escaped would be a better word. Bless India's heart, but this was making me squirm in my apron.

"Listen," she went on, "I am ashamed to say that I ran like a rabbit when Allison Chamberlain first gave me the opportunity to be part of this ministry. But when I finally allowed myself to get to know these amazing women and see how hard they're working to better themselves, I couldn't run. I didn't want to run. And I know, because I know you, that most of you are far better people than I am. You're not going to disappoint me and run off from this."

She waited as if she could see them adding zeroes to the obligatory amounts they already had in mind. I, on the other hand, witnessed them eyeing one another in a supreme effort not to look as if they were waiting to see what the others would do. I could imagine them doing the same thing forty and fifty years ago when somebody in the cotillion broke into the Watusi in the middle of the dance floor. India waited some more, and a few reached for their Louis Vuittons and their Montblancs.

But suddenly, I didn't want their zeroes.

Will you do it now, Allison? Will you?

As India continued to talk, I leaned over the porch railing to Desmond. "Go tell Hank I need as many big pitchers as she can find. Tell her to fill them with water."

Desmond flipped his towel over his arm and headed inside. I crooked my finger at Owen.

"Can you find me some buckets?" I hissed. "Maybe four or five?"

"How big?" he said.

"Big enough for a pair of feet."

I went to stand beside India, who still had her arm firmly around a stiff Mercedes.

"Will you go find some towels, Merce?" I said.

India blinked. Mercedes nodded and pulled away as if she'd just been released from custody. The crowd fidgeted as India feigned delighted surprise.

"I just never know what Miss Allison is going to come up with," she said.

She should have, in my view. She should have known I was going to say, "Put your checkbooks away. That isn't what we want from you."

I went down the steps and stopped at the group from the Garden Club. "Would any of you well-connected ladies be willing to hire one the Sisters of Sacrament House," I said, "or recommend them for employment?"

I didn't wait for an answer because I knew there wouldn't be one. I stood before the Junior Leaguers. "Would any of you successful women give a few hours of your time every week to teach the Sisters job skills? Help them learn how to present themselves the way you do?"

I did wait this time. The expected silence was deafening.

I turned to the United Daughters of the Confederacy sprinkled jarringly among the HOGs. "What we need are more people to drive them to doctor's appointments and go to court with them to settle their past mistakes. Are any of you influential members of society available to do that?"

Owen came up behind me, clattering buckets. "Where do you want these, Ally?"

I took two and nodded for him to follow me with the others. I set one down in front of a now white-faced member of the UDC, another in the flustered midst of the Garden Club, a third with the Junior Leaguers whose fingers were poised over their cell phones, Facebook on the screen. The fourth bucket I took up the steps and placed before Ms. Willa.

"What do you intend to do with that?" she said.

"I intend to wash your feet, Ms. Willa."

"Why on earth would you want to do such a thing?"

"Quite frankly, I don't," I said. "I imagine you've got corns for days and heels like the soles of cowboy boots."

She narrowed her already screwed-tight eyes. "Go on."

"I'm not going to wash your feet because I think I'll enjoy it. Heaven knows it will be probably be fairly disgusting."

"You've been talking to my podiatrist," she said. A tiny star formed in each eye.

"I'm washing them because I want you to know that I'm here to serve you, no matter how nasty and gross and full of fungus that service might turn out to be. It's what the people of God are called to do for each other." I turned to the mismatched crowd on the lawn. "It's what all human beings ought to do for each other. I—no, *all* of us in the Sacrament House ministry are here to wash your feet. Literally. Maybe then you'll experience the kind of love it takes to come to the table with more than your money. What we want goes deeper than that. We want to wash you so you can become part of the story. Our story. The big story."

I squatted in front of Ms. Willa and slid off one of her pink ballet flats. Mercedes leaned over me.

"You want we should wash some feet?" she said. "For real?"

I looked up, expecting the mother of all eye rolls. What I got was a smooth smile and a look full of knowing.

"For real," I said. "Wash any feet that are willing."

I went back to Ms. Willa and her white knee-highs. I heard Mercedes take the steps and say, clear and strong, "Whose feet needs washing today?" Beyond her, Jasmine's laughter bubbled up and Stan said, "Over here."

"Is that water cold?" Ms. Willa said.

I hadn't thought of that. For all Hank knew, we were going to drink it. But when I dipped my finger into the pitcher, I felt myself break into a full-body grin. It was just the right temperature for a satisfying bath.

I swung Ms. Willa's knotty-toed feet into the bucket and poured the water over them.

"You don't know what I'm doing, Ms. Willa," I said. "I'm not sure I do myself. But just by doing it, maybe God will let both of us understand how to really love."

The hard sole softened in my palm. She nudged my hand with her other foot, and she spread her toes as I massaged the swollen joint below her big toe. I could feel the sigh in her muscles.

When I'd pulled her feet from the bucket and wrapped them in the Harley Davidson beach towel Mercedes had provided, India tapped my shoulder. Her lips were so close to my ear they brushed at my lobe.

"I thought we agreed you'd tell me if you were going to do things like this," she said almost inaudibly.

I stood up. "I would have if I'd known," I murmured back as she stood with me. "It just came to me and I had to go with it."

Actually, it hadn't *just* come to me. God had been trying to get me to do this since Ash Wednesday when I'd first felt it in my soul. I couldn't apologize for going with it when I finally got it. Not with Ms. Willa looking at me with the wisdom of the ages in her eyes.

"Well, I'm sorry," India said, "but it's a train wreck."

I picked up the bucket and turned to look out over my front yard. I could see how India might interpret it that way. Surely Not and her sorority sister were hurrying, arm-in-protective-arm, toward the Lincoln they'd arrived in. Trish Whatever-Her-Name-Was had her sizeable purse over her shoulder and was headed for the gate with her equally sizeable checkbook still in it. The entire pack of forty-somethings must have left en masse with their iPhones the minute I poured the water into the bucket because all their seats were empty. One of the chairs was even upside down on the grass, as if its occupant hadn't been able to get away fast enough. India was right: The scene could qualify as a vehicular disaster.

If Sherry weren't bathing the hair-tufted foot of Ulysses, while Rex waited, socks off, for his turn.

If Liz Doyle weren't kneeling before a UDC member with a severe bun, quietly sponging a callus I could see all the way from the porch.

If Desmond didn't have Miz Vernell's feet in a five-gallon bucket with water up to her doorknob knees, going on about how he didn't have no neighbor better than her, 'less maybe it was Mr. Schatzie, but, then, everybody couldn't be Mr. Schatzie, could they?

This wasn't a train wreck. This was a body of people who were so on track, the speed of it took my breath away.

"I need to get fresh water in those pitchers," I said, and started for the steps.

India caught my arm. "You realize that I can never ask any of those women for money again. Not just for us, but for anyone."

Her eyes smoldered, but it wasn't anger I saw. The film of tears, the confused blinking, that could only be fear. I put my bucket-free arm out to hug her neck, but she stepped back, nearly trampling Sherry, who was on her way out of the house with clean towels.

"If we make one dime off of this, I'll drop my teeth," India said. "And if we get a single volunteer, you can order my casket because I will probably drop dead." Her voice caught. "So I don't see what you accomplished today, Allison, except to make everybody feel so guilty they won't even look us in the eye, much less give us any kind of support."

"Not everybody," I said.

Because right behind us, Ms. Willa had the young prostitute's legs across her lap. The girl's feet were soaking the pink flowered pants, but Ms. Willa didn't seem bothered as she reached an almost transparent blue-veined hand for the towel and used it to get between those grimy toes.

"I know you say you don't use drugs," she said to the girl. "But you can't hide what's on your breath, and that will get you into just as much trouble if you overdo it. My first husband took to drink when Troy Irwin walked away with everything he had and he couldn't stand the pain. But you—" Ms. Willa stopped rubbing and looked into the young woman's stunned eyes. "You have a chance."

Ms. Willa's hands seemed young now, ropeless and smooth, and I felt like I ought to kiss them, and possibly even her feet. She could give us a check or not. Because the old money of a St. Augustine matron had just washed the filthy feet of a St. George Street hooker and shown us Jesus Christ.

I turned back to India. "How will anything really change if the way we do things stays the same?" I said.

She swallowed hard and walked away.

The washing of the feet went on until every foot that was willing to be clean had been bathed. Not every one of the people who stayed took part. The Reverend Garry Howard watched curiously from the side porch, though I didn't see a *tsk-tsk* in his eyes, necessarily. Chief had his boots off and his jeans rolled up, but he never actually got to have his feet bathed. He was involved in a conversation with Owen by the gate that went on for some time. A few of the Garden Clubbers weren't keen on removing their shoes, but Bonner and Hank didn't press them. Hank brought out some walnut oil from the kitchen and massaged their hands instead. Erin O'Hare would allow Desmond to wash her feet only if he would let her wash his. A reverent stillness fell over the property when she dried them with her hair.

And then, of course, she broke the spell when she looked up at us, laughing, and said, "Don't anybody report me to the Board of Education. I've just broken so many rules, I'd be in court for the rest of my life."

"It's all good, Miss All Hair," Desmond said. "I know me a good lawyer."

I looked for Chief again. He and Owen had finished talking and he was poking something into his cell phone. I wouldn't have been surprised if he was dealing with the health department, probably called by one of the women who had also seen the footwashing as an

Amtrak pileup and escaped before she could be caught in it. There was nothing sexier than Chief handling a crisis without so much as twitching an eyebrow.

He looked up suddenly, as if he felt me watching him. I felt myself blush like a teenager. Actually, I'd never blushed as an adolescent. Not even when the boy I thought was the love of my life—who turned out to be the hate of my life—smiled at me across a room, over the heads of all the other girls who would have jumped him in a heartbeat if he'd given them a sideways glance.

I shuddered. Ms. Willa was right about that poison.

"What's going on, Classic?" Chief said.

"I was just about to ask you the same thing," I lied.

He took my elbow and edged me away from the small circle of people who had pulled the wicker furniture into a circle in the center of the yard and were lingering over Hank's *panforte.* There was plenty of it left, since more than half the guests had departed before dessert was served.

"Owen told me he saw that car today 'that's been cruising past here on a regular basis.' Any particular reason why you haven't mentioned that to me?"

I shrugged. "I haven't actually seen it myself, and you know how Owen is. He believes everybody wants to buy Palm Row out from under us."

"He thinks there might be more to it than that."

"Oh?"

"He said Desmond asked him about it the night we went to the beach with the HOGs. Owen sensed he was more freaked out by it than he was letting on."

I couldn't help smirking. "Owen used the phrase 'freaked out'?"

"No. He described it as 'putting a mask on it. Putting up a front. Going at it by the way of Cape Horn.'"

"Right. No wonder you were talking to him for so long."

"That's not the half of it." Chief consulted his phone. "He gave me twenty minutes worth of him getting the description of the car."

"He told me that. Beige Mercury Sable?"

"Yeah. And how he didn't want to stare at the driver too long in case the person caught him and thought he was a peeping Tom, an old Becky—"

"Stop," I said.

Chief's eyes laughed. "So he and Desmond went and asked Miz Vernell, who has no problem with being mistaken for a voyeur. She said she'd been watching the woman through her binoculars."

"Of course she had."

"And as soon as Desmond heard it was a woman, according to Owen he dropped that burden like a ton of bricks, like the weight of the world had just been lifted from his shoulders, and, my personal favorite, like Sisyphus letting go of the boulder."

"You're enjoying this, aren't you?" I said.

"He's better than Comedy Central. But ..."

"I knew there was one in there."

"When Owen saw her drive past three times today, which was no small feat with all the cars parked here, he wasn't comfortable with that, so he took the risk of looking like a nosy neighbor and got a real good look at her face. He said she was madder than a wet hen, et cetera." Chief tilted his head at me. "I know Owen's an alarmist, but he seemed genuinely disturbed. I think it's worth looking into if you don't object."

"Looking into how?" I said.

"I got the license number. I can have it checked out."

"You don't have to do that."

"Just taking care of what I care about."

"Miss Allison."

I was never less excited about having a conversation with the Reverend Garry Howard than I was at that moment, and that was saying something. Chief was stepping away from a promising conversation, and for that I could have cheerfully clobbered the good reverend with a bucket.

But I closed my eyes for a few seconds and made a space for God, somewhere around my tongue.

"It's been a while," I said.

Garry gave his head of winged white hair a pastoral nod. "Too long," he said. "I took Bonner's invitation as a sign that you might be open to talking with me again."

"I've been open," I said. "I just wasn't sure we'd get much further than we have before." And then because his eyes dropped at the corners, I added, "I'm sad about that. You were good to me when I needed you."

Reverend Garry cringed visibly. "You make it sound like our relationship is all in the past tense."

I didn't have a reply for that. He pulled his hands behind his back and clasped them there.

"This was very powerful today," he said. "Very moving."

He looked about as moved as an anvil, but I nodded.

"I don't think our ministries are as diametrically opposed as you do," he went on. "And I'd like to show you that."

"Show me how?" I said.

"Tomorrow we're breaking ground for the Christian school we're building."

I stiffened. "The one Chamberlain Enterprises is giving the money for."

"The Chamberlain Foundation," he said, as if that should make a difference. "I know you have issues with that." He put his hand up to stop the barrage about to burst from my mouth. "And I respect that. But it would mean a great deal to me for you to experience the spirit of what we're doing, just as I've done here."

I felt my eyebrows shoot up. "Did you experience it?" I said. "Did you have your feet washed?"

"No, I didn't do that."

"Talk to any of the Sisters?"

"I did talk to one woman, yes." He turned and pointed to Jasmine, who was currently dancing barefoot with Desmond in the grass. "I invited her to come and she said she'd have to talk it over with Miss Angel."

Did you tell her it's going to be a celebration of the same money that's being used to threaten the program that's saving her life? I wanted to say. I even tried to say it, but the words caught in my throat, caught deeper than that, where a contraction squeezed away my breath.

"It's at ten a.m. tomorrow," Reverend Garry said. "We're holding our worship service there."

"And where is 'there'?" I said.

"A very convenient location for you. Right at the corner of San Luis and Old Moultrie."

Three doors down from Sacrament House. I'd forgotten that, or maybe I'd just hoped Troy had, once he'd gotten the satisfaction from my flipping out over it last December.

He reached over and patted my hand. "If we're going to be neighbors, Miss Allison, we should get to know each other in a new way."

Once again the words I wanted to say caught in my gut, or I would have spewed them out in one long venomous stream. *I know all I want to know, and that is that you have taken the thirty pieces of silver.*

The ones I needed to say made their way through.

Wash their feet, Allison. Wash all *their feet.*

"I'm sorry," I said to the Reverend Garry. "I can't be a part of what you're doing because I think it's wrong." I put my own hand up before he could protest. "Like I said, we've been through this before and there's no need to go there again. But I want you to know, we're about loving the people who are most separated from God."

"I'm not quarreling with that, Miss Allison. These women and that boy of yours, they need what you have to offer."

"I'm not talking about them, Reverend Garry. I'm talking about you."

After Garry Howard left, wings ruffled, I didn't have a chance to talk to Chief again until the place was cleaned up and everyone had left, including the Sisters in the van and India in Stan's truck with all of her furniture piled in the back. I didn't have a chance to talk to her either—by her design, not mine.

"It's a lot for her to process," Hank said to me. "After all, you did basically tell her she's going to have to reconfigure her entire approach to society. You might as well have told her she must now be a man."

"I didn't tell her she *has* to do anything," I said.

"Yeah, you did, Al," Hank said. "Yeah, you did."

As for Ms. Willa, she must have left while the Reverend Garry had me cornered. I didn't look into the helmet someone had passed, but Bonner hadn't said anything about a big check finding its way in there. She must have taken me at my word when I said I didn't really want their money. Come to think of it, Bonner hadn't said anything at all to me. And no wonder.

So it was only Chief and me in the living room at almost midnight. Desmond had protested going to bed until I relented and told him he could sleep in his tuxedo. It was so covered in red sauce and grass stains, it was going to have to make a trip to the dry cleaner anyway.

By the time I was curled up in the red chair-and-a-half and Chief was putting a cup of cocoa in my hand, I wasn't sure I had the energy to continue the conversation Garry Howard had interrupted.

"Did you make this?" I said.

"Hank did. I was under strict orders to warm it up in the micro-wave and make you drink it."

He actually stood over me until I took the first sip. Then, as I'd hoped, he parked himself on the ottoman, just an arm's length away. Even that was too far, but I settled for it.

"You never got your feet washed today," he said.

A sip's worth of cocoa startled over the edge of the cup and onto my fingers. Chief wiped it off with his hand and smeared it on his jeans.

"Why was that?" he said.

"Why was what?"

"Why was it that no one washed your feet?"

"I guess it just didn't occur to anybody," I said.

"It occurred to me."

I could only gaze at him, all contradiction and paradox and everything else I couldn't figure out. Why was it at such times that the phone always rang or some random person inserted himself into the conversation? This time it was the front doorbell that nobody ever rang.

I started to climb out of the chair, but Chief shook his head at me and went himself. He was back in a matter of seconds, his face grim.

"I think you better come," he said.

Heart dropping to my feet, I untangled myself from the chair and went to the door. Standing in silhouette was a willowy figure, bowed over as if the wind were beating it down. The eyes that came up to me were almond shaped. And as swollen as the cheeks that came up to meet them even as I stared.

"Can you help me?" said the St. George Street hooker. "I've been raped."

CHAPTER NINE

I got her into the red chair, where so many before her had sat wrapped in blankets and shock, and joined Chief in the kitchen, where he was putting water on for tea. I pulled my cell phone out of my pocket.

"Who are you calling?" he said.

"Nicholas Kent."

"You sure?"

I stared at him as he opened the canister of chamomile tea bags. "Of course I'm sure. A prostitute's been raped. Do you really think anybody else in the police department is going to take that seriously?"

"*He* isn't going to take it seriously either until we know what we're dealing with." He cut off my next sentence with his eyes. "I know a rape is a rape, Classic. I get that. But if we don't talk her through this first, *whoever* interviews her is going to think she had it coming to her."

"Okay," I said. "Just as long as *you* aren't thinking it."

He dropped the tea bag into the cup and without looking at me said, "I can't believe you even had to ask me that."

"I didn't," I said. "I'm sorry."

He didn't say anything. I went back to the living room, muttering, "Why don't you ever show up in my conversations with *him,* God?"

The girl in the chair had shriveled in my absence. Chief was right. If I didn't get her mind wrapped around whatever had happened to her, she was going to lose it in the deep hole she was already sinking into.

"Chief's making you some tea," I said. "You need another blanket?"

"I can't get warm," she said. Even her voice was shivering.

"We're going to need to get some ice on your face," I said, "but let's wait on that. Here."

I motioned for her to lean forward so I could tuck an afghan around her. I stifled a gasp when I saw her back, exposed by the undersized jacket and an angry, ripped opening in the leopard pants. The skin on either side of her backbone was striped with gashes, each the width of a fingernail. The blood that still bubbled in them told me this travesty had taken place no more than thirty minutes ago. I shifted into triage mode so I wouldn't fall into the same hole she was headed for.

I finished wrapping her and sat on the ottoman Chief had vacated. Her hands plucked at the fibers, so I took them into mine. They were cold as death.

"What's your name?" I said.

She searched for focus for a full ten seconds before she said, "Ophelia."

"Ophelia what?"

"Sanchez."

"I'm Allison," I said, because I wasn't at all sure she really knew where she was.

"You're the one," she said.

I decided not to follow up on that.

"Have you washed your hands since this happened?" I said.

She shook her head numbly.

"Have you used the bathroom? Wiped yourself?"

"No."

"You haven't tried to wash in any way."

"I came right in when he dumped me here," she said.

I heard Chief enter, but I put my hand up to stop him from handing her the tea. I had to catch this before she disappeared before our eyes.

"Who was 'he'?" I said.

"The man who raped me."

Chief set the tea on the table and nodded for me to go on.

"Do you know who he was?" I said.

Ophelia tried to lick her lips, but I could see that her tongue was coated and dry.

"Water," I whispered to Chief. To her, I said, "Ophelia, do you know who he was?"

She shook her head and winced.

"Ice, too, Chief," I called toward the kitchen.

"I never saw his face. Only his shadow."

"You said he brought you here. Can you tell me what happened?"

Ophelia pulled her gaze from her lap and lifted it to the wall above my head. This time she didn't find her focus. I knew before she got one syllable out that she was going to say the three words most likely to suck the life out of her case.

"I don't remember," she said.

Chief handed me the water. "I don't think we should treat the swelling until they've seen her in the ER."

Ophelia's head jerked back down to me. "No hospital. And no police."

"We need to—"

"They won't believe me. They won't do anything about it."

I scooted forward on the ottoman and kept my eyes on her until she couldn't look away anymore.

"Do you want our help, Ophelia?" I said.

"Yes," she said. "*Your* help. Not somebody who's gonna tell me it was just a john who got too rough. It was not a john. Randi fired me because she said I got us kicked out of our place. I haven't turned a trick since that day."

I put the glass of water in her hand. "Do you remember where you were when this guy—what? Came up to you someplace, maybe?"

She bowed her head. "I was drunk. I couldn't handle what happened to me here, today, so I drank. And I went someplace." She tried to squeeze her eyes closed, but they were nearly swollen shut already. "And all I remember is him dragging me into a car and hitting me and raping me and then it was all black."

I felt Chief's hand on my shoulder. Only then did I realize I was shaking, from someplace inside myself and out to the legs that quivered against the footstool and the hands that pressed, trembling, against my mouth. My face ached with every punch this jackal had inflicted on her.

"Ophelia, is it?" Chief said.

She flinched, as if she was seeing him for the first time. He took a step back and another until she nodded at him.

"Ophelia, we're going to take you to the hospital." He continued over her moan. "You need treatment, and you're going to want them to gather information that'll help them find out who did this to you."

"They won't believe me," she said again.

"But we do," I said.

"I know!" Her voice cracked open. "I don't know why he brought me here, but I came in because I saw something here when they were washing the feet."

"What did you see?"

"You," she said. "I saw you and I knew you were the one."

"The one?" I said.

But she covered her ravaged face with her hands and then she pulled them away, as if touching herself was too painful. There were no tears, and I knew why because I couldn't cry either. We were both too bruised to weep.

While Chief went back to the kitchen to make phone calls, I took the glass of water and put the warm mug in her hands, but she didn't seem to know what to do with it. I was spooning tea into her mouth when he came back.

"They'll be ready for us at the ER," he said. "Nick Kent's going to meet us."

"Have you figured how we're getting there?" I said. "The Sisters have the van, and I can't take her on the bike. Obviously."

"I called Hank. She's coming over with her car and she'll stay with Desmond."

I love you, I told him with my eyes. But he was at the window. I turned to Ophelia.

"You're not alone," I said. "I'll be with you every minute. With the doctor, the police officer, everything. When it's over, I'll bring you—"

I stopped when Chief turned sharply to look at me over his shoulder.

"I'll bring you back here," I said, my eyes on him. "And then we'll decide what to do."

"Can I be in the house?" she said.

"This house?"

"Whatever house you were talking about today. That house."

"Sacrament House?" I said.

"Can I be in it?"

"Yeah," I said thickly. "You can be in it."

When I looked back at Chief, he had turned to the window again, his eyes closed in the reflection.

Ophelia's prediction was absolutely correct. None of the doctors or nurses or rape counselors said it outright, but their lack of faith in her story was clear in the way they took down her answers and gathered evidence from her body for the rape kit, all without actually seeing her. Every time I started to tell them they were unfeeling pieces of coal, Chief squeezed my shoulder or touched my elbow or told me with the lines around his eyes that it wasn't worth it for me to blow my cool with people who already thought I was nuts for even being involved in this.

Only Nicholas Kent showed any compassion when he questioned her, but he didn't glean any more than we had.

"I asked them to do a blood test and see if she'd been drugged," he told us when Ophelia was in the restroom. "They told me this is what they consider 'an occupational hazard,' and I told them ... Well, I pushed. And there was enough evidence for a DNA sample."

"How long will it take to get a match?" I said.

"Forever if there's nobody to match it to. She can't even lead us to a suspect."

"She's traumatized," I said, hackles rising.

Chief put his hand right on the back of my neck as if he'd seen the hair standing up. "Do you think she'll remember more when she comes out of shock?"

"She might," Nicholas said. "Unless she *was* drugged. In that case, she might never be able to recall anything." He looked at me closely. "You okay?"

I was shaking again, and this time I couldn't hold down the bile that rose from the clench in my stomach. I barely made it to the trash can.

Even after I'd retched, I stayed there, bent at the waist with the blood crowding painfully into my head. There was no denying what was going on here. I was feeling everything Ophelia was so very obviously going through, just as I had with Zelda the day she was arrested. I told my mind to get it together, that what was happening to them wasn't happening to me. But I couldn't convince my body.

When we got home, I tucked Ophelia in on the couch, where she promptly fell into an exhausted sleep. When I got back to the kitchen, Hank said, "Desmond stayed crashed out through the whole thing."

"Good."

"What are you going to do about this, Classic?" Chief said.

I'd already been there several times on the way home with Ophelia's head lolling on my shoulder in the backseat.

"I have to keep her here tonight," I said. "She's been through too much for me to do whatever I would do if I even had an idea."

"And what about after that?" Chief said. "Vickie Rodriguez would pull those adoption papers in a New York minute if she found out you had a prostitute staying here with Desmond in the house, recovering or otherwise."

"That's kind of ironic, isn't it?" I said. "Desmond grew up on the streets with hookers who, unlike this one, never had any intention of changing." I pressed my fingers to my temples. "Don't get me started."

"Here's my suggestion," Chief said. "Desmond can stay with me for a few days until you get something figured out for Ophelia."

"Are you sure?" I said. "It could take more than a few days. I can't put her in Sacrament House yet. She's not ready, and I'm not sure there's room anyway. What if we get Zelda back?"

"You going to keep chasing your tail, or are you going to let me give you a chance to take this one ride at a time?"

I couldn't help smiling at him. "You've been spending way too much time with Owen."

"I'll come back tomorrow around ten and take him home with me. We'll go out to the beach first. I promised him that."

"He's going to be thrilled." My voice was thickening again. "You just have to promise to let me have him back."

I'd seen Chief look like he wanted to kiss me enough times to know it wasn't just wishful thinking on my part. But Hank was there, and in spite of her tactful exit into the pantry for no apparent reason, Chief just squeezed my neck and gave me a look that stole my breath. "See you tomorrow, then."

Almost before the door to the side porch closed behind him, Hank poked her head out.

"For somebody who has it all together in almost every other area of his life, that boy is dense as a brick when it comes to romance."

I thought I was going to laugh, but what came out was something between a wail and a sob as I slid down the cabinets to the floor. My shoulders caved as she put her arms around them.

"This isn't about Chief, is it?" she said.

"No. It's all this stuff I feel that I shouldn't be feeling because it isn't my stuff."

"You're going to have to give me a little more to work with, Al."

I raised my head to look at her. "I wasn't the one who was raped tonight. I didn't snort up a speedball and drive somebody's car up a pole. But here I am, feeling like I've been punched in the face and handcuffed to a wall and it isn't like I'm just imagining it." I pressed my hands to my abdomen. "It's physical, Hank. Only I can't treat it with ice or a pain pill. It's throbbing and I can't do anything about it."

I finally stopped for air. Hank stepped into the pause.

"You know how you hear things from God," she said.

"Yeah, again, finally."

"I hear them too, only in my case they aren't prophecy. They're … Let's call them insights. It just so happens that most of them are about you."

I drew the snot from under my nose with the side of my hand and looked at her.

"I know," she said. "Go figure, right? And here's the insight I'm getting now. If you want to hear it."

"Are you serious? Tell me before I lose it completely."

She handed me a paper towel. "You're gifted with a sensitivity to God's presence, not just in the cosmos, but inside other people."

"This is a gift?" I said.

"Oddly, yes. It's always been part of any prophet. "

I blew my nose. "Well, you know what? This is one of those times I wish God had given my gift to somebody else."

She folded her hands in that no-nonsense way she had and said, "Then it's a good thing for all of us that wishing doesn't make it so."

Hank left shortly thereafter. There wasn't a whole lot more to say, and I needed to at least try to get some sleep.

But I didn't go to bed. I sat wrapped in blankets in the red chair-and-a-half the way Ophelia had just a few hours before and watched her sleep the sleep of the beaten-up.

I went over the events of the day, asking God the obvious questions and getting no direct answers. I'd resigned myself to the fact that *wash their feet* was going to be the background music in my soundtrack from here on. But the feet had been washed, and here I was, with no place to bathe the rest of this woman who was on my sofa, or the others who walked West King Street or rode in cars with johns this very night and would drink and shoot themselves up to kill the pain before the sun came up on it. Here I was, in this big house with many rooms I wasn't allowed to fill.

I sat up in the chair.

This big house. A house some woman in a beige Mercury Sable apparently wanted to buy so much she was mad when I had a party that prevented her from seeing it.

I could almost feel Sylvia in the room, giving me the stare that could melt confessions out of me for crimes I hadn't even committed yet.

"I know I promised you," I whispered. "But if you could feel what these women feel, Sylvia … I'm just going to find out how much this person offers. I'll just ask."

I got no sense of approval from Sylvia. Or, for that matter, from God. All I knew was that I had to provide for Ophelia and Zelda and Jasmine and Mercedes and Sherry and the rest of our Sisters who were making their journey toward us. Because the pain wasn't going to leave me alone until I did.

When my phone rang the next morning, I was still in the chair, twisted in some kind of impossible sleep position I could hardly get out of to answer it. Not that I wanted to answer it. Every time a bell rang it seemed to start an avalanche.

But Chief's voice was calm. "Is Desmond packed yet?"

"Is he going somewhere?"

Chief gave a throaty laugh.

"Oh, yeah." I scrubbed at my face with my free hand. "I thought you weren't coming until ten."

"It's eleven."

"You're not serious! Why didn't you call me sooner?"

I threw off the afghan and tried to find the floor with my feet.

"I did. Desmond said you were still asleep, so I told him not to wake you up."

"Desmond was in here answering my phone?"

I bolted up in the chair. Then he'd seen Ophelia, who, I realized, was no longer on the couch.

"Did you tell him he was coming to stay with you?" I said as I sprinted for the kitchen.

"I did. And he's already given me a list of food I need to buy. I'm going to need to take out a second mortgage."

I stopped just short of the kitchen door and cupped my hand around mouth and phone. "I'm a terrible mother. I didn't even get up in time to talk to him about this before he saw Ophelia." I shoved my hair out of my face. "I don't know how I'm going to handle this with him."

"Have you seen him yet?'

"No."

I could hear the almost smile. "I think you'll find him handling it himself. I'll be there in ten."

I stuffed the phone in the pocket of yesterday's dress pants and pushed open the kitchen door. Desmond sat at the bistro table across from Ophelia, pouring orange juice into a tall pilsner. She was curved like a question mark in the bistro chair, but half of a toaster waffle was missing from her plate. The other half swam in about a half a bottle of Mrs. Butterworth's. Desmond's Mother D persona was gone, along with the tuxedo, but he was certainly putting the servers at the Waffle House to shame.

"Hey, Big Al," he said. "We was fixin' to starve half to death so I went ahead and cooked us some breakfast. You want some?"

My stomach still felt like I'd eaten bad shrimp, so I shook my head. "I see you've met Ophelia."

"Met her yesterday," he said. "Only I almost didn't recognize her since somebody rearranged her face."

"You have such tact, Desmond," I said.

Either Ophelia hadn't heard or she didn't see the point in being offended. Her right eye and cheek were less swollen than the night before, but her skin was now a heinous shade of purple. My own face throbbed.

"You want coffee, Ophelia?" I said. "I'm going to make a pot."

"She done that already," Desmond said. "Me and her on our second cup."

I gave him the death stare. "Tell me you did not consume caffeine."

He grinned. "Gotcha, Big Al."

"Wretched child," I said. "Are you packed? Chief'll be here in five minutes."

"I got it all in two trash bags."

I poured what looked like liquid mud into a mug. "And you're planning to get that into Chief's saddle bags?"

"I was thinkin' you could bring it over later and I could fix y'all a candlelight dinner."

There was so much awry in that statement I didn't even answer. I filled the space in the mug with milk and nodded toward his room. "Get your leathers so you'll be ready."

"We goin' to the *beach,* Big Al," he said, voice rising to that range that would soon have dogs howling all over St. John's County. "I don't need no—"

"No leathers, no ride."

That came from Chief, now blocking out the sun in the side

porch doorway. Ophelia slid out of the bistro table and whispered, "Is it all right if I take a shower?"

"Absolutely," I said. "I showed you where last night. I'll be up in a minute with fresh clothes for you."

She seemed to evaporate from the room.

"Leathers?" I said to Desmond.

He glanced at Chief's legs, which, bless the man, were clad in chaps. "They in the garage," he said, and went out the side door.

"How's she doing?" Chief said.

"I really don't know. Those were the first words I heard her say. She made coffee, though." I frowned into my mug. "At least, I think it's coffee. And she asked to take a shower. Every other woman who's come here I've had to put in a half nelson to get them into the tub."

"She's not a drug addict," Chief said.

"She's an alcoholic, though, or at least she self-medicates with it." I looked at the kitchen door that still swayed slightly in Ophelia's wake. "She needs to recover from something, I know that much."

"Then she's come to the right person."

I kept my eyes on the door, but my mind saw the look I heard in his voice. When I turned to him, it was there, and I couldn't breathe.

He had just made love to me.

Right on cue, the side door banged open and Desmond bolted through it and toward his room almost in one noisy motion. One of the bistro chairs tottered as he rammed between it and Chief.

"We've got all day," Chief said drily.

But Desmond slammed his door behind him, and I heard his

headboard knock against the wall. That was the sound of him throwing himself across his bed, a move usually reserved for me announcing his next dentist appointment.

Chief shot up an eyebrow.

"He's going to fight this leathers thing to the very end," I said. "Oh, and by the way, while you have him with you, would you have a talk with him about his 'women'? I don't think …"

I stopped because Chief was looking past me and through the front window, eyes trained on something that brought the lines in tension. I turned to follow his gaze, in time to see a beige vehicle back out of the short driveway in front of my garage and head toward the exit from Palm Row.

"Was that the car?" I said.

Chief was already looking at the notation he'd made in his phone. "Yeah, same one."

"Shoot. I wanted to talk to her."

"About …" he said, eyes narrowing.

"I just want to see how much—"

"No, Big Al!"

I whirled around to see Desmond standing in his doorway, chest heaving, eyes bulging from his head. He flung himself in the direction of the snack drawer, but he didn't touch it. Nor did he yank open the refrigerator door, although he showed every intention. When he made an aimless dive for the pantry, I knew that if I waited he would eventually proclaim me the best listener on the planet, but I feared for the condition of my canned goods.

"Desmond, what is it?" I said.

He hurled himself into the pantry anyway and then did an

about-face that knocked a container of olive oil from a shelf and sent it bouncing and denting under the table.

"Don't have nothin' to do with that woman," he said to me. "Just don't."

"Do you know her?" Chief said.

"I just know she evil."

"Does she look evil?" I said.

Desmond swallowed so hard I could almost hear his Adam's apple hit bottom. "Yeah. She jus' look like she ain't got nothin' good on her mind. Like she nothin' but trouble for us."

I rifled back through what I'd just said to Chief. Had I actually gotten out that I was going to ask her if she was interested in buying the house? Or had Desmond just picked up on her interest in Palm Row property from my conversation with Owen? The boy was, after all, everywhere he didn't need to be, hearing everything he didn't need to hear. I supposed that was how a kid like him survived on the streets.

"Would it make you feel better if your mom promised not to talk to her?" Chief said.

I glared at him. Nice. Use the boy for your own agenda.

"If she cross her heart and hope to die right here on the floor." Desmond's eyes swelled again. "No. You don't got to die. Just cross your heart and hope to spit."

I glanced out the window. "She's gone anyway," I said. "Now both of you, quit doggin' me and go to the beach."

Desmond wriggled his shoulders as if he were shaking himself back into place. Chief, on the other hand, suddenly looked uncharacteristically embarrassed.

"There's going to be a slight delay, pal," he said. "I put my sis—backrest—on Allison's bike until the new one came in and I forgot to pick it up."

"I don't need no backrest thing."

We both looked at Desmond. He put his white-palmed hands up in surrender, but I could see he was going to come right out of his skin if he didn't get on that Harley in the next seven seconds.

"Take my bike," I said to Chief.

He looked doubtful.

"Just to go pick up the bar. Then you can bring it back here and put it on and you guys can be on your way."

"Imma go wichoo, right?" Desmond said to him.

Chief's lines flinched, but he nodded. "All right. Get your stuff."

Desmond took off out the door as if he had a pack of dogs after him. Chief tilted his head at me. "I don't like riding somebody else's bike."

"You've ridden mine before," I said. "It's just a couple of miles. And you are not leaving that kid here with me to scrape off the walls. Besides, I have …"

I pointed to the ceiling. I could hear the shower running in the upstairs bathroom.

"You're pretty persuasive, Classic," he said.

His lips brushed my forehead.

"Did I mention that I will have your head in a handbasket if anything happens to my bike?" I said.

What I wanted to say was, *I can't stand this anymore. I love you. Now will you please kiss me?*

I didn't, and he left with my kid and my bike. But I made a

vow as I watched them from the side porch that I would tell Chief that the next moment I laid eyes on the man. No matter who else clattered into the room while I was doing it.

I was still standing there, listening to my Classic fade into the Sunday sounds of St. Augustine, when another vehicle turned into Palm Row. The Mercury again, tires squealing. The driver rocked it to a stop right in the middle of the lane and threw open the door with the bell still ringing to tell her the keys were in the ignition.

Apparently she didn't care. Her eyes found me on the porch and she marched through the gate and across the lawn, a lace-trimmed dashiki flapping around her. Her head was so tightly wrapped in a dark blue scarf, her eyes stretched unnaturally at the corners. Even at that, they were huge eyes that seemed to take up half her face. I'd seen eyes like that before.

And as soon as she stopped on my bottom step and opened her mouth, I knew where.

"Allison Chamberlain," she said, as if I dare not try to deny it.

"Who wants to know?" I said.

"Priscilla Sanborn," she said. "I am Desmond's aunt, and I have come to see about him."

CHAPTER TEN

They were Geneveve's eyes. Only my sweet friend had never looked at anyone with those eyes the way this woman was piercing me with hers. I didn't need a mirror to know I was piercing right back.

Although she was small-framed like Geneveve, she stood tall, as if she could somehow shrink the rest of us if she tried hard enough. She straightened entitled shoulders and marched, uninvited, up the steps. I moved not at all subtly to put myself between her and the kitchen door. If this woman even thought she was coming into my home—

Okay. Pull it back. Respond in love.

If that was God, he had to be kidding. But I did respond in coldly polite.

"Have a seat?" I said, slicing a hand toward the swing.

She pulled the African lacy thing across her chest. *Yeah, lady, it's chilly out here in March—deal with it.* The closest I could come to responding in love was not saying that out loud.

The woman finally sat like a plank on the edge of one of the Adirondack chairs and clasped her hands together in a fold halfway between praying and dealing with indigestion. It reminded me that prayer would be a good thing right now.

God, please don't let me push her off the porch.

"You said you wanted to see about Desmond," I said. "He's not here."

"I am well aware of that." She pronounced every consonant with the precision of a needle. Hours of practice had obviously gone into erasing any trace of a Southern accent. "I just witnessed him leaving on the back of your motorbike with your boyfriend."

She couldn't have made it sound more like a trailer-trash event if she'd tried. I did nothing to correct her.

"I have been watching you."

"We're all aware of that," I said. "If you hadn't made your intentions known soon, the police would have been called."

Surprise flickered through her eyes. Had she expected me to talk like a redneck?

"I was not trespassing," Priscilla said. "I have a right to see what kind of life my nephew is living."

"Then why didn't you just knock on the door and ask?"

She refolded her hands. The indigestion was apparently trumping the prayer. "It has been my experience that people are much more themselves when don't know they're under scrutiny. Let me just get to the point, Miss Chamberlain: I do not like what I see here."

"I'm sorry," I said. "I don't recall arranging for a critique."

"I don't believe you understand the seriousness of this situation. I am Desmond's only living relative, and I do not approve of his current lifestyle. He is being driven around like a member of a motorcycle gang. It is Sunday, yet this morning or any other Sunday I have not seen him being taken to church. And despite his living in this blue-blood neighborhood, he is still exposed to his mother's unsavory friends." She pursed her lips until they resembled a raisin. She was looking less like my beautiful Geneveve by the minute. "Your way of life embodies everything that is despicable about this town's wealth and power, and I cannot stand by and watch Desmond be brought up under this kind of influence."

"I see," I said.

"*Do* you?"

"I think so. Here's what strikes me." I resituated myself against the porch railing so I could face her squarely. "You can't stand by and watch Desmond be surrounded by love, by people who are living healed, healthy lives despite their pasts. You can't stand by and see him taking part in a Christian community that worships at least once a week if not more. You can't stand by and watch him exposed to male role models who embody integrity and generosity." I put my hand up as she unraised her mouth. "But you *could* stand by and let his grandfather, your father, die in a nursing home without his family. You *could* stand by and watch your sister try to raise the boy on the street when you knew she wasn't capable of it. Oh, wait. You *didn't* stand by. You went to Africa or someplace to do heaven knows what while this nephew you're so concerned about tried to survive with absolutely no tools in the bag until his mother came to me and asked for help." I pulled my face back. "Yes, Miss Sanborn, I do see."

She sat stone still, and I watched her will every syllable I'd uttered to roll from her like so much water off a duck's behind.

"You are not black," she said finally.

"That's the first true thing you've said since you got here," I said.

"Joke if you want, but that is a significant fact. Desmond is not being raised in his own culture."

"What culture is that? If you want to split hairs, his father was white."

"The white world is not going to accept him as one of them."

"You seriously have not heard a word I've said."

Nor did she hear any in *that* sentence. The door from the kitchen fell open, and a forlorn figure wrapped in a towel stumbled onto the porch. Ophelia grabbed for support and landed against the swing. It knocked her to the ground where she lay, towel open, naked and raw.

I went to my knees beside her and pulled the towel across her body.

"Need I say more?" Priscilla said. "You will be hearing from my lawyer."

I didn't bother to answer her. Ophelia was weeping into my lap and clawing at my pants like she was trying to dig a den to crawl into. Cries threatened in my throat too, but I ordered them back with a hard swallow and pulled Ophelia up to rock her in my arms.

"I was in the shower," she sobbed into my chest. "And I felt like it was happening all over again. I can't get away from it."

"I know," I said.

"I want a drink. But I don't want to want a drink."

She dug her fingernails into my arm until I was sure she was drawing blood, but I didn't pull away. It might have been the only way she could keep from crawling to my kitchen and breaking every bottle until she found something that could take away her agony. Chief was wrong. I couldn't be that something.

"I'm going to call somebody who can help us," I said. "You just stay right here with me while I call."

"Don't let them take me away."

I found Leighanne's number in my phone and pressed it with my thumb while I smashed my other hand against Ophelia's wet hair.

"You're in the House now, Ophelia. No one's taking you away."

Leighanne was there with Nita in less than fifteen minutes. By then I had Ophelia in a terry-cloth robe in the red chair. At first while they talked to her, she clung to my arm like a baby koala. But when Ophelia finally began to shape her story with her hands as she talked to them, I tiptoed out to the kitchen and looked at the clock.

Chief and Desmond should have been back by now, unless they'd decided to take my bike to the beach, which was fine. Actually the longer they stayed gone the better. We needed to get Ophelia past the crisis, and I needed to discuss with God just what I was supposed to do about Priscilla Sanborn.

The woman hadn't actually said she was going to try to take Desmond from me, but then, she didn't say she hated my guts either, and it was obvious that she did. I had everything going against me as far as she was concerned. I was white. I was a Chamberlain, although a Livengood or a Todd or an Irwin would apparently have been just as despicable.

But I was also the woman who made sure her father *and* her sister were given decent burials, and the one who had kept her nephew out of the foster-care dead end, not to mention out of his felonious father's clutches. She didn't seem to recognize any of that, which was like a jagged piece of glass that refused to fit back in the window it was smashed out of.

I peeked into the living room. Ophelia was crying again, but softly, and she appeared to be pouring her heart out to Nita. I needed to do some pouring myself. Chief probably wouldn't hear his phone, but if I left a message he'd call me. But he was with Desmond.... Or I could call Hank.... No, she was still at church. Bonner, maybe? Ten to one he was still trying to convince India to ever speak to me again.

The avalanche still hadn't hit bottom.

Okay, leave Chief a message telling him not to come by here, and then concentrate on finding a place for Ophelia. That's what I would do.

I didn't have a chance. The kitchen window was suddenly framing a police cruiser with Nicholas Kent at the wheel. I knew from the reluctant way he pulled himself out of the car that he was coming to tell me something I wouldn't want to hear. When I met him on the side porch, his freckles stood out in bas-relief from blanched skin.

"Tell me," I said.

"There's been an accident, Allison," he said.

I shook my head even as I said, "Chief and Desmond."

"Yeah."

"Are they ..."

"Desmond's injuries seem to be minor."

"Chief?" I clapped my hand over my mouth.

"He's alive, okay?"

"But it's not good, is it?"

"I can't tell you that."

"Stop it, Nicholas—yes, you can!"

Nicholas rubbed the back of his neck. "He's unconscious. They've taken them both to Flagler."

"Okay," I said. And then I said it at least a dozen more times as if saying it would make it so.

"I can take you to the hospital," Nicholas said.

"Why don't you let me do that?"

Owen was suddenly on the porch with us. In the blur of pain, I nodded.

By the time we got to the ER, I discovered a tunnel of sanity to crawl through, so that when I found Desmond sitting on the edge of an examining table with his arm in a sling and his face in a stoic stare, I didn't sink into a puddle of okay-okay-okay. I hiked myself up next to him and let my legs swing with his.

"You all right?" I said.

"I got a broke collarbone," he said.

"I know. The doc told me. He said if you hadn't been wearing a helmet and leathers, it would've been a whole lot worse."

"That didn't help Chief none," he said.

I myself knew nothing about Chief's condition. No one would tell me anything because I wasn't a relative. I had a feeling Desmond's conclusions were drawn from being there.

"I couldn't make him wake up," Desmond said. "He just lyin' there, and I couldn't get him to answer me."

"He's not dead," I said.

He turned his face to me, eyes as angry as they were frightened. "Don't you lie to me, Big Al. I can't stand it if you lie and I find out."

"I'm not lying, son. I promise you. Officer Kent told me he's still alive."

The Adam's apple swelled. "He gon' be all right?"

I sucked in air. "I don't know. But you and I are going to do everything we can to get him there."

"What *we* gon' do?"

"We're going to love him," I said. "And nobody can do it like you and me."

"I thought you was gonna say, 'We gon' pray.'"

"That's what I did say. Love *is* prayer."

His mouth hardened, and he looked away.

"What?" I said.

He tried to shrug.

"Don't you lie to me, either," I said. "What's going on?"

It came out in a blurt. "How I'm s'posed to pray to God when he let this happen to Chief? When he let people—"

He choked himself off and jittered his feet so hard the table absorbed his anxiety and vibrated under me.

"He let people do what?" I said. "Maybe we should start with what people we're talking about."

"Nobody," he said. "I don' feel like talkin' no more, Big Al. I don't remember nothin' anyway."

Owen appeared then, muttering about not being able to find a parking place. For once he was without similes.

"Will you stay with Desmond?" I whispered to him. "I'm going to get the doctor."

At his nod I slipped out and headed for the nurse's station where the still-pimpled resident I'd talked to earlier was staring into a computer screen.

"Could Desmond be suffering memory loss?" I said. "Or is he just traumatized, do you think?"

He looked at me blankly.

"We just talked a few minutes ago," I said, "I'm Desmond Sanborn's foster mother? He says he doesn't remember what happened in the accident."

"Right. That's entirely possible," he said. "Most people don't, whether they suffer a head injury or not. He's still in shock, and I'm looking here …" He turned back to the computer. "We haven't done a CT scan because we didn't have your permission yet. The sling was just first aid."

"Fine," I said. "Please do it. What do you need me to sign?"

He motioned to a nurse behind the counter and she handed him a form. "He might recall some details in the next few days, or he might not." He smiled the smile that had probably gotten him into medical school, the one that would make him a great doctor when he grew up. "Some details are better not remembered, you know?"

That seemed to be the consensus among everyone in my life who'd been kicked in the stomach in one way or another in the past two days. I'd love to forget some of it myself.

When I got back to Desmond's cubicle, they were taking him off for his scan. I asked Owen to go with him and I went in search of the nurse who had told me she couldn't tell me anything about Chief. My own shock was wearing off, and I was ready to yank somebody up by the front of her scrubs to get her attention.

Nicholas Kent met me at the double doors marked TRAUMA and pushed them open as I approached.

"You can see him through the glass," he said, "but they're still working on him."

"What does that mean?" I said to his back as he led me down an eerily shiny hallway and into a dimly lit area where the only light came from the other side of a window.

"I'm not sure," he said. "Except that he's alive and they think they can do something for him?"

His youth curled itself right around my heart. He was trying so hard to be kind. I started to cry without a sound.

He nodded toward the window at the long limp form that I could only assume was Chief. No one actually seemed to be "working on" him. There were certainly no more orifices they could put tubes into, no more veins they could open to needles, no more wires they could attach to computers to make them blink green lines and numbers that meant nothing to me.

"Which one is the heart monitor?" I whispered to Nicholas.

"I think that one," he said, pointing.

A fragile line moved in what seemed to me an untrustworthy rhythm across a screen. I watched it go until I couldn't see it for the tears. As long as that line continued its path, no matter how erratic, I could still breathe. But without Chief, I didn't know if I could.

Shoes squeaked on the floor behind us and I steeled myself to resist being tossed back into the waiting room. But an unthreatening voice said, "Are you Allison?"

The shoes belonged to a man in his late forties wearing rumpled scrubs and a surgical cap from which gray curls poked their way wherever they could find an escape.

"I'm Dr. Doyle," he said. "I understand you and my sister know each other."

I couldn't put that together.

"Liz Doyle."

"Oh, of course, I'm sorry."

"No worries." His eyes blinked rapidly. He wasn't making it up; he was definitely related to Liz.

"You're Mr. Ellington's significant other," he said.

"I … Yeah, that would be me."

"I think HIPAA would consider you a relative. Would you like to know—"

"Yes, and in the next ten seconds, starting with if he's going to live."

He didn't give me the unqualified yes I knew my face begged for.

"I can't assure you of that," he said. "But I can tell you the next best thing, and that is that we don't know."

How that could be the next best thing I had no idea. I wanted to grab him and shake him and make him tell me something better. What I wanted more was for Chief to be standing next to me, touching my elbow to keep me from doing it.

"First of all, it's good that he was wearing a helmet or I guarantee you he wouldn't have made it. However, he is in a coma."

I gasped.

"I know that word is frightening, so let me just try to explain it for you."

I thought I said, "Okay."

"Your brain sits in a kind of soup. It isn't attached to your skull. When your head comes to a stop abruptly, like in an accident such as this one, your brain can bang against the inside of your skull, which is what more than likely happened to Mr.—"

"Chief," I said. "He likes to be called Chief."

"Good to know. I'll tell the nurses that when we get him into ICU. They'll want to call him by the name he's comfortable with when they talk to him."

"When he comes out of the coma," I said.

"While he's in the coma."

"Which is going to be for how long?"

"I honestly don't know. The CT shows a great deal of swelling, and what we're worried about there is that the pressure of the brain against the skull will deprive the brain of its blood supply."

"You're saying he could have brain damage."

"He could. There's also a chance he won't. No way to tell until he wakes up, and again, I don't know when that will be."

So, basically, he didn't know anything that could stop my heart from trying to slam its way out of my chest.

"There is one piece of excellent news, though," he said.

"Yeah?" Nicholas said.

I'd all but forgotten he was there.

"The swelling doesn't involve the brain stem, so he's able to breathe on his own. We feel like he's stable enough for surgery on his leg."

"His leg?" I said.

"He suffered a fracture, so we're going to have to stabilize it with a rod. Then we'll take him to Neuro-ICU." His face softened beneath the pokey curls. "I'll put you on the list of people who can spend short periods of time with him, and I encourage you to talk to him as if he's awake. Studies have shown that's associated with positive outcomes. If you and his family can rotate so there's someone with him for some portion of every hour, that would be optimum."

I nodded, but I was wondering for the first time if Chief even had any family. I knew so little about him.

"Any questions for me?"

I knew my face was vague. All I could do was look at him.

"This is a lot to absorb," he said. "I need to go consult with the orthopedic surgeon, but please get my number from the nurse at the desk. You can call me as questions come up in your mind. Okay?"

I suddenly wanted to lean right into this unkempt man and stay there until Chief woke up. When did I become so needy? When did I get to the place where I was strangled by the very thought of losing someone?

"How's your boy doing?" Dr. Doyle said.

Desmond. I had to get back to Desmond. And I couldn't do it groping for air.

I tried to straighten my shoulders. "Okay, I think. I need to go see how his CT scan went."

He shook my hand and Nicholas's and squeaked off down the hall. Nicholas kneaded his uniform hat between his palms.

"Can I do anything else for you?" he said.

I took his hint and moved with him to the double doors. "I want to know how this happened, Nicholas. Chief is an expert rider. He and that bike are like one. Oh."

"What?" he said.

I stopped with the door pushing against me. "They were on *my* bike. I made him take it. This is my fault."

Nicholas nodded at the disgruntled nurse who was staring at the open door and gingerly touched my arm to steer me toward a waiting area.

"I don't see this being your fault," he said. "In the first place? I mean, I don't know him that well, but I'm not sure anybody makes Jack Ellington do anything he doesn't want to do."

"Then what happened? Desmond doesn't remember anything. At least, that's what he tells me."

"You think it's true?"

"I don't know why he'd lie. He usually tells me more than I really want to know about anything."

Nicholas tried a smile on me. I saw it and burst into tears again. Big sobs that made him look like a new father with a screaming infant on his hands.

"Is there somebody I can call?" he said.

"I'll be okay," I said, snot already pouring from my nose. "I need to focus on Desmond."

"I'll see what I can find out from the officers on the scene." Nicholas straightened his shoulders. "You want me to walk you back to the ER?"

I shook my head. "I just need to sit here for a minute."

I waited until his footsteps faded before I sank my face into my hands. The fact of my aloneness contracted inside me, a pain that went on and on until I nearly cried out *Dear God*.

He answered anyway. He said, *It hurts, doesn't it?*

I knew it would. I knew it would hurt to love like this. That was why I had pushed it away for so long, because I knew it could make me writhe like I was in an endless act of giving birth.

"Why did you change me?" I whispered into my palms. *I was doing what you asked of me. Why couldn't I do it without ...*

I don't do my work without love. How can you?

The next spasm went so deep I doubled over in the chair.

"Are you all right?"

I pulled my head up and found myself nose to badge with Detective Kylie.

"Sorry to disturb you, Miss Chamberlain," he said. "I need to ask you a few questions."

CHAPTER ELEVEN

That was Detective Kylie. It was so like him to go directly from "Are you all right?" to "You have the right to remain silent." At least it felt that way, even when he said, "I know this is a bad time, but I only need a few minutes."

"I don't have a few minutes," I said. "I need to get to my son."

"He's okay. I just talked to him."

"Without me there?"

"His grandfather was with him."

"His gr—" I stopped myself. He had to be talking about Owen. Detective Kylie shrugged. "All he would tell me was that one minute they were riding and the next minute they weren't."

"Then that's all he remembers," I said. "And from now on, don't talk to him without me present. Are we clear?"

My own clarity was a surprise to me. The Chief-pain dulled to an ache as my mind came to a point on Desmond.

"I understand your concern," Kylie said. "Did he tell you any more than that?"

"No."

"If he does, I would appreciate your letting me know."

I didn't answer.

"Look, I know you and I don't see eye to eye on some things, but I'm trying to determine whether we need to be looking for a hit-and-run driver."

I sat up straight. "You mean, someone caused the accident and then took off?"

"We're not even sure it was an accident. Two witnesses at the scene said they thought the other driver deliberately caused Jack to swerve and lose control."

The pain wrenched at me again. "Why would someone do that?"

"That's where I hoped you could help me out. Do you know anyone who would want to see Jack ... out of the picture? Maybe a disgruntled former client?"

"Good grief, no. He's not even a criminal lawyer. It's not like he puts people behind bars."

"Anything of a personal nature? An old boyfriend of yours who's jealous of your relationship with Jack?"

"No. Look, everyone likes Chief. He's a paragon of integrity in this town."

Detective Kylie closed his notepad. "Some people hate integrity, especially when it gets in their way."

"To my knowledge he hasn't gotten in anybody's way." I fought to keep my voice steady. "But if I find out anything I *will* let you know. And when he wakes up, he'll probably be able to tell us exactly who it was. Chief is always aware of his surroundings. He doesn't miss anything."

Kylie drew his eyebrows together.

"What?" I said.

"Both witnesses said just before the car went for them, Chief turned his head like he was trying to look at Desmond."

I tried, but I couldn't imagine Chief doing that. I pulled in air, once, twice, but I couldn't push back the pain. I always thought I would be the one to have the unexpected dismount that landed me in the ICU. Not Chief.

"Who were the witnesses?" I said.

He hesitated before he opened his pad again. "Ulysses Hickman and Stan Wentworth. The officers said they both sat with Desmond because he wouldn't leave Jack's side for the paramedics to assess him. They had to do it right there."

I clamped my hands behind my neck and stared at the ceiling and wished he would go away before he told me one last thing that might send me over the edge.

"That's it for now," he said. "I might want to question you about this rape you reported last night, but that can wait."

Could it? I thought, as he left me in the waiting area squeezing my elbows together to keep from coming apart. Could any of it wait? Ophelia's rape. Zelda's sentencing. Priscilla Sanborn's intentions for my son. Was all of that going to take a hiatus while I kept a vigil at Chief's bedside and begged him to come back? Each one of those desperate things stretched its hands out to me, but even as I stretched back to them in my mind, my fingers couldn't reach them. If they had, I knew we would only end up in a tangle of need I couldn't meet.

One creamy-palmed hand did touch mine from the end of a lanky adolescent arm. I got up and went to find it.

The sun was just leaving Matanzas Bay to a silhouette of boat masts when Owen got us back to Palm Row. All the way Desmond sat in a curl in the backseat saying nothing, which of all the things I'd experienced in the last twenty-four hours was the most disturbing.

Owen filled me in on the interview with Detective Kylie, including his posing as Desmond's grandfather. It had gone down just as Kylie said, which instilled a fragment of trust there.

Owen offered to take Desmond home with him, but I declined. I needed to keep him next to me. I hadn't told anyone about Priscilla's visit yet, but somewhere in the painful reality of the day, the stark realization had come to me that Desmond must have recognized her that morning. Hence, "Don't have nothin' to do with that woman."

Desmond went straight to his room and I let him. We needed to be alone before I broached the subject with him, and the house was full of people. Nita and Leighanne had taken Ophelia out to eat, but Hank was in the kitchen preparing a meal for Desmond and me, and Jasmine, Mercedes, and Sherry were gathered in the dining room, heads bowed around the table, lips moving soundlessly.

"They've been praying for an hour," Hank whispered to me.

The smell of leather led me to the living room, where Stan and Rex sat with Ulysses in front of an untouched loaf of Italian bread and a saucer of olive oil. I sat on the arm of the red chair and Stan put his arm around my waist. All my reasons for usually smacking him for doing that blew away like dust.

"We've been going over it and over it," Stan said. "And we just can't figure out what happened to save our life."

I wanted them to go over it one more time, for me, but what came out of my mouth was, "We have to be his family."

"You got that right," Ulysses said. "He doesn't have much of one. An ex-wife's all I know about."

Stan gave a grunt. "We won't be calling her."

I thought with a stab that I didn't even know there was one not to call.

"No parents, no siblings," Ulysses said. "You're right, girl, we *are* his family."

"Who sign for his treatment?" Rex said.

They all looked at me, but I had to shake my head. "All I know is that someone can be with him for fifteen minutes every hour, and that when we're there, we should talk to him like he's awake. They say that'll maybe bring him out faster."

They waited while I pulled my voice back from the edge it tee-tered on. Their respect for my pain made it even harder to speak.

I managed, "Do we know anybody who would want to see Chief hurt?"

"No," Stan said, "but I know who I want to hurt when they find him, and that's that limo driver."

"What limo?" I said.

Ulysses frowned at Stan. "It was a Lincoln Town Car."

"Yeah, but they were using it like a limo. Who sits in the back-seat while somebody else drives unless it's a limo?"

"How could you see anybody in the backseat?" Ulysses said. "The windows were tinted."

"Because the dude in the back rolled his window down about that much." Stan held his index finger and thumb several inches apart. "I couldn't see his face. He had on shades and a hat. But there was definitely somebody sitting back there."

"*What* limo!" I pressed the heel of my hand against my forehead. "I'm sorry. I'm a little freaked out."

"The car that ran Chief off the road," Stan said. "It was a limo,

Town Car. Whatever." He gave Ulysses a look. "With a driver in front and a guy in the backseat."

"And you saw him?" I said.

"Just the top of his head basically. I was too far away for a good look."

"Dinner's almost ready," Hank said from the doorway. "You people need nourishment. We have a long haul ahead of us."

She rested her dark eyes on me and I had to nod. I didn't know how I was going to eat with my insides cramped into a knot, but I didn't know how to get out of it either. Not with Hank speaking her love language all the way to the table.

Nita brought Ophelia back around eight. I hadn't had time to figure out where to put her, and at the moment, whether Vickie Rodriguez approved was at the bottom of my priority list. With Priscilla Sanborn now in the picture, Vickie was likely to hear all kinds of tales that would top that anyway. I got Ophelia settled in the bedroom I'd used for Geneveve and later for Zelda, and hoped the outcome would be better for her.

I bade her good night and started to snap out the light by the door, but from the bed she said, "I heard them calling you 'Miss Angel.'"

I tried to smile at her. "It isn't because I am one, I can tell you that."

She looked into her lap. Her dark hair grazed her shoulders. "I just want to know if I have to be one."

"If that were true, none of us would be in the House, including me."

"What *do* I have to do, then? To stay here."

I opened my mouth and hoped something coherent would come out.

"Be honest," I said. "With us. With yourself. With God."

"I have to believe in God? Nita and them, they told me I needed a Higher Power. They didn't say it was God."

I so didn't want to have this conversation right now, but I crossed to the bed and put my hand on her forehead and said the only thing that came into my too-crowded mind.

"If you have issues with God, we'll sort that out," I said. "For now, knowing you can't do it alone is enough."

She nodded and closed her eyes. Her breathing was deep and even before I got to the door.

I hoped I could follow that advice myself.

I certainly didn't fall asleep the way she did. It was after eleven when everyone left, and I was so exhausted I couldn't even climb the stairs, much less talk to Desmond. He was blessedly asleep anyway.

Yet after I stretched out on the couch and stopped my shivering with three of Sylvia's afghans, I could barely close my eyes. When I did doze, dreams immediately haunted me—of the Reverend Garry flying over the footwashing on white-haired wings, Priscilla doing a tribal dance on Geneveve's grave, and squealing tires sending my son and my love hurling into the air. When I awoke to screaming,

I thought the cries were my own. But they were coming from Desmond's room.

One of the afghans caught on my sweats and dragged behind me as I groped through the dark to the kitchen. I expected to see the boy in the doorway sobbing, but his door was closed the way it had been from the moment we got home. He'd slept through the time for his pain pill, and I was wracked with guilt as I pushed open the door. The poor kid was probably in agony.

But I knew the minute I saw him cringing against the head-board, eyes darting sightlessly, that he wasn't even awake.

"Desmond," I said.

I touched his good shoulder, and he jerked away and spewed out a jumble of sentences I couldn't understand. I didn't need the words to know he was seeing something that terrified him.

"Desmond," I said again. I tried to keep my voice calm, despite the terror climbing up my own throat. "You're dreaming, son. It's okay."

His breathing slowed, but he remained so taut I would have to break his legs to get him unwound from his frightened fetal position. I reassured him, over and over, that it was just a dream, that he was asleep, that no one was going to hurt him. I wasn't sure which one of us I was trying to convince.

When he finally went limp, I eased him down under the covers and pulled them up to the base of his marvelous pyramid of hair. If it hadn't been under a helmet that day, I wouldn't be sinking my fingers into it right now. But I was, and I stayed there the rest of the night.

He woke up the next morning still quiet—for Desmond—until I told him he was staying home from school. That lifted his spirits enough for him to consume two bowls of the Froot Loops I kept hidden and allowed him handfuls of only on special occasions. I plugged him into a movie on my laptop while I took a shower and tried to figure out how to talk to him about Priscilla. I was no closer to a decision when Stan showed up with the new sissy bar for Chief's bike.

"Thought you'd need it so you can get around," he said.

"I appreciate it, Stan," I said. "But I don't think I'll be taking Desmond out with a broken collarbone. Besides, I can't ride Chief's bike."

"You probably can, but maybe you shouldn't until you feel up to it."

"I look that bad?" I said.

"Uh—yeah. But Chief looks worse."

"You've already seen him?"

"I did my fifteen minutes before I came over here." Stan's eyes swam. "I told him we'd all take care of you until he was up and around again."

I put my arms around his neck and held on until we could both pretend we weren't crying.

Things went that way for the next few days—that way of unexpected people doing unexpected things.

Owen stayed with Desmond several times a day while I went to be with Chief.

Hank cooked meals in my kitchen and made me eat them.

That wasn't unexpected, but Jasmine and Mercedes cleaned my house and did my laundry and reported that Nicholas Kent drove down Palm Row every couple of hours.

As was par for Nita and Leighanne, they took Ophelia to AA meetings, but the rest of the time Ophelia chopped and peeled and diced things for Hank and helped Desmond with the homework Erin O'Hare gathered and brought by for him. The doctor said he could go back to school, but I knew he wasn't ready. On the days I suggested it, the following night was filled with nightmares he didn't even seem to remember having the next morning. Though he did the work without complaint, perhaps a sure sign that he truly was unwell, I couldn't even interest him in returning to campus so he could check on his women. That only served to remind me that I hadn't had another chance to ask Chief to discuss that issue with Desmond, and that sent me into another paroxysm of pain. There was actually very little that *didn't* connect me back to Chief—the things left unsaid, the things I might never get to say.

The only relief for that was my time at the hospital. Chief showed no change as the days went by, and I stopped asking what that meant because the answer was always the same: We had to wait and see. I clung to the fact that although his face was bloated and pale and looked nothing like my eagle Chief, he was still breathing on his own, and that the bruising on his head turned from angry purple to a less disconcerting yellow-green at the same rate Ophelia's did. The leg that hung in traction with the alien rods protruding from it was reportedly healing, and that was reassuring too.

I mentioned to God countless times that surely the leg wouldn't recover if the man wasn't going to. How could that be?

Yet how could it be that Chief was even in that bed, relying on IVs and nurses and round-the-clock one-sided conversations to keep him from slipping away forever? Chief didn't *need* like this, and that alone was enough to wake me up in the middle of every night in a sweat of anxiety.

But it was also enough to bring me to his side four and five times a day. I always waited until the nurse left before I pulled the stool close to his bed and rested one arm on the pillow above his head. The other arm I kept in my lap where I could squeeze my own knee if I started to cry. If he could hear me, I didn't want him to know I had doubts.

Most of my monologues were renditions of Desmond's latest outrageous statements and the lack of progress Detective Kylie was making on finding the driver of the hit-and-run vehicle and the lack of anything at all happening with Ophelia's rape. When that got too depressing, I assured him I wouldn't ride his bike, even though *he* had wrecked *mine,* although it occurred to me by Thursday—Day Five of the Coma—that maybe if I told him I *was* going to ride the Road King, he might snap out of it.

It didn't work, and for some silly reason I couldn't handle that.

"Please, Chief," I said, tears pouring shamelessly down my face. "You have to come back. How am I supposed to make any decent decisions without you? Huh? Don't you see that I need you? Do you think I'd be admitting that if I weren't desperate to have you open your eyes and say, 'Classic, I'd advise against that.'"

I fixed my eyes on the screen that traced his brain activity, as if it could tell me that any of this was registering. Maybe I was looking in the wrong place. Maybe it was the line on the heart monitor that would bring him awake if he knew.

I leaned on the stool until it was only on its front two feet, until I could get my lips close to his ear, until perhaps he could feel my breath in it, the way I loved to feel his in mine.

"I'm afraid you don't love me the way I love you, Chief," I whispered. "But I can't let that keep me from telling you. I love you enough to walk away if you wake up and tell me you don't feel that way. I love you enough to hurt for you."

"I think he knows that."

I put my hand up to the one that rested on my shoulder.

"How can you say that, Bonner?" I said.

Bonner squatted beside me and brushed the tears from my cheek with the corner of his handkerchief, the kind only Bonner Bailey would carry. "I saw it on his face."

"When?"

"You remember that night at O. C.'s ?"

"You had the oysters."

"Yeah."

"And he and I were arguing." I turned to look up at Bonner. "I sure didn't see any love on his face that night."

"Oh, it was there. He said, 'I'm not going to let you do this, Classic.' And you didn't argue with him. I expected the engagement ring to come out next. "

I laughed for the first time in days. It was a snot-filled, snorty sort of thing, but it mixed with my sobs until it all came out as hope.

"We're going to get in trouble if they find two of us in here," I said.

"Nah. Your Dr. Doyle told them to lighten up for you." He nudged my shoulder. "You're getting a lot of mileage out of rescuing Liz in high school."

"Yeah, who knew, huh?"

"God?"

"Maybe."

Bonner tucked his chin in. "Just 'maybe'?"

"I'm struggling, Bonner," I said. "I just keep thinking that all this stuff that's happened is because of my doing what I thought God wanted me to do."

"And now you're not sure it's what God wanted."

"I think I am. I wouldn't have bought a Harley on my own— or started Sacrament House or got people washing each other's feet in buckets on my front lawn." I dragged my fingers under my eyes to make room for more tears. "How far is it really getting us, though?"

"Maybe farther than you think," Bonner said.

Chief's nurse stepped in and began to adjust his IV. Although she smiled at us, Bonner motioned for me to follow him out into the hall.

"I found out about Zelda," he said.

"You did?" I said. "How?"

"That's my assignment."

"Your what?"

"We all have assignments so you can concentrate on Chief and Desmond." He shrugged lightly. "You want to hear about her?"

"Tell me."

"She wants to come back."

"And you know this how?"

"I went to see her."

The image of Bonner in a starched Oxford shirt looking through a glass at Zelda clad in county orange stopped my tears in their tracks.

"Seriously?" I said.

"I took her some toiletries, put a little cash in her account so she could at least get a candy bar."

I blinked to make sure it was still Bonner I was looking at. He merely blinked back.

"So how is she doing?" I said.

"She looks like death eatin' a cracker, as Mercedes would say, but she's hanging on to the chance that she can come back to the House."

"What about God?"

Bonner tilted his head.

"The last time I saw her, she was spitting at him."

"Spitting? At God?"

"Literally. And ever since then she's refused to see me, and I know it's because she doesn't want to hear about the heart and soul of this whole ministry." I rubbed at my forehead. "I don't know, Bonner. Can we take her in just because she sees that Sacrament House is a better deal than jail?"

"It may be a moot point anyway," Bonner said. "We don't really have a place to put her yet."

My mind flipped back through the days like it was going through a Rolodex.

"Is that house across from Sacrament up for sale yet?" I said.

"I think the owner's real close to putting it on the market. We did take in some cash at the Feast, but not enough."

"I want to sell the Palm Row house," I said. "That'll give us more than enough."

Bonner rested his chin on his knuckles.

"Don't try to talk me out of it," I said. "It's what I want to do. I have to."

"Allison."

"Make the guy an offer contingent on the sale of my house. Zelda probably has another thirty days before her case even comes up in court, right?"

"About that, yeah. That still isn't enough time."

"Can't we work it out somehow? Rent the house from the guy until mine sells and closes? You said he was already fixing it up."

"You've thought this through?"

"Truthfully? No. I'm making it up as I go along." I wrapped my fingers around his cuffed wrist. "I don't see any other way, Bonner. And in the meantime ..."

"In the meantime, I'll see if I can get her to stop spitting at God."

I kissed him on the forehead. When I drew back, he was swallowing hard.

"I hate it," he said. "That house is yours. Where are you and Desmond going to live?"

"I haven't gotten that far." It was true. Every time I tried to think of us finding a new place, I had to wonder if I would even have him, if Priscilla Sanborn really was going to get a lawyer and try to take him from me. That was one pain I couldn't allow right now, or I knew it would kill me.

"All right," Bonner said. "I'll start the paperwork. How much are you asking?"

"I'll leave that up to you. What's wrong?"

A shadow was crossing Bonner's face as he looked over my shoulder toward the nurses' station. I turned, and felt a darker shadow fall across mine. The Reverend Garry Howard was showing his ID to the charge nurse.

"What's he doing here?" I said.

"I think we're about to find out," Bonner said.

Garry came toward us, tucking his wallet back inside his jacket. All I could see were his white wings of hair, just as they appeared in my fitful dreams.

He dispensed with hellos and put his hands in his slacks pockets. I was tempted to say, *Who are you and what have you done with the Reverend Garry?* I had never known him to show a single sign that he didn't know what to say in any situation. Right now, it was written all over him.

"I was here visiting a few people and I saw Jack Ellington's name," he said. "I've gathered you two are close, Allison." He pulled his shoulders up to his ears. "I'm so sorry."

"Thank you." I searched his face for an agenda. I found none.

"What can we do?" he said. "Do you need meals? Shall I call Mary Alice?"

Mary Alice. I had the immediate image of my multi-chinned friend sitting across from me in my living room the day after Sylvia died, pulling a needle in and out of a piece of embroidery in a hoop and listening to me while I talked and cried. And another of her bringing casseroles to try to fill my empty place when Geneveve was murdered. It wasn't much of a leap from there to the rest of my Wednesday Night Watchdogs—who prayed and coached and fed me for seven years as I discovered who Jesus was. They were the people who at one time I would have turned to in a crisis like this—Frank Parker and Mary Alice Moss and—

"You seem to have a praying community."

I blinked back to Garry.

"We do," Bonner said.

"I suppose I just came by to show my—our—support." Garry pulled his hands from his pockets as if he wanted to do something with them. When he couldn't seem to decide what, he put them back again. "No matter how far you've wandered, Allison," he said, "your church family still loves you. Anything you need—"

"We're fine," Bonner said.

The pause that ensued was torturous. The Reverend Garry seemed to take all he could and then hurried down the hall.

Bonner let out an exasperated sigh. "He had me until 'no matter how far you've wandered.' You're right, Allison: He's—"

"Where is India, Bonner?" I said.

He let the anger slide from his face. "At work, I would assume."

"You know what I mean. Is she that angry with me that she hasn't even come by?"

"Do you want her to come by?"

"Of course I do. Do you know what's going on?"

"No, but I know who does." Bonner rubbed my arm. "Look, I'm on it, okay? Like I said, you focus on Chief and Desmond."

Yeah. As if I had a choice.

That night Desmond had another nightmare, and this time I was able to ferret out that somebody in the depths of his dreams was trying to take him. All week there hadn't been a single moment that seemed like the right one to bring up his aunt's visit. I'd even been able to convince myself at times that if she hadn't sicced her lawyer on me by now, she probably wasn't going to. Now, with Des screaming, "You can't have me!" I knew I couldn't put it off any longer.

But when he got up the next morning and announced that he wanted to go to school, I mentally rescheduled that discussion for the afternoon.

"You must be feeling better," I said.

"I got to pick up somethin'," he said. "Then maybe I'll knock off early."

"It's not a job, Desmond, it's school." I bounced my hand off of his hair. "You can't just 'knock off' whenever you want to."

Fear shot through his eyes.

"But if you get to feeling bad, call me," I added quickly. "I'll be with Hank this morning and I'll always have my cell with me."

He nodded uncertainly.

"Tell you what: If you feel like you need to come home, just go to Miss O'Hare and have her call, and then stay with her until I get there."

He seemed okay with that. He did load a second baggie full of Oreos into his lunch. But the swagger was missing when I watched him walk across the schoolyard, even when two junior coeds ran to him squealing. Even with them cooing and dancing, he looked back over his shoulder until his eyes found mine behind the windshield of the van. I gave him a thumbs-up, which he answered with only half a grin.

I was so ready for my weekly talk with Hank I caught air with the van going over the speed bump at the entrance to the parking lot behind St. George Street. Hank was standing there, helmet in hand.

"It's not a Harley, hon," she said when I climbed out.

"I know. I'm not sure I'll ever ride one again."

She peered at me over her sunglasses as we walked toward St. George Street. "Why not? Insurance is paying for a new one, right? That's what Bonner told me."

"It is. But I don't know if I have the heart."

Hank stopped me on the corner and waited for the blaring voice of the tour bus guide to take his spiel on up to Orange Street.

"I don't have to think very hard to know what Chief's going to say when he hears you say that. And I'm not even the prophet."

I sagged against a light pole. "You really think he's going to wake up? Be honest with me. It's been six days now, and even Dr. Doyle said the longer he's out, the less likely it is that he's going to make a full recovery."

"Then it sounds like you've had about all the honesty you can handle," she said. "Let's opt for some faith instead."

She crooked her elbow through mine and pulled us both down St. George at Boston speed.

"Where are we going, anyway?" I said. When I'd asked her the day before where we should meet now that the Spanish Galleon had closed, she just said we'd figure it out in the parking lot.

"Little place that just started serving coffee and breakfast," she said. "The food's not much, which means we'll probably have the whole thing to ourselves."

I let her haul me along, although my mind wasn't making much progress.

"Faith," I said.

"Yeah."

"I hope you don't mean faith that God is going to snap the Divine fingers and this is all going to be peachy. I'm not buying that."

Hank grunted. "If that were the way it worked, why would he have made all this happen in the first place?"

"You think God did?"

"Absolutely not."

"Then why are we even talking?"

She twitched her lips at me. "You brought it up, Al."

"I love you, Hank," I said.

She stopped again, and put herself in front of me, and took both of my wrists in her hands. The face she turned up to me was tender.

"That's the faith I'm talkin' about, Al," she said. "That's what's going to get us all through this and on top of it. God's got the love and God's pouring it out. Now, can we eat?"

I looked up at the sign above us.

"The Monk's Vineyard?" I said. "Lewis and Clark are serving breakfast now?"

"You've been here before?"

"This is where I found Ophelia."

And where I'd last seen Kade Cacciatore, or whatever that scoundrel's name was. I hadn't thought much about him since, which was actually fine.

"Miss Chamberlain!" a voice sang out from the porch.

Hank gave me a look.

"Long story," I said. "Hi, George."

"Not a long-enough story, far as I'm concerned," he said, shaking his head and with it his impossible mop of curls. "What do you say we fix that? Tell me what's been going on with you."

"Some menus first, please, George?" Hank said. "And a table would be good too."

The air was a little March chilly, but the street was quiet before the expected onslaught of kids on field trips, so we picked a spot on the porch and let George regale us with the specials. None of it sounded particularly appetizing to me, but I ordered a sausage biscuit and let him persuade me to try the latte Lewis was perfecting.

When he was gone, I felt Hank looking through me. I might as well tell her before she guessed.

"I'm putting the Palm Row house up for sale," I said.

She stared.

"I have to," I said.

That was as far as I got before my phone rang. I scrambled it out of my bag, sure it was Desmond already knocking off for the day. But it was Bonner.

"Hey, we were just talking about you," I said. "Or getting ready to, anyway."

"I don't know if this is good news or not," he said. "But the owner of that house on San Luis has accepted our offer, contingent on the sale of the Palm Row house, like you said. You and I need to sit down and really talk seriously about what you want to ask for it."

"What if we offered him a straight trade?" I said.

Silence didn't fall. It crashed.

"I know I'm not Chief," he said finally. "But I am not going to let you do that, Allison. I'm just not. I won't represent a deal like that."

"Okay," I said. "It was just a suggestion."

"And I'm going to pretend you never made it. When can we meet? How about I take you to dinner tonight?"

"I don't—"

"You need to get out and Hank needs a break from feeding you."

"I heard that," Hank said. "I don't need a break, but I'll take it."

"What about Desmond?" I said.

"I'll take him, too," Hank said.

I frowned at her but she waved me off. "Go—it'll do you good. Maybe Bonner can talk you out of whatever it is you're trying to do."

I told Bonner I'd go and hung up with Hank still staring at me.

"I just want to know one thing," she said.

"Okay," I said.

"Are you getting this from God, this selling your house idea?"

I rubbed a smudge from the screen on my phone.

"You're not," she said.

"Not directly. But Hank, I have to do something. Now I have Ophelia *and* Zelda to find places for."

"And you and Desmond?"

The phone rang again.

"Speaking of Desmond," I said.

For once his timing was perfect.

Desmond did look as if he were in pain when I picked him up, though he was vague on the details. When we got home he went straight to his room, and when I peeked in later, he was bent over his sketchbook.

"I'm liking this," I said. "I haven't seen you draw since the accident."

He flipped the cover closed and tossed the book aside.

"I wasn't going to try to look at it," I said. "I always wait for you to offer."

"It ain't no good," he said.

I tried to appear casual as I leaned against the doorframe, arms folded, but my heart lurched. I had never seen Desmond be anything but downright cocky about his work.

"If drawing's not doing it for you, you could come out here and have a snack. Or you could just ram around the kitchen until whatever it is comes out and then you can tell me what a good listener I am."

"Or I could just take a nap," he said. He turned his back to the doorway and lowered himself to the mattress.

Okay, so I blew that.

"Allison?"

I jumped. Nicholas Kent was at the screen door. I must have left the main door open when Desmond and I came in through the porch.

"Hey, come on in," I said.

His freckles were folded into a frown as he let himself in. "I don't advise you to leave that unlocked when you're here."

"Sorry, I'm just a little—okay, I'm a complete mess. You want some tea?"

That seemed to befuddle him momentarily, but he nodded. The boy was learning.

I nodded him toward the bistro table and put the kettle on. He wasn't wearing his uniform, so I knew whatever he'd come for wasn't of an official nature. There was that anyway.

"They got the DNA back on the rape case," he said.

I stopped, tea bag in midair. "Are you serious? That was fast."

"Some friend of Mr. Ellington's. Said it was the least he could do."

I hiked myself up onto the other bistro chair. "Why doesn't this sound like the good news it's supposed to be? I know we don't have anybody to compare it to yet."

"That's the bad news," he said. "The department is doing a half-hearted job of coming up with any suspects. If we can't get some more from Othella—"

"Ophelia, Nick," I said. "Her name's Ophelia."

"Look, I'm trying, okay? And I'm the only one who is, so just cut me some slack."

I chewed at my thumbnail.

"Sorry," he said. "I don't know why, but this case has got under my skin or something."

"I'm sorry," I said. "I told you, I'm just a mess. What were you saying?"

"If we can't get her to give us more about what happened, they're going to shelve this as a cold case."

"Do you want to try talking to her again?" I said. "She's upstairs."

"No. I'm here."

Ophelia moved across the kitchen, her hand out to Nicholas. He made no attempt to hide his outright astonishment as he shook it and watched her flow over to the stove and pour our tea. I really hoped this kid didn't play poker.

I couldn't blame him. With her hair brushed and swinging down her back and her sweet figure clad in jeans and a top that didn't offer her breasts up as a condiment, she looked like a different person than she had the night of the rape. She was still teeming with history beneath her caramel skin, however, and I didn't want Nicholas to get his hopes up about how forthcoming she was likely to be.

"Officer Kent needs to ask you some more questions," I said. "Are you up for it?"

It was my turn to be astonished. "I remembered something just today, just when I was waking up."

She still had her back to us, and I put my hand up to Nicholas. He nodded.

"What did you remember?" I said.

"I remember a profile." Ophelia turned as if to demonstrate. "It was no features, you know, just black."

"Like a silhouette," I said.

"Yes. That's the word."

"Can you describe it?" I said.

"It was handsome," she said. "But ugly."

I could feel Nicholas all but groaning.

"Handsome because of the nose and the chin, but ugly because—of what he did."

Ophelia's eyes filled, and I knew we were about to lose her into her pain again. I could feel my*self* falling, for that matter. But I had an idea.

"Desmond!" I said.

"I'm sleepin'," he answered from the bedroom.

"Wake up. I have a job for you."

Nicholas looked at me quizzically as I vacated the seat and nodded at Desmond, who appeared in his bedroom doorway.

"You'll need your sketchbook," I said. "It's police business."

I held my breath as he disappeared back into his room, but he came out with the book under his arm and a pencil behind his ear. He nodded at Nicholas and took his place on the chair, all with a glimmer of his cocky self in there somewhere.

"Ophelia's going to describe a person to you," I said, "and we need for you to draw it as best you can from her description."

He squinched his cheeks up to his eyes. "I don't get to see this person Imma be drawin'?"

"No," I said. "Is that a problem?"

"Yeah, it's a problem, Big Al. I always got to see who I'm drawin'."

Something about that didn't ring true, but I didn't have time to go there. "Just give it a try, okay? Ophelia, why don't you sit where Officer Kent is …"

For the next several minutes, Nicholas and I watched as Ophelia closed her eyes and, judging from the tightness of her forehead, strained to see that handsome-ugly profile yet again. Tears slipped from under her eyelids, but she finally began her description.

Hair smooth, only coming up like fingers right in the front.

Forehead that ended at his regular nose.

"Ain't no such thing as a regular nose," Desmond told her. "You gon' hafta looka here at what I'm drawin' and tell me is it right."

From that point on she stood at his elbow, making the picture with her fingers and watching as Desmond transferred it to the paper. After several false starts, she watched him sketch and shade for a long time until she gasped and grabbed for the table. I caught her before she made it to the floor.

"That's him!" she said. "That's him, Miss Angel!"

"Okay, you did good," I said. "You did great. Desmond, can you help Ophelia into the living room and stay with her till I get there?"

"You need the big chair, Miss Ofeelins," Desmond said as he took her from me—with far more therapeutic expertise than a twelve-year-old should have.

"There you go," I said to Nicholas.

He shook his head at the drawing. "It's pretty amazing that he can do that, but I don't know how much it's actually going to help us. Like you said, it's just a silhouette. Unless we see this guy standing sideways in a dark alley."

"Don't you think that's exactly where we *are* going to see him?" I said.

He scratched at his head. "I don't know. I keep thinking about how she said he dropped her off in front of your house. I don't see some West King Street wino driving her here. Besides, not to sound racist, but does this guy look African American to you?"

"Not typically, no. Whatever that is. Okay, so it's a long shot. Do what you can with it. I'm going to make a copy and give it to a guy I know. Maybe he can get them to print it in the paper."

"Good luck with that."

"Y'know what, Nicholas," I said. "Luck has nothing whatsoever to do with it."

My phone rang and I held up a finger to him. "We're not done," I said. "Hello, this is Allison."

"Miss Chamberlain, it's Doug Doyle."

Nicholas Kent and everything else around me disappeared down a tunnel.

"What is it?" I said. "What's wrong?"

"No, it's good news," he said. "Your Chief is awake."

CHAPTER TWELVE

Doug Doyle stopped me at the nurse's station, and it was all I could do not to knock him down and trample over him so I could get to Chief. But then my stomach turned over and I grabbed his sleeve.

"What's wrong? Is there brain damage?"

"No—"

"What is it—why won't you let me see him?"

His face fought a smile. "I'm going to let you see him. I don't think I have much choice."

"Okay. Then what?"

"You just need to keep it low key," he said. "He still doesn't remember much."

"Will he know me?"

He looked at the nurse behind the counter.

She glanced up from her computer. "The first thing he said when he opened his eyes was, 'Where's Allison?'"

Dr. Doyle let the smile win. "I think that's conclusive."

"So …"

"Don't ask him a lot of questions, and if he drifts off to sleep, that's okay. We want him to rest. I know it seems like all he's been doing is resting, but it's a different kind."

I left him giving the neuro-lecture to the nurse and bolted for Chief's door. I stopped just inside, and I closed my eyes, and I felt the pain in my gut release, just enough so that I could breathe. Just enough to hear—

It is good, yes?

Yes, God, it is very, very good.

Chief's face was as mushy and soft as a three-year-old's in those first fuzzy moments after a nap. His eyes stayed closed long enough for me to wish I could crawl in with him, and pull him onto my lap, and kiss the backs of his hands. When he opened them, all I could do was grin.

"Where have you been, Classic?" he said.

"Don't give me grief, dude. I've been here every day. I can't help it if you waited for me to leave before you finally decided to wake up."

"I know."

"You know what?" I heard my voice threatening to crack.

"I know you were here. But you never stood across the room."

I laughed like the teenager I never was and went to the bed. His hand groped for mine.

"How's our boy?" he said.

"Ornery as ever," I lied. "He's just about milked all the sick leave he's going to get out of that broken collarbone."

"They weren't lying then. He wasn't hurt that bad."

Not physically, I wanted to say. *But, Chief, he's not the same.*

I was glad his eyes fluttered closed because I knew he would have read it in mine. I blew out some air.

"Your bike," he said, eyes still shut. "Was it totaled?"

"Yes. That's the last time I'm letting you ride it. And just so you know, I still have yours."

He opened his eyes to slits and gave me a half smile.

"I'm not riding it, though," I said.

"You can. You should. You can do it."

"Are you sure you're not still in a coma?"

He squeezed my hand. It was surprisingly strong, that squeeze.

The need to hold him, all of him, pounded in me, and I had to do something, even if it was wrong.

"You said you knew I was here," I said. "Do you remember what I told you?"

"No. I just knew when you were here and when you weren't."

My Adam's apple rivaled Desmond's as I swallowed. "Y'know, I hate to repeat myself—"

"Had a personality transplant while I was asleep, did you?"

"Jack?" a male voice said behind me.

I wasn't that crazy about Detective Kylie under any circumstances. Right now, I could have ripped out his nose hairs.

"Just need to ask you a few questions," he said.

He nodded at me as if he expected me to step out, which would have taken an act of Congress at that point. I didn't move from my spot next to Chief, which necessitated Kylie going to the other side of the bed. In the meantime, Chief's eyes closed.

"What's the matter?" Kylie said. "Is he out again?"

"Must be," I said. "Darn the luck, huh?"

"Classic," Chief said.

Kylie shot me a look and leaned over Chief.

"Just need to ask you about the accident and then I'll leave you alone."

"I don't remember anything."

Kylie's eyebrows met over his nose. "Nothing?"

"I feel like Humpty Dumpty." Chief's voice grew drowsy. "Everything about that day is lying on the ground around me and I can't put the pieces back together again. Don't bother with the king's horses and the king's men."

"I don't follow," Kylie said.

Chief didn't answer. His breathing was restful and easy and rhythmic.

"He's just asleep," I said.

"Which is right where we want him to be." The nurse from the station stepped briskly to the foot of the bed. "The doc says no more talking until tomorrow. Let him get a good night's sleep and you can pick it up from there."

As Detective Kylie left, I wondered if he'd be able to pick up anything at all. I wasn't quite believing Chief remembered absolutely nothing. I might not have known that he had an ex-wife or that the HOGs were his only family, but I did know Chief's honest, no-nonsense voice, and that whole thing about Humpty Dumpty? That wasn't Chief at all.

I turned toward the door.

"Classic?" Chief said.

"Yeah?"

"Bring Desmond tomorrow. I want to see him."

"You've got it," I said.

I didn't tell him that Desmond had been surprisingly willing to let me come alone. That wasn't the Chief-worshipping Desmond either.

Hank met me on the side porch when I got home in the van.

"I'm going to go ahead and take Desmond," she said. "I think you still ought to go out to dinner with Bonner."

"We'll see."

"Um, and you have a visitor."

Her tone stopped me midway to the door. "Who?"

"Vickie Rodriguez."

"Vi—she's not in there talking to Desmond, is she?"

"No, he's in the shower. But she *is* talking to Ophelia."

"No."

"Yes. I tried to get rid of her."

"No, it's okay. It was only a matter of time." I tried not to go completely concave as I added, "Yeah, please take Desmond."

"I won't bring him back until you give me the all clear."

I left her to Desmond and made the dreaded walk to the living room. Walk, nothing. I might as well have been riding a roller coaster.

Vickie sat on the edge of the couch, observing the room like it was a crime scene. Ophelia was nowhere in sight.

"If you're looking for Miss Sanchez, she went up to help Desmond find a clean towel."

Why did the floor not open up and swallow me into the pit I was going to end up in anyway?

"Well, he's male," I said. "They can never find anything, even if it's right where it always is."

"She seemed to know its location just fine."

I sat in the striped chair. The chair-and-a-half was where I let myself be vulnerable. This was no time to be putting myself there.

"Look, I know you know she's staying here right now," I said. "Otherwise you wouldn't be here."

She shook her head, still as sleek as before. Come to think of it, she might also be wearing the same outfit she had on the last time. Or maybe she just lived in a closet and wound herself up everyday.

"I'm here because I've had a visit from Priscilla Sanborn and her attorney," she said. "You're acquainted with Ms. Sanborn, I understand?"

I forced myself not to sink back in the chair. "She came by here about a week ago."

"And you didn't think it would be a good idea to call and tell me she intended to try to get custody of Desmond?"

"I thought she might just be blowing smoke, especially when I didn't hear from her again."

"It's more than smoke. She's serious about this."

I pressed my fingers to my temples. There was no point in trying to keep up the front. "She can't take him, can she? We do have Geneveve's signed document."

"I hope that stands up in a court hearing."

"A hearing? I thought we were just going before the judge, a formality, you said."

"It's an entirely different ballgame when someone contests the adoption. This woman is going all the way."

"You have to stop her!"

"How am I supposed to do that when you have a woman living upstairs who was recently raped? Whether she is a former prostitute or not isn't going to make much difference."

"How did you know about that?"

"Our office received an anonymous tip, which, honestly, I was going to ignore until the Sanborn woman showed up. I really wish you had told me."

"Would it have made any difference?"

"I wouldn't have been blindsided. I wouldn't have had to sit there looking like a complete idiot while she ran down a list of all the reasons that you are an unfit mother."

"I'm not!"

"I know that!"

A vein stood out on her forehead, which was now scarlet. I was stunned.

Vickie pressed her palms together at her chest, and for a moment I expected a *namaste* to escape from her lips.

"Please hear me," she said, voice once again perfectly modulated. "I want to see Desmond with you. But I've just seen too many good adoptions go south because things got misconstrued. I have an obligation to you and Desmond to keep everything absolutely aboveboard. Do you see?"

I nodded.

"If you want to keep your son, you're going to have to find another place for Ms. Sanchez."

I felt my head tilt. "It's black and white, isn't it?"

"In some aspects, yes."

"I don't even know if I can think that way anymore."

"That's my job," she said. "If you'll give me what I need to do it."

I tried to smooth out my forehead with my hand. "I'm sorry I put you in a bad position with Priscilla Sanborn. I know what's it's like to be, what did you call it?—blindsided by her."

Vickie stood up and eased invisible wrinkles from her pencil skirt. "Well, you've had a few other things on your mind. How is Jack, by the way?"

"Out of his coma," I said, "and thankfully there's no brain damage. He was as cryptic as ever."

"Good. I imagine that's what you love about him."

I was still staring at her, gape-mouthed, when she added, "Do you have someone else to represent you?"

"We haven't gotten that far. He just woke up today."

"Let me know. Yes?"

She watched me until I nodded. And then I watched *her* from the front door until her Mini Cooper—not the car I would have put her in—disappeared from Palm Row. She was definitely human after all. I wanted to tell Chief.

While I was still standing there, Bonner drove up. It wasn't until then that I realized Hank's car was gone, which meant she and Desmond must have stolen out like thieves while I was talking to Vickie. I knew Bonner was going to be disappointed, but I really didn't feel like going out to dinner. Maybe he'd settle for leftovers with Ophelia. Heaven knew there were plenty of them. Hank had cooked enough food that week for Desmond and me to live on for a year.

If we had a year.

I turned from the doorway to get the cramping pain under control. When I went back to greet Bonner, he was already inside, and he wasn't alone. India stood next to him.

A rather diminished version of India. While she wore the usual class-act outfit and her hair was its customary mass of enviable waves, her eyes looked washed out, and there was a pallor to her skin that made her seem to have aged ten years since the day of the Feast. But, then, hadn't that actually been about a decade of anguish ago?

"Oh, honey," she said. "Do you forgive me?"

I just held out my arms to her and she fell into them. Nearby, I heard Bonner blowing his nose on his inevitable handkerchief.

When India pulled away from me, she held me at arm's length. "We have a lot to talk about," she said, "but we need to get down to business."

"What business?" I said. "Come on, give it to me. Nothing can surprise me at this point."

"Liz Doyle called me," Bonner said. "Vickie Rodriguez called her—"

"Bottom line," India said. "You need a place for Ophelia, and I want to take her home with me."

I was wrong. I was surprised, enough to sink to the old church pew in the foyer and stare.

India knelt beside me and folded her hands on my knee. "I know I don't have your wisdom," she said. "And I'm not one of the Sisters or the NA people. I haven't been through what they have. But, darlin', I think I can help Ophelia." She glanced downward. "Unless you don't think I can."

I ran my hand across her head. "There is nobody in the world who would be better for Ophelia. Nobody. Just one thing though."

"What?"

"Do I need to go ahead and order your casket?"

The glow shimmered back into her eyes. "No. I don't think I'm gon' drop dead after all."

So India packed Ophelia up and took her home. Ophelia held me hard and cried before she left, but when I whispered to her that India could teach her things I couldn't—like how to dress, maybe—she smiled into my eyes.

I hoped Bonner would leave with them, but he didn't. Which maybe was fine, since I would have been left alone with Sylvia's memory, looking at me like I'd just broken curfew and saying, "Now, about you putting our home up for sale." At least Bonner I could argue with.

Still, I turned my back to him and headed for the kitchen before I said, "You're going to try to talk me out of this sale, aren't you?"

He stopped me in the dining room with a surprising tug at my sleeve. "How can I not?" He looked down at the table. "I sat right here and helped the Sisters pick out the colors for their rooms at Sacrament House."

"Don't do that," I said. "It isn't easy for me, either."

"So hold off. At least for a while. Now that Ophelia's taken care of—"

"What about Zelda? She's not going to be in rehab forever. "

Bonner folded his arms and stared at them.

"What?" I said.

"I would do just about anything for you, Allison. You know that."

"Unless it went against your own conscience."

His face came up abruptly. "How did you know I was going to say that?"

"I don't know. I just did. But I don't get why selling this place for me would put you crosswise with your integrity."

"There's just something about it that seems wrong. I can't put my finger on it."

I shrugged. "Well, until you do—"

"Until I do, I don't know if I can even list it for you."

I stared at him. "We have a contract for the Taylor place!"

"You haven't signed it yet. And neither have I."

"You're just going to let the deal fall through?"

"There are other Realtors."

"None that I trust like I do you!"

"Then don't do this." Bonner pressed his hands into the table and leaned toward me. "I believe in Sacrament House every bit as much as you do, Allison, but I also have to trust my gut. And it's telling me there is something just not right about this."

He didn't pull his gaze from me, even when I rolled my eyes and turned away.

"Do I do that to you when you get a Nudge?" he said.

"No."

"So you're the only one who can have them?"

I looked back at him. There was fear in his face—fear that I'd give him the answer he knew was wrong. That I knew was wrong.

"Where's the contract?" I said.

He closed his eyes as if I'd slapped him. "In the car. I'll go get it. There's a list of other brokers with it."

"No," I said. "How long do we have without signing it before the Taylor deal's off?"

"Forty-eight hours."

"Keep it for forty-eight hours, then."

"And then what?"

"I don't know." I swallowed the lump I couldn't explain. "A lot can happen between now and Sunday night."

"I hope a lot does," Bonner said.

He left without mentioning the dinner we were supposed to have together, and I was fine with that. I needed to be alone, at long last, to sort things out.

But the minute he left, the stillness attacked me. I had to do something—something I couldn't screw up.

I took a stab at cleaning out the refrigerator, but Hank's assortment of leftovers made that too overwhelming. Laundry. I'd do laundry.

I ventured into Desmond's room to collect his clothes from under the bed and over the chair and in the bottom of the closet. One random sock even hung over the side of his trash can. When I bent over to retrieve it, a penciled eye seethed up at me. I'd already drawn back my hand when I realized I was looking at Desmond's eye-patch caricature.

I dumped the dirty underwear on the floor and pulled out the drawing. It had been crumpled, savagely, so that even after I smoothed it out, the cratered forehead was twice as disturbing as before. Who *was* this person? Or was it even human? The piece of Desmond's artwork I treasured most was his depiction of God: a figure on a Harley who looked suspiciously like Chief. Could this be his rendition of Satan?

I shivered and started to re-crumple the paper, but I decided against it. I should probably show it to Chief and get his take on it.

So the clothes went into the washer and the drawing went under the cushion in the red chair and I went back to imagining Sylvia drumming her fingers and waiting for an answer.

"I don't have one," I said out loud. "And I'm about to flip my stuff all the way out."

I was grateful for the sudden thought that I hadn't told the Sisters about Chief yet. I grabbed my leather jacket and my Harley key and was all the way out on the porch before I realized I was functioning on automatic pilot.

You can.

I grinned. That wasn't God's voice. It was Chief's.

You should.

I zipped up my jacket. I needed a ride. It had been so long since I'd felt that energy under me, so long since I had let my prayers and my questions roll themselves out with the throttle.

You can do it, Chief had said.

I had to trust him on that.

Chief's Road King did feel different from my bike, heavier, maybe, and somehow more responsive to my touch. As I left the Spanish-moss-blowing-in-the-breeze part of St. Augustine behind, the soft night began to wrap itself in fog, covering the Magic Moment clientele in the gutter who had already called it a night, and leaving only the hopeful picture of old Maharry turning off the lights in C.A.R.S.

I felt *There is good, yes?* soothing my face in the cooling air.

Yes. There is some good.

But I didn't feel the good when I pulled up to Sacrament House and cut off the engine. Every light in the place was on and the shades and curtains were drawn and pulled like the Castillo de San Marcos preparing for attack. As I hurried up the walk, someone pulled back the front drape a quarter of an inch.

"This is not good, yes," I whispered to God.

Mercedes opened the door, eyes flashing.

"Come in, Miss Angel. Everybody freakin' out in here."

I stepped inside the door, and her face immediately changed.

"You got somethin' good to tell for once," she said.

They would speak of nothing else until I gave them the news about Chief. Although Jasmine cried and Sherry hugged my neck and Mercedes said mmm-*mmm* at least five times, whatever they were holding back bled through.

"All right, ladies," I said. "Give it up. What happened?"

"It wasn't anything," Sherry said.

"Yes it was!" Jasmine cried.

"All right, just hush up." Mercedes stared at them both until Sherry jerked her face toward the wall and Jasmine plucked a Kleenex out of the box.

"I don't want you to hush up," I said. "I want one of you to tell me what's going on. Please."

"They were already here when I got home from work," Sherry said. "So I don't know anything."

"They aksed you questions too," Jasmine said.

"*Who?*" I said.

Mercedes rolled her eyes. "It was two cops. Asking us if we knew anything about what happened to Ophelia. Like we would, like just because we used to be on the street we know everything about every hooker ever lived in this town."

I couldn't stop a sigh of relief. "That's a good thing. It means the police are finally getting serious about finding the person who raped her."

"Huh," Sherry said.

"What does that mean?"

She tightened her ponytail, inspected her nails, did everything but answer. I looked at Jasmine, who melted under my gaze.

"I don't much like that Ophelia girl," she said. "She was a high-price ho thinks she better than us. But it was still like a insult to all of us, the way them cops was actin'."

"Which was how?" I looked at Mercedes.

"Anybody with two eyes could see they didn't give a rip 'bout Ophelia bein' raped. They just want to put it on somebody so they can go about they business."

"What kind of questions were they asking?" I said. "Wait. Nicholas Kent wasn't one of them, was he?"

"That freckle-face boy?" Jasmine shook her head. "Unh-uh."

"Officer Kent wouldn't treat us like we trash," Mercedes said. "They was all like, 'we know don't nobody change that much. You can get us samples from johns and we can wrap this up.'"

"Samples?" I said. "DNA samples?"

"They think we're still working the streets," Sherry said. "I'm over there slaving my butt off with my father, trying to stay clean, and they come in here telling me to turn tricks so they can 'wrap it up.'"

I was sure my head was going to explode if I didn't physically hold it together with both hands.

"What did you tell them?" I said.

Sherry sniffed. "I didn't tell them anything. I don't talk to cops unless I absolutely have to."

"Mercedes?"

"I was afraid to open my mouth."

"They threatened you?"

She licked her substantial lips. "No. I was scared I was gon' threaten *them*. It was Jasmine set 'em straight."

"What did you say to them, Jazz?" I said.

"I just tol' them Sacrament House Sisters don't sell they bodies no more. Not for nobody."

Mercedes finally smiled. "She tried to tell 'em about Jesus, but they didn't want no part of that."

I wasn't sure Jesus wanted any part of them either, whoever they were. And whoever they were, I was going to find out.

Once I was sure the Sisters were finished freaking out, I left the House and hurried to Chief's bike, my cell phone already in my hand. Nicholas didn't answer, but I left him a message and hoped he could hear the fury in my voice. Maybe it was a good thing he didn't pick up. I might not have been able to refrain from calling his brothers in uniform what no woman of God should call anybody. Even if they *were* jackals.

I had to sit on the Road King for a good five minutes before I felt safe to ride. Even then I took off too fast and almost lost it on the first turn. I was shaking when I got to West King and headed back toward the historic district. That was probably why I didn't notice at first that the car behind me was way too close.

"Come on, back off," I muttered into my helmet.

I tried slowing down, hoping the driver would get frustrated and pull around me. There was virtually no traffic at that hour. It wasn't like he couldn't pass.

But the more I geared down, the closer he crept to my tail pipe.

If I lost any more speed I wasn't going to be able to keep my balance. Ahead, the light at the St. George Street intersection turned yellow. I rolled the throttle and bulleted through it. The driver of the car gunned its engine and ran it right behind me.

Tentacles of fear threatened to wrap themselves around my brain. I had to get away from this loser before my already unsure riding landed me in the gutter.

Toques Place was only a few yards away. I still hated those alleys on a bike, but I waited until the last second to downshift and made the turn without dumping it. The only light ahead of me came from the beam from the Road King, which meant I narrowly missed that same line of trash cans I'd almost taken out before. Using up the last morsel of my wits, I reached out and grabbed one as I rode by. I had to speed up to keep from hitting it myself, so I wasn't altogether sure it fell over. I didn't dare look back, though, not until I reached the other end. I could only steal a glance before I rounded the corner onto Hypolita. The car still sat there, behind a domino pile of garbage cans.

Even through the lifting fog I could see it. A black car, with black windows.

CHAPTER THIRTEEN

Although the dark car didn't find me to follow me home, it chased me for hours in my dreams, and I woke up at dawn marinating in my own sweat. Someone else was evidently awake, too, because I was just stepping out of the shower when my phone rang.

I hoped it was Nicholas Kent, who still hadn't gotten back to me, but it was Ms. Willa, who greeted me with, "How is a person supposed to sleep with you roaring through the back alley like a Heck's Angel in the middle of the night?"

Not knowing which part of that to try to unpack, I just laughed.

"I fail to see the humor," she said, though I could hear it in her yippy bark. "Why didn't you stop by while you were in the neighborhood?"

I grabbed my bathrobe and struggled into it with my one free hand. "Like you said, it was practically the middle of the night."

"Well, what about now?"

"I'm sorry?"

"I said what about now? I want to talk to you."

Since Ms. Willa seemed to get whatever she wanted, I said I'd be there in thirty minutes. Besides, twice I'd thought she was going to write a check for Sacrament House. Maybe the third time was the charm.

"And don't bring that noisy piece of machinery with you," she said.

"Yes, ma'am," I said.

I got dressed and was about to go out the door when I saw

Desmond's silhouette of Ophelia's rapist on the bistro table with a Post-it note attached.

Opie Taylor made this copy and left it for you. Hank

It took me a second to realize she was talking about Nicholas. There was so much going on that I couldn't keep up with, I didn't even try to figure out when all of that had taken place. I rolled the drawing carefully and stuck it in my bag and took off on foot for Ms. Willa's.

It was one of those late-March mornings in north Florida when the air is so soft you wear it like a cashmere sweater. With the sun playing against the coquina walls and the moss roses starting their journeys through the flower beds, I had a hard time believing this was the same labyrinth of dark alleys I'd ridden through with my heart up to my tonsils the night before. I wondered if maybe I'd just overreacted.

The disgruntled man in bermuda shorts and a canned tan picking up trash containers at the end of Toques told me otherwise. I hurried past and turned onto Cuna, the cashmere air forgotten.

Speaking of fine fibers: When I arrived, Ms. Willa was already decked out in a chartreuse silk number that did nothing for her complexion. I was glad to see she hadn't gone for the matching hair today. Just as before, she didn't get out of the chair. The same unsmiling Hispanic woman let me in, and Ms. Willa told me to sit on the brocade love seat and pour the tea.

Like I said, Ms. Willa was used to getting what she wanted.

"I see you didn't waste time dressing for the occasion," she said.

"You told me to come right over," I said. "I don't wake up looking like I'm ready for the Easter parade the way you obviously do. Sugar?"

"Milk. That's the only way to drink tea."

I handed her the china cup, but she just looked at me.

"You're right attractive when you aren't telling everybody to go to hell," she said.

"I never told anybody that!"

She pondered the tea for a moment. "No, I guess not. That was probably me. I get the two of us confused. We're on the same mission."

"Are we?" I put two cubes of sugar in my tea and then wished I hadn't. Their failure to dissolve indicated they might have been in the bowl since Ms. Willa's society debut. "And what is our mutual mission?"

"We both want to see Troy Irwin go down."

I sagged. "That's not my mission, Ms. Willa," I said.

She ignored me as she attempted to peel the newspaper from the piecrust table at her left elbow. The old fingers looked stiffer than usual this morning, and the length of the nails didn't help. I was about to offer to get it for her when she was finally successful enough to get it into her hand and wave it toward me.

"Page Two, Column A," she said. "Read that."

I set down my tea and looked at the section she already had it folded to. The paper smelled like it had been soaked in Ms. Willa's lavender talcum powder. I stifled a sneeze.

"'Alleged Rape Reported'?" I said. "Is that the one you want me to read?"

"That's one of your girls, isn't it?"

"It is. Ophelia Sanchez. You washed her feet."

"Was she assaulted?"

"She was."

Ms. Willa jabbed her arthritic index finger at me. "Then why does it say 'alleged'?"

"Because—"

"I will tell you why. They think she's lying. The police, the doctors, everybody. They think because she was a—how did they put that? Let me see it."

She snatched the paper back and squinted at the print. "Right here. 'Sanchez'—they couldn't even call her by her first name—'has been arrested twice for solicitation.' Why don't they just come right out and say she was a—"

"You've got me, Ms. Willa," I said. I stood up and went to the window, but the sunlight dancing through the lace had lost its charm. "What I don't understand is why it's just now making the paper. It happened a week ago."

"Because this town is so determined to keep its so-called image, the powers that be will do anything to cover up a stain." She dropped the newspaper back on the piecrust table in disgust. "This has Troy Irwin's fingerprints all over it."

I turned from the view of the town in question and returned to the chair. "As much as I would love to blame anything I can on Troy Irwin, I don't get the connection."

"My word, child, he owns the *Record* and everybody who works there. The chief of police has his hand in Irwin's pocket. He bought that new wing at the hospital, so everybody in a white coat bows down to him." Ms. Willa's eyes seemed to grow closer together. "I like that girl. She shows promise. But she won't amount to a thing with this following her like a bad smell. I want to help you take Troy Irwin down."

There was something about this I wasn't understanding. I folded my hands under my chin. "Maybe it would help if you told me what exactly it is that you have against him."

She licked her dry lips as if she relished the opportunity. I might regret asking, but I settled in to hear.

"I was only married to my late second husband, Quincy Livengood, for fifteen years," she said. "Married him when I was sixty-four, and he died five years ago."

There was nothing wrong with her arithmetic.

"Before that I was Willa Renfroe for thirty-five years."

Renfroe. That was a name I recognized, vaguely. It made me uneasy enough to have belonged to one of my father's associates.

"Now he was my first husband, you understand."

I wasn't sure I did. It was hard to keep up.

"Harold Renfroe built a successful financial firm in St. Augustine from the ground up, and he never borrowed a dime to do it. He was a man of integrity and a genius with money." Ms. Willa's voice went from proud to shrill. "And then Chamberlain Enterprises put him out of business, and it killed him." She worked her mouth, forcing the web of lines into a sad dance. "I held your father personally responsible, not only for Harold's death, but for my being left virtually penniless."

I rubbed at the ache in my chest. "Unfortunately, Ms. Willa, you weren't the only one that happened to. My father was a ruthless man and I'm ashamed to be related to him."

"I know you're nothing like him or we wouldn't be having this conversation."

I looked around at the camelback sofas and the Lladró clowns watching us from the china cabinet. "If you were left with nothing—"

"I was rescued by Quincy Livengood. He was a bachelor of some means."

Ya think?

"And he promised to support me and help me seek restitution from Chamberlain Enterprises." Her eyes nearly met over her nose. "By then it was being run by Troy Irwin, who still had peach fuzz on his cheeks. But he was evidently trained by the best, or the worst, I should say."

"My father," I said.

"Quincy was never successful in taking Irwin down. He left me everything, and I know I should be satisfied with that."

Again, ya think?

"But I still lie in the bed sometimes with a bitter taste in my mouth because that company cost my first husband his life, and not just his, as you say. Troy Irwin is still undermining everything that ever *was* good about the people of substance in this town. He doesn't think of us as people. You saw him at Cordova that day. He didn't even know who I was."

Ms. Willa let out a long, uneven breath and caved slightly into the chair. Her face was gray, and I was sure that wasn't due to wearing an all-wrong shade of green.

"You don't have the money," she said, "but you've got the good. I'm a bitter old woman, but I do have the means. Together, we can stop him."

I pushed out a long breath of my own. This would be the answer to so much of what was roiling around in my life. In all our lives. Bonner wouldn't have to list my house. Desmond and I could stay there. There would be a place for Zelda and Ophelia and more. *Wouldn't there, God?*

I got nothing. Except the image of India having a stroke if she heard what I was about to say, what I *had* to say.

"Ms. Willa," I said. "There is a part of me that wants to storm the Bastille and march down St. George Street with Troy's head on a pole."

"Now you're talking," she said.

"But I can't take your money and use it for that. If you give to Sacrament House, it has to be so we can buy a second house for more women who need help, not so we can outbid his investors and buy up all the businesses on West King Street. Your money has to be given to what we are *for*, not what we're *against*." I shrugged. "Besides, although I'm flattered, I don't know why you think I could pull off what neither of your husbands were able to do, and they were financial wizards."

Ms. Willa jerked forward in the chair so sharply, I thought she was the one having a stroke. "They didn't have your passion," she said. "That's what this town needs."

"Then this town needs God," I said. "Because that's where it comes from. It's not me."

The old head shook. "I don't understand you, Allison Chamberlain," she said. "But I think I admire you."

Evidently not enough to write a check. Or make an offer. Or tell me she'd think about it. The meeting was clearly over, and I left more confused about Ms. Willa than ever.

One thing I was grateful to her for, and that was for bringing the pathetic excuse for a newspaper article to my attention. On my way home, I stopped at the Monk's Vineyard. It wasn't open yet, so I left the rolled-up silhouette on the doorknob with a note for Lewis, explaining what I needed him to do. I hoped the old journalist was better at convincing editors than he was at making lattes.

At noon, Desmond and I headed out to see Chief, with one false start.

When I wheeled the Road King out of the garage, I tossed Desmond his helmet, which didn't bear a scratch from the accident.

"I shouldn't hear any whining today," I said. "I can't make you wear your leathers. We're going to have to replace those. They kind of took it heavy in the accident."

I stopped because he was shaking his head, harder than he had to for just about any reason.

"What's wrong?" I said.

"I don't wanna ride no bike without leathers," he said.

I faked a smile. "*Now* you start listening to me. Okay, wear your old ones. They're a little short, but they'll work.

He still shook his head.

"Nobody's going to give you grief for wearing high waters," I said.

"It ain't that!"

His voice shot up into the atmosphere and with it his cocky confidence. A little boy stood before me, all but scraping his toe in the dirt.

"Desmond, are you afraid?" I said.

He didn't answer. He just looked miserable.

"Anybody would be," I said. "That was a scary experience. Look, I'm sorry. I didn't even think about whether you'd be ready to get back on a bike."

"S'all good."

"No, it's not. But you need to speak up about stuff like this, all right? I'm a lousy mind reader."

Actually, I wasn't. I could see right through his helmet of hair to the fact that riding a Harley wasn't the only thing scaring him into silence.

"We can take the van, no problem," I said. "We might need to pick up some stuff from Chief's place anyway, so we'll need it. Is that cool?"

"That's cool," he said.

But I was right. He was still scared spitless.

He was no more at ease when we got to the hospital, which completely mystified me. I couldn't figure out why he wasn't tearing down the hall ahead of me to see Chief. But I didn't ask because I wasn't sure he even knew.

"Is it okay if we go in?" I said to the nurse on the new floor they'd moved Chief to.

"The social worker's in there with him," she said. "But you know what, go on in. I think it would be a good idea."

I was about to ask her why, but Desmond tugged at my sleeve. "How come Mr. Chief need a social worker?"

"You got me."

"I don't like social workers," he said.

Evidently Chief didn't either. He was sitting up in bed, still-massive arms crossed over his chest, eyes piercing a somewhat lumpy-looking middle-aged woman. Chief was back in full force.

"I can manage fine at home," he was saying.

"No, Mr. Ellington, you can't," was her reply. She didn't have the voice or the physicality to compete, but then, he was attached to a bed by traction, and she wasn't. It would have been amusing if smoke hadn't practically been coming out of Chief's nostrils.

"She better look out," Desmond muttered to me.

"Keep quiet and I'll take you to Sonic later," I muttered back.

This was not the time for Desmond to come out of his sullen silence and slip back into his outrageous self.

"Hey," I said. I didn't usually do breezy, but it seemed like a good choice at the moment.

The social worker gave me the official this-does-not-concern-you look, but Chief waved me in.

"This is Allison Chamberlain," Chief said. "She's handling things for me until I go home, which is where I'm going straight from here."

"And why wouldn't you?" I said.

"He is going to need round-the-clock care for several weeks." The woman tugged her too-tight blazer over her stomach, but to no avail. "Maybe you can get him to choose a convalescent home, because that is where he's going to need to go."

"You talkin' 'bout a nursing home?" Desmond said.

Sonic evidently didn't have the power it once had.

"My granddaddy was in one of them," he said. "Them places is nasty."

"My point exactly," Chief said. He grinned at Desmond, who grinned back, shyly, timidly, and every other adverb that had never matched the boy before. Not when it came to Chief.

"There are some excellent facilities covered by your insurance," the woman said.

"I didn't catch your name," I said.

"Barbara Bush. And spare me the jokes. I've heard them all."

Yeah, Chief had definitely sucked the delight out of this conversation.

"Ms. Bush, just so I'm clear, why is it that Chief—Mr. Ellington—has to go to a rehab facility?"

"Rehab?" Desmond said. "He ain't on drugs. You ain't, right, Chief?"

"*Physical* rehabilitation. That leg is not going to be completely healed and usable if he doesn't have physical therapy."

"Can he do it as an outpatient?" I said.

"Yes, but he can't drive himself there. He can't see to his basic needs. With no one else residing with him—"

"What if he stayed at my house?" I said.

To be honest, it wasn't me who said it. My mouth was used, but the words totally came from someone else.

I had never seen Chief look dumbfounded before. But his frozen-in-the-unexpected face was no match for the expression on Desmond's. He looked as if I were coming after him with a hypodermic needle. Yeah, we *were* going to Sonic, and we were staying there until I got out of him whatever was eating him up. I mean, for Pete's sake, I was inviting his idol to be accessible to him 24/7.

"Classic."

I turned to Chief. He was beckoning me over with both hands. When I reached his side, he put his hand on the back of my head and pulled me close to his face, as if neither my twelve-year-old nor the First Lady of Social Work was in the room.

"Are you sure about this?" he said. I could feel his breath on my mouth.

"It was a Nudge," I said.

He studied my eyes before he turned his head toward the woman still waiting with her clipboard.

"Start the paperwork," he said.

I expected her to quiz me about whether I was really willing to cart him to physical therapy every day, see that he was bathed … oh, sheesh, *bathed?* But she just clicked her pen and stood up and said, "I think you can handle him."

That wasn't the problem. I wasn't sure I could handle *me.* This was God's idea, so God better know what God was doing.

"Hey, Big Al," Desmond said when the woman had bustled out to fill in forms. "I'm feelin' faint. I think I need to visit the vending machine."

"Get me something too," Chief said.

I gave Desmond a handful of change and pondered his exit.

"He doesn't want to talk to me," Chief said.

I perched on the edge of the bed. "Then it's not just me. I don't know what's going on with him. Well, I know why he's freaked out around me. I haven't even had a chance to tell you this."

I filled him in on both Priscilla Sanborn's visit and the one from Vickie Rodriguez.

"We have to go to court now, and she says I need somebody to represent me."

"I'll take care of it," Chief said.

"You just came out of a coma."

"I said I'll take care of it. Unless you don't trust me, now that I'm nursing-home material."

I loved the mischief in his eyes. But, then, what didn't I love about him? Except the fact that he wasn't pulling me into his arms this very minute.

"Of course, I trust you," I said. "I just don't want you to take on more than you should right now."

"Classic. Enough." He touched my arm. "If you want to get in somebody's business, find out what's going on with Desmond. You might start with the elephant that's in the middle of the room."

"You mean Priscilla."

"That. And what he remembers from the accident."

"He says he doesn't remember anything, but, Chief, he never lost consciousness."

"Is he drawing?"

"Not that much. Oh—" I told him about the silhouette, and about my conversation with Ms. Willa, and about the cops going to Sacrament House. I thought I knew how much I'd missed him, but I'd only known the half of it.

"You're tired," I said when I was almost hoarse. "Get rest. And eat healthy. And do what they tell you."

"I may want to rethink staying with you," he said.

"You have no idea," I said.

Desmond decided he didn't want to go to Sonic. His excuse was that he filled up on a Snickers bar and couldn't do an order of cheese fries justice. I didn't have to be a brain surgeon to know he didn't want to be confined with me in a space he couldn't get out of. So when we got home, I didn't let him out of the kitchen.

"Okay, Clarence," I said after I'd ordered him to the bistro chair. "Here's what I'm thinking, and I could be wrong, but I know you'll set me straight if I am."

He looked at me suspiciously, but he nodded.

"I'm going to talk first and you're going to sit there, but after that, feel free to move about the cabin."

"Huh?"

"The kitchen." I swiveled in the chair so I wasn't looking him directly in the eye. "I think you're freaked out because that woman who showed up here in the beige car is your aunt Priscilla."

"She ain't my aunt," he said.

"She's your mother's sister," I said. "That makes her your aunt."

"That don't make her family. You and Mr. Chief and Miss Hankenstein and all them? That's my family. She can't take me."

"So you've already figured out that's why she came here. To try to stop me from adopting you."

"She can't," he said again, with even more authority, "'cause my bi-o-logical mother left a letter. It's final."

"That's what we're hoping for," I said. "Chief is still going to—"

For the first time in the conversation, fear flashed through his eyes. "Mr. Chief s'posed to make sure it happens?"

"He's our lawyer," I said slowly. "And he loves you."

"He can't!"

Desmond sprang out of the chair and was headed I wasn't sure even he knew where. I grabbed a handful of sweatshirt and pulled him back until I could get him by both shoulders.

"Desmond, he's okay. He can do this."

"He ain't gonna want to! Not after he remembers!"

"Remembers what?"

"That I made that accident happen!"

He struggled to get free, but I held on.

"Tell me what you mean," I said.

"You won't want me neither if I do."

"Are you serious?" I shook him. "It wouldn't make any difference to me if you held up the Walmart. You are my son. Bottom line. Now talk to me."

He went so limp I had to plant him back in the chair, where he stared dismally at the salt and pepper shakers.

"Start from the beginning," I said. "Desmond?"

"I was all freakin' out 'cause that woman came here."

"Priscilla," I said.

"Yeah. I know you say we ain't s'posed to use the H-word."

"The H-word."

"Hate."

"Oh, that one. Right."

"One time, she said she'd take me and my mama to the clinic 'cause we both sick. This when we was livin' with my granddaddy, and he was too sick to take us hisself."

"So you were about, what, seven, maybe?"

He held up his hand, fingers fanned out.

"Five," I said.

"But I remember it, it ain't like I was too little. My mama, she throwin' up in a trash can, and I was jus' throwin' up on my*self*, and she—"

"Priscilla."

"Miss Prissy, I called her in my head, 'cause she always drawin' in eyebrows on herself with a pencil and—stuff—like that. When I got older, I left out one of the letters, but you won't let me say that word so I'm not gon' tell you what that was."

"I appreciate that," I said.

"So she get us in the door, and she says, 'Geneveve'"—his voice sounded remarkably like Priscilla's—'you go on in now, and I'll pick you up later.'"

"Did she have to go to work or something?" I said.

"No," Desmond said in falsetto. "She jus' didn't want nobody to see her in that place. I climbed up on a chair and look out the window, and there she was, sittin' in her car. And there's me with throw-up all over me."

I thought I might throw up myself.

"She done stuff like that all the time. You don't even know. But *I* know this: She don't want me. Come to think about it, I ain't even worried about her."

"But you were freaked out at the time," I said.

He looked as if he'd been caught with his hand in the Oreos.

"That's what you said a minute ago. You said you were all freaked out the day of the accident."

"Yeah. That's right."

It clearly wasn't, but I let him go on.

"So me and Mr. Chief was riding and I was all fussing over it in my mind and then I saw that car and I yelled or jerked or somethin' and I distracted Mr. Chief like you and him always tellin' me not to do and he didn't see the car and he run into the pole. I coulda' killed him, Big Al."

So he did remember. And from the way it was gushing out of him he hadn't just suddenly put it all together. He'd had this in his head since the day it happened.

"Okay, just listen to me now," I said.

He nodded. I noticed tiny beads of perspiration on his upper lip. I always broke into a sweat after I threw up too.

"Chief doesn't remember any of that, and I'm going to leave it up to you whether to tell him. But if you do, I guarantee you he isn't going to stop loving you. Love wins out every single time. You got that?"

"God tell you that?"

"God tells us all that, all the time," I said. "It's what God's about."

"He ain't never told me nothin'."

I drew in air. The potential for getting this all wrong was huge.

"Have you ever asked him anything?" I said.

"Yeah, and he ain't never answered, which is why I ain't doin' no baptism." Desmond stopped, waited. "You not gon' make me, are you, Big Al?"

I shook my head. "That's not the kind of thing you make somebody do," I said. "That's between you and Jesus. But I will say this: You're not going to find out if that's what he wants for you if you don't talk to him."

He seemed to consider that, although what came out of his mouth next was, "When Mr. Chief comes here, he can stay in my place and I'll move upstairs. He can't be goin' up and down them steps with his leg all messed up."

"Great idea," I said.

"His leg gon' be a'right, ain't it? He gon' ride his Harley again?"

"That's the plan."

He nodded again, and then stuck up his fist to knock it against mine. "Imma start movin' my stuff," he said.

I started in on a long relieved sigh, but I thought of something.

"One more question," I said.

He turned from his doorway.

"Did you see the car that Chief swerved to miss?"

The air went dead.

"No," he said. His door snapped shut behind him.

I would have felt like Claire Huckstable herself right then, getting all that information out of him and turning him around, if I didn't know from that single syllable that there was still a piece of something stuck inside him that he wasn't letting go of. And it was stuck inside me too.

Monday morning came, and the moment I got back from taking Desmond to school, Bonner was there with a briefcase and a long face. It took me a minute to remember *why* he was there. I'd been right: A lot could happen in two days.

My heart sagged, but I waved him in and put the kettle on.

I could feel his uneasiness as he hoisted himself up to the bistro table.

"How is Zelda?" I said.

"Holding her own. Allison—have you decided?"

"No," I said.

"Our time's up. I don't think Taylor has a dozen prospective buyers knocking on his door, but it isn't fair to keep this tied up."

I sat across from him. "I didn't say there was no decision. I just said *I* hadn't decided."

"You're losin' me here," he said.

"Okay. You aren't going to list my house because something tells you not to. I get that."

He nodded slowly.

"And I don't want to list it with anybody else because something tells *me* not to. Well, not just 'something.' It's your integrity. The same thing that won't let you list it."

"So where does that leave us?"

"What if we sign the contract, saying our purchase of the house is contingent on the sale of mine. Only we don't list it." I put up my hand to stop his protest. "And we tell Mr. Taylor we're not listing it. If somebody else comes along and wants to buy his place, he can sell it to them. But if this one sells, we get his for the deal that's in the contract."

Bonner just stared at me.

"It's legal, isn't it?"

"Yeah."

"This way it's up to God."

Bonner sat back in the high seat and watched his leg dangle.

"What?" I said.

"Wasn't it up to God when you decided to sell in the first place? Wasn't it a Nudge?"

I opened my mouth. And then I closed it.

"Seriously, Allison?" Bonner said.

"I'm desperate, Bonner," I said. "There's just so much, so many people to save from the lives they're living. I just have to find a way."

"You do? Not God?" He shook his head at me. "I thought that was what we were doing here. And you're the reason for that. You're the one that keeps plowing ahead on nothing but faith. And that's it."

"That's what?"

"That's why I can't list this house. That's what's wrong. It's not coming from God. It's coming from you trying to second-guess God."

There was nothing in that I could deny. Not even the shame that burned my face.

"If we're going to give it to God," he said, "I think we have to give him the whole thing. Tear up the contract. Tell Taylor we'll buy when we can if his property is still available. If God sends somebody to buy this house, totally without advertising, then so be it. Meanwhile, there will be another way." He pressed his hand down on mine. "There will be, Allison."

"Okay, Bonner," I said. "You want tea?" I squeezed his hand. "I'm having humble pie with mine."

❧

Dr. Doug Doyle said Chief would be released Sunday. He pointed out with a twinkle that that was April Fools' Day. Yeah, well, the thing didn't feel like a joke. Every time I thought about it, I got the shakes.

The meeting with Vickie and Priscilla Sanborn and her attorney was scheduled for Thursday the twenty-ninth, but Chief kept reassuring me he was handling it.

"You aren't going to make me go in there alone, are you?" I asked on the morning of the twenty-eighth. "Don't tell me you're going to be there via Skype or some such ridiculous thing. I *will* fire you."

"Oh ye of little faith." He glanced at his watch. "I've hired a guy. He's doing my legwork. In fact, if you aren't busy, he'll go with you this morning to meet with Stan about your bike and the insurance. "

"And tomorrow?"

"He'll be with you at the meeting. I'll be a phone call away in case he needs me. I'm still the attorney of record."

"Am I going to meet this person?" I said.

"He should be here anytime."

"Now? Why didn't you tell me?"

"Why? Did you want to have your hair done or something?" He pointed at me. "I didn't tell you in advance because I knew you'd do what you're doing right now."

"Which is what?"

"Building a little wall around you."

I stared. "Do I do that?"

"Sometimes." His eye lines crinkled. "I enjoy taking it down, brick by brick."

Oh, for Pete's sake, get a wrecking ball and let's get on with this.

I was still trying to catch my breath when someone tapped on the door.

"You could have at least told me his name," I whispered.

But he didn't have to. When the door swung open, Kade Capelli walked in.

CHAPTER FOURTEEN

The kid appeared as self-assured as he was the first time I met him. He gave no indication of caring that I'd seen him being thrown out of a prostitute's room. Ophelia's room. Our Ophelia. Did he actually think I wasn't going to turn to Chief and say, *Get this little jackal out of my sight?*

But on closer inspection, as he crossed the room and shook my hand to the tune of Chief's explanation of how he'd taken my recommendation and called him, blah, blah, blah, I saw the question in Kade's clear blue eyes: Was I going to out him or not?

"I interviewed him right before the accident," Chief said.

"World's longest wait for a job offer." Kade was still watching me.

"You happier now?"

I looked at Chief.

"Does this make you feel better?" he said. "You obviously saw something in the guy, which I did too."

I wanted to scream, *Did you see that he's a complete phony?*

But Chief was looking pleased with himself. The lines that had deepened in his long sleep relaxed around his eyes.

"You've checked his credentials, I assume." I tried to sound light, but I hoped Kade could hear through that.

"Harvard Law Review. Great recommendations."

"Great bedside manner," I said.

The door opened and a hefty guy in scrubs came in already talking. "I hate to break this up, but it's time for Jack's PT."

"You say we're meeting Stan?" I said to Chief.

"He said he'd catch up with you two wherever."

I smiled my best smile at Kade. "How about the Monk's Vineyard?"

Only because the color drained from the kid's face did I not spill the whole thing to Chief.

"Let him know we're on our way," I said.

I swished past Kade and headed down the hall. I wasn't sure what I was actually going to do or say once we got to the parking garage, so I took the stairs instead of the elevator, with Kade's footsteps echoing behind me. I couldn't wrap my mind around this, even as right as Chief was about us needing help. I couldn't be Chief-right. I had to be me-right. God-right. I only knew one way to get clear on that.

"We should talk," Kade said when I stopped.

"We will," I said. "I'll drive."

"I have a car."

"I have a Harley." I pointed to the Road King. "Get on."

"I don't have a helmet."

"Florida law says you aren't required to wear one if you're over twenty-one and have insurance. You do have insurance?"

"Yeah."

"Then let's go."

I didn't give him a chance for further argument. I stuffed my head into my helmet, poked my fingers into my gloves, and fired up the bike. He finally swung one trousered leg over and pressed his soles onto the foot pegs. He was, of course, heavier than Desmond, and I hoped he knew how to be a passenger. Otherwise, this was going to be my worst dismount yet.

I took off out of the parking garage as fast as I dared and wove through the back streets to US 1. My mind was in a higher gear than the bike.

Could this be any more ironic? What was the deal? It wasn't even April Fools' Day.

If it was, Kade didn't get the joke. His body was so stiff I wondered if he was still alive back there. I was fine with his being freaked right out of his tasseled loafers.

As we passed West King and turned onto Valencia, I slowed down. This was only getting me more stoked for a fight with the kid, and I had to admit that verbal fisticuffs weren't going to get us anywhere. The meeting was tomorrow. I couldn't do it without legal representation, not if I wanted to keep Desmond, and there was no *if* about that. We'd get through this and then I could tell Chief. Or maybe he would be ready for court by the time of the hearing that Vickie Rodriguez would surely have moved under the circumstances. Or maybe this kid was sharp enough to eliminate the need for that altogether.

That was too many maybes. When I pulled into a parking space on the St. George end of Cuna, I sighed a prayer into my helmet.

Please show me what you want me to do, because I have no idea.

"Can I get off now?" Kade said.

"Yeah," I said.

He did, and stood white-faced on the sidewalk looking at me. "When we set out on the motorcycle to Whipsnade zoo, I did not believe that Jesus Christ is the Son of God, and when we reached the zoo, I did."

I felt my jaw drop. "C. S. Lewis," I said.

"Yeah," he said. "I never understood that before."

"Huh," I said. Now there was a surprise. Either that or he was just a well-*read* phony.

We started off toward the Vineyard, threading our way among the school groups shouting their way toward the Schoolhouse.

"Are you going to tell him?" Kade said above the babble.

I waited until we were standing by the Monk's bottom step before I answered. "That depends on why you were here that day."

The color returned to his face, all the way into his scalp. "It wasn't what you think."

"What do I think?"

"What anybody would think if they saw a guy coming out of a, uh, room belonging to a woman of questionable reputation."

"How long have you been practicing that?" I said.

"All the way over here. Look—" He moved his neck as if his collar had suddenly shrunk. "We didn't even—nothing happened. I just wanted to ask her some questions."

"So it was a job interview," I said.

"Research," he said.

"You really know your way around a euphemism, don't you?"

"I wanted to find out about you."

I rocked back against the porch railing and folded my arms. "I can't wait to hear what you do with this."

"After I met you that day, I googled you and I saw what kind of work you do. It relates to the kinds of cases I want, representing people trying to get their lives together. I wanted to find out if you were the real thing, so, yeah, I thought I'd ask somebody who might know."

"You're nothing if not creative."

"I offered to pay her."

"Ophelia," I said. "Her name is Ophelia."

He went scarlet again. Not the reaction I expected. "When I started asking questions, she thought I was an undercover cop and she threw the money back at me and showed me the door. That's when you showed up." He actually grinned. "At least I knew I'd come to the right place."

"I never met Ophelia until that day. Why didn't you just come ask *me* if I was the 'real thing'?"

"I tried to, that day at the restaurant when you kicked Troy Irwin's butt."

"I did not kick his butt," I said. But the fact that he seemed to find that delicious softened me up a little.

"You acted like you didn't have time for a conversation," Kade said, "and you handed me off to Chief. So yeah, here we are."

"Yeah," I said. "Here we are."

Kade parked his hands on his hipless hips and tilted his head back as if he were examining the grapes carved into the sign above us. "You can believe me or not about any of it, and that'll be what it is." He lowered his gaze to me, blue eyes clear. "But if you don't trust me to be there for you at the meeting tomorrow, tell me now. I don't want to waste your time."

I nodded toward the porch and went up the steps. He followed me to the table in the corner.

"You know C. S. Lewis," I said.

"I've studied him."

I raised an eyebrow. "At Harvard?"

"No. When I was an undergrad. I was trying to figure some stuff out."

"Did you?"

"I'm still working on it."

Allison.

I know, I know. Wash his dadgum feet.

I sighed, somewhere from the vicinity of my own feet. "All right then. I guess we'd better talk about tomorrow before Stan gets here. You want to order something?"

"So does that mean ..."

"Yeah. And don't get the latte."

He smiled, teeth white and square as Chiclets, eyes lit up with an assurance I didn't have at twenty-six. It wasn't a cocky smile, but he wasn't cowed by me either.

Which he proved as he pushed aside the silverware-wrapped-in-a-napkin, rippled his fingers on the table, and said, "Tell me why you want to be a mother."

"I'm sorry?" I said.

"In case it comes up tomorrow. Mr. Ellington already knows, I bet, but I don't, and I might need to be able to think on my feet. Kind of hard to do without all the information. So, yeah."

"I don't want to just be a mother," I said. "I want to be Desmond's mother."

"Because his biological mother signed him over to you?"

"Y'know, I don't like your tone."

"It's not my tone," Kade said. "It's the tone the lawyer's going to use when he cross-examines you."

"I feel like I'm being cross-examined right now."

"That's the point."

He sat there, hands flat on the table. I put mine there too.

"I don't just *want* to be Desmond's mother," I said. "I have to be, and not because his mother signed him over like a used car. Because he is already my son here." I pointed to my head. "And here." I pressed one hand against my heart. "I get him, and I love him, and I am making a good life for him. I don't see anybody else being able to do that."

A slow smile spread across Kade's face. "Now that's what I'm talkin' about."

"Miss Chamberlain?"

I knew it was Nicholas Kent before I turned around. He couldn't send me a text but he could track me down at the Monk's Vineyard?

He nodded at Kade and switched his coffee cup to the other hand so they could shake. Okay, so he hadn't tracked me down. Nice to see business was picking up for Lewis and Clark. Maybe they wouldn't have to give up the expedition after all.

"Didn't you get my message?" I said.

Nicholas's face colored, filling in the spaces between the freckles. "I had a little incident with my cell phone."

"Let me guess," Kade said. "You dropped it in the toilet."

"No, bathtub. Dude—so embarrassing." Nicholas turned to me. "You left me a message?"

"You want to go in and order us a couple of coffees?" I said to Kade.

He scoped us out with a look and then nodded and disappeared inside. I told Nicholas about the cops at Sacrament House. His eyes grew cloudier with every sentence.

"I don't know anything about it," he said when I was done. "In fact, I didn't think the department was even pursuing the case. I'm not in on it if they are."

"I don't get it, then."

"Neither do I. But I'll find out."

I liked the set of his jaw. He was looking less like Opie Taylor all the time.

"It's about time you came in to say thank you."

Lewis set two coffees on the table, virtually elbowing Kade as he tried to get back into his seat.

"What am I thanking you for?" I said.

The mustache seemed to expand. "Don't you take the paper?"

"No."

"George!" he said.

George was already behind him, planting a folded newspaper in front of me. There was a lot of that going on lately. I really was going to have to think about subscribing.

"Front page," Lewis said, "Above the fold. I didn't know I still had that kind of pull."

I stared at the picture he was proudly thumping with his finger. It was Desmond's silhouette of Ophelia's rapist.

"Good article too," Lewis said.

I started to scan it to see if they'd used the word *alleged*.

"I've been following this," Kade said when Lewis had returned to the kitchen with Nicholas to get his to-go order. "You know your connection with it could affect our case."

"Then it's your job to see that it doesn't," I said.

"And your job to tell me everything I need to know. So, yeah, let's get started."

By the time Stan showed up, I felt almost like I'd been on the witness stand already. I hated to admit it to myself, but young Kade Capelli might be able to handle this after all.

Nicholas called me early the next morning to tell me that the department was already receiving a flood of phone calls since Desmond's drawing made the *Record*.

"Any leads, then?" I said.

"Most of them are crank calls, people saying it's everybody from Henry Flagler's ghost to their brother-in-law they always thought was a pervert. One thing is for sure, though."

"What's that? And please tell me it's good."

"It could be. The chief's on the hot seat now because the mayor doesn't like this kind of thing on the newsstands when tourists walk by."

Ms. Willa would have several paragraphs to say in support of that theory. "Any luck finding out who those jerks were that went to Sacrament House?"

"Nobody's talking. Frankly, I think whoever it was is ticked at me for raising a stink about investigating this, even before it got on the news. It makes more work for them in what they think is a nothing case."

He went quiet.

"What?" I said.

"Nothing. I was just waiting for you to blow up."

"What would be the point, Nick?" I said. "Would it help?"

"Maybe." I imagined his freckles getting lost in a blush. "It's you blowing up that got this whole things started. If you stop popping your cork now, we might not get *any*where."

"Popping my cork,'" I said. "I like you, Nicholas."

"Yeah, well, listen, I'll keep you posted."

Bless his heart. He was probably one big freckle by now.

Just as I was headed for Desmond's room to wake him up for school, the phone rang again. It was Vickie Rodriguez this time.

"I hope you're calling to tell me Priscilla Sanborn has gone back to Africa," I said.

"No, I called to tell you that you need to bring Desmond to the meeting this morning."

I stopped, my hand ready to tap on Desmond's door. "*Now* who's being blindsided."

"I just found out myself. Her lawyer called and said she wants to see him in person."

"What hasn't she seen? She's been spying on him for weeks."

I heard Vickie take a deep breath. I couldn't be a terribly easy client for the poor woman.

"Okay, we'll be there," I said. "I just wish I had more time to prepare him."

"We could set up another meeting to do this, but I'm not thinking we want to face this woman any more than we have to."

I took solace in the fact that Vickie seemed to share my opinion of Miss Prissy. Still, before I woke Desmond, I called Chief, just to hear his voice.

"I hate that I can't be there," he said. "But Kade told me you had a good session yesterday. He's ready."

"I'm not sure I am," I said.

Desmond, on the other hand, was surprisingly cavalier at the prospect of coming face-to-face with his aunt.

"She can't take me, so I ain't worried," he said for about the third time when we were crossing the parking lot to the FIP building. "I know how to handle her."

I stopped him on the sidewalk. "I want you to be yourself at this meeting," I said. "But both of us are going to have to hold back on telling Priscilla what we think of her. As in, no insults, no 'you left me puking on myself'—none of that. We have a new lawyer. He works for Chief so it's like having Chief there, and we need to let him do most of the talking unless somebody asks us a question. Can you handle that?"

"Ain't nobody like having Chief there," he said. "Just so you know."

Desmond bore that opinion out when we met Kade in the lobby. I thought Kade looked older than his years, and capable, and a whole lot calmer than I was, but Desmond pulled back from him as if Kade were carrying a sign saying, "Don't trust me. I'm bad news."

It wasn't lost on Kade.

"I know I'm not Chief," he said, "but I'm here to help."

"Can I see some ID?"

"Desmond!" I said.

But Kade was already digging in his pocket. "Not a problem. I like a client who's cautious."

He pulled out his wallet and presented his driver's license to Desmond, who studied it like he worked for Homeland Security. I didn't know whether he was satisfied or not when he handed it back to Kade.

"Are we good?" I said to him.

Desmond closed one eye. "*You* cool with him?"

"Yeah."

"Then I guess itta be a'ight. I got to use the restroom."

I pointed the way and turned to Kade. He was wiping a grin from his face with his hand.

"Sorry about that," I said.

"No, it's fine. He definitely trusts you. I think the jury's still out on me."

He seemed young again, so young I had to say, "He does trust me, so don't mess this up."

When the three of us entered Vickie's office, Priscilla Sanborn was already there with her lawyer, a Mr. Quillon. Older man. Balding with dignity. Wearing a suit that was worth more than my entire wardrobe. What did this woman *do* in Africa? Mine diamonds?

The question sent me into a mental tailspin. What if the judge decided she would be the better mother because she could afford to give Desmond more than I could?

"Relax," Kade whispered to me.

I rubbed my palms on my thighs and turned my attention to Desmond. He was already chatting it up with Vickie Rodriguez, personality seeping from every pore.

"This a *nice* office," he said. "You got you some good taste."

"Thank you," she said. I was grateful for the absence of isn't-that-cute in her expression.

"Sorry I'm late," Liz Doyle said as she burst in, eyelids batting.

Desmond was on her in a heartbeat, arms around her, kissing her resoundingly on the cheek.

"Are you behaving?" she said to him.

"Yes, ma'am," he said, and wiggled his eyebrows.

"Desmond. Aren't you going to speak to me?"

I watched Desmond's backbone straighten as if each vertebra were a Lego being stacked on the one below it. When he turned to face his aunt, his eyes were so blank I shivered. "Whachoo want me to say?"

"We could start with hello. And a hug."

"Hello," he said. The request for a hug went unrequited.

"I think we can get started," Vickie said.

"Lemme start." Desmond pulled out the chair across the table from his aunt, sat himself down, and folded his hands so close to the way Hank did I felt a pang. "You don't want me," he said to her.

"Of course I want you." Her voice was so condescending, it set my teeth on edge.

"No," Desmond said, "you jus' think you want me. But you don't know me. I'd be way too much trouble for you, I can tell that by the fancy way you dressed and the way you holdin' your chin." He leaned into the table. "Only people can handle me is Big Al and Mr. Chief. And Miss Hankenstein, and Mercedes-Benz. I got way more people here can handle me than you even *know*. I am doin' you a favor tellin' you this, so you don't got to go to all this trouble." He took a breath and smiled up at Vickie. "We done, then?"

She smiled back at him. "You are," she said. "That was a huge help, Desmond. I'm going to have Miss Doyle take you on to school."

"If you need me, you know where to find me." He followed Liz happily to the door and turned back to Priscilla. "Have you a good trip back to wherever it was you went to when you lef' me and my mama in the street. I bet it's way nicer there."

All the air went out of the room as he and Liz exited. She put her head back in.

"Yes?" Vickie said.

"Before I go, as the foster care manager for the county, I am *not* recommending that Desmond be placed into foster care between now and the hearing."

"Was that even a possibility?" I said.

"That would be news to me," Kade said.

Vickie shook her head. "Although Ms. Sanborn suggested that, I never seriously considered it. Desmond is obviously in good care and in no danger right where he is."

Liz bugged her eyes at me and left. Priscilla Sanborn barely waited for the door to close before she said, "He most certainly is in danger—of never being able to speak like a normal human being. Did you hear the grammar?"

"Four months ago he would have been dropping F-bombs in here," I said. "It's all relative, ma'am." I covered a smile with my hand as I realized for the first time that Desmond was right. She did draw in fake eyebrows with a pencil.

"All right." Vickie pressed her hands together. "Ms. Sanborn, you have seen your nephew, and despite any reservations you may have about his verbal skills, you now know that he is in good health, he's obviously self-assured, and he knows that he's loved."

"He knows he's indulged," Priscilla said.

I opened my mouth, but Vickie shot me a warning look. "Our concern is in determining what is best for Desmond."

"If I may," Kade said.

"Please."

"According to a ruling by Judge Baker on December twenty-sixth of last year, what is best for Desmond has already been determined. That decision was arrived at not only with the information that my client had already been caring for him for several months, but by the legal document signed by his mother giving custody to Ms. Chamberlain in the event of her death.

"And if *I* may," Mr. Quillon said.

He sounded so like my father I cringed. Even though he was at least twenty years younger, he was of the same vintage. He'd definitely been trained to be Southern gentleman on the outside, serial opportunist on the inside.

"The boy's mother"—pronounced *mu-thah*—"was a known drug addict. We can't be sure she was even in her right mind when she agreed to that."

"She didn't agree to it," Kade said. "She initiated it. And she'd been clean for months at that point."

"I'm sorry, son," Mr. Quillon said, making a show of flipping through his papers. "I've been remiss. I don't seem to have the document that says a drug test was administered that day."

I was sure they could all hear my teeth grinding.

"There's no way of proving that either way," Kade said smoothly. "The point is that Miss Chamberlain has already shown herself to be a more-than-adequate mother to Desmond, and a judge has agreed.

Only under very unusual circumstances is His Honor going to over-
turn a ruling."

"You know, I'm glad you used that phrase, *unusual circumstances,*
because that is just what we have here."

"And those would be?"

Mr. Quillon smiled, showing a neat fence of capped teeth. I'd
seen smiles like that when I was growing up, smiles put on when
there was really nothing to smile about.

"Harvard Law, was it, Kade? May I call you Kade?

"You can call me whatever you want if you'll get to the point,
Clyde."

I cringed again. I was right there with Kade, but Chief hadn't
coached him in the finer points of plastic Southern etiquette. "There"
wasn't a place you wanted to take a hometown boy like Quillon.

Mr. Q. gave a laugh that matched his nonsmile. "You're a Yankee
for sure, aren't you? That's a sly Harvard Law tactic, trying to tease
our case out of me before we get into the courtroom."

"Clyde, please, the point?"

Oh, dear. It was all I could do not to get Chief on the phone.

"The point. The point is that those unusual circumstances are
exactly what we are going to bring before the judge."

"You seriously intend to put your client through that," Kade said.

I glanced at Priscilla, but she seemed unconcerned about being
put through anything. Her face was a complete blank, until she
caught me watching her. Even then she only stiffened and refused to
meet my eyes again.

"It's your client I'm concerned about." Mr. Quillon gave me a
paternal look. "Little lady, I knew your daddy."

There were so many retorts I wanted to throw at him like darts, starting with *Dude, I am neither little, nor a lady,* but I had to undo the damage Kade didn't even know he'd done. I left all the sarcastic possibilities in the quiver and said, "Did you, now? You couldn't have been more than a boy when he passed away."

"I had just graduated from Stetson Law," he said. "You familiar with that school, Kade?"

"Yeah. Great school. Look, I'm sure your résumé is stellar, but I don't see what this has to do with the case at hand."

Mr. Quillon winked at me. "They're always in a hurry up there north of the Mason-Dixon, aren't they?"

"Now we're revisiting the Civil War." Kade looked imploringly at Vickie.

"Mr. Quillon, we really do need to wrap this up."

"That's is exactly what I'm trying to do." Quillon stopped grinning and let his eyes sadden dramatically at me. "The only thing I wanted to do when I passed the bar was work for Chamberlain Enterprises. I had an interview scheduled with your father for the day after he was murdered. I didn't have the heart after that. I opened my own firm, been very successful, but I never got over it. Did you?"

"Ms. Rodriguez is right, Clyde," I said, voice stony. "You need to wrap this up."

The Southern smooth slid from his face and left his eyes cold and his mouth hard. "We goin' to trial, Miss Allison. Mr. Capelli, if I were you, I would advise my client to drop this case, because I am going to hate humiliating her."

"Mr. Quillon, there will be no threats here." The vein in Vickie's forehead was throbbing.

"Oh, that is not a threat, *Señorita.* That is a promise."

"Enough." Vickie stood up and made no attempt to slow her breathing. "The hearing will take place as scheduled on Thursday, April fifth. You will both have an opportunity to present your arguments and provide witnesses. But I warn you: Judge Atwell will not tolerate attempts at intimidation. Watch yourself, Mr. Quillon."

He gave her the smile. "No bias here, I see. That's why we're going to court. We will see you all there."

Kade and I were the first ones out. I was afraid if I stayed any longer I'd wind up sharing a cell with Zelda.

"That went well," Kade said when we were safely entombed in the elevator. "How does he get away with that?"

"It's the South," I said. "And he's a good ol' boy in a designer suit. I'm sorry nobody told you they play by different rules down here."

"They play dirty." Kade rubbed the back of his neck. "I hate to do this to you, but if you have any skeletons in your closet, you need to tell me about them now because I guarantee you they're going to come up in court and I need to be ready to deflect them." The doors sighed open and he put his hand on my back to usher me out, mind obviously still going like an Intel processor. "If you've got any dirt on her, I need that too."

I stopped him dead in the middle of the lobby. "No," I said.

"No, what?"

"No, we're not going to play that game. And if you don't get that, you can't represent me."

"They're going to dredge up things in your past that didn't even happen and make them sound like the truth."

"Then let them." The words freed themselves from the stuck place and flowed out. "If I'm capable in the present, there's no need to bring up the past. Hers or mine."

I waited for the protest. But Kade only grinned. "Chief warned me," he said.

"About what?"

"He told me not to push you when you get that God-look in your eyes."

I was still trying to respond to that when he spun out through the revolving door.

On Sunday, the HOGs and Hank and a team of physical therapists moved Chief into my house, traction and all. Although Desmond had offered his "place," we turned the living room into Chief's domain and the dining room into the PT area for the therapist to work with him when he came daily.

"Casa de Chief," Nita said when she and Leighanne and the Sisters came to celebrate Palm Sunday with us.

"I don't know nothin' 'bout no casa," Desmond said. "This here's HOG Heaven."

"Shall I have a sign painted?" Bonner said.

India looked at me in horror. I couldn't keep a straight face.

"Let's just call it home for now," I said. "Y'all need to get those palms out so we can get started. I'll get the bread."

Bonner followed me into the kitchen. "For now?" he said.

"Slip of the tongue," I said.

"You haven't told Desmond you might sell?"

"No."

"Chief? He might want to be making other arrangements in case somebody buys it right out from under his hospital bed."

"I haven't told anybody except Hank." I set her homemade communion bread on the counter and leaned over it. "Last week I thought Ms. Willa was going to come through, but she wants me to use her money to get into some kind of war with Troy Irwin."

Bonner looked at me over the tops of his glasses. "I thought you were already in a war with Troy Irwin."

"I don't know, Bonner. I just don't feel like I can say the H-word anymore."

"The H-word?"

"*Hate*. I mean, don't put me in the same room with the man, but for as angry and frustrated as I am, I can't go at this like an attack on him. You're the one who told *me*: this has to be for God or I can't do it. I physically can't. I don't know how to explain that to you."

"You don't have to," he said. "You look like you're having an attack of appendicitis."

"It feels more like labor pains." I added quickly, "Not that I would know what that felt like."

"Unless you tell me not to, I'll just keep praying that we'll get the funding for Sacrament Two and you won't have to part with this place."

"Do it," I said. "Can I ask one more thing of you?"

"Anything. Except for me to change Chief's bedpan. I draw the line there."

"Will you keep me posted on Zelda? I haven't given her any support. I know you go there, and that's a lot. Still."

"The girl's getting more support than an eighteen-hour bra."

"I'm sorry?"

Two splotches of color appeared on Bonner's cheekbones. "Bad analogy. People have been to see her. The Sisters are over there praying with her every Sunday. I'm on the phone with her daily. Hank tried to take her communion but they put the kibosh on that." He craned his neck toward me. "Allison? What's with the tears?"

"I have no idea, Bonner," I said. "Just hand me a paper towel, would you?"

We had our Palm Sunday celebration standing in a circle in my living room with our palms. Chief didn't have much of a choice but to join us, parked as he was in the middle of it all. But I saw him listening, his eyes intense, as I talked about the week that lay ahead of us.

"It's Holy Week," I said. "The marking of Jesus' last seven days on earth. Seven remarkable days. These days need to be remarkable for us too. There are feet to be washed, my friends. Many, many feet."

"*Mmm-mmm*," Mercedes said.

On Monday the physical therapist came to work with Chief. It was apparently grueling, because Chief let out so many groans I had to go out on the side porch to keep from, to use Desmond's words, punching the therapist in the face.

That was where Troy Irwin found me.

I didn't hear him coming. He must have coasted the Beamer into Palm Row. I considered diving back into the house, but it was too late for that. Troy stood at the bottom of the steps, hands in the pockets of his Dockers. That seemed to be the preferred posture for men who were trying to look like they didn't know what to say. I wasn't fooled. Troy Irwin always knew what to say.

He has feet, Allison.

I gritted my teeth. *I know. Really dirty feet.*

"Out for a stroll, Troy?" I said. Even I could hear the icicles hanging from my voice.

"No," he said. "I came to see you."

He wore a white polo shirt and a matching long-sleeved thing tied around his shoulders with a casual air that must have taken him half an hour to achieve. His sandy-going-gray hair barely spiked in the wind coming off the bay, and the sleeves dangling across his chest were just as cooperative. He already had a tan.

"Been to the islands?" I said. Did civility covering disgust count as a footwashing?

"Just got back, and to some disturbing news. Do you have a minute?"

No, I thought. "Yes," I said.

I nodded him toward the swing, but like every other person who wanted to take control of a conversation on this porch, he opted for the Adirondack chair. I leaned against the railing on Miz Vernell's side. If I took a swing at Troy, she'd call the cops. I was counting on that for self-control.

"So what news has disturbed your world?" I said.

"I won't go into all the ins and outs. I know you hate the corporate thing. So I'll keep it simple."

Nothing was simple with him, but I nodded.

"It's come to my attention—" He stopped and tilted his head at me. "Do I really have to be this formal with you? It just feels wrong."

"Whatever way you want to be it's going to tick me off, Troy, so just get on with it." Not nice, but it was better than a kick in the teeth. And it was honest.

"Right. I've learned that an attorney at the firm that represents Chamberlain is also representing a woman who's trying to take your boy from you."

I willed myself not to move.

"I don't know the man personally, but he's connected to me through …" Troy leaned forward, arms on his thighs. "Look, Ally, I don't agree with most of what you're doing. Matter of fact, I think it's pointless. You know that."

"You've made that clear," I said. "And in some pretty threatening ways. The last time I saw you, you were smearing my reputation in the middle of 95 Cordova. The time before that you were threatening me at my best friend's funeral. So forgive me if I'm not sure what else there is to say."

"There's this: I don't think you adopting the boy *is* pointless. I actually think it makes a tremendous amount of sense." He punched his knuckles softly against his mouth. "It's ironic, isn't it?"

"What?" I said.

"How much you hated having your father as your father, and how he was the only father I ever wanted."

It was such a complete non sequitur it gave me whiplash, but I felt the Nudge to go with it.

"How was yours that much different from mine?" I said. "I always thought they were interchangeable."

"I thought they were too. When I thought about them at all." He eased himself back in the chair. "You and I were both allergic to our fathers as kids, if you'll recall."

My upper lip wanted to curl. "Only one of us was cured of that allergy."

"There was one major difference between your father and mine. I saw it when I came back after college and sat down in the same office with the two of them." Troy gazed at the ceiling as if he were watching the memory on video. "That's when they told me Chamberlain had bought out Irwin. Not a merger. An acquisition."

I hadn't known that. Hadn't actually cared. But the skin around Troy's eyes was tightening. If we'd been playing poker, I'd have upped the ante.

I said, "My father didn't give him a good deal, I take it."

"It was a great deal. My father died a rich man. My mother's in the best Alzheimer's facility in the state." Troy looked me full in the face, his blue eyes simmering. "The difference was, my father didn't fight. I don't care how good the deal was, he built that business up from nothing. He even forced me not to marry you when you were pregnant, just to save the reputation of Irwin Inc. And then he just let it go for money."

For the flicker of a moment, I saw something real in Troy's eyes. Not the real of a man who would wash the feet of a down-and-out human being, but the boy who would've held a pool party for them all and been the first one in. The boy with sunshine in his cowlick hair and dreams in his eyes. Real dreams.

When I blinked, it was gone.

"What does all this have to do with Desmond's adoption?" I said.

"He ought to have the right parents. One at least. It can make all the difference."

"Well, that's one thing we agree on," I said.

Troy twisted his ring. "This is something I've wanted to say for a long time. I'm sorry I made you get an abortion."

I stopped breathing.

"You would have been a wonderful mother. That's why I want to help." Troy slanted toward me, forearms on his knees. "I can call this guy off, this Clyde Quillon. I can get the whole thing settled out of court. Forget Doyle and Rodriguez. Forget Judge Atwell. I can make it disappear."

My insides were contracting so hard I had to clench the railing. This pain went too deep for me to grab at anything very much below the surface. I went for the shallow end. "How is it that you know every detail?" I said.

"I've told you this before, Ally: I make it my business to know everything about you."

"And I've told you before: Don't call me that."

Troy spread out his hands. "What am I supposed to do, pretend the past never happened to us? Maybe you can, but I can't."

The sun caught his eyes and he had to look down—the way he used to cast his eyes away from me when he had to leave, to hide the longing because he couldn't get enough of being with me.

I trusted that back then, although even at sixteen I knew Troy Irwin had finesse he hadn't even used yet. This wasn't finesse. This was a full-out acting job.

It was pathetic, but I felt a wave of despair. Not my despair. His.

"What's in it for you, Troy?" I said. I was surprised at the softness in my voice.

"Very little," he said. He had the nerve to smile. "All I want in return is San Luis Street."

"All you want," I said. "All you want is everything."

"It's one block."

"For now. I can't fight you on West King. I don't have the stuff. You're going to take it over and there's nothing I can do about it. So why my street too?"

"My street and your street can't coexist. I need that property."

"For Pete's sake, how freakin' rich do you have to be, Troy?"

"Look, I don't have a black heart, Ally—Allison. I'll relocate the program for you. I'll build you a whole complex."

"Where?" I said.

"I have three hundred acres outside Palatka. You can rehab all the prostitutes you want."

"No," I said.

His fists doubled. "What is so wrong with my money?"

"Your money's not the problem." I slid off the railing. "It's the fact that you have no regard for these people as human beings that makes the whole idea of taking a nickel from you revolting to me."

"I have regard for your relationship with the boy. And yet you're telling me that you would pass up a guarantee that the adoption will go through because you have some principle."

I took a breath and prepared to say the same thing I'd had to say far too many times. The thing that whisked valuable solutions right out of the room.

"It's not my principle," I said. "It's God's."

I had never seen a conversation shut down so fast. The look that came over his face was pure contempt. And yet I couldn't stop.

"I have a personal relationship with the people you want to relocate. They have memories and hungers and regrets and smashed-up dreams. They've all but given up. I focus on the thread they still hang on to, and that thread isn't the hope of being taken away to some rehab facility out in the swamp. It's rebuilding their lives here, where they live. Where they have a right to live."

Troy's look was long and stony.

"There was a time when you would have been part of it," I said.

"Part of what? Your little footwashing?"

He spat the words like they were phlegm in his throat.

"Go," I said, "before I say the H-word to you."

"Are you telling me to go to—"

"No, Troy," I said. "I think that's already taken care of. It's me I'm worried about."

His exit was punctuated with the squeal of BMW tires. Miz Vernell poked her head out of her screen door and glared him all the way to Artillery Lane. I just stood there, feeling homesick, wishing the man would remember the boy. Wishing I could stand up in some boardroom where this heartless shell of a person served and tell them who he used to be.

And then it stabbed me to the heart that nobody in a corporate boardroom would care about either one.

Although the good that God reminded me of showed itself in the next few days—India and Ophelia bonding like soul mates, Liz Doyle and Lewis both writing editorials about the rape case, Desmond ceasing having nightmares—I felt like I still had Troy Irwin on my skin, clinging like a cobweb. I couldn't shake him off, so I carried his stuff on me along with everybody else's as I moved on. There was a lot to move on to.

Nicholas Kent asked me to meet him at the Monk's Vineyard Monday night when his shift was over. I didn't inquire over the phone what kind of news he had. I could hear the bad in his voice.

For once George and Lewis were perceptive and left us alone in our corner of the porch after George served us a pair of Lewis's reportedly new and improved lattes on the house. I barely sipped mine as Nicholas talked.

"I finally got a couple of guys to admit they know who went to see your women," he said.

"Who?"

"They wouldn't give me names. All these guys told me was that the officers went on their own, not under orders from the department."

"Why would they do that?"

"You got me. I'm still working on it."

"Working on it how?" I pushed the cup aside. "Look, I don't want you getting into any trouble, Nick. I appreciate your help, but you've got to watch your own back too."

He blushed to the roots of his wonderful red hair. It didn't occur to me until then how much I really liked this kid.

"What I want to do is bring over a photo array and have your—what do you call them?"

"The Sisters."

"Are they like nuns now?"

"Uh, no," I said drily. "Just Sisters in Christ."

He nodded. "Anyway, they could look at the pictures and identify the two guys. That's our best shot."

"Let me ask them," I said. "I'll get them on the phone right now."

"Before you do that." Nicholas dug into his pocket and pulled out a slip of paper. "Do you know a Marcus Rydell?"

"No. Who is he?"

"He's the guy who rented the car your Zelda crashed into the pole."

"Wait. He rented a car and she stole it from him when she was blown out on cocaine?"

"That's what it looks like. We traced the car to Hertz, and they said a Marcus Rydell rented it and then reported it stolen."

"Where was it stolen from, did he say?"

"Nightclub out at the beach."

"What?"

"Yeah, right? No way Zelda stole it from there. Not unless somebody else drove her out there."

"It makes absolutely no sense."

"Does she remember anything?"

I looked down at my now lukewarm coffee. "She's not talking to me."

"Oh. Sorry."

He actually did look sorry. Before I could start bawling, I dialed the number for Sacrament House. Mercedes answered, and before I got my question about the photo array all the way out, she was giving me a no.

"I know that red-haired boy is on our side," she whispered, as if he were listening in. "But when it come to police and courts, I just had it with all that."

"Can you speak for everyone?"

I heard her click to speakerphone. I repeated the request.

"I'm sorry, Miss Angel," Jasmine said, with tears not far behind.

Sherry was the most vehement. "Don't ask me that again, Miss Angel, or I might have to move out. I'm serious."

"No need to do that," I said. "Subject closed."

I didn't even have to shake my head at Nicholas. He was already shaking his.

Bonner's news was better.

Hank and I were having coffee Tuesday morning in my kitchen, listening to Chief bite back expletives in the dining room while the physical therapist put him through his paces. He was done with traction, but that apparently meant his workouts could be stepped up. Hank smothered a snort every time he broke out with "son of a biscuit eater."

"Looks like he's going to have a cheering section today," she said.

The screen door opened and Bonner appeared with Liz Doyle.

"You playing hooky?" I said to her.

She shook her head, blinked, and dumped her armload of stuff onto the floor. Bonner stopped to help her, but he got caught in the crossfire between a hairbrush and the purse she was trying to toss it back into. He came up rubbing a rapidly rising bump on his forehead.

"Let me," Hank said to him. "Sit. Have a biscotti. Have two."

"Tell her the *good* news," Liz said from the floor.

"We just came from court," he said. "The judge is releasing Zelda to us for a probationary period. If she stays clean, he'll consider it time served."

"Where is she now?"

"Being processed."

"Don't you love the terminology?" Hank said, putting a mug into Bonner's hand. "They make it sound like we're ordering something on Amazon."

"*How* is she?" I said. I searched Bonner's face.

"She's not spitting at God, Allison," he said.

"So what do you think?"

"I think we have to go with that."

I let out a slow breath of air. It had been so long since I'd felt relief, I barely recognized it.

Liz stood up, purse under her arm, hands full of cosmetics. "Zelda's scared. Which she probably should be. She has a lot of work to do."

"Wait," I said. "How is it that you know all this, Liz?"

"I've been spending some time with her." She shoved a compact into a purse pocket and looked at Bonner. I was so used to seeing her blink like a strobe light it took me a moment to realize she was doing battle with tears.

"What's going on?" I said.

"I want to work for you."

"You mean at Sacrament House?"

She nodded so hard, my heart dove.

"I wish we could *afford* to hire you," I said. "I'd take you away from FIP in a heartbeat if we had the funds. As it is—" I looked at Bonner with what I knew bordered on helplessness. "I still don't know how we're going to take care of Zelda."

Liz raised the hand that was holding a lipstick and a Sharpie.

"Idea?" I said.

"Plan," she said. "I want Zelda to come stay with me."

"Oh, Liz. Really? I mean, think about it."

"I already have. We can go to Sacrament House for meetings and all, but at my place she'll have her own room and my full attention until you get the second house."

"But we can't help you financially."

"I have some savings." Liz hugged the restuffed handbag to her chest. "Please, Allison, I want to do this. I have to."

I looked at Bonner again, just in time to catch him gazing at Liz with tender eyes.

Well, go figure. I really *had* been out of the loop.

"We'll give you all the help you need," I said. "Bless your heart—this is—"

"God," Liz said. "It's God."

Everyone was gone when Chief finished up his PT session. I was convinced they timed their exit so they wouldn't catch the backlash of the mood he would have to be in after an hour of whatever kind of torture went on in there.

But he looked rather pleased with himself when he pushed open the swinging door and rolled into the kitchen in a wheelchair, leg sticking out like a cannon in front of him.

"Look at you!" I said.

"I needed some wheels under me," he said.

"Wait till Desmond sees you. You know he's going to want to put pipes on that thing."

"Probably give it a nickname."

"Ya think? Anybody who spends five minutes with him gets one. He's started calling Kade Cappuccino."

"That's our boy."

"Yeah," I said.

A funny silence fell. I collided with myself rushing to break it.

"Should we celebrate? There's still a ton of food. Or do you just want coffee? Tea? How about tea? Tea would be better."

"Classic."

"Tea, then?"

"Thank you."

"For what?" I laughed like a fifteen-year-old. "I haven't given you anything yet."

Chief held out his hand to me. When I took it, he pulled me close to the wheelchair and looked up at me. Even then, he seemed larger than my life.

"You've given me everything," he said.

"Yes. My special burnt toast. A twelve-year-old so you won't be bored."

"Like I said—everything."

He tugged at my hand and let it go.

"So, tea?" I said.

And Hank thought *Chief* was romantically challenged.

Yet things had already taken on a rhythm. I felt something just as good as romance, something I couldn't name, but it was there. When I was preparing mac and cheese out of a box for him or adjusting the blinds while he napped so the sun wouldn't wake him. The word for it didn't come to me until late that afternoon when Desmond decided they were going for a HOG ride, broken leg or no broken leg. I sat at the bistro table, "bustin' a gut" as Desmond himself put it, while he pushed Chief through the house, both of them clad in helmets, making engine sounds that rivaled any bike down at the HD dealership.

"Imma pop a wheelie," Desmond called from the dining room.

"Try it and you're dog chow," I called back.

"Busted," Chief said.

That was the moment I gave the feeling a name.

It was home.

In the evenings that week, however, home turned into command central. With the hearing looming on Thursday—Maundy Thursday, I realized—Kade was there every night, working with Chief and me after Desmond went to bed. He came earlier Tuesday and Wednesday, though, so he could hang out with Desmond, who had decided Cappuccino was part of Hog Heaven.

"What changed your mind?" I asked Desmond when I saw him to bed Tuesday night.

"Don't know," he said. "He give me the prickles at first, like I knew him before or somethin', but now—it's all good."

So good, in fact, that before Kade got there Wednesday, the night before the hearing, Desmond did a caricature of Kade that was all teeth and sticking-out hair.

"Dude, I look like some kind of twisted George Clooney," Kade said when he arrived. He tried a grin as big as the drawn-in one and came up several molars short.

"Looks like a used car salesman," Chief said. "I wouldn't buy a vehicle from this guy."

"Say somethin', Big Al," Desmond said. "They dissin' my art."

I didn't say what actually came to me as the face in the drawing laughed into mine. Those were Kade's clear eyes, on steroids, and his handsome, symmetrical features to the hundredth power. That was his New England pluck that fell just shy of smug, and his boyish appeal, which even in two dimensions vacillated toward the man in him and came back again. What I couldn't name was a thing that made him familiar, as if Desmond had captured déjà vu with his pencil.

"Big Al, you killin' me here," Desmond said.

"Your talent makes all words meaningless," I said.

"Imma put this on the refrigerator." He headed for the kitchen, tripping over a piece of PT equipment on the way.

"Are you joining us when Hank and everybody comes over?" I said.

"Not unless you make me," he said, and pushed through the door. It swung hard in his wake like a tattletale classmate. Did you hear that? Did you hear it?

"What was that about?" Chief said.

"He's decided he doesn't want to be baptized," I said. I watched the door until it stopped telling its tale.

Kade looked up from the coffee table, where his files were spread out solitaire fashion. "I remember those days."

"What days?" I said.

"When my mood flipped around like that. I'd be messing around with my mom in the kitchen, y'know, juggling the eggs or something, and then she'd, like, look at me wrong and I'd tell her she didn't understand me and I'd go sit in my room in the dark like Heathcliff."

I perched on the arm of the red chair. "Heathcliff?"

"*Wuthering Heights.*"

"You read *Wuthering Heights?*"

"I thought that was only adolescent girls," Chief said.

Kade shrugged. "Anybody can read Brontë."

"No, I thought only adolescent girls had mood swings like that."

I elbowed Chief, whose wheelchair pulled up next to me. "You probably didn't. Matter of fact, I can't even imagine it. You're like a rock."

My rock, I longed to say. Because he was looking at me with that steady gaze, a smile waiting for just the right instant to grab my breath and make off with it so I would chase him to get it back.

"We should probably get to work if you've got people coming over," Kade said. "We have less than twenty-four hours left."

"You don't want to talk about *Pride and Prejudice?*" Chief said.

"I'm not into Jane Austen, dude," Kade said. "I like a little more passion in my literature."

Chief pulled the smile into a line. "You're going to need more than passion for this hearing."

Kade looked at me, eyes twinkling. "I think we're getting to work."

I slid from the arm down into the chair and sat cross-legged. "Look, guys, I don't know why we need to keep going over this. I've let you turn my private life inside out, and there isn't anything left that the judge doesn't already know about from when I was trying to get guardianship in the first place."

"We can't go into this thing without a plan," Chief said.

"What plan do I need to tell them I love Desmond and he's supposed to be with me?"

Kade and Chief exchanged glances.

"What?" I said.

"This one's yours," Kade said to Chief.

Chief hitched himself up in the chair, winced, and gave his leg an annoyed frown. The irritation stayed on his face, and I had a feeling it wasn't all directed at his uncooperative limb.

"Quillon is going to get as much mileage as possible out of his client being some kind of social worker in Botswana. Then he's going to bring in a platoon of witnesses to say you can't hold a candle to that. And he's going to make hash out of whoever Kade brings in to testify on your behalf." He lapsed into a believable imitation of a good ol' boy. "Former hookers, little lady?"

"They won't come within a hundred yards of a courthouse anyway."

"Bikers?"

"The HOGs we hang out with are professional people!"

Chief shook his head. "In the hands of a shyster like Quillon, they're going to look like the Hell's Angels up there. And don't think he won't do the same kind of thing with Nita and Leighanne—'Lordy ... recovering addicts'—"

"What about Hank?" I said. "India. Bonner. They're ... stainless."

"Motorcycle Mama. Bleedin' heart liberal. Former boyfriend with a bias as slanted as the Tower of Pisa."

"Get serious."

"I am, Classic. What we have to plan for is what's going to happen when *you* take the stand."

I leaned in to meet the gravity of the gaze he was lowering on me. "I'll tell you what's going to happen. I'm going to spend tonight the way I spend every other night—trying to empty myself of everything but God. And then I'm going to sit on that stand and I'm going to open my mouth and let the words come out, just like I do every time I'm in a situation where I have absolutely no control of the outcome."

"Can we count on that being an objective utterance?" Chief said.

"Objective's not a word I'd necessarily use for God."

"Con*found* it, Classic."

Chief pulled his hand into a fist, skin whitening over his bones. His jaw muscles clamped down on the words his eyes couldn't hide. I'd never seen him want to tell me I was crazy before.

"How did you *think* I was going to approach it, Chief?" I said. "How have I approached this entire ministry?"

"Your ministry isn't going before the judge. *You* are."

"I can't separate myself into little compartments. It's all God. You know that."

He held my gaze with his confounded one until Kade spoke.

"If I could just sort of mediate here?" he said.

"Knock yourself out." Chief turned his face toward the window. He might as well have slammed a door.

Kade put his hands up like goal posts. "What I'm hearing you say, Allison, is, well, exactly what you said. You live your life listening to God and doing what God says, so why should this situation be any different? Am I getting it right?"

I listened for irony, for sarcasm, for the slightest hint that he was patronizing my faith. All I heard was the faint echo of reverence.

"Yes," I said. "That's what I'm saying. Thank you."

He turned to Chief, whose face was still closed. "What I'm hearing you say, Chief, is that you support the ministry but you don't quite buy into the theology behind it, so relying on God in *this* situation doesn't make sense to you."

"No," Chief said, "it doesn't make sense to me to sit back and expect 'God' to swoop down and work this all out so that woman doesn't get our boy and take him to the other side of the world where we'll never see him again, which is exactly what's going to happen if we don't go in there with something more than 'God will put the words in my mouth.'"

He twisted back to face me. But his gaze went past me, and closed as if he saw something he couldn't bear. I turned to see. And I couldn't bear it either.

Desmond was standing there, his face stiff with Chief's words.

"Desmond," Chief said. "Come here, buddy."

"I jus' come in to tell you Miss Indiana and them's here." He gave me an empty look. "I'll be in my room."

I couldn't even look at Chief, and he didn't try to get me to. As the happy chatter of the Sisters and Hank and India and Ophelia rose in the kitchen, Kade scooped up his files and inserted them into his briefcase.

"We'll finalize everything in the morning," he said to me. "We've got until one."

I nodded, but I felt like something had already become final.

Kade glanced at Chief's back and looked at me sadly. "I'm sorry if I—"

"Don't," I said. "It's not your fault." I squeezed his shoulder and pointed my voice toward the kitchen. "We're meeting in there, y'all. The dining room's too full."

"I'll see myself out the front," Kade said.

We left Chief in the shaft of light from the lamp by the chair. I turned off the dining room light and started for the kitchen, where Ophelia was already opening the door, eyes shining.

Until they locked on something behind me. Before I could turn around she clutched at the doorframe as if she were falling off a bridge, and her face contorted in terror.

"That's him!" she screamed. "That's the man who raped me!"

I whirled to see a perfect silhouetted profile. Kade's profile.

CHAPTER FIFTEEN

The silence was strangling, as if the thoughts in all our heads couldn't find their way past our throats. I struggled for air as I stared at Kade, and I knew my face was no longer soft.

"Ophelia, honey," I heard India say. "What's wrong?"

"She said that guy right there is the one who raped her," Sherry said. Her voice was like a verdict.

India pushed her way through the knot in the doorway and grabbed Ophelia by both shoulders. "Honey, is that true? You think that's him?"

"I know it is! It's that same silhouette, just like I saw it."

My head turned in dizzying slow motion to look again at Kade. He was giving us a full frontal, his face ashen in the shadows.

"Someone turn on a light," I said.

Amid the gathering chaos the overhead went on and caught us all in shocked starkness. Faces registered everything from horror to bewilderment. Kade's registered all of it.

"She's wrong," he said. "She's wrong. I didn't rape her."

"Yes you did!"

"I haven't seen you since the day at Monk's Vineyard."

"That's how I know you. I remember now!"

India had to dig her fingers into Ophelia's arm to keep her from clawing her way to Kade's face. If Hank hadn't taken hold of her, too, she might have succeeded.

"I swear," Kade said to me, his lips trembling, "I have never touched her. I told you, I didn't even touch her that day."

"Kade. Shut it, man." That came from Chief, whose voice smacked us all into obedient silence. "Kade—Ophelia—Allison—in here. Kade, not another word."

He was using his lawyer tone. As far as I was concerned, he could use any tone he wanted if it quelled the tide of panic that swelled through the house. And inside of me.

"Hank," I said, "will you—"

"I'm on it," she said, and herded Mercedes, Jasmine, and Sherry back into the kitchen.

"And Desmond—"

"Done," she said.

Ophelia wasn't letting go of India, so there were three of us joining Chief in the living room, where he already had his head bent with Kade's.

"He's going to try to make up a story to make it look like I'm lying," Ophelia said. She let go of India with one hand and clamped it around my arm. "You can't let him do that, Miss Angel."

"Nobody's going to lie," Chief said. "Nobody."

Ophelia tossed her head. "I am not lying."

"Didn't say you were. Allison."

"Yeah."

"I think you should call Nicholas Kent."

Kade threw his hands up. "Come on, man, this is—"

"Is there something about 'shut it' that you don't comprehend, son? We need to determine the best way to handle this, since obviously something isn't making sense here."

"It makes perfect sense to me," India said. "It doesn't to you, Allison?"

"You going to make that call?" Chief said to me.

I nodded and took my phone into the stairwell. I could feel India staring, confused, at my back, as well she might. I would have stared at me that way too.

Nicholas answered on the first ring with "Everything all right?" instead of hello. I told him it wasn't and why.

"I'm on duty," he said, "so that's good. Here's what you do: Get both of them to the precinct, but in separate cars. Don't let them talk to each other."

"We're working on that," I said. I could still hear Ophelia shrieking and Chief saying, "Kade, dude, I'm telling you, not a word."

"You think this is our guy?" Nicholas said.

"I hope not," I said.

"Why?"

"Because he's my lawyer. We're going to court for the adoption hearing tomorrow afternoon."

Nicholas swore into the phone.

"Yeah," I said. "My sentiments exactly."

We decided India should drive Ophelia to the station. India gave me an acid look when I said I would take Kade, but she pulled herself up and said, "At least that way we'll be sure he doesn't skip town."

"She thinks I did it," Kade said when they were gone. He studied my face. "Do you?"

"I don't know what to think. My gut tells me you'd have to be a complete narcissist to rape one of our women and then hang out here." I pressed my palms against my face. "But why would she pull you out of thin air?"

"She said I looked like the silhouette."

Chief shook his head. "Half the male population looks like that silhouette. Kent even told us it wouldn't do much good. It definitely wouldn't hold up in court."

Panic seized Kade's face.

"It won't go that far if you just keep your cool," Chief said. "One thing they're going to ask you is whether you have an alibi for that night. Where were you?"

"When was it?"

"March seventeenth," I said. "It was a Saturday. Check your phone. You've got everything in there."

"Do it on the way," Chief said. He glared at his leg. "I wish they'd question you here. Listen, if it even looks like they're trying to corner you, just ask for your attorney. We'll figure it out from there. Like I said, it won't go that far."

Kade nodded and looked at me. "Do you mind if we don't go on the Harley? I don't think I can handle that right now."

"Pull your car up out front," I said. "I'll be right there."

He left like a truant schoolboy. The air of self-assurance had been snuffed out.

"You really think it'll go nowhere?" I said to Chief.

"I do, and I'll tell you why if you promise not to blow a gasket. You need to be prepared for this anyway."

"You're going to say they'll never believe the hooker over the lawyer."

"You aren't going to help either one of them if you fight that battle tonight. We'll get to it. Just not now."

He was right, of course. Chief-right, and judging from the settling of the confusion in my chest, God-right.

"Call me if you need me," he said.

I nodded, but we couldn't look at each other. We'd driven a wedge between us, and I didn't have time to knock it out.

When Kade and I got to the station, after a silent ride, Nicholas Kent told us Detective Kylie was already questioning Ophelia. India was pacing a trench in the hallway with her pumps, but she stopped when she saw us. She glared at Kade until he took a seat several feet away and sat with his head in his hands.

India still towed me down the hall and even then spoke in a whisper. "Now, honey, I know you're right fond of that boy and he's been wonderful and all that, but I do not see how you can defend him. Your loyalty is to the women in this ministry."

"My loyalty is to the truth," I said. "And we don't know what that is yet."

"Don't include me in that we." India's eyes flashed. "I have spent the last ten days sequestered with that child. I've stayed up till all hours listening to her story, and spent the rest of the night wishing I hadn't because it's so horrible. I've taken her to work with me because I was afraid to leave her alone with her own thoughts. I've held her head while she had the dry heaves over the commode, trying to get rid of all that mess inside of her."

"I know how it goes," I said. "I've done it with all of them."

"Then you'll believe me when I say I *know* her. I would be able to tell if she was making up a story, and she is not."

"I didn't say she was."

India spread her hand on her chest. "Then you think he did it."

"No, I think she believes he did it."

India blew out exasperated air.

"I'm sorry, something just isn't right about this," I said. "That's why we're here, so maybe somebody objective can sort through and figure out what that is."

India floated her arms into a fold. It occurred to me how jarring her elegance was in this block-wall place. "You do not seriously think that we're going to find somebody objective here."

"I know that's a problem, but Chief says if we don't go through the proper channels …"

"All right. But I just want you to stick this right in the center of your mind: If Ophelia thinks for a minute that you don't believe she's telling the truth, it will break her heart in twenty-five places. That girl thinks you hung the moon. You and this ministry are all that's holding her together right now. Without that support, she's completely lost."

"Of course we're going to support her, India," I said. "Her. Even if what she says about Kade turns out to be a mistake."

Her eyes narrowed. "And what about him? Are we going to support him if he's the one who's made a mistake?"

"Miss Angel!"

Ophelia stumbled toward us, hands over her face, and flew into my chest. I could see how her sobs could be mistaken for those dry heaves India talked about.

"What happened, darlin'?" India said. "Honey, were they rude to you?"

Ophelia shook her head against my jacket.

"What did they say?"

"Do you just need to cry for a minute?" I said.

Ophelia pulled herself back and looked at both of us, eyes bitter. "They said, 'Thank you for coming in.'"

India drew Ophelia into her arms and raised her eyebrows at me over the top of Ophelia's head. Chief had been right to warn me. I did want to blow a gasket.

"You go on home with India," I said. "I'll take care of it."

Ophelia grabbed my wrist with a clammy hand. "Thank you for standing by me."

"You don't have to th—"

"You are, aren't you?" Ophelia's face went wild, as if she were seeing the rape all over again. "Why don't I feel that?"

"Come on, darlin'," India said. "You're so worn out you can't think straight."

She tucked Ophelia under her arm and half-carried her down the hall without a glance back at me. I waited until they were gone before I went to the empty chair where I'd left Kade and sat in it until Nicholas Kent joined me.

"He's in with Detective Kylie," he said. "I don't think this is going to amount to anything."

"I wonder if he has an alibi," I said. My voice fell flat against the cement floor.

"Sorry?"

"He was supposed to check his calendar on the way here to see where he was the night of the rape, but he ended up driving, so he didn't do it then."

"Most people don't have anything airtight. Look how much

time we all spend doing things nobody sees us doing, or remembers they've seen us."

I cocked my head at him. "You don't want him to be guilty."

"I'm trying to be totally unbiased."

"I hope somebody can be."

"I've got some other news for you. It's not that helpful either, but …"

"Tell me anyway."

"I finally got to one of those officers who questioned the Sisters."

I straightened. "And?"

"He'd had a few beers when we talked so I'm not sure how accurate it is, but he said they didn't come up with the idea on their own. Somebody outside the department paid them."

"Let me guess. He wouldn't tell you who."

Nicholas checked out his thumbnail.

"Are you serious? He told you?"

"He told me what he knew. He said they met with the guy at the Waffle House out on US 1. The guy tried to be all clandestine—hat pulled down over his face, sunglasses in the middle of the dang night. Sorry. I know you don't like swearing."

"So was the guy young? Old? White?"

"White guy. Probably in his late twenties, early thirties. Maybe older. He looked like he was in good shape, which can make a person look younger. The hands usually give it away, but he was wearing gloves."

"What about his voice?"

"He said the guy mumbled." Nicholas gave a disgusted grunt. "I think they were so interested in the money, they weren't paying that much attention. It could've been a woman and they wouldn't have noticed."

"Okay," I said, "so, correct me if I'm wrong, but the only person who would pay cops to mess with a rape investigation would be the rapist himself. Right?"

"Or somebody who didn't want to see the rapist get caught, which is just as much of a crime in my opinion."

Yeah. I really liked this kid. I didn't tell him this time because his face was already frustration-blotchy.

"What's wrong?" I said.

"I hate it that guys who call themselves officers of the law would get mixed up in something like this. Thing is, I can't do anything about it. The officer I talked to said he'd deny it if I said anything, and even if I did, he told me when he was about wasted. IA would laugh in my face."

"Internal Affairs," I said.

"Yeah."

I had a few internal affairs of my own, and they weren't laughing. They were squeezing the life out of me. I crossed my arms over my stomach and tried to rock unobtrusively.

"You okay?" Nicholas said.

A door opened down the hall and Kade came out and started toward us. Detective Kylie walked with him, one hand in his pocket, the other gesturing like he was describing a basketball game. There were no handcuffs in the mix.

"Take him home and pour him a drink," Kylie said to me. He clapped Kade on the shoulder. "Don't lose any sleep over this. Just keep in mind what I told you."

"What did he tell you?" I said when both Kylie and Nicholas Kent were gone.

Kade went for the door, and I had to practically run to keep up with him.

"You don't want to know what he told me."

"Was it along the lines of 'she's just a hooker and this will never stick'?"

"Almost word for word."

Kade didn't speak again until we were out on the steps. He seemed to take no notice of the drizzle that collected on his shoulders. "He actually apologized when he swabbed my cheek for DNA. I doubt the sample will ever make it to the lab."

"And if it does?" I said.

I held my breath.

"I don't blame you for asking that," he said. "You don't even know me. I could be a *serial* rapist for all you know."

That hadn't occurred to me, but I said, "You could be. I don't sense that about you."

Kade searched my face, his usually clear blue eyes cloudy with a chance of imminent showers. My throat tightened.

"What *do* you sense about me? I need to know."

I hugged my arms against the dampness. "You're an honest person who's searching for something he can't name. Something you're not even sure you really want. And sometimes when you get close to it, it scares you half to death so you run off to find something else."

His face was incredulous. "You can sense all that?"

I laughed. "No. I recognize it. I *was* you until about seven years ago."

He turned away so sharply I thought he was going to take off. It took me a minute to realize that he was throwing up over the side of the porch. It was all I could do not to join him.

"You okay?" I said.

"Yeah. I feel like an idiot."

"I'm sure older and wiser people than you have tossed their cookies in front of the police station. I think the older and wiser you are, the more you recognize the need to puke."

"Do you still want me to represent you tomorrow?"

"Yes," I said, without hesitation, without considering how India was going to react or what I was going to say to Ophelia or whether Chief would approve. I never took any of that into consideration when I got the word from God. Why start now?

Kade was still shaken when he dropped me off on Palm Row, but he didn't want to come in. I decided it was probably better for me to face Chief alone anyway.

But, alas, he wasn't alone. Desmond was parked on Chief's bed, and Chief was still in the chair.

"What are you still doing up, Des?" I said.

"We got somethin' to show you." He picked up a drawing from the bed without the usual flourish. It was the one he'd done of Kade.

"Did you make some changes on it?" I said. I looked at Chief, *Did you tell him?* in my eyes.

Didn't have to, was in his.

Of course. How could Desmond have missed Ophelia's screaming? People in Jacksonville probably didn't miss it.

"I didn't make no changes," Desmond said. "Me and Mr. Chief was just comparin' it to this one."

He held up the newspaper with his silhouette on the front page. My heart dove.

"What did you guys decide?" I said.

"We didn't decide nothin'. Pichers don't lie."

He placed the two drawings side by side on the bed. I sat on the edge and forced myself to look at them.

"It's hard to tell," I said, "since one of them's a profile and one's almost head-on."

"That's what we said, right, Mr. Chief?"

The hope in his voice matched mine. But, then, there was the hair—spiky in both—and the nose, strong but proportioned. That described a lot of noses, didn't it?

"What do *you* think?" I said.

"I think if Idda drew that one"—he pointed to the silhouette—"from a real person 'stead of from what Miss Ofeelins told me, we could tell if they was both Cappuccino." He shrugged his bony shoulders. "'Course, if Idda drew that from a real person, we'd know who it was and he'd be in jail."

"That's it," Chief said. "You're going to law school."

"Yeah, well, before that, you have to go to middle school." I gave Desmond a gentle shove. "Get to bed so I don't have to drag you out and throw you under a cold shower tomorrow."

Desmond went all too readily, as if he wanted to get away from this topic. I wished I could have avoided it that easily.

"He came out on his own after you all left," Chief said.

"No doubt he heard the whole thing."

"So did Owen, by the way. He came over to check on us. Said he'd be there tomorrow."

I stood up and fluffed Chief's pillows.

"We need to talk about tomorrow," he said.

"I don't want to go over all that again."

"Is Kade going to be there?"

"Yes," I said. The sheets needed straightening too.

"If the judge gets wind that Kade was even questioned, it might not bode well."

"It'll be what it is, and please, I don't want to talk about objective utterance and my lack of ability to utter it. I'm not changing my mind."

"Unless God changes it for you."

There was nothing scornful in his tone. It was the lack of it that made me stop fluffing and straightening and look at him. His face just waited for an answer, like an attorney assessing his client. And nothing else.

"Let's be clear," I said. "I may lose the power of will to God when he asks me to. But I don't lose the power of mind. I'm not crazy."

The eye lines tightened. "I never said that, Classic."

"You didn't have to," I said. "Come on, I'll help you get in bed."

"I'm not ready yet," he said. Stiffly. "If I doze off here I'll be fine."

I took the stairs two at a time and barely made it to my room before I started to cry. I shouldn't have said it. I should have tried to talk it out with him. But if we were going to come to the same impasse, what was the point? What was the point in prolonging the pain I could hardly bear for one minute?

I curled into a fist on my bed, my back curled hard against the thoughts, against the loss. Against the rolling contractions that were never going to bring new life.

The next morning I dug out the makeup I hadn't used since …
well, from the looks of it, since Mary Kay was a pup, and tried to
disguise the dark circles under my eyes. I hoped the crying bags
would shrink by the afternoon so I wouldn't look hungover in front
of the judge. I pushed aside the fear that it wouldn't make any
difference anyway.

That put me behind in getting Desmond off to school, so I was
simultaneously pouring Cheerios and making him a ham sandwich
when Vickie Rodriguez called. For once I was glad for the interrup-
tion. The thought that this could be the last time I did any of this for
Desmond was waving its ugly hand in my head.

Vickie didn't do much to help.

"Allison?" she said. "Do you lie awake at night thinking of ways
to sabotage this adoption?"

"You've already heard," I said. "Did it make the paper?"

"Having your boyfriend move in with you is not media material.
Mr. Quillon called me with that news."

I set down the mayonnaise jar. "I'm confused."

"Is Jack Ellington living with you right now?"

"He's convalescing here, yes."

"And the two of you never considered how this was going to
look?"

"No. For Pete's sake, Vickie, he's not my boyfriend. I brought
him here so he wouldn't have to go to a rehab facility."

"You know as well as I do Quillon isn't going to present it that
way."

"So what do you want me to do—set him up out on the street real quick before I come on over to the courthouse?"

Her sigh sounded suspiciously like a laugh. Either that, or I was finally snapping.

"We just need to meet before this afternoon, you and Mr. Capelli and myself, so we can figure out how he's going to spin this."

Spin. Was there no end to this debate?

Desmond pushed open the door to the dining room and stuck in his out-of-control head of hair. *Dear God, why didn't you remind me to get him another haircut before today?* Next thing I knew Priscilla Sanborn was going to demand that he be checked for head lice.

"Mr. Chief says take the phone in here," Desmond said, gesturing toward the living room like he was bringing in a 747.

"Allison?" Vickie said.

"Just a minute. I think Chief … Hold on."

I pushed the phone against my chest and let Desmond haul me into the living room. Chief was, indeed, still in the chair, looking drawn and haggard except for the urgency in his eyes.

"I'm talking to Vickie," I whispered. "There's a problem."

"I caught that. Let me talk to her."

I felt like a piece of lead as I handed him the phone. I tried to get ready for, *Don't worry about it. I was already halfway out of here already.*

"I can make other arrangements," he was saying to her. "Yes, today." He looked at me and then at Desmond.

Right. Get the kid out.

Before I turned, hand on Desmond's head, Chief motioned that he was tossing me his cell.

"Get Kade on the phone," he whispered.

"Go brush your teeth," I said to Desmond.

"You know Imma hear every word y'all are sayin'."

"Brush loud," I said.

I tapped Kade's name on the screen and held up my palm to Chief.

"It's a matter of one phone call," he said to Vickie.

"Hey, Chief, what's up?" Kade said.

"It's me," I said.

"Chief okay?"

No, he's losing his mind. Right now he was scribbling something on a piece of paper, which he shoved toward me.

"'Move in with Chief,'" I read out loud. "'This morning.'"

"What the—"

"I get it," I said.

"I don't! What's going on over there?"

I locked eyes with Chief. He nodded as I talked.

"Okay, short version: Quillon's going to try to use Chief staying here to make it look like we're shacking up, so he wants you to move into his place this morning, and then he's going to have somebody transfer him over there. But we have to do it before the trial starts or we'll be committing perjury if we say this all went down when it didn't."

I gave Chief a questioning thumbs-up. He nodded and smiled.

Curse the man. Just—curse him.

"Yes, I'm sure," Chief said to Vickie. "I'll get you an affidavit, signed and notarized ... Do I sound like I'm kidding? ... Because I don't want to be the reason Desmond isn't adopted by Allison." His eyes came back to mine. "I love the kid too much."

Hearing that from halfway down the stairs was the only reason Desmond agreed to "let" Chief go. It wasn't as easy for me. He didn't love me too much.

Hank came over to help with the move, she and Stan, who was the only HOG who was off work. She left him packing up Chief's stuff, yet again, to join me in the kitchen where I was just getting off the phone with the PT people.

"They aren't happy with us," I said.

"They don't have to be," she said. "Have you eaten today?"

"I couldn't eat if you stuffed it down my throat."

"Don't tempt me. Sit down. I'll fix you some toast."

I basically needed a crane to hoist me into the bistro chair. I hadn't even been able to drag myself to the van to take Desmond to school. Owen took him, and promised he'd have him at the court-house by twelve forty-five.

"I wish Desmond didn't have to be subjected to all this," I said.

"He's not going to sit in the courtroom while they give you the third degree, is he?"

"No. He has to wait outside until it's his turn. I don't know why they can't just ask him what he wants and be done with it. Shoot, Hank, I'm going to cry again. All I *do* is cry."

"Cry and writhe in pain."

I looked up at her sharply.

"You think I don't see you bracing yourself like you're in labor?"

My gasp brought her up from the cheese drawer. She closed the fridge and climbed into the other chair.

"Then I'm right," she said.

"It's exactly that, Hank. It feels just like it did—"

"When you gave birth."

I groped through my memories of conversations with Hank across coffee shop tables. "Did I tell you?"

"That you didn't have that abortion? No. Until just now."

I smothered my whole head in my hands. "I can't think about that today, Hank, or I'll die. I swear I'll die. I feel it, physically, all of it—Desmond—Ophelia—Zelda—Kade—"

"Chief."

I felt my face crumple as I looked at the kitchen door.

"That might be the worst of it," she said. "You loving a man who doesn't get God."

"I thought he *was* getting it. What's the point in even talking about this? I have to focus on Desmond."

"This from the woman who can't put herself in little compartments."

I gave her another look.

"Chief talked to me about it," Hank said. "Not in detail. Just his frustration and his fear that this adoption isn't going to work out the way you're approaching it."

"Great. So I get to feel everybody's pain, all the time. This helps how?"

"Is it their pain you're feeling?" Hank said.

"It's more than mine. Who else's pain could it be?"

"I think once you figure that out, you'll have your answer."

"My answer to what?"

She folded her remarkable hands on the table. "To how you can help God get what God wants. That's what you're here for, my precious prophet."

I folded myself over the ache in my womb. "What about what I want?"

Hank didn't answer until I raised my head. "What makes you think they aren't the same thing?" she said.

She slid from the chair and left me in the kitchen alone. With God. Whose waiting pulsed across the room like the heart line, the one I'd watched in Chief's room, hour after hour racing and slowing and jerking with things I couldn't know.

I felt my hands on my lips before I knew I had put them there.

"Is it yours?" I whispered. "Is it your pain?"

Speak through it, Allison, said the throbbing in my forehead and the burning in my throat and the stabbing in my chest. *Speak through it. And you will give birth.*

CHAPTER SIXTEEN

It didn't dawn on me until I was a block from the courthouse that Kade had actually sounded upbeat on the phone that morning. It must have been his version of compartmentalizing. I hoped he was still doing it, after packing up all his belongings from his hotel, dumping them in Chief's garage, and rustling up a notary public, all in the span of four hours.

Whatever compartment he was in, Kade felt confident in it. Or at least it looked that way when he met me on the other side of security, wearing a dark blue suit worthy of a Harvard Law graduate and a red tie that clearly said *bring it on.* In a Massachusetts accent. The self-assurance had snapped back into place.

"You look great," he said.

I had Hank to thank for that. She wasn't any more into clothes and makeup than I was, but she did prevent me from walking out the door in sweats, with mascara running down my face.

"I guess anything would be an improvement over the usual, huh?" I said.

"Stop."

Kade brought me up short, right in the middle of the hallway.

"What's wrong?" I said. "Look, what you see is what you get."

"Stop," he said again. "Stop running yourself down. You have to go in there like the Allison Chamberlain I know."

"There's only one."

"Yeah, the one who takes nothin' offa nobody. Except God." He didn't toss it off like the gratuitous prepositional phrase he thought would get him points.

"That's all you have to do," he said. "That, and trust your lawyers."

"'Lawyers' plural? Do you have Chief on Skype or something?"

"Or something," he said. "Let's go."

He took my elbow so much the way Chief always did—always used to—I bit down on the inside of my cheek to keep from putting my mascara in jeopardy again. That stopped working when we got about halfway down the aisle and I saw Chief at the table in a wheelchair. He looked gaunt and drawn, perhaps like an aging eagle, but he was there, sitting tall, making everything around him fall into place.

"Are you serious?" I whispered to Kade.

"He's not up to taking first chair," he said. "He's here as advisory counsel." I didn't care if he was there as window dressing. My palms stopped sweating. I made it the rest of the way down the aisle.

"Thank you," I said as I took my place beside him.

"Don't thank me. I'm here to bust you if you try to take anybody down."

"Good luck with that."

"If you get the urge to kick somebody's tail, write it on here," he said, and pushed a legal pad toward me.

"Why?" I said.

"Because I don't believe in luck," he said.

I hoped he believed in something, because Priscilla Sanborn swept in then, wearing the usual ankle length tunic over baggy pants, both in a self-righteous shade of gray. As always, she strode as if the waters had parted in expectation of her arrival. There was nothing different from the persona I'd seen before. No trace of anxiety in her hands. No hint of angst in the way she took charge of her table. No indication that this day was even a variation on any other.

It hit me like a punch in the stomach: She didn't care enough to be afraid.

I put my lips next to Kade's. "We have to win this," I said.

"You're going to walk out of here today with your son," he whispered back.

I knew after the first thirty minutes it would take more than a miracle to get a final ruling today. The Honorable Charles Walton Atwell the Third, a man of elongated features, who had possibly been a classmate of Ms. Willa's, spoke at the speed of a snail and felt the need for frequent long, digesting pauses. He spent fifteen minutes telling us all that this was not a trial but a hearing, which he intended to conduct informally but with dignity. Endless pause. Each side would have an opportunity to speak and bring witnesses if they deemed it necessary. However … *interminable* pause … we were all to keep in mind that no crime had been committed and that no one was going to be indicted.

Evidently Mr. Quillon didn't get that memo. His opening statement to the judge began with, "It is our intention, Your Honor, to show that the defendant, Allison Chamberlain—"

"Mr. Quillon." His Honor pulled down on his already lengthy chin with his hand. "There is no defendant…. I only want to hear why your client claims to be the better parental choice for this child."

"That was exactly where I was headed, Your Honor," Quillon said.

Right after he made that U-turn, I scribbled on the pad.

Mr. Quillon escorted Priscilla Sanborn to a chair near the judge's bench. You couldn't really call it a witness stand. She made it look more like a throne.

After he established Priscilla's relationship to Desmond and, for the record, everything about her except her blood type, Mr. Quillon puffed out his chest as if he alone were responsible for this woman's achievements and said, "Ms. Sanborn, please tell His Honor what you do for a living."

"I am the director of a small home for the orphans of deceased AIDS victims in Botswana," she said. "My staff of five and myself are responsible for the well-being of thirty children. We have more than two hundred on our waiting list, many of whom will die from the disease themselves before we have room for them."

Kade scribbled furiously on his own pad. I set my pencil down on the table.

Quillon looked at Judge Atwell as if he were giving him an opportunity to applaud. His Honor just pulled on his chin.

"It sounds like your plate is already rather full, Ms. Sanborn," Quillon said. "But you're willing to take on the care of your nephew as well?"

"Desmond will have a place of his own," she said. "He will not be living with the orphans—"

Kade circled something on his pad.

"—although seeing the work we're doing will certainly build his character. How better to develop integrity in a young man than to have him experience firsthand what it means to sacrifice for the good of the helpless and hopeless?"

I glanced at Kade's legal pad, where he was writing, *And what the *&$%^ do you think AC is doing?*

I put my hand on his. When he looked at me, I shook my head.

"Now, in terms of that sacrifice you spoke of …" Quillon glanced at the judge. His pauses were growing longer than the judge's. "You don't earn a great deal of money in your line of work. How will you support Desmond?"

"I am financially compensated by generous donors," Priscilla said. "It has been my experience that when you open yourself up to the universe in a positive way, the universe opens itself up to you."

Chief handed me my pencil, but I couldn't take my eyes off of Priscilla Sanborn. It was like looking at an alternative brand of myself, done up in a more appealing package, with a far more aggressive marketing plan behind her. It didn't make me hurt. It left me cold.

Kade pushed his pad toward me. *She almost had me with the orphans,* he'd written.

"The bottom line?" Priscilla was saying. "My nephew has spent the first twelve years of his life surrounded by addicts and prostitutes and drug dealers, and, granted, that has been on both the street side and the rehabilitation side. But as the only living member of his family, I see it as my responsibility to see that he spends the next six years at least away from the haunting memories of his past, in a place where he is surrounded by children his own age and mentors who will provide him with a safe, healthy environment."

I broke the pencil in half.

"Do you have reason to believe that his current environment is not healthy and safe?"

"I do."

Judge Atwell was gathering himself up, but Mr. Quillon said quickly. "We are not putting Ms. Chamberlain on trial, Your Honor. But we would be remiss if we did not provide you with a picture of what Desmond Sanborn's life looks like in her care."

Kade stood up, but the judge pressed both hands down in the air and waited for Kade to sit.

"As long as you can do it without attacking Ms. Chamberlain," he said to Quillon.

Mr. Quillon selected a regretful expression and put it on. "Sadly, Your Honor, we won't have to say a word."

He moved solemnly to the table and picked up a brown envelope. The I-hate-to-have-to-do-this look was still on his face, but his eager hands betrayed him. He was barely containing his glee as he slid a stack of photographs from the envelope and stepped up to the bench.

What is THAT? I wrote with the now-stubby end of my pencil.

Kade scrawled a question mark and leaned forward to take the set Mr. Quillon offered him. My heart went into a slow, excruciating fall as Kade passed them to me one by one.

Desmond sitting on the porch at the Monk's Vineyard, sipping what looked like a glass of champagne.

Desmond chatting at that same location with a barely clad Ophelia.

Desmond coming out of the hospital with Hank—she in leathers, he in a sling. Desmond on the beach, alone except for the two figures in the shadows, on the verge of a kiss. Chief and me.

These weren't taken from the window of a Mercury Sable. Or caught by luck at random times. Someone had to have watched us constantly to get these pictures. My skin crawled right up my spine.

Quillon gave a theatrical sigh. "A picture is worth a thousand words, isn't it, Your Honor?"

"That may be so.... But I am going to give Miss Chamberlain a chance to use some words when it's her turn. Anything else?"

"I think that pretty much says it all," Quillon said.

"Mr. Capelli, do you have any questions for Ms. Sanborn?"

I tapped *She almost had me at the orphans* on his legal pad and frowned at him.

"Trust me," he whispered.

A deluge of what-were-you-thinking? flooded over me. He was too young. His finesse was too shallow and his fervency too deep. I looked at Chief with what I knew was panic in my eyes. He picked up my pencil stub and wrote, *I think I know where he's going.*

"One question, Ms. Sanborn," Kade said. "You indicated that some of the orphans you take care of suffer from the AIDS virus themselves."

"That's correct," she said.

"So, I'm sure you have a way of ensuring that Desmond doesn't become infected as well."

"Desmond won't be coming into contact with the children at the center."

"I'm sorry, I must have heard you wrong." Kade consulted his pad. "No, I think you said Desmond would be surrounded by children his own age."

"Not those children."

Kade waited for her to go on, but she simply gave him an impassive stare.

"Then … to which children are you referring?" he said.

For the first time, her gaze wavered as she glanced at Mr. Quillon.

"Do you mean the children at the school he'll be attending?" Kade said.

"Yes."

"In Botswana."

"No."

The formerly loquacious woman had become verbally anorexic. I sat up uneasily.

"Where is the school you'd be sending Desmond to, Ms. Sanborn?" Kade said.

"I have already made the arrangements," she said, "with a school near London."

Chief dispensed with the pencil and went straight for my shoulders, pressing me back into the chair I was already coming out of.

"So what you're saying is that you want to take Desmond out of the loving environment he's already in to put him in a boarding school, away from you, in a foreign country …"

"England is hardly a foreign country."

Kade let that sink in. When she jerked her face away, he said, "No more questions, Your Honor."

"I need a recess so I can go throw up," I whispered to him when he returned to the table.

But Judge Atwell was already pulling himself out of a pause. "Is there anyone else we need to hear from, Mr. Quillon?"

"Yes, Your Honor. The Reverend Garrett Howard."

"Do you know this guy?" Kade muttered to me.

"Apparently not," I said.

He motioned for me to make some notes for him, but I couldn't even get my fingers around what was left of the pencil. I could only watch Garry Howard take an oath to tell the truth and hope he knew what the Sam Hill it was.

The white hair was in perfect order, the conservative tie neatly knotted, as Garry rested his hands on the arms of the chair. Then folded them in his lap. Then used them to smooth the unruffled wings. All proof that he was ill at ease. That, and the fact that he had yet to look in my direction.

By the time my heartbeat slowed down, Mr. Quillon had gotten the reverend through the preliminaries and was moving on to his relationship with Ms. Sanborn.

What relationship?

"I had never met her until she came to see me several weeks ago."

"Do you remember the date?" Mr. Quillon said.

"Monday, March nineteenth."

Two days after the footwashing.

"Why did she seek you out?"

"She wanted to talk to me about Allison Chamberlain."

"Why you?"

"I am—was—Allison's spiritual mentor."

That was stretching it.

"Past tense?" Mr. Quillon said, looking for all the world like he didn't already know.

"Allison has drifted from the church in the last several months."

"Several. Would that be two, three … ?"

"Four. About the time she took in the boy."

"Desmond."

"Right. And his mother, who was a prostitute and a drug addict. And may I just say that I applaud Alison for doing that. She has a very big heart. She's the soul of compassion."

Mr. Quillon's eyebrows lifted on cue. "I sense some hesitation there, Reverend."

I didn't sense any hesitation. I sensed a script.

"It's just that Allison's compassion has become somewhat misguided."

"In what way?"

The Reverend Garry closed his eyes.

"This is difficult, I know," Quillon said.

Quillon's voice was grounds for losing my breakfast. But Garry's torment was all too real. When he opened his eyes, they were red-rimmed and wet.

"It *is* difficult to see a beautiful soul like hers taken over by pride."

"Meaning?"

"She calls herself a prophet."

I went cold.

"A prophet. She claims to be able to tell the future, then?"

"No, no. She tells what's wrong with the present."

Mr. Quillon leaned casually against the table. I wondered how long they'd rehearsed this scene. I might have been amused if I weren't seething.

"Is that such a bad thing?" he said. "There are certainly plenty of things wrong with the present. Political pundits regale us with that information on a daily basis."

"There would be nothing wrong with it," Garry said. He worked his lips like his mouth had gone sour.

"If?" Mr. Quillon said.

"If she didn't claim she was getting it all directly from God."

The words came out in an anguished rush. Garry put his hand to his mouth, as if their exit had burned his lips. I felt Chief watching me for signs of eruption, but I had no desire to explode. Garry had just spoken the truth.

"As a pastor, Reverend Howard, don't you hear God's voice?"

"I get a sense of His will, yes," Garry said. "But the things Allison claims she hears from God are false teaching."

I gripped the edge of the table.

"God doesn't tell people to purchase motorcycles and pretend to be Jesus and wash people's feet in her front yard. He doesn't tell them to stand in the way of the work of the church—" His voice broke and he shook his head. "I'm sorry. It's just very disturbing for me to see one of my own use God's name to raise herself up. The Bible says 'beware of false prophets, who come to you in sheep's clothing but inwardly are ravenous wolves.'" Garry stiffened his face. "That is all I want to say about this. May I be excused?"

That was clearly not in the script. Mr. Quillon had to scramble for his next line.

"Of course, Reverend. You've been a great help. Thank you."

"Just a moment," Judge Atwell said. "Mr. Kade, any questions?'

"I do have one," Kade said.

He got up without conferring with me. I couldn't have spoken anyway. I was smothered in pain.

"Reverend Howard, are you familiar with the Reverend William Sloane Coffin?"

Garry blinked himself into focus. "Of course. He marched with Dr. King. I don't agree with some of his politics, but he was a godly man."

"Would you agree with this statement of Reverend Coffin's?" Kade said. "He said, 'Some Christians use the Bible in the same way a drunk uses a lamp post: more for support than illumination.'"

Chief's shoulders shook. I covered my mouth, just in case I was still capable of a grin.

"What exactly am I supposed to do with that?" Garry said.

"Nothing, sir," Kade said. "I have no further questions."

As Garry made a hurried exit, Judge Atwell turned his long-and-growing-longer face to me. "I'm a little concerned about this, Miss Chamberlain.... I've heard mixed reviews about your work, but I personally haven't seen anything wrong with it. Anybody who can turn a drug addict around is fine by me, no matter how you do it ... however ..."

What? For Pete's sake, what "however" could there be?

"Hearing voices and claiming to be the next best thing to God ... I find that somewhat disturbing when I'm considering granting you an adoption."

"Your Honor," Kade said.

"Let me finish."

And then, of course, he didn't, for another fifteen seconds, while I fought back a scream.

"The rest of this—these photos, the child's current environment— that's all easily explained, I'm sure. I'm not worried about that....

But this … I'm going to want a full explanation when we reconvene tomorrow morning. Bring in witnesses, bring in a psychologist, whatever you see fit.… But if you're going to convince me that this child belongs with you, Miss Chamberlain, then you'd better make me believe you are of sound mind. Bailiff—next case?"

"We'll talk outside," Kade murmured to me.

That was optimistic. I wasn't sure I could utter a word at that point.

We wheeled Chief to a corner down the hall and stood in a knot with our backs to the rest of the courthouse world.

"Here's what I'm thinking," Kade said, "because I don't get the sense that this judge is religious."

Chief nodded him on.

"We're not going to convince him that *anybody* hears God, and I don't see Allison denying it."

"Can we not talk about me like I'm not here?" I said.

"Sorry. Look, I don't want to put you up there and ask you if God talks to you because you'll have to say yes."

"Where are you going with this, son?" Chief said.

Kade consulted the ceiling. "Okay, I'm just going to be blunt. We present it as, 'She may be a wacko, but she's a good wacko.'"

Chief was already reaching for me, but I eluded his grasp and put myself in front of Kade. Right in front, so I could see straight through those blue eyes.

"Do you believe in me?" I said.

"Look—"

"Just answer the question: Do you believe in me, in what I stand for, in who I am?"

I didn't wait for the words. I was looking for what his eyes had to say.

They didn't flinch.

"Yes," he said. "The same way you believe in me. Without proof."

"Good answer," I said. "Because there *is* no proof. There's only my word. If you can't work with that, then you can't represent Desmond and me."

I heard someone else step up behind us.

"Nick," Chief said.

"Mr. Ellington."

I pulled away from Kade and leaned against the wall.

"You got a minute?" Nicholas said to him.

"Does he need his lawyer present?" Chief said.

Nicholas shook his head, and Chief nodded for Kade to follow him. I waited until they were gone before I let myself cave, just a little.

"There is one alternative, Classic," Chief said.

"What?" I said.

"It depends on how much you're willing to give up for Desmond."

"I'd give up anything, you know that. I can't just let her take him off to freakin' *London* and drop him off!"

"What about your job?"

"With Sacrament House?"

"No," he said. "With God. Would you give up your place as prophet?"

I stared at him. "What are you suggesting?"

"I'm not suggesting anything. I'm asking you the question you need to ask yourself between now and tomorrow. And while you're at it, you probably ought to ask God."

I didn't blurt out the automatic answer. There was a check in my soul, a catch in my heartbeat.

"That's what it's going to come down to, Classic," he said. "And we both know it."

Kade rejoined us, hands jammed into his pockets. My mind jumped back to him.

"What happened?" I said. "Was that about Ophelia?"

"They did a PCR-based test on my DNA. It wasn't a match."

"Of course it wasn't," I said. "Now I have to deal with her some-how, but I'm not even relieved, y'know. I knew—"

I couldn't finish the sentence. Kade was very clearly struggling with something.

"I'm sure he told you PCR isn't conclusive," Chief said. "But what it *can* do is rule you out." He leveled his eyes at Kade. "Take a little time to shake it off. Use my workout equipment if you want. But then you and I have work to do."

"What do you want me to do?" I said.

Chief turned his gaze on me. "Whatever you need to, Classic."

Hank met me downstairs with Desmond in tow. He was more than a little disgruntled that he'd gotten "all dressed up like a preppy" only to hang out in the lobby.

"We didn't get to your part," I said.

Hank didn't ask me any questions, which meant I was wearing my angst all over my face.

"We'll talk tonight," Hank said as we split off at the corner of St. George and King so I could get ice cream for Desmond.

"What's tonight?" I said.

"Maundy Thursday at Sacrament House," she said. "Six o'clock."

I wasn't sure I could handle even my Sisters in the shape I was in. Especially Ophelia, who was now going to be faced with the fact that her accusation had been unintentionally false. Maybe Ophelia wasn't the one I was really worried about. Maybe it was India.

But Desmond and I showed up at the House at six, in the van because he still wouldn't get on Chief's bike. On the way, he didn't ask me any questions about my day in court, and I decided that was about more than him not wanting me to go off about the whole thing. When we pulled up to the curb, I said, "Okay, so here's what happened today, and I promise not to blow—"

"I don't wanna know," he said.

The pain in those four words shredded me. Was this how God felt all the time, watching us make such a mess out of things? Was that what I was supposed to tell the judge, that I not only heard him, but I felt pain, too? I might as well put Desmond on a plane to London right now.

"I do got one question."

I pulled myself back and took a breath. "Go for it."

"We gon' be talkin' to God tonight?"

"Probably." I steeled myself for the usual list of excuses.

But he considered the windshield for so long I felt like I was in a car with Judge Atwell. Finally, he said, "You think God gonna swoop down and work it out so that Prissy woman don't take me away somewhere you can't find me?"

I turned off the ignition.

"That's what Mr. Chief said he *don't* believe. He said God wasn't gon' put words in your mouth to keep her from takin' me. So who I'm s'posed to believe, Big Al? Him or you?"

I rubbed my palms on the steering wheel. Now I knew why Atwell let so much silence fall.

If you want the right ones to come out, God, now would be a good time to put them in my mouth.

"If you don't even know, then why we goin' in there to eat that bread and all?" Desmond's voice rose with his precious Adam's apple. "I don't even know—"

"Okay, here's the deal," I said. "You can believe both of us, Chief *and* me."

"How Imma do that when y'all sayin' two different things?"

"We're not," I said. "*I'm* saying we need to talk to God and listen to what God's telling us. Chief's saying God isn't going to do it all *for* us, God's not going to swoop down like a fairy godmother."

"Oh, I *know* God ain't no fairy."

"Chief's right about that. That's why I listen for God to show me what to do, so I don't mess up when I'm doing it."

"What about them words comin' out yo mouth?"

"Sometimes they do and sometimes they don't," I said. "Chief's nervous that they won't come out when I need them. He wants to have a backup plan."

"What is it?"

"What is what?"

"His backup plan."

I closed my eyes. *There is one alternative, Classic. It depends on how much you're willing to give up for Desmond.*

"You don't like that plan, do ya?" Desmond said.

"No, pal, I don't," I said. "But I might not have a choice."

He gave the windshield another deep survey. I got the feeling his problems with God weren't solved.

"We better go in," I said. "You don't have to participate, Des. Just be with the people who love you."

I got out of the van before my face could betray me.

There were more people who loved him, and me, in the House than I was expecting. Besides Hank and the Sisters, including Zelda, Ophelia, and India, Bonner was there, and Liz Doyle. Yeah, I always thought those two should get together. She was looking less frazzled than I'd ever seen her.

"We ready for y'all," Mercedes said from the doorway.

The table had been moved out and another, lower one, moved in with the fresh bread and the juice in its pottery chalice and the snowy white linens ready to catch the crumbs and drops of our ritual. Everyone, including a reluctant Desmond, was gathered around it on pillows on the floor. All except Zelda. She was on her knees next to a big pitcher and a white porcelain bowl.

At last, Zelda.

In some ways she looked very much as she had the day she left Sacrament House. Her hair was still forced into a cruel ponytail that pulled her eyes back to her temples. Her skin was still a jailhouse pale that wasn't all that different from her former drug-induced pallor. And the bones in her wrists still protruded like dresser-drawer knobs.

But her eyes were someone else's. Someone who had hope.

"I done missed the big footwashin', Miss Angel," she said. "But my Sisters and Miss Liz been washin' mine all week."

Liz squeezed my arm, exuding heat she couldn't contain.

"But they tol' me only one person didn't get they feet washed." Zelda's look was wide. Unslitted. "And that's you. So if you'll let me, I'd like to wash them now."

Some of the pain eased from me, leaving just the right space for me to say, "I would be honored."

So my feet were washed by the woman who'd stood in the muck of West King Street and slashed my face with her desperate claws. The one who had slammed my head into hers and spit at my back because I made her think of God. The woman who taught me I wasn't the only one who could heal people.

And that same night I shared in the symbolic body and blood of the one who washed everybody's feet, all the time. I shared it with everybody, except young Ophelia. She stood back while we partook in the reenactment of the Last Supper. She wouldn't even look into my eyes when I offered her the cup. But I could feel her pain. God's pain.

India, on the other hand, showed me all of her pain. She caught up to me when Desmond and I were walking down the front walk at the end of the evening. Her face was drawn so tight, no amount of elegance could smooth it over.

I handed Desmond the keys. "Wait for me in the van, okay? And do *not* start it up, or you'll never see another Oreo for the rest of your life."

India watched until he was out of earshot, though for Desmond that could mean Miami Beach.

"What am I supposed to *do* now, Allison?" she said. She curved over her folded arms. "Hank told me about the DNA, and I tried to break it gently to Ophelia, but she just fell completely apart. She still says she's telling the truth and she doesn't see how she can stay now."

"Oh, India, no," I said. "We can't let her go. Do you want me to talk to her?"

"No—no, no." India brushed her hand against my cheek. "I don't want to hurt your feelings, honey, but you are the last person she wants to talk to. She's convinced you think she's a liar. And here's what I've been thinking. Just because we know it wasn't your Kade, that doesn't mean the real rapist isn't still out there. Are we going to stop looking now?"

I shook my head firmly. "Definitely not. Nicholas Kent is still on it, although without more information, he's sort of at a dead end."

I thought of the officers on the take, but I didn't say anything. India probably wouldn't have heard it anyway. Her face was a wreath of grief.

"How do you do this all the time, Allison?" she said. "I feel like it's happening to me. I don't know if I can take it."

"Okay, look." I curled my fingers around her wrists and pulled her closer to me. "This is Ophelia's pain, so don't take it on. Just let it speak to you."

"I don't understand."

I wasn't sure I did either, but I let it unfold the rest of the way.

"This isn't going to end for her until she gets it all out. You said it yourself—she gets the dry heaves, she wants it out of there so bad."

"Right …"

"I think those memories are in there. They didn't find any trace of drugs in her body the night of the rape, and her blood alcohol content was only point zero eight. I don't think it's that she can't remember what happened. I think she just doesn't want to because it's too painful."

"So you want me to try to get her to go in there and pull it up?" India put her hand to her throat. "What if she can't handle that?"

"Don't do it alone. Get Hank to be there, or Nita. I would, but—"

"No, no—honey, you have enough going on. We'll take care of Ophelia. Oh, Allison." She put her graceful arms around my neck. "I love you. I don't understand you and I don't know if I ever will, but, honey, I love you."

"I love you," I whispered. I hugged her back and looked over her shoulder at Sacrament House. A lone figure sat just outside the shaft of light from the porch lamp. Ophelia. Still wrapped in God's pain.

And what about your pain? That was the question I asked hours later, after Desmond was in bed and I was on my side porch in the swing, smelling Miz Vernell's gardenias, missing Chief, missing the vision that had seemed so clear to me, missing the certainty that Desmond was going to be mine.

You told me to speak through it and I would give birth. But he's the only son I want.

I pushed the swing harder. *I gave up one son. Please don't make me give this one up too. If there's any other way …*

I couldn't think anymore. Through the screen door I heard Desmond whimper in his sleep. Across the side lawn, Miz Vernell's porch light winked out. She was done observing the crazy lady for the night.

"Maybe I am crazy, Miz V," I said out loud. "Maybe all this pain makes a person do and say crazy, crazy things."

Someone sighed. The long, slow breath was almost out before I realized the someone was me. It left me limp and drowsy on the swing.

"All right, then, God, so be it," I said. "Crazy it is."

CHAPTER SEVENTEEN

When Desmond and I arrived at the courtroom Good Friday morning, there was standing room only in the hallway outside. The first people I picked out of the crowd were the Sisters, who were hard to miss, gathered in a circle holding hands. After I got over the fact that Jasmine, Mercedes, and Sherry were within a mile of anything connected with the judicial system without being in handcuffs, I found Hank, who *wasn't* hard to miss among the HOGs.

"What's going on?" I said.

"Support, Al," she said. "We thought you could use some."

"What are the Sisters doing?"

"Holding a prayer vigil. They've been here since the doors opened."

I felt my face starting to crumple. "Leave it to you to think of that."

"I didn't," she said. "It was Zelda's idea. She said them praying for her at the jail kept her from—how did she put it—"

"Flipping her stuff all the way out?"

"That's it."

There was so much I wanted to say to Zelda. So much I wanted to ask her. Where did she get the stolen car? Did she know Marcus Rydell? Was he the Satan she was talking about? Did he give her the drugs? And why on earth would he do such a thing?

But it wasn't just about that. I wanted to know how it felt to her when she knew God was there. I needed to know that. For Ophelia.

Later, though. For now, it was all about Desmond.

"You know what, Mr. Chief, we got a lot more room here than we do at home. You have got to get you some *bad* pipes on this thing."

Desmond was rolling Chief toward us, making engine sounds en route. I knew he *would* pop a wheelie in this venue if I didn't intervene.

"I'll take over," I said.

"I'm going to sit out with Desmond until they call him," Chief said.

Anxiety lapped at me.

"Kade's got it handled, Classic."

He was Chief-right. Although Kade had bags under his eyes the size of small carry-ons, the eyes themselves were bright when he greeted me at the table.

"Were you up all night?" I said.

"What night?" He glanced at the still vacant judge's bench. "We only have a minute, but I just need to make totally sure you want to go this route."

"Yes," I said. "I know that makes it difficult."

"Big Al," he said. "Step back and watch me work."

He tucked his mischievous grin away as Judge Atwell took the bench. When, the preliminaries had been dispensed with and Kade stood up to speak, he was pure professionalism.

"Are you prepared to convince me that Ms. Chamberlain has the mental stability to raise a child, Mr. Capelli?"

"Yes, sir."

"Then you're going to give me a rational explanation for this prophecy situation."

"No, sir."

Judge Atwell drew his chin toward his chest. "This is not a game, counselor."

"I fully respect the court, Your Honor," Kade said. "I am completely serious."

"Your client claims God speaks to her, tells her what to do. That does not sound like mental stability to me.... That sounds like—"

"She's submitting her will to a higher power?" Kade said. "Because that's what Miss Chamberlain does."

"My concern is what happens if this higher power one day tells her to send the boy back out on the street where she found him."

"Miss Chamberlain gives up the power of the *will*, sir. Not the power of the mind. That is what we hope to show you."

Mr. Quillon made a noise that may have been a laugh. Judge Atwell lowered his chin at him. Quillon's next noise sounded like strangulation.

"I'll hear what you have to say, Mr. Capelli. Just keep in mind that my purpose is to decide what is best for Desmond."

Kade gave him a respectful nod, and called Henrietta D'Angelo to the stand. Once in the chair, Hank set him straight on the name thing, mouth twitching. Kade asked her to explain her relationship with me.

"When I first met Allison, she didn't know she was a prophet." Hank looked at Judge Atwell. "Like you, Your Honor, she considered the possibility that she was hallucinating. But the effect of her paying attention to what she felt was God was so positive, she finally accepted her role."

"So she was reluctant at first."

"She still is at times. Allison is very conscious of being over-whelmed by God, but she's able to respond sanely."

"An example might help," Kade said.

Hank folded her hands in her lap. I relaxed in spite of myself.

"God's Nudge has led Allison into some of the darkest corners in this city. She has seen the women she reaches out to overdose on cocaine and heroin, she's nursed them when they've been beaten and raped, she's held one in her arms in an alley while she died from a gunshot wound. She has suffered shock most of us would crumble under, and yet she heeds the call to effect change. That is what separates her from a psychopath."

Kade nodded his thanks and turned to the judge.

"Do you have any questions, Mr. Quillon?" Judge Atwell said.

"No, Your Honor," Quillon said. "I'm just enjoying the show."

The judge's face came to a severe point at his chest. "There will be none of that here, sir. You will respect the dignity of this court."

"I apologize, Your Honor. I didn't realize that's what we were doing."

Quillon just received a look this time, one that would have cut me in half. It only served to make Quillon adjust his tie. The jackal.

Hank patted my shoulder going by. Kade was announcing our next witness.

"I would like to call Mercedes Phillips."

I startled in the chair as Mercedes made her way to the witness stand. She wore a black skirt that shivered at her knees, and her hands clasped and unclasped inside the cuffs of the white blouse someone had pressed for her. She couldn't possibly have done it herself, not without losing control of the iron from perspiring palms. Hers had to be sweaty; mine were oozing through my slacks on her behalf.

When she'd agreed to tell the truth and sat stiff as a ruler in the chair, she found me with her eyes. I prayed my hands under my chin. She prayed hers back.

Kade spoke softly to her, as if he were taking care not to upset the tenuous balance she was somehow maintaining. "Has Allison Chamberlain ever told you she was a prophet?"

Mercedes shook her head.

"We're going to need you to speak your answers, Miss Phillips," Judge Atwell said. "Just for the record."

She nodded, and then said, almost inaudibly, "No."

I hoped Kade didn't have too many questions. What was he thinking, putting her through this?

"She doesn't talk about her gift of prophecy?" Kade said.

"No. She don't have to. It's not about what she says, it's about what she do."

"Have you ever seen her do anything that you thought was crazy?"

Mercedes rolled her eyes at Kade. "No. I've known me some crazy people in my life, and Miss Angel—Allison—ain't one of them."

"How do you know that?" Kade said.

"If she was one of them crazies think they prophets standin' on the corner wavin' signs sayin' the world gonna end tomorrow, she wouldn't be able to do what she do with us."

Her voice was headed for the courtroom ceiling, and she was wagging her head back and forth. I rested my chin on my hands. Mercedes was taking charge of the room.

"And what is it that she does?" Kade said.

"Miss Angel teach us not to be afraid, not by what she sayin', by her whole attitude in what she doin'." Mercedes slanted forward and planted her hand on her chest. "She can do that because she feel what we feel. I just don't see nothin' crazy 'bout savin people's lives."

Kade smiled at her. "Thank you, Miss Phillips."

Mr. Quillon stood up. "Your Honor, if I may."

My backbone bristled. Chief might regret not being here to hold me back. When Judge Atwell nodded Quillon on, I saw Mercedes set her jaw. I wasn't sure if I was more nervous for her, or for him.

"Just one question," Mr. Quillon said.

He didn't ask if he could call her Mercedes. At least he wasn't a complete moron.

"It's a point of clarification, actually," he said. "Did I hear you refer to Allison Chamberlain as Miss *Angel?*"

"I don't know if that's what you heard, but that's what I said."

"So, she is not only a prophet, but an angel, too?"

Mercedes gave him a look that should have shriveled him inside his Armani suit. "It ain't like she sprouts wings. She just does what angels do—and that's the will a God." Mercedes looked him up and down. "Seem like some other people could take a lesson from that, now."

Mr. Quillon looked at Judge Atwell with mock helplessness. The judge nodded at Mercedes.

"That will be all, Miss Phillips. Thank you for your time."

But it was Kade she looked to for permission to go. When he smiled at her again, I expected her to bolt, and I wouldn't have blamed her. She stood, however, with the grace of the magnificent creature she was and walked out carrying the courtroom dignity she had brought in with her.

I was still gazing at the image when Kade called Desmond's name. My eyes went directly to Priscilla Sanborn.

All morning I'd avoided looking at her. Her face had registered very little of anything the day before, even when she was on the stand, so I hadn't seen the point in trying to read her when Kade or Hank or Mercedes was speaking. Even now she was staring at the wall behind the judge as if all of this were an extreme waste of her time. But I had to see how she reacted when Desmond entered the room.

He came down the aisle with his usual swagger, and although he grinned at Stan and pointed at Rex and gave Erin O'Hare a one-sided high-five, he didn't stop to exchange fist bumps with Ulysses or tackle Liz Doyle with a hug. Chief must have coached him well. Even now Chief followed Desmond down the aisle in his wheelchair, leg stuck out at the boy's behind.

While Kade got Desmond settled and sworn in, I looked again at Priscilla. She was watching Desmond, I had to give her that. And there was something other than disdain on her face. Her head tilted a few degrees, and she drew the penciled-in eyebrows together inquisitively. She had come halfway around the world to rescue this nephew, and the most she displayed was curiosity.

And who was the crazy person here?

Kade was already into his first question. "So, you remember, Desmond, that later on you'll have a chance to tell the judge your feelings about being adopted by Allison Chamberlain."

"I got that," Desmond said. "I *don't* get why I hafta wait, but I get that we ain't goin' there right now."

"Fabulous," Kade said.

Any minute now they were going to be smacking each other in the head and saying, "I love you, bro."

I loved it.

"You're here so you can help us clear something up," Kade said.

"Right. Which is that the judge think Big Al might be crazy, and I'm here to tell him she ain't. Isn't."

"Excuse me, son," Judge Atwell said. "When you say, 'Big Al'— who are you talking about?"

Desmond pointed to me and grinned. "My mama. Miss Allison *Cham*ber*lain*."

The judge looked at me. "Miss Chamberlain, I wonder that you can remember your own name."

"That's easy," Desmond said, looking around the courtroom as if for a vote. "I call her Big Al, Miss Hankenstein just say Al, Sisters call her Miss Angel, and Mr. Chief, he—"

"Thanks, Desmond," Kade said. "So, about Big Al being a prophet. Does that ever scare you?"

"*Scare* me? No. She don't scare nobody don't need scarin'."

"You want to tell me what you mean?"

"She don't even yell at people that's messed up. She just makes 'em feel sorry 'bout theirselves. Makes 'em wanna do better, like clean up they act. It's like she know if they *see* how messed up they are, they gonna turn their self around."

"You ever see that happen at all?" Kade said.

"Yeah, I seen it happen," Desmond said in falsetto. "I seen it just about every day, even in me. " He jabbed his thumb at himself.

"I ain't nothin' like I used to be, all runnin' the streets and sayin' the H-word and the S-word and the—"

"Got it. Thanks."

"But I will tell you what scares me about Big Al, now."

Kade looked wary. This evidently wasn't in the plan.

"What scares me is when she catch me with my sorry hand in the Oreo cookies. She can give you some looks make you want to run under the table *real* quick." He grinned at me. "Jus' kiddin', Big Al. I ain't scared a that neither."

Kade stuck his fist out and Desmond met it with his and started to get out of the chair. Quillon stood up.

"Question, Mr. Quillon?" the judge said.

"Your aunt and I were just wondering, Desmond, how do you feel about Chips Ahoy?"

Desmond gave him the why-do-you-have-two-heads look. Judge Atwell's expression wasn't much different.

"Chips Ahoy," Mr. Quillon said. "The cookie?"

"Yeah?" Desmond said.

"Never mind, son. It was just a joke."

"I don't see nothin' funny 'bout no Chips Ahoy," Desmond said to Kade.

Laugher rippled through the courtroom, and Judge Atwell half-heartedly rapped his gavel. I checked to see if Priscilla Sanborn was capable of humor and found her whispering furiously into Quillon's ear. He straightened and looked at Desmond.

"I know that your mother didn't give you what anybody would call a normal life."

"You talkin' about my first mama," Desmond said.

"All right. That's one way to put it. And the life you have now probably isn't like the life most of your friends have with their families, would you say?"

"I don't know," Desmond said.

"You don't go to your friends' houses to spend the night?"

"You askin' me if my life and Big Al's is normal, right?"

Mr. Quillon smiled so sweetly I wanted to slap him. Just slap him.

"Yes, son, that's what I'm asking."

"Then let me jus' tell you, it's normal for me. And if God was talkin' to you all the time like he is to Big Al, which God obviously is *not,* you wouldn't seem like you was normal neither."

"Your Honor," Quillon said. "What am I supposed to do with that?"

"Don't do anything with it," the judge said. "We'll take a recess for lunch—"

"Can I say one more thing, Mr. Your Honor?"

The courtroom turned unanimous eyes on Desmond.

Judge Atwell gave him the nod.

"If I got to talk to him again"—Desmond pointed to Mr. Quillon—"I would appreciate it if he would stop callin' me son. I ain't his son, and I sure ain't hers." The point was for Priscilla this time. "Only person has the right to call me son is my mama, and that is Big Al." He nodded his wonderful head at the judge. "Thank you."

Judge Atwell covered the smattering of applause with his gavel. "We will reconvene in one hour," he said.

Kade brought Desmond over to the table, where Chief was parked on the other side of me again.

"You were fabulous," I said.

Desmond just shrugged and said, "What are we doin' for lunch?"

"Anybody up for Chips Ahoy?" Chief said.

I pawed around under the table for my purse. We were all behaving as if it was perfectly natural for us to think about food when Desmond's future was dangling over our heads. Or was that just normal for us?

"What does everybody want?" I said.

Kade picked up his briefcase. "Nothing for me. I've got some stuff to do. I'll be back at twelve forty-five."

"One would hope," I said.

Chief had his cell phone in his hand. "I'll order a pizza."

"They deliver here?" Desmond said. "Sweet."

"Actually, the judge would like you to join him for lunch, Desmond."

I looked up at Vickie Rodriguez, who stood at the end of the table, tailored and trim and—wet-eyed?

"Why?" I said. I tried not to sound like I was about to lose it, but if Vickie Rodriguez was crying, we were done.

"It's customary," she said. "He likes to have some time with the ... Desmond, so they can talk things over."

Desmond scowled. "I already said all I got to say."

"Good," Vickie said. "So maybe you'll let him do some of the talking."

"What are we havin' for lunch?"

"Whatever you want."

"Later, y'all," Desmond said and went off placing his order with the bailiff before I could even say good-bye. Every time he left my side now, I ached like it was the last time.

"I'll bring him back when he's done," Vickie said.

"Hey," I said.

She squatted beside me.

"What's with the tears? If there's something wrong, you just need to tell me."

"It just got to me is all. What Desmond said, what they all said. If this doesn't go through, I may quit. I mean it."

"Do you think it will?" I said. "Be honest."

"It all depends."

"On what?"

Vickie looked at me squarely. "On what you say when you get up there."

When she was gone, I turned to Chief.

"I don't want pizza," I said.

"What do you want?"

You.

"I just want to sit here," I said.

He didn't say anything. He just sat there with me.

We were *still* sitting there, the two of us, at 12:58. Owen had already taken Desmond home with him. The courtroom crowd was settled in, and Priscilla and her lawyer had long since returned to their table. Everyone was there but the judge.

And Kade.

"What if he got into an accident?" I said.

"He's not answering his phone," Chief said. "Could be a long line down at security."

"If he doesn't show, can you do it? Can you question me—get me through this?"

Chief pulled his searching gaze from the courtroom doors back to me.

"Who gets you through, Classic?" he said.

"Sorry—"

Kade dropped into the seat next to me. For someone who was breathing like he'd just run from Boston, his face was dead white. I'd seen it like that before, just before he hurled in front of the police station.

"Are you all right?" I said. "What is *wrong,* Kade?"

"Nothing. I have good news—fabulous news."

The courtroom was coming to its feet. Kade pulled me up by the elbow and got his mouth near my ear, eyes on the bench.

"We have a donor. He's buying the Taylor place for Sacrament House."

"What?" I said through my teeth. "Who is it?"

"Anonymous. Shh—"

"Mr. Capelli?"

Kade gave me a downward push toward my chair and straightened his tie. "Yes, Your Honor?"

"I don't know what your plan is, but I'd like to hear from Miss Chamberlain."

"That *is* our plan, Your Honor. Miss Chamberlain is ready."

Miss Chamberlain was so not ready she could barely stand up. If I opened my mouth at that moment, Judge Atwell would not only deny the adoption, he'd have me committed.

Somehow I got to the witness chair. Somehow I was able to state my name. Somehow I managed not to grab Kade Capelli by the necktie and ask him what he was *thinking* telling me that right before I had to take the stand.

"Mr. Capelli, before you begin," Judge Atwell said. "I want to remind you once again that all I am interested in is …"

Whether I can prove that I'm not a nut bar with delusions of grandeur. If not, this entire courtroom was going to watch me disintegrate right before their eyes.

And then I looked at their eyes. George's and Lewis's, on either side of Ms. Willa like a pair of gentleman bookends. The HOGs, out from behind their shades for a whole day so I'd know they had my back. Erin O'Hare's bright, intelligent eyes and Liz Doyle's dewy greens. The ones watching me like frightened deer in the back: the women beaten by the system, who swore they'd never come near a courtroom for anybody, anytime. Not a single pair of eyes said, *You're insane.* They all just waited. Waited for me to—

"Miss Chamberlain."

I turned to the bailiff.

"Do you swear to tell the truth?" he said.

The truth. That was what they were waiting for.

"I absolutely do," I said to them.

"Miss Chamberlain," Kade said.

His face was still like porridge, and his voice was a half step higher than it should have been. I wasn't sure it was me he was seeing.

"You can call me Allison," I said.

Kade stared for a second, until a smile came into his eyes. "Allison," he said. He took a breath. "Can you tell us what happens when you hear from God?"

"I can try," I said, "but it isn't going to make any sense."

Kade's wince was almost imperceptible. Making sense was evidently just what he wanted me to do.

"It isn't like we have deep conversations," I said. "Sometimes I get a Nudge—like someone is physically poking me to get my attention. Sometimes I hear a voice—not exactly hear it, I sense it—I know the words."

The poor kid was blanching again.

"And sometimes," I went on, "it's a feeling—a strong feeling—okay, it's pain. How can I tell you—something happens that gets God in the gut, and it gets me in the gut too."

If Kade had another question in mind, it was now lost in the panic I saw in his eyes.

Thank you, God. How could I wax so eloquent in front of a crowd of strangers, and yet sound like an imbecile when I was fighting for the one person I couldn't live without? Kade looked so miserable, my heart broke for both of us, as India would have said, in twenty-five places.

"Your Honor," someone said.

"Yes, Mr. Ellington."

Chief rolled himself out from behind the table. "May I ask a few questions, as advisory counsel?"

"Please do." Judge Atwell looked at Kade. "Do you mind, Mr. Capelli?"

"Not at all" was a marvelous cover for "If you fix this, Chief, I will give you my firstborn child."

Chief parked his chair just a few feet from me and drilled his eyes into me.

"Miss Chamberlain, can you prove that God is speaking to you?"

"No," I said. "I can't."

The courtroom rustled. Mr. Quillon stared at the back

of Chief's head as if I wasn't the only one whose sanity was in question.

"You can't even take a stab at it?" Chief said.

I stared at him too. Whose side was he on?

And then I saw the lines crinkling around his eyes.

Work with me here, they said.

You got it, mine said.

"Look," I said out loud, "the burden of proof doesn't rest on me. I'm just a witness for God, not his attorney."

"All right, so if you yourself can't even prove it's God you're hearing and feeling and being Nudged by, how do you know it's God?"

"Because if it weren't God, believe me I wouldn't be doing what I'm doing. I couldn't have cared less about the plight of the poor until God sent me down to West King Street on a Harley. I didn't sign up to do any of it. This prophecy thing was not my idea."

"So *you're* convinced," Chief said. "Now convince us. Prophesy for us right now."

"I can't do it on demand. Not someone else's, anyway. It isn't like I'm getting this constant influx of news from above. It's not some divine version of CNN. The messages I get from God are sudden and they're intermittent. They come when God needs them, not when I think *I* need them. They're extraordinary. They're irregular. Why wouldn't someone think I was crazy? You would be crazy *not* to think I was crazy." I moved to the edge of the chair. "But what I think is crazy is seeing all that is sick about our society. About this town. And ignoring it, thinking it'll all go away if we pretend it isn't there or blaming the sickness on the people it's happening to. That is what's crazy, and that is what God won't let me do."

"What if you did ignore it?" Chief said. "Would God strike you down?"

"He wouldn't have to," I said. "I would just go back to being the shriveled sack of nothing I was before." I was almost off the chair now. I had to hold on to its arms to keep from getting to my feet. "I don't go into some mysterious realm. The pain I feel is very real. It orients me to the cruelty and the evil that exists right here in this city, and it forces me say, 'Look at this! Let's do something about it!'"

Chief folded his arms. With his leg extended, he looked like he was sitting in a chaise lounge, enjoying himself immensely.

"You know, Miss Chamberlain, a crazy person doesn't usually know she's crazy. Have you ever considered the fact that you might be deluding yourself into thinking you can really change anything?"

He waited, eyes drilling again, telling me, *This is it, Classic. Take your shot.*

"False prophets and crazy people prophesy out of their own minds," I said. "I prophecy from God's."

It was out now. I'd said it in a court of law, where I had vowed to tell the truth, where if I tried to take it back, I would be thrown in jail. I couldn't take it back. I wouldn't take it back.

Even if it meant I might lose my son.

"Any questions, Mr. Quillon?" Judge Atwell said.

Mr. Quillon stood up and beamed at him. "No, Your Honor. I think Mr. Ellington has done my job for me."

"Thank you, Miss Chamberlain."

I returned to the table, where Kade sat like a rod, his professional veneer barely covering the defeat in his shoulders.

It's all right, I wanted to whisper to him. *I guess I just didn't want you to have to make me hang myself.*

The courtroom held its collective breath as Judge Atwell looked up from his endless pause.

"I know that you would like to have my decision before we adjourn," he said, "… But I can't do that in good conscience, not without more serious contemplation…. And I have another concern."

Something worse than that the adopting applicant is a crazy lady? I studied Clyde Quillon, but his face was quizzical.

"According to young Desmond … He has not spent any significant time with his aunt since he was a small child."

If you could call dropping him off puking at clinic significant.

"I think it's important that we remedy that … Ms. Rodriguez?"

Vickie stood up a few rows back.

"Please arrange for Desmond and Ms. Sanborn to spend a few hours in each other's company this weekend."

Both Kade and Chief pinned my arms to the table.

"Certainly, Your Honor," Vickie said. "And I request that the time be personally supervised by me."

"That would be my recommendation, yes. We will reconvene at nine a.m. on Monday. You will have my ruling then." Judge Atwell lifted his gavel, left another endless ellipsis, and swept his eyes over the room. "Have a happy Easter," he said.

As soon as the judge turned to exit, Vickie was on me before I had a chance to stand up and scream, "Are you *serious?*"

"Don't worry," she said. "I will be there the entire time."

"He's going to throw a fit."

"Good. I'll love reporting that to the judge."

"Excuse me—Ms. Rodriguez?"

At least Quillon didn't call her *Señorita* this time.

"Ms. Sanborn would like to be involved in the arrangements."

I craned my neck to see around him. Priscilla didn't look like she would like to do anything. In fact, she seemed rather put out. I hoped Vickie would put that in her report too.

"Actually, Mr. Quillon," Vickie said, "I will be making those arrangements. Desmond and I will meet Ms. Sanborn for supper at six o'clock." She glanced at me, and I nodded. "I'll call her and let her know where."

Quillon sniffed. "You don't have that planned too? You seem to have no trouble making decisions for everyone."

"That decision is left up to Desmond," Vickie said. "Again, I will call Ms. Sanborn with a location."

There was definitely something to be said for being an ice queen. Vickie gave Quillon a stare so chilly, I thought I saw him shiver before he walked away.

I shivered too. If God felt this kind of fear when he was about to lose one of his children, then I truly did feel what God felt.

I had never been more sure of it.

CHAPTER EIGHTEEN

I had been to Chief's place only a few times before that night, and then just to drop Desmond off for an afternoon of basketball on TV or some other completely boy thing. Desmond always referred to it as their man cave, but it was far from cave-like. Set on a slight rise overlooking Matanzas Bay, it was all windows on the water side, and its inside walls were a vast cream-colored mat for a few well-placed pieces of thoughtful art. A Georgia O'Keeffe print. A Celtic knot of twisted copper. A sepia-toned photograph of a lone Harley rider, leaning into a far-off turn. Chief always said it wasn't homey like my place on Palm Row. But that evening Palm Row felt nothing like home, and so at Chief's invitation, Hank and I went there to come down from the day.

Although how much further down I could go, I wasn't sure. Despite Hank's chicken alfredo and Chief's selection of Coltrane for background and both of their assurances that my testimony had not blown my chances, I was headed for a pit I couldn't stay out of unless I paced Chief's floor without stopping.

"What if she tries to kidnap him?" I said.

Hank gave a grunt. "Right under George and Lewis's noses. I have a life-sized picture of that happening. I have to say, I love that Desmond picked the Monk's Vineyard for this little rendez-vous."

"I'm serious. For all we know they could be on a plane for Gaborone right now."

"Vickie Rodriguez is with them," Chief said.

"Have you *met* the woman? Priscilla could take her out and keep moving."

"She's not so tough. One little"—Hank flicked her index finger off of her thumb—"and that glass case she's in would implode." She seated herself on the floor in front of the coffee table. "My theory is Priscilla's reinvented herself into whatever she thinks is the complete opposite of where she came from. Trouble is she's working from the outside in, so she hasn't even touched what's really going on with her."

"I can't get a feel for what that is," I said. "The only time she gave me anything at all was when she was talking about the AIDS orphans. I think that was real. But I don't sense pain in *her,* and that's what scares me." I threw my hands up. "Listen to me: If a person's angst isn't sending me into labor, I think *she's* messed up." I picked up my pace past the desk where Chief sat, files stacked around his laptop.

"You're going to need sustenance if you hope to wear a dent in that tile, Allison," Hank said. "Eat. Both of you. What—did I cook this for myself?"

Chief didn't look up.

Hank grunted. "Am I *talking* to myself?"

I paused at the coffee table but ignored the pasta-filled fork she pointed at me.

"Where's Kade?" I said. "He took off out of there this afternoon, with *no* explanation about this anonymous donor."

"He said he had to go follow up," Chief said. "I asked Bonner to see what he could find out from Dexter Taylor." He picked up the reading glasses I seldom saw him wear. "I assume you're all right with me doing that?"

"Why wouldn't I be?" I said.

Uh, because that honkin' huge wedge we drove between us is still there? You think that could be it?

"What are you doing over there anyway, Chief?" Hank said. "It's Friday night and you're shuffling papers."

"Got a lot to catch up on. I had my secretary print out some e-mails, little things I was handling before the accident. I can only remember about half of—"

He peered through the glasses at a slip of paper, and I saw his eyes startle.

"What?" I said.

"License plate I must've asked a buddy of mine to run … Mercury Sable registered to—"

"That's the car Priscilla was driving," I said, "when she was stalking us."

"This says it's registered to a rental company."

The hair stood up on my arm. "It isn't Hertz, is it?"

"No. Reliable Rentals. Small private company, it looks like." Chief clicked the keys on the laptop.

"It would have to be a rental," Hank said, "unless she brought it over on a ship from Capetown. Has it struck anybody else that for somebody who says she basically works *pro bono,* she has a lot of cash to throw around? Did I tell you Joe and I saw her at O. C.'s the other night? Of course, Quillon was with her—"

"Whoa."

"What 'whoa'?" I said.

Chief smeared his hand across his mouth. "It *is* a private company. Subsidiary of Chamberlain Enterprises."

Hank tugged at my pant leg. "Don't go postal, Al. Anybody can probably rent from them, and Priscilla does like the best."

"No," Chief said, "their cars are not available to the public. They can be rented by employees of CE only. They probably keep it as a separate company because ... Forget that." Chief took off the glasses and looked up at me. "This doesn't necessarily mean that Troy Irwin is somehow involved in this."

"Why would he be?" Hank said.

I closed my eyes and I was on my porch, thinking I saw something real pass through Troy Irwin's eyes. *I can call Clyde Quillon off. I can make the whole thing disappear. All I want in return is San Luis Street.*

"He is involved," I said.

Chief gnawed at his earpiece and watched me. "Not everything that smells fishy comes out of Troy Irwin's pond."

"This did. He offered to get the adoption suit dropped if I would step back and let him buy up the whole street." I jerked as the last piece slammed into place. "I guarantee you he's behind this donation of the second house. I know it with everything that's in me."

"All right," Chief said. He was using his "do not blow, Allison" voice. "Like I said, I've got Bonner on it."

"I don't care if the Sisters and I have to camp out in tents in the middle of the freakin' street," I said. "We find out he's connected with this in any way and it is *off.*"

"Kade did say there were no strings attached."

"Oh, come *on,* Chief. You know as well as I do wherever Troy's involved, there are strings attached. He's the dadgum St. Augustine puppeteer."

"Not this time."

I didn't know how Kade had managed to get to the entrance from the foyer without us hearing him, but he had obviously heard *us*. His face was devoid of color again, only this time, I didn't feel sorry for him.

"It's him, isn't it, Kade?" I said. "You made a deal with Troy Irwin. He's the anonymous donor."

"Listen—"

"No, *you* listen. How could you be in my presence for five minutes and not know I—will—not—take—anything … *anything* … from that man? Or his company? Or his foundation? How did you miss that?"

"I didn't miss it. I just used it."

"Then go unuse it." I dragged my hand through my hair all the way from my hairline to the back of my neck. "I don't believe you did this."

"You have to let me do this for you," Kade said. "I know I screwed things up in court today and if it hadn't been for Chief—"

"So you want to make up for it by making a deal with the devil?"

"He's *giving* you the house!"

"He never gives anybody anything unless there's something in it for him. You don't know this man, son."

"Okay, fine." Kade's hands went up between us, but I could still see his face, wringing itself out. "I'll go make it right. But I'm telling you the same thing Desmond said in court."

"What?"

"Don't call me son."

He was out the door before any of us could find a breath.

"Somebody cuss for me," I said. "I just completely blew that. But what was he *thinking?*"

"Let him calm down, Classic," Chief said. "Then we'll find out."

"Unh-uh," I said. I snatched up my helmet from the couch. "I'm going to find out now."

"Al," Hank said.

"*What?*"

"Don't get on that bike strung out like this."

I looked at Chief, but he didn't add that it was his bike I was getting on. His eyes understood.

"I'll calm down," I said. "But I just need to go set this straight."

"How will you even know where to find him?" Hank said.

I pretended not to hear her as I went out the front door. I would have had to lie, and so far I'd managed not to do that. I'd just said I was going to go set it straight. I just didn't say with whom.

St. George Street was in high Friday-night gear when I elbowed my way through the rudderless crowd of spring breakers, trying to get to the Vineyard. Across the street, a sax player juiced up the coeds spilling from the Irish pub, and a beefy frat boy with his shirt half off crowed like a rooster on the shoulders of a skinny kid who was too drunk to know he was going to wake up the next day with hairline fractures of L1 and L3.

If I hadn't been so bent on taking Priscilla's head off, I would have found an entire stand-up routine in the image of her and Vickie Rodriguez ordering appetizers on Lewis and Clark's porch with

Sigma Nus bellowing below. But it's hard to find anything amusing when your stomach is splitting open.

I stepped onto the sidewalk in front of the Marble Slab Creamery two doors up and sat down on the far end of a bench occupied on the other end by a passed-out freshman. I couldn't storm into the Vineyard with my teeth bared. Desmond was there, for one thing, and for another, I had to catch Priscilla off guard. With the full armor she wore at all times, that was going to require all the concentration I could pull together.

Besides, I needed a minute to listen. To know exactly who the pain in my gut belonged to. I couldn't act on it if it was anybody's but God's.

The fury stopped pounding in my head. The crushing pressure on my chest drew back as if it were glad to have someone else do its light work. The knot in my left side went slack and waited for further orders. Only the deep ache in my heart went on.

At the other end of the bench, the wasted freshman moaned.

"I hear you, dude," I said.

I let the ache guide me down the street and up the steps of the Vineyard.

Desmond was at his usual table by the railing. Actually he was *on* the railing, holding the other guests captive with some tale. Vickie Rodriguez sat below him, eyes streaming, mouth open in a big long guffaw. Priscilla was across from her, snapping her fingers at George as he maneuvered behind her with a tray held over his head.

She appeared to be asking for the check. George appeared to be finding her invisible. I got between him and the door and pulled his face close to mine.

"I need a quiet place," I said, and jerked my head toward Priscilla.

"Hallway," he said. "I'll have her there in two."

"You're a prince," I said.

I ducked into the hall where Lewis had taken me the day I first met Ophelia. I set aside the image of Kade exiting her room. One ride at a time, as Chief would say.

One pain at a time.

"If you'll just wait right in here, ma'am," I heard George say. "I'll fix that problem with your check."

"I don't understand," Priscilla said.

And then she did. George gave her a gentle push and closed the hallway door behind her. Before she could turn away from me, I said, "You're going to want to hear this."

"This is inappropriate," she said.

"You don't know the half of it," I said.

"The judge will hear about this."

"Oh, I don't think you want that, but I'll let you decide after you hear me out." I paused. "Unless …"

"Unless what?"

It came to me so suddenly I didn't have time to question it.

"Unless this is cutting too far into your time with Desmond. You haven't had that much."

Her penciled eyebrows practically inverted. "I don't appreciate your sarcasm."

"I'm not being sarcastic," I said, and I wasn't. I was only giving her one more chance to show me something. Anything.

"There's obviously some problem," she said. "You might as well tell me what it is."

There it was. Or wasn't. The ache in my soul filled in the rest.

"Troy Irwin isn't quite as careful as he led you to believe," I said.

Only her eyes moved.

"He didn't totally cover his tracks, which I think is what happens when a person thinks he's above the law."

"I have no idea what you are talking about."

"Then let me clarify. Troy contacted you in Africa. The man has connections, I'll grant him that. And he paid your way here, has paid all of your expenses—rental car, attorney. I don't know that picking a lawyer connected to Chamberlain was the wisest choice, but like I said, a person in his position gets careless when he's used to everything going his way."

The adamant denial in the knot of Priscilla's lips was the most emotion she'd ever betrayed to me. I knew I was no longer guessing.

"He's promised to support your program in Botswana," I said. "He'll give you enough to build—what does he like to call it?—a state-of-the-art facility, right there in Gaborone. I have no doubt he convinced you he had only the orphans' best interests at heart, and Desmond's, of course, but did he ever tell you what was really in it for him?"

"There is nothing in it for him."

She tripped too late. I didn't stop to do a victory dance.

"This is all purely to get to me, Priscilla," I said. "To use the one thing he knows I would sacrifice everything for, so I would step aside and let him continue to build his kingdom, especially when I was starting to get support from the same well he was trying to draw from."

"You could have had all the money you needed for *your* program too," she said. "And Desmond as well."

"I'm sorry?"

"You're so smart, you figure it out." She took a step forward. "But I'll lay this part out for you, Miss Chamberlain: You will never get anywhere with this little mission of yours if you pick and choose who you accept money from. I know what kind of man Troy Irwin is, but the dying orphans who are depending on me don't care if he's a *serial* killer."

"What about *my* orphan?" I said. "Was the money for your orphanage the only reason you tried to adopt Desmond? Is that why you had it all planned for him to go to boarding school in London, so if you won you wouldn't have to deal with him?"

"There was no boarding school in London," she said. "We thought you would fold when you heard that and take Troy's deal. We also thought you'd give in when they said you were crazy."

"Well, now I don't have to give in, do I?" I said. "Do you get it? You've committed fraud, perjury—"

"You can't turn me in."

"Are you *serious?*"

"I'll lose tens of thousands of dollars for the orphans. If I go to jail, they'll die."

"You know something? I really think you see it that way."

"Tell Troy you'll take the deal. Keep Desmond, and retract later. I'll have the money in an offshore account by then."

"There is no deal anymore," I said. "For some reason I haven't figured out yet, Troy is buying the property we need and donating it to Sacrament House." I shrugged "He doesn't need you now."

Light shot across her face as the door from the hallway opened. Her eyes were pools of fear.

"Miss Rutabagas say she got to take me home." Desmond stopped and grinned at me. "Hey, Big Al. You got Mr. Chief's bike? I could ride with you. Oh, wait, I don't got my helmet, 'less you brought it—"

He was cut off by Priscilla Sanborn shoving past him to get to the door to the street. Before he could peel himself from the wall, she was swallowed up by the caterwauling crowd on St. George.

"Somethin' I said, Big Al?" Desmond said, and then his grin faded. "She ain't takin' me, is she? I can't go live with her, now, I can't."

"She's not taking you anywhere, Des. We were just having a little … chat."

"Chat nothin'. She look like you kicked her—"

I put my hand up and my phone rang at the same time.

"Where are you?" Chief said. His voice was taut.

"I'm at the Vineyard with Desmond."

"You're not with Kade, then."

"No."

"India just called. He's outside her house, pacing up and down the sidewalk talking to himself. She thinks he might be drunk. Ophelia is hysterical. It's a mess over there."

"I'm on it," I said. "If Hank can meet Vickie Rodriguez at my place and stay with Desmond—"

"I don't wanna go home, Big Al," Desmond said. "There is a *party* goin' down here."

"Why are you with Desmond?" Chief said.

"I've got to go—"

"Classic."

I closed my eyes. "I came to talk to Priscilla."

"You what?"

"I'll explain it to you after I get this thing at India's settled down."

"And then I'm going to explain some things to you."

There was dead air. I didn't know which of us hung up first.

I sent Vickie on her way to Palm Row with Desmond and my house key and a minimum of explanation. I would have been amazed at how little Vickie demanded, if my stomach hadn't been in a square knot. Kade drunk in front of India's. How had he had time to tie one on in the half hour since he left Chief's? He was sober as a judge then. And why India's?

I forced myself not to conjecture as I rode up San Marco Avenue. I had to concentrate on getting there first.

It was my night for going to homes I seldom visited. India had a two-story Spanish villa, and she invited me over at least once every time I saw her, but I seldom went. Troy's parents had lived in this neighborhood. He'd spent his teenage years here, the years when we were always at each other's houses, although we spent more time at mine than his because my parents left us completely alone, and his were always in our faces. It hadn't dawned on me until years later that that was because the Irwins actually gave a rip about *their* child.

The area had changed very little since then. It was still pretentious and closed-off and proud of its stuffy oldness. Even the tile roofs looked down snub noses at those of us who didn't have the social wherewithal to live there. I'd hated it as a kid, and I hated it now.

I turned onto India's block and slowed down. She had the lights on, all of them, and even though I knew she'd done it to reassure Ophelia, they made her house look open-armed and welcoming and full of places at the table. The Irwins would have been uncomfortable in her house. They would have been the misfits.

The lights served another purpose: Kade was fully illuminated, slumped on the sidewalk against a fire hydrant. My engine sound brought his face up to squint into my headlight beam, and he bent his legs to get up. He only got as far as his knees when I lurched the bike to a halt and pulled off my helmet.

"I just want to talk to you," I said. "I promise: no yelling, no 'son.' Okay?"

He nodded and dropped back to his seat. I didn't need a Breathalyzer to know he wasn't drunk. His face was stricken with a pain you couldn't feel unless you saw something all too clearly.

I left my helmet swinging from Chief's handlebar and sat next to Kade on the grass. There was only room for one leaner on the hydrant, so I rested on an elbow.

"You okay?" I said.

"No," he said.

"You want to talk about it?"

"I have to talk to Ophelia, but India won't let me near the front door. She threatened to call the police on me." Kade glanced over his shoulder at the house. "I could hear her screaming in there."

"Ophelia?"

"Yeah."

"Look, India knows I'm here now. Chief called her. So let's just take a few minutes to talk this out and maybe we can come up with a plan."

Kade glowered at the hands flopped over his knees, each picking at the nails of the other. "Why?" he said. "I thought you were done with me."

"I'm sorry. You have to understand, when somebody brings up Troy Irwin, I go ballistic. Inside or out, doesn't matter—something blows."

"You hate him."

"That H-word," I said. "I try not to. There's not much left of the real him to hate, so I guess I just hate what he does."

"I hate him."

That stopped me. I wasn't even aware that Kade knew Troy until an hour ago.

"You have some kind of relationship with him?" I said.

"No. I never wanted to have anything to do with him after I found out what he was. The only reason I went to him was because I wanted to help you."

"I don't get why you thought anything connected with Troy Irwin could help me. There's a lot you don't know—probably don't need to—but he has done things to me—"

"I know."

I shook my head at him. "What on *earth* does this have to do with Ophelia?

"From the DNA test. Kent told me the DNA belongs to a close male relative. Most likely my father."

"Your *father?*" I said. "I thought he was in Boston."

"Not my adopted father." Kade turned his stricken face to me. "My biological father."

My hands went to my mouth.

"When Nick told me the DNA results, I went to the—to Irwin and told him I wouldn't turn him in if he would buy the Taylor place and donate it to Sacrament House, no strings, no nothing. If he left you alone from now on, I'd keep my mouth shut." He rocked forward. "When I saw how you reacted, I realized I was as bad as he was."

"Kade, stop." I pressed my hands to my lips, harder, until my teeth cut into my mouth. "You were born in 1986? Brigham and Women's Hospital?

He nodded. There was none of the surprise that should have sprung into his eyes.

"You know, don't you?" I said. "You know I'm your mother."

"I do," Kade said. "That's why I came to St. Augustine."

CHAPTER NINETEEN

Surely someone had thrown a handful of hot tacks in my face. Surely that was what happened.

Surely this boy had not told me he was my son.

But he was there, Kade was, stunning in the light from India's house, with his clear blue Irwin eyes and his squared-off Chamberlain chin. He made it impossible to believe I hadn't seen it in the spike of his hair, heard it in the husk of his laugh.

Or nailed that chiseled profile, just the way Ophelia had.

"Okay," I said, "we have to put this somewhere for right now. I can't even—"

"Please—"

"No, okay? What about Ophelia? Did you come to tell her?"

"Yeah. I couldn't go through with the Irwin deal."

"All right. So … how were you going to handle it?" My head was spinning to the point of nausea, and I put my hand over my mouth again.

"Are you okay?" Kade said.

I stuck the other hand up and breathed until I was halfway sure I wasn't going to vomit into India's azaleas. "Did you have a plan?" I said.

"No. After I left Chief's I just lost it."

"Well, you'd better find it."

He blinked, hard, where my words stung. They stung me, too.

"Okay," I said. "Ophelia. Focus."

"I am."

"I'm talking about me. "

The whys, the hows, the ifs were dizzying. I closed my eyes and breathed again. The wheel stopped on the what-do-we-do-now.

"All right," I said. "I'll get us in the door and make sure Ophelia's coherent. Then you tell her just the basics, all right? She doesn't need to know you made a deal or any of that."

"I know," he said. "I won't tell her about you."

I stood up and waited for Kade to join me. We walked, strides matching, arms swinging in rhythm. It had been there all along, as close and clear as my own reflection.

India opened the front door for us before we even reached the metal gate.

"Chief called," she said. "I've got her calmed down for the moment, but if she sees him—" She looked at Kade. "Is this really necessary?"

"It is, India," I said. "Trust me."

She showed us into the living room, all Saltillo tile and Italian leather. I looked around a column for Ophelia.

"She went to wash her face," India said.

She gestured Kade to a chair. Distracted as she was, she was still more gracious than I could hope to be on my best day. And this was definitely not my best day.

"You know what's really strange?" India said as she tugged me onto the couch with her. "Just this evening she told me she'd started remembering things."

"About the rape?"

"She said she remembered she was sitting on the steps at Sacrament House and then she was leaving, walking down the front walk, when this man pulled up in a car."

"That came back to her last night," I said, "when we were all there. I thought she was just uncomfortable with *me.* "

"That *is* where it happened," Kade said.

India recoiled. I put my hand on her arm.

"He told me that," Kade said.

"Who? Allison, what is going on?"

"He said he'd had a few drinks and he was ticked off at Allison so he drove over there to … how did he put it? Something about claiming his territory." Kade bit off the words. "Sort of like a dog lifting his leg up and down the street, I guess."

"I am *so* confused," India said. "Who are we talking about?"

"We're talking about Troy Irwin," I said.

India's eyes rounded. "Troy *Ir*win! Mother of Jefferson *Davis!* Why would Troy Irwin commit … *rape?*"

"He didn't plan it," Kade said. "He was half-drunk and mad, and he saw a chance to bring Allison down."

I stopped breathing. Something was kicking me, hard, between my hips, again and again.

I doubled over.

"Allison! Honey, what is it?"

I could feel India's frantic hands on my back.

"Oh my Lord, Kade! Allison—do you need an ambulance?"

I shook my head. I didn't need paramedics. Not to tell me that Troy Irwin wasn't seeing our sweet Ophelia when he violated her.

He was seeing me.

"I'm calling nine-one-one," India said.

I sat up and put my arm across hers. "No, it's okay," I said. "It just got to me. I'm all right. Just go on, Kade."

"You sure?" he said.

"Yes. Go."

He gave me one more reluctant look. "He said he dragged her into the car. You know, assaulted her—"

"Then hit her in the face," India said.

"He knocked her out so she'd stop screaming. And then he dumped her off at Allison's. Told her that was where she belonged." Kade dropped his head and pushed out a long breath.

"Finish it, Kade," I said.

"That's enough, isn't it?"

"Just finish it."

Kade closed his eyes. "He said she belonged there with the rest of the whores."

One last kick in the pelvis. I folded both arms against it and rocked.

"He *told* you all this?" India said to Kade.

"He did."

"I cannot comprehend why he would tell *anybody*, but surely not the person that was being accused. I hope you recorded that conversation."

Kade just looked at her miserably.

"Then it'll just be his word against yours. I don't understand any of this—I just don't."

I stopped rocking. "There's DNA. Now they'll have someone to match it to." I nodded toward India's hallway. "But they'll need probable cause to even test him."

"Oh," India said. "Honey, Ophelia still swears it's Kade, which now I ..." She stopped and squinted at Kade. "Does he favor Troy to you, Allison? I never saw it, but I could see how *she* might. Or am I just imagining that?" India put her hand to her forehead. "I just can't even think right now."

"Miss Angel?"

I turned to the soft Latino voice behind me. Ophelia stood there like a waif. Her dark eyes were bright, almost feverish as she looked at Kade.

"It wasn't him," she said. "I thought it was, but it wasn't."

She came out from the behind the couch and crossed over to him. When she knelt down in front of him, he pulled himself back, but she brought her face close to his. I watched his knuckles whiten on the arms of the chair. Her hair swished between her shoulder blades as she shook her head.

"I couldn't see it before. I was afraid to look close enough, but it's there."

"What's there, honey?" India said. She glanced uneasily at me.

"Miss Angel," Ophelia said. "*That* man didn't have Miss Angel in *his* eyes."

Kade's very skin trembled. He was on an edge I couldn't let him go over, not right now, or I was going over it with him.

"Okay," I said. "India, help us."

"Come here, darlin'," India said.

Ophelia turned from Kade and went to India's open arms. "I'm sorry," she said—again, and yet again. "I'm sorry."

"It was an honest mistake, honey," India kept telling her, until I took hold of Ophelia's chin and tilted it toward me.

"You can fix it," I said. "India said you were remembering things?"

"*Some* things."

"Enough that if you saw the man who hurt you, you would know him now?"

She closed her eyes.

"Ophelia."

"I can see it," she said.

Her face collapsed, as if she were succumbing to the picture behind her eyes.

"We want to send this man to jail," I said, "so he never does this to anyone else. If we're going to do that, we need to take you back to the police."

Ophelia opened her eyes. The right one was still stained yellow, heightening the hysteria that rose in them.

"I can't go through that again. Please. They treated me like … like what I was. Only I'm not that now."

"No you're not," India said. "Allison, really?"

Ophelia started to cry. "They didn't believe me before, Miss Angel. Why will they now?"

"Because," I said, "we're going to do things differently this time."

⚍

Ulysses and Stan met us at the police station with Chief, Ulysses claiming he was sick of hauling Chief's sorry behind all over St. Augustine. Their faces were grim, though, as they left us in the hallway to wait while Chief and Ophelia went into a room to talk to Detective Kylie. Chief insisted on a conference room, not an interrogation room. His client, he said, was the victim, not the suspect.

India wafted up and down the hall a little less frenetically than she had two nights before. Kade and I sat side by side in eggshell silence. It was as if even a thought would crack us.

After twenty minutes, Detective Kylie came for Kade. They were both back out in ten.

"You do realize the can of worms you're opening here, don't you?" he said to me.

"It's not my can," I said.

"But you're wielding the opener." He heaved a man-sigh I couldn't sympathize with. "I'm going to call Mr. Irwin, and I'm going to ask him to come down here to answer a few questions. But you better prepare yourself for the backlash." He set his teeth. "This is going to cost me big time."

"What about what it cost that young woman in there?" I said. "And so help me, if you say it was an occupational hazard—"

"I suggest you take her out for some fresh air, Mr. Capelli," Kylie said, "before she gets herself in trouble."

He gave me one more warning look before he yanked open the conference room door and slammed it behind him.

"Allison?" India said.

"It's okay," I said, "just wait here for Ophelia, would you? I'll be out front if you need me."

Kade followed me through the glass doors to the front steps of the station where we'd shared that magic moment of regurgitation. There wasn't a trace of déjà vu. I was certain this scene had never taken place before, anyplace, anytime.

I sat on the marble balustrade and pulled my jacket tight across my chest and held it there with my arms tucked into me. The air was warm and close, but I was shivering.

Kade sank with his back to me onto the top step. "Do you want me to talk?" he said. "Or do you want me to shut up?"

"I want you to tell me why you lied to me."

"I didn't lie."

"You just didn't tell me the truth, which is the kind of distinction your father makes."

"He is not my father."

I could almost hear his jaw muscles straining.

"That was nasty," I said. "I'm sorry. I don't even know how to *be* right now.... Kade, why didn't you tell me?"

"Because I had to find out if I even wanted to know you. I had to find out if you had a really good reason for giving me up."

"I would have told you if you'd asked me," I said.

He went very still.

"I would have told you there *is* no good reason for giving up your child, unless you're completely incapable of taking care of him, and that didn't apply to me."

"Then why did you?"

"Because I was young and scared and had no support."

"He said you didn't even tell him about me. Was he lying?"

"See, that's the thing about Troy. He only tells enough of the truth to make himself look good, or at least like the injured one. I told him I was pregnant. He told me to get an abortion."

Kade jerked around to look at me.

"That has to hurt," I said. "But if we're going to make any sense out of this, we have to be honest with each other." I leaned back on the column. "Your turn."

"What do you want to know?"

"Why come here now?"

Kade curved over his hands and studied them. "My mom died. My dad barely waited a year before he got married again. Don't get me wrong, He's a great guy. He just couldn't do it alone. And then he was all wrapped up in her and I felt, I don't know, adrift."

I knew about adrift.

"So I went to the adoption agency in Boston. I thought it would be a dead end, but you left instructions, I guess, saying it was okay for them to give me your name if I ever asked."

"Yeah, I did."

"His name was on the original birth certificate too. I googled both of you and got all this stuff, about him, mostly. There were a couple things on you. Newspaper articles."

"Showing me in the best possible light, I'm sure," I said.

"I'd just passed the bar exams. I didn't know what I was going to do next, so I took out all my savings and came down here."

"How long have you been here?"

"Since February twentieth. I spent the first week checking him out. Pretended I was interested in investing so I could talk to his people. Hung out at the 95 Cordova. He eats lunch there about three times a week, cocktails after hours. So yeah, took me, like, two days to get him nailed."

"And then you checked me out by going to a prostitute to get my résumé. The part about wanting to help the same kind of people I do was a nice cover." I pulled away from the column and tilted toward him. "How do I even know *this* explanation is the complete truth?"

"You don't, okay? So why am I even bothering?"

"Because you owe me at least that much," I said.

Kade whipped around. "I owe *you?*"

"Did you have a good childhood?"

"Yeah."

"Parents who were nuts about you? Who instilled confidence in you, helped you believe you could do anything?"

"They were great parents."

"Then I'm sure they made certain you got a great education, taught you how to get along with people. Was *anything* missing in your upbringing?"

"No."

I sat back against the column again. "Then you had a heck of a lot better life than I could've given you."

"Better than the life you're giving Desmond? Because, see, after I got over thinking you were a whack job I didn't want to be related to, I found out you were the kind of crackpot I'd give my right arm to be. Only I couldn't tell you because by that time I'd figured out you were all about the truth, and that you hated Troy Irwin's guts. What was I supposed to do then? Say, 'Hey, I've been posing as your devoted lawyer, but actually, I'm the kid you had with your worst enemy'?"

Something struck me, hard.

"Did you know Troy was behind Priscilla contesting the adoption?" I said.

For the first time he swiveled all the way around to look at me. "Are you serious?"

"Don't lie to me."

"I've done all the lying I'm going to do. What does *he* have to do with it?"

"He instigated it. Paid for it. I wouldn't be surprised if he's already paid off Judge Atwell. Clyde Quillon is definitely on his payroll. Now I know why he could offer to make it all go away if I gave him San Luis Street."

I watched Kade's eyes. If I was going to see the truth, it was going to be there, where he couldn't seem to hide anything now.

At the moment they were staring at the top of the column, as if his files of folders were open up there.

"Then he must have been the one who hired a photographer to follow you and Desmond around. Dude was a freakin' sniper. I thought Quillon did that."

"I think those were taken way before he was hired. I think Troy used them to persuade Priscilla that I was an unfit mother. As if she cared."

"If he doesn't go down for the rape, we can get him on this."

"With what?" I said. "The only way I know all of this is because Priscilla told me, and I had to pry it out of her. You've only scratched the surface of the kind of power Troy Irwin has in this town."

"There's no *way* he's getting by with all this. I can't just let it go. I mean, can you?"

There it was, what I was waiting to see in his eyes. Slowly I shook my head. "No, I can't," I said. "Because I'm just as sickened by it as you are."

Kade chewed at his thumbnail, probably a habit he'd had all his life.

"I wanted to help you," he said. "Especially after you believed that I didn't rape that girl."

"You *were* helping me. You stood up for me in the courtroom. Why did you feel like you had to go to *him?*"

"Because I was screwing it up in the courtroom! If Chief hadn't stepped in, the judge would probably have handed Desmond to that Sanborn woman right then. I can't have conversations with you like the two of you do—where you just look at each other and you know what you just said."

"If you want to beat yourself up, fine," I said. "You're right. I am all about the truth. But did you get the part where I'm also all about forgiveness?"

"Are you?" Kade said. "Are you really? Because I'm not feeling that right now."

The pain went all the way down. I felt it for both of us.

"Aw, now what's this, a little family squabble?"

A shudder went straight through me.

Troy strolled up the walkway, arms swinging, as if he were making his way to his table at the yacht club. Kade rose from the steps and moved to the other side of the portico.

Troy watched him, eyes amused. "I see it's not going well. Our son's a little hard to reason with, Ally."

"There is so much wrong with that statement I don't even know where to start," I said. "So I'm not going to." I jerked my head toward the door. "They're waiting for you inside."

"So I hear."

Troy took the steps at a trot and came to the wide place where I was still sitting. He put one foot on it, inches from my thigh.

"Do you know why I raped that girl?"

I only stared at him for a shocked second before I gathered myself up and shoved my body into his shin. It knocked him only slightly off balance, just long enough for me to stand up and get my hand into the middle of his chest.

"*Get* away from me," I said.

I tried to shove him again, with my palm, but he grabbed my wrist and pulled me close to his face.

"I'll tell you why." His tone was low, too low for anyone beyond the porch to hear him, but if they had, he wouldn't have cared. That was clear in the play of his lips. "I did it to show you that you are never going to change things."

"No you didn't."

At the sound of Kade's voice, Troy loosened his grip enough for me to wrench my hand away. But he still blocked my way, trapping me against the balustrade with his arrogance.

"Why did I do it, then, counselor?" Troy said.

"Because you couldn't stand the thought that anyone could have more power than you do."

Troy put his finger to his lips where the smile still played. "Keep your voice down, son. You don't want the whole town to think your father's a rapist."

"Don't call him son," I said. "He hates that."

Troy gave me a quick look. "You're pretty cavalier about this whole thing, aren't you?"

No. I was trying to keep Kade's pain from exploding from my throat.

"They're going to know anyway," Kade said.

"How so?" Troy said. "If they do charge me, it won't stick."

"Maybe not. But in the meantime, it's going to be all over the newspaper—"

"I own the newspaper—"

"Do you own the broadcast networks? The Internet? Facebook?"

"What about YouTube?" Troy said. "Do you have a clip of the rape you can download?"

"Dear *Lord!*" I said. "Have you completely separated from your soul?"

I tried to lunge past him, to get away before I heard any more. Troy stepped sideways, once more blocking my way.

"You are not going to ruin me by smearing this story all over the social network," Troy said. "You don't have the clout."

Suddenly, out of nowhere, Kade smiled. "I haven't told you about my father—my *real* father—have I? He's the editor of *Fortune 500*. You know? The magazine? Well connected, my dad." He unfolded and held out empty hands. "Do I look like I was raised by a plumber? Not that that would be a bad thing. Matter of fact, it would be a *whole* lot better than being raised by you." The clear eyes bored into Troy. "I thank God I wasn't."

"All right, you've made your point," Troy said.

Kade definitely had. I was close enough to see that despite the shift into his boardroom voice, Troy's face was covered in a fine sheen of perspiration.

"Here's what we'll do," he said, voice still low. "I will vest you in CE—substantially. You can open your own firm, practice any kind of law you want. Pro bono yourself all over town. You'll be a success your old man will be proud of, if, and I say this not as a criticism but as a piece of hard-earned wisdom, if you learn the true art of using your advantage." His eyes hardened into scorn. "Did you seriously think you were going to blackmail me for the rest of my life?"

"What am I, a chump?" Kade said. "I was going to turn you in as soon as the house was in the ministry's name."

"Kade, Kade, Kade." Troy gave him a contemptuous smile. "I'm afraid you've gotten the worse of the two contributors to your gene pool."

"How's that?"

"Don't, Kade," I said. "He's just trying to bait you."

"No, I'm giving some fatherly insights. From me, you inherited your bent for manipulation, though it could use some fine-tuning. Unfortunately, from your mother here, you came by a naive belief that people are essentially good, which will prove your undoing. Especially if you buy into her higher-power bull—"

"Kade—no!"

My cry came too late. Kade was already across the porch, grabbing Troy by the front of his shirt and shoving him into the column. I got hold of one of Kade's arms with both hands, but there was no pulling him off.

"He isn't worth it," I said.

Kade's grip tightened until his hands shook.

"Don't do this to yourself, Kade. I'm serious. Or you're as bad as he is."

"Nobody's as bad as he is," he said.

"Right. So let him go."

Kade released his fingers, but his eyes held on to Troy like a vice.

Troy shook out his shirt and smoothed it with his hand. The smile was gone. Game over.

"Now," he said, "I'm going to go in there and make this whole thing go away, and everybody will eventually be happy. Except maybe you, Ally …"

He gave Kade one last look before he turned to me. His eyes were ruthless.

Pain slammed into my pelvis.

"Yeah. You will just have to live with the fact that I raped your girl."

"Stop," I said.

Troy backed me into the column. "I know you, Ally. It will always be there, eating you up. And there is not one thing you can do about it."

"Maybe she can't. But I can."

Troy didn't move. I turned my head and looked below us. Nicholas Kent stood, face upturned, recorder in hand.

"Let's go, Mr. Irwin," he said.

Troy tried the smile, and it failed. "And where am I going?" he said.

"Down, sir," Nicholas said. "You're going down."

CHAPTER TWENTY

When my doorbell rang the next morning, I didn't want to answer it. I was sure it was Nicholas Kent, come to tell me that I had only imagined the things that happened the night before.

That Ophelia had identified Troy Irwin as the man who raped her.

That he had refused to give a DNA sample, and asked for his attorney and exercised his right to remain silent, even though Nicholas and Kade and I each gave statements about his admission on the station steps, right there between those stately columns.

That when Troy passed me in the hall, flanked by two clones of Clyde Quillon, the indifference in his walk was obscene. Or that when he met me with his eyes for one transparent moment, he showed me our future: If his brittle image shattered, the pain it held back would find its place in me.

It was a prophecy I couldn't deny.

As I ran down the stairs now, tying my bathrobe, I could see through the window that my ungodly hour visitor wasn't Nicholas Kent, but Vickie Rodriguez. That might be even worse. Hank said Vickie wasn't thrilled with my drive-through at the Monk's Vineyard last night. I felt like I was playing one of those stupid arcade games, where every time you hit a gopher with your mallet, another one pops out of a hole. I wasn't even awake enough to consult God yet.

When I opened the door, I was met with probably the largest Easter lily east of the Mississippi. Vickie peeked around it.

"Is this for the grave I'm going to want to crawl into after we have this conversation?" I said.

"Happy Easter to you, too," she said.

"Wait," I said. "It *is* still Saturday, isn't it?"

"Yes. Do I have to wait until Sunday to come in?"

"Sorry," I said. "Come on. I'll make some coffee."

She followed me into the kitchen and put the plant on the bistro table. It made an odd juxtaposition with the empty Oreo package and an equally empty pesto jar.

"Look, I'm sorry about last night," I said. "How do you like your coffee? Strong? Medium?"

"I think you're going to want champagne."

I turned slowly from the coffee canister, scoop in my hand. "Why?" I said.

"I got a call from Clyde Quillon at six a.m. Priscilla Sanborn called *him* at nine thirty last night and said she's dropping the custody suit. She wanted to come by right then and sign the necessary papers."

Nine thirty. Two hours after our confrontation at the Vineyard. The woman wasted no time.

"You don't look surprised," Vickie said. "I was at least expecting the happy dance." She stood facing me at the counter, hands on her negligible hips. "What did you say to her last night?"

"It's more what she said to me." I saw Vickie's eyes narrow. "I didn't threaten her or bribe her or anything."

"That never entered my mind. I just want to know what it felt like to out that little witch."

I spit out a laugh.

"You would have enjoyed the phone call from Quillon," she said while I wiped my saliva from her blouse with a paper towel. "His biggest concern was whether he's still going to get paid."

"That is such a long story. It's like an epic." I tossed the paper towel into the sink and felt my face sober. "What about Judge Atwell? Even with Priscilla gone, he's still worried about whether I'm too crazy to keep Desmond. I may actually *go* nuts if I have to wait until Monday."

"You don't," Vickie said. She nodded at the Easter lily, trying to maintain its dignity amid the common clutter. "I don't bring flowers for nothing."

"What are you saying?"

"The judge made his decision when I called to tell him about Priscilla. He said, and I quote, 'If everybody were as crazy as Allison Chamberlain, this world would be a better place.'"

"He's mine?" I said. "Vickie—Desmond's *mine*?"

She smiled, and for the first time in my relationship with this little mystery of a woman, she looked shy. "I don't know about the world," she said, "but I'm a better person because of you."

"Big Al! You hear that?"

Wearing only a pair of Harley boxers and a T-shirt of Chief's that dropped off one shoulder, Desmond burst from his room and jumped up into the sink to look out the window.

"Morning, Desmond," Vickie said.

"Sorry, I ain't got time, Miss Rutabagas." He smacked his hand happily against the glass and scrambled off the counter, headed for the side door. "It's what I thought!"

I stepped between him and the door and pulled the T-shirt up over his shoulder. "What?" I said.

"It's the Classic, Big Al! It's back!"

There was no keeping him from dodging around me and out onto the porch.

"Stan the Man!" he cried. "You rock!"

"The craziness continues," I said to Vickie.

Still barefoot and swathed in chenille, I picked my way across the gravel to the garage where Stan was leaning a Red Hot Sunglo Heritage Softail Classic on its kickstand. It wasn't my original. She'd suffered fatal injuries. But if Desmond were to tell it, she was Classic reincarnated. For the first time since his accident, I watched him climb onto a motorcycle with his face glowing as only the face of a boy enraptured could do.

"She's all yours, Miss Allison," Stan said. "Ulysses broke it in for you, so you can go right out and ride it like you stole it."

"Imma put my leathers on right now," Desmond said.

"After I have at least three cups of coffee," I said. "You want some, Stan?"

He nodded absently, his gaze on the side porch. "Who's that pretty little thing?"

Vickie was waving from the steps. "Your cell phone's ringing, Allison."

It was Ms. Willa, who had clearly been awake long enough to get the morning grog out of her voice. She was yipping like a bull terrier.

"I want you to come by here this morning," she said. "I'm ready to make you an offer."

"That's … that's great, Ms. Willa," I said, head reeling again. "What time?"

"Now."

I turned to look apologetically at Stan, but he was already on the porch, giving Vickie some of his best stuff.

"Let me just have my coffee," I said to Ms. Willa.

"Coffee's bad for you. You can have tea here. And bring your boy with you. I like that child's attitude."

She made a tiny snarling noise before she hung up. If I wasn't mistaken, Ms. Willa Livengood had just laughed.

Desmond was in his leathers so fast I was sure he had put them right over his boxers. We were looking at a summerlike April day, but he donned gloves and boots and skullcap as if he were afraid one small deviation from the rules would cancel the ride. The coffee never got made. Stan and Vickie left for the Monk's Vineyard to see if George and Gracie had any ready, and if I'd kept Desmond waiting any longer, he might have suffered the first stroke in adolescent history.

Once I fired up Classic Two, the need for caffeine disappeared. She gave me a low, reassuring growl when I rolled the throttle, and her gears clicked under my left foot like the soothing clucks of a mother's tongue. I eased her into the turn off Palm Row and felt Desmond lean with us. We were three-in-one again.

Make that four. Because a Nudge guided us up St. George Street. A hand cool as a salve loosened my shoulders to let me weave us through the flower-lined maze that was the St. Augustine Ms. Willa knew. And a whisper told me, *One ride at a time.*

There was still no buyer for the Second Sacrament House. Still no room for Zelda and Ophelia. Still no wrapping my mind around the appearance of the son I'd given up. No end yet to the battle with the H-word Troy Irwin constantly forced me into. And no assurance that I would be allowed to keep Palm Row. Or Chief.

The hum of the bike beneath me roused the pain of all those things. But the Nudge and the Hand and the Whisper kept me upright, kept the engine's good-natured grumble as my song. For now, for this one ride, I didn't have to be afraid of unexpected dismounts.

Until we rounded the corner into the alley behind Ms. Willa's house, and a large vehicle leaped at us from the other end like a panther lying in wait. I squeezed the front brake before I saw the gravel sprayed across the asphalt. I applied the rear brake, hard, and I might have been able to stop without losing it, but Desmond screamed his chilling nightmare scream, and I jerked the handlebars. As the Harley went into her downward slide, the scene I hadn't been there for flashed behind my eyes.

The driver boring down on my red Classic. Desmond crying out in terror. Chief reacting like the father he was, turning, swerving, losing control …

The car swished past so close its steel brushed my leg. The Classic hurtled into the row of trash cans, and the engine screamed a protest and died as bike and Desmond and I fell against the cans. They clattered across the stones and echoed against the alley walls with the scream, "You can't have me!"

I felt Desmond's hands claw at the back of my jacket and I reached back to grab him—but someone else already had.

With Desmond's screams in my ears, I lashed out at metal and garbage and my own panic and tried to drag myself from under the bike. Pain seared through my left leg, but I yanked at it with both hands. I could only raise my head high enough to see black shoes skidding and grasping for traction and dark hands closing over leather sleeves—and Desmond's body sliding away from me. His legs kicked up from the knees that dragged and bounced across the stone pavement, connecting only with the air.

With the same tortured exhale I screamed, "Let him *go!*" and tore my own leg free. I crawled, trying to get to my feet, but the black shoe smashed into my side and kicked me over onto my back. Just beyond, Desmond's cries were abruptly snuffed out. Mine ripped from my throat.

Somehow above the clamor I heard the hum of the car window lowering. I struggled to get to my feet again, but the pain in my side flattened me back to the stones. I could only lie there as the black tint gave way to a face I'd recoiled at before, just as I did now. A black patch over one eye, the other empty with evil. A forehead misshapen with scars.

"Mama!"

Desmond's voice shot through me, brought me straight up through the pain, hurled me onto the back of the man who was trying to throw my child into a car and take him away. And nobody was taking my baby away.

The man shifted his massive shoulders and shook me off. On the way down I caught a handful of his hair and hung on, but it was slick and I slid away. Free of me, he shoved Desmond's head down and lifted him up by the seat of his leathers.

The monstrous mouth in the back snapped an order I couldn't hear over Desmond, his pitch now so shrill and frantic I could feel his panic in my veins. The man gave a final heave and Desmond was shot across the driver's seat. I heard him crumple into the door on the other side. And then I heard my own body slam into the man's back again, heard my nails scrape down his face, heard him swear—

And then I heard a *crack* that whistled above our heads, above the car, and ricocheted through the alley like a squalling cat.

The man went to the ground. With the last nerve I had left, I crawled over him and hauled Desmond out by his feet until I could get him upright and shove him under my arm, screaming, "*Run!*"

The trash cans ahead were our refuge and I dragged Desmond toward them, sliding and stumbling until I was close enough to push him behind one and throw myself on top of him. Behind us, the car door slammed and the engine tacked up to a livid whine. For a horrified moment I thought it was backing toward us, and I pressed myself into Desmond, my face buried in the back of his glorious head. *Dear God. DearGoddearGoddearGod.*

But the tires screeched their way out of the alley and cried through the maze until all we could hear was a window opening above us. And then a screen creaking out. And a terrier of a voice barking.

"Did I get him?"

I pulled myself off of Desmond and realized I could barely breathe for the pain in my side. But I managed to say, "You just chased him off, Ms. Willa. That's good enough."

"You all right?" she said.

I looked down at Desmond, who turned his face to me and peeled a blackened banana skin from his cheek.

"Are we all right?" I said.

His marvelous lips trembled and his eyes were only a few blinks this side of madness, but he said, "You kicked butt, Big Al."

"Yeah, Ms. Willa," I called to the window. "We're all right."

"Then you better come in here and have some tea and pick up this check."

"We need to call the police," I said.

Her answer was drowned out by the whoop of a siren at the other end of the alley.

Two lanky arms came around me, and a fuzzy head burrowed its way into my neck. "You know somethin', Big Al?" Desmond said.

"What?"

"I think I better get myself baptized."

When the two police officers got to us, they found me laughing big old sobs into my son's hair.

"Why don't you just get a uniform and show up for roll call every-day?" Detective Kylie said to me.

"I don't look good in blue," I said. "Hank, where's Desmond?"

Hank got up from the couch and started for the stairs. "He said he was going to take a shower."

"He's bathing? Did you threaten him?"

Hank's lips twitched at me from the bottom step. "No, I just informed him that he had an eggshell smashed on the back of his neck. He's been in there for thirty minutes."

Detective Kylie looked annoyed. "I just need to ask him some questions."

Hank headed up the stairs, already calling. "Desmond! Let's get the lead out."

I sank back into the red chair and held up my hand to Detective Kylie. I could either talk or breathe, but not both at once.

"What did they say? Broken rib?"

I held up two fingers. "And a messed-up knee. Desmond didn't even get a scratch, which is all I care about."

Kylie looked at his notepad. "What you've told me is pretty much the same as what we've been able to piece together from the first accident."

"You think it was the same driver."

"Same driver, same scenario." Kylie drew his eyebrows in. "Same motorcycle, basically. Same passenger."

I didn't want him to say what I already knew. Maybe coming out of my mouth it wouldn't sound so certain.

"They're after Desmond," I said.

"Were. We picked up the driver out on I-95. He was headin' south." He shrugged. "We have the DNA from the skin under your fingernails. If you can ID him, he's done."

I turned my head and listened. The shower was still running, and Hank was continuing her litany of, "Let's go! You're going to shrivel up in there."

"What about the man in the backseat?" I said.

Kylie shook his head. "No sign of anybody else in the car."

"He rolled down the window. I saw him."

"Rydell claimed he was alone. That was right before he lawyered up. Now he's not saying anything—"

"Rydell?" I said. "Marcus Rydell?"

"I thought you said you didn't know him."

"I don't. I just know *of* him." My mind was spinning. "He rented the car that Zelda supposedly stole and crashed into a pole."

"Who's Zelda?"

I gave Kylie a hard look. "She's the woman who was obviously set up by the same people who just tried to run me down and take my kid. You need to let her ID him too. "

"Just for the record, only one person tried to run you down."

"So … I was hallucinating about the man in the backseat," I said. "People are lining up to report that I'm crazy."

Kylie sighed. "Can you describe him?"

"I can do better than that. I can show you his picture. But you have to promise me one thing."

"Why not? I feel like I'm working for you anyway."

"Swear that you won't mention this in front of Desmond. He doesn't know this person was in the car, and I want to keep it that way."

Cringing at the pain, I reached under the chair cushion and pulled out Desmond's drawing. Its days under the weight of my angsting and praying had left it smooth except for the flattened wrinkle-scars of Desmond's attempt to forget.

I handed the drawing to Kylie, and waited for the smirk, the eye roll, at the very least the patronizing *We'll look into it.* I didn't care. I had to take it as far as I could, or Desmond's nightmare was never going to be over.

But Detective Kylie looked at me with perhaps the first authentic expression I had ever seen on his face.

"This looks like Jude Lowery," he said.

"Jude Low—*Sultan?*" I moved from Kylie's startled gaze to the eye patch and the hideous head. "No. No, I've seen Sultan. This isn't him."

"When did you see him?"

"The night he was killed."

"Before that?"

"I only saw him the once."

"Well, I've spent most of the last fifteen years of my career studying his face in photographs and staring at him across interrogation tables and watching him in court." He tapped the drawing with the back of his hand. "He's looking a little the worse for wear, but—"

"Worse for wear! The man is dead."

"Do you know that? Because I never saw his body. Neither did the coroner." He let the drawing drop to the ottoman between us. "Looks like he's lost an eye. Has some scars he didn't have before. Typical injuries for a man who's been shot in the head and lived to get his revenge."

"On Desmond? He had nothing to do with Sultan being shot."

"No," Kylie said, "but you did."

I gripped the back of my neck. "This is absurd. There was enough blood in that parking lot to prove he couldn't possibly have lived."

"And yet his biological son drew *this.*"

"From the nightmares he's been having, yes."

"Sultan didn't look like this before he was shot. You said that yourself."

"You're saying he's *seen* him?"

"How else would he know what he looked like now?"

"But if Sultan wanted to get back at me, why not just shoot me in the alley? Why try to take Desmond?"

He didn't have to answer. I knew from the place in my soul that wouldn't have survived if that car had driven off with my son in it.

I reached across the ottoman, ribs on fire, tendons screaming, and grabbed the detective by the rolled-up sleeve of his shirt.

"You cannot breathe a word of this to Desmond. Please. He can't know."

He paused for too long. I tightened my grip.

"I'd like to know where he saw Sultan," Kylie said. "We could get some kind of clue to where he's staying, how he's operating."

"I can tell you that," I said. "I admit it's a guess, but just hear me out."

Kylie nodded me on.

I closed my eyes and watched the pieces move together, forming the picture Desmond had been drawing for us. Then I opened my mouth and shaped it into words.

Desmond coming back more than once from lunch recess to Miss O'Hare's class, shaken and distracted, one day too terrified to take his history test. Desmond doing a caricature to manage the fear of a man in a car with tinted windows, a man whose threats were spoken in the screams of his nightmares. Desmond being far less frightened of being taken by Priscilla Sanborn than by this man who had come back from the dead.

Until the day he and Chief set out on my bike. Until he thought the accident was his fault, not because he distracted Chief but because he knew the black car with the tinted windows. Because he knew it was after him.

How had he survived these last weeks? Afraid Chief would remember, afraid to go to school because the car might be there at recess, afraid to get on a motorcycle because it might come after him again?

"Today he wasn't afraid to ride with me, though."

"The stalking must have stopped as long as your bike wasn't on the road," Kylie said. "But he didn't put that together."

"Sultan knows where I live. He could have come in here and kidnapped Desmond any time, right out from under my nose."

Detective Kylie fanned the pages of his notepad.

"What?" I said.

"This guy is a psychopath. He wants it his way or no way, and his way is so twisted you and I can never understand it, much less come up with it. He wanted it the way it was supposed to go down this morning."

I pulled my good leg up to my chest. "They were waiting for us in that alley," I said. "How did Sultan know that was where we were going?"

"Have you been there before?" he said.

"Yeah, a few times."

"Were you ever followed there?"

I caught my breath.

"I'll venture to say they watched you. When you headed out in that direction today, on your bike, with Desmond, all the conditions were right. They probably took an educated guess and got there before you. If you hadn't shown up, no problem. They could try again later."

"What if they do try again later? What's to keep Sultan from getting another driver?"

"Best-case scenario? Word gets out that we're onto him and he'll be hard put to find somebody to chauffeur him around. He's powerful, but he's getting less so all the time. If he can't get out there and muscle people anymore, no one's going to put their life on the line for him. Especially the caliber of the loser we picked up today. Rydell didn't have the brains to tell the difference between you and Jack Ellington on a motorcycle. I'm thinking now they would have grabbed Desmond the day of the accident if they hadn't realized you weren't there."

I searched Kylie's face. "Do you really believe that? Because if you don't, I have to take Desmond and move somewhere else."

I shook my head and buried it between my hands as I choked on the pain.

"I believe it," he said. The gruffness softened. "I think you ought to tell him, so he can report to you if he sees anything. He's going to need protection until we nab Lowery."

I brought my head up. "I don't want him living like he has a specter chasing him."

"Maybe he does."

"Then, please, let me take it on."

A door opened upstairs, and Desmond's voice filled the stairwell.

"I ain't got time for a buncha questions," he was saying to Hank. "I got to go get baptized."

Detective Kylie turned toward the stairs.

"Please," I whispered.

Desmond appeared, swaggering and working his eyebrows and otherwise thinly veiling the apprehension I saw lurking.

"We got to make this fast," he said. "They's stuff I gotta do."

Please. Please.

Detective Kylie stood up. "Y'know, your mom's given me every-thing I need. You're off the hook."

Desmond eyed him. "For now?"

"Forever, unless you get yourself in trouble."

"Oh, now don't even be thinkin' that. I don't do the T-word."

Kylie looked at me.

"Trouble," I said. "But I will call you, detective, if I find any more of my Oreos missing."

"I didn't eat alla them, now. Miss Rutabagas done ate her share."

"I'm not even going to ask," Detective Kylie said.

I must have talked to everyone I knew in the next two hours. Various HOGs called to tell me they'd seen Troy making his statement to the press in front of the police station, saying he had compassion for the disturbed individual who had set out to frame him. India came by with an envelope from Ms. Willa, who couldn't get it to me when I was surrounded by sirens and paramedics. Ophelia, India said, was vulnerable, but she'd be there to watch the baptism. Lewis phoned to say he had his letter to the editor drafted; George chuckled in the background. Bonner came by on his way to set up for the Sisters' baptisms—and now Desmond's.

He had Zelda with him.

We didn't have much time to talk. They were on a mission to get flowers and I could only get a promise of five minutes out of Bonner as he lured Desmond into the kitchen in search of

Pop-Tarts. We spent the first thirty seconds stumbling over each other's sentences.

"I'm sorry, Miss Angel—"

"Did I push you too hard, Zelda—"

Finally, I grabbed both of her hands and looked as far as I could into that small, straining face.

"We have plenty of time to help each other heal," I said. "But there are two things I need to know."

She nodded.

"Did you steal that car?" I said.

She looked away. "I can't tell you that, Miss Angel."

"Why?"

"'Cause I don't wanna go back to jail."

"You're not going back to jail. This is between you and me."

She gave me a long look before she said, "I drove it 'cause Marcus tol' me to. He said it was his, only I knew it wasn't, so that's the same as stealin' and I know it."

"You knew Marcus Rydell?"

"Me and him was livin' together 'fore I come to Sacrament House. He's the one done throwed me out so I didn't have no place else to go."

She tried to pull her hands away but I held on.

"This is your chance to get it out," I said. "Get it out and give it up or you will wind up back in jail."

"I knew it was stupid, goin' back to him when I lef' the House that day. I didn't even mean to do it. He just saw me walkin' down King Street and picked me up. I didn't even know he still around."

"And he had those expensive drugs," I said.

"That's not why I went with him." She shook her head, a thin sheen in her eyes that she tried to blink away. "It was that car. I always liked me a fine car."

"The one you wrecked."

"No. Not that one. This one a black Lincoln, almost like a limousine." Zelda shook her head again, this time as if to muddy the thoughts within.

"Keep going," I said.

"I can't, Miss Angel! Just like I couldn't that day at the police station when I did everything I could to get you outta there so you wouldn't aks me these questions!"

It was my turn to blink.

"I didn't mean none of what I said. I just wanted you to get outta my face, and that was the only way I knew how."

"Yeah, well, it's not working, is it?" I said.

She closed her eyes.

"That's it. Look at it. You need to do this."

"I thought Marcus done struck it rich, but he just drivin' that limo for Satan. That's who give me the drugs, tol' me I'd forget all about you and my old life and—"

"Satan? Was that his name, or—"

"That's what Marcus always call him, but not to his face. He don't really have much face. Marcus said he got messed up in a shootin' or somethin'. I don' know. He knew him before. I didn't know him then and I don't wanna know him now." Zelda shuddered. "That's all I can do right now, Miss Angel. I'll do more later, I promise. But Miss Liz say I don't got to do it all at once."

"Miss Liz has got it going on," I said. "We're good, Zelda. And thank you."

"What's the other thing?"

"I'm sorry?"

"The other thing you wanted to aks me. You said there was two things."

I let go of her hands and wiped mine on my shorts. "I just need to know if you'll help Ophelia."

"That girl got raped?" Zelda said.

"Yeah."

"You want *me* to help her?"

"I think you can."

"Why?"

"Because you two have a lot in common."

Zelda pulled in her chin. "She way more high class than me, Miss Angel. You should be the one to help her."

"No, see, that I learned from you," I said.

"Whachoo learn from me?"

"That I'm not the only one who can help. Besides, it's all God anyway."

I waited and watched.

"Maybe it is," she said.

That had to be good enough. For now.

So the only two people I didn't hear from that day were Kade and Chief.

Chief had left the station with Ulysses and Stan the night before without a word to me. I was left to wonder what things he'd warned me he was going to explain to me. Maybe I didn't want to know. Maybe I never would.

As for Kade, he'd disappeared after he was questioned about Troy. I didn't ask anyone else about him or Chief. I was too afraid of the answers, and God's only input was the empty ache that made it hard to get out of the chair after Zelda left.

I realized as I sat there that I hadn't opened the envelope from Ms. Willa. If the check was enough for at least a down payment on the second house, that would be a good thing, yes, God?

But there was only a letter folded into the envelope, written in Ms. Willa's own hand, by the looks of it. There weren't that many flourishes at the bottom of the Declaration of Independence. *Dear Spunky Allison*, she'd written.

> *I've thought long and hard about this. Every time I've come to a decision about what I wanted to donate for your young women, and why I wanted to do it, you've given me a shake and I've had to rethink. At my age, you can't count on waking up for another day of thinking, so my decision is now final. I will not be giving you money for a house.*

I tried not to feel like I'd just been blindsided by a buffalo, and then decided I had a right to. How many times had this woman invited me in for tea and a donation and sent me home empty-handed? And I was rattling *her* cage? I almost crumpled the paper.

Except that there was the whole business of her saving my life. And Desmond's.

Yeah. She'd given me enough.

So I went back to the page for the sign-off. But there was more.

> *I've taken your policy to heart, and I agree that these women need to do the work of getting back on their feet themselves. Here is what I propose. I will purchase a building on St. George Street that is currently owned, and just barely, by some old friends of mine. They call it the Monk's Vineyard or some such nonsense. I told them years ago it would never fly. You and your women can start a business there, perhaps two, one upstairs, one down. I'll provide you with the capital for the first five years. I trust by then you'll have everybody off the streets.*
>
> *I look forward to watching this grow, Spunky Allison. I'll expect you for tea weekly.*

She signed it, *Yours very truly, Willa Renfroe Livengood.*

At least I thought that was how she signed it. I couldn't see it through the blur.

"You cryin', Big Al?"

I looked up at Desmond. He had put on clean jeans and a T-shirt with no writing on it and a plain metal cross on a leather cord I had never seen before.

"Where did you get that?" I said.

"Mr. Chief gave it to me," he said.

"When?"

"That day we was washin' everybody's feet."

"O-kay," I said. "Did he tell you why?"

"Yes."

"Any particular reason why I haven't seen you wear it before?"

He couldn't quite contain a small smile. "You gotta wait to hear that, Big Al. You and Mr. Chief are gonna be sur*prised.*"

I closed my eyes and massaged my temples. "Listen, Des, I haven't heard from Chief today. I don't know if he's coming. I mean, he doesn't even know you decided to be baptized."

"'Course he does. I called him." Desmond let the smile go all the way across his face. "He tol' me he wouldn't miss it for nothin'."

I blamed my shakiness on the broken ribs and the torn leg and the crutches I had to hobble out on when Owen escorted us to his car to drive us to Sacrament House. In truth, every wobble and quiver came from the wavering between dreading and hoping.

"Ally, I think you need to retire that motorcycle. You're like a poodle on a circus bike with that thing. You're like—"

"Owen," I said, "stop. Seriously. Just stop."

He didn't look at all offended. In fact he smiled like the proverbial canary-swallowing cat as he settled me in the backseat with my crutches and checked Desmond's seat belt three times in the front before Desmond said, "If it get any tighter Imma choke, Mr. Schatzie."

When we pulled out of Palm Row, Owen was still beaming at me in the rearview mirror.

"All right, I give up," I said. "Give me the rest of the metaphors. I can handle it."

"Metaphors? No, I'm smiling because I bought something today."

"You gettin' a Harley, Mr. Schatzie?" Desmond said. "Cool, dude! You got to let me pick out the color. You got to get you one of them hot paint jobs—"

"Des," I said. "Mr. Schatz isn't buying a Harley. You're *not,* are you?" Come to think of it, the man would do just about anything for Desmond.

"No. I bought a house."

"What's wrong with the one you got?" Desmond said. I saw his head extend over the top of the seat. "You ain't movin'? Mr. Schatzie, you can't be movin', now."

"It's a second house," Owen said with exaggerated patience. "In fact, that's what I think it should be called: the Second Sacrament House."

"I don't get it," Desmond said.

"Owen?" I said.

"I had breakfast with Bonner Bailey this morning and made him my offer. I buy the house and donate it to your ministry you have going, and you don't sell your house." Owen pulled up to the light at St. George and King and flashed his dentures again into the rearview. "He thought you'd agree to that."

"Oh, Owen …"

"You think that's a yes?" he said to Desmond.

"I think that's a 'I'm fixin' to cry so don't ask me no more questions till I get myself back together.' And then she usually say yes after that."

"Well, that's a good thing, because we're headed for that new house right now."

"What about my baptism?" Desmond said.

"Like I said, that's where we're headed."

When we turned onto San Luis, cars lined the street on both sides. Owen drove all the way down to the other end of the block before he concluded there were no more parking places.

"I'll turn around and drop you off," he said as he pulled into the deserted construction site on the corner. "Then I'll see if I can't find a space over on—"

I didn't hear the rest of his plan. A figure had caught my eye, someone standing beneath the skeletal framework of a building yet to be, hands in his pockets.

"Let me out here, Owen," I said.

He stopped the car and looked at me yet again in the rearview mirror. "I'm not going to have you going all the way down this street on crutches."

"You can wait for me, then," I said. "There's somebody I need to talk to."

I refused his attempt to help me out and got the crutches untangled and under my arms. I heard him back the car out as I swung my way to Garry Howard.

He didn't look up until I had almost reached him. A shock of white hair fell over his forehead, but it didn't conceal the deep lines in his brow. I'd never seen the Reverend look unkempt and vulnerable. I almost wished I'd cleared my throat to give him a chance to recover his dignity. That must be why Bonner always did it.

"Are you here to say I told you so?" he said.

"No," I said. "I'm just … here."

He gave me a frail glance and returned his gaze to the half-framed structure. "I had a vision," he said.

"I know about those."

"Not just for the school. For Troy."

"I'm sorry?" I said.

"I always thought I could get through to him somehow, help him be a better man. He did so much for us, I thought I could do that for him. I knew he had his flaws, but I thought I saw good." The Reverend Garry bowed his head. "Foolish," he said.

"I can tell you that there was good, once," I said. "But evil cut to the root of the good somewhere along the line, and the flaw became tragic."

"You were wiser than I was."

"I didn't come up with that. Anything remotely coherent that comes out of me is all God."

I waited for the frown. The Bible quote. The insistence that if I would only come to church, I could be healed of such blasphemy.

He only gazed up again. I could feel the hurt etched in the long creases of his face.

"I don't know what to tell my church," he said. "They had such high hopes."

"Tell them you feel God's pain for Troy."

He looked at me, startled.

"As long as we can still feel God's pain," I said, "there's still hope for the church."

"Big Al!"

I looked behind me at Desmond, who was hanging halfway out of the car window.

"I got to go get *bap*tized!"

"There's still hope, Garry," I whispered.

I left him staring at his broken vision.

It wasn't until Owen dropped us off in front of Sacrament House that I saw everyone was gathered not there, but across the street. Old Maharry Nelson, Bonner and Liz, India and Hank, Nita and Leighanne, and the man-HOGs in leathers had formed a circle on the front lawn. Ophelia sat willowy and quiet on a lawn chair. Zelda was beside her, looking awkward and dutiful. Hank was there too, whisking Desmond into the house that I could only stare at.

Blossoms of freesia and pinks festooned the porch railings and trailed down either side of the front path as if they'd been dropped there by frolicking flower girls. The late afternoon light made pink shafts across the communion table on the porch and cast the long playful shadows of my family on the grass.

"Hobble on over here, Al," Hank said from the steps. "A little help, yes?"

"You don't have to carry me," I said to the platoon of HOGs who mobilized outside the car. "Seriously, guys."

There was no stopping them. I was all but CareFlighted up the drive and inserted into a lounge chair. When they stepped away, I saw the pond.

Someone had scrubbed the slimy green into smooth white stone; that action had Mercedes's MO all over it. Fungus-less water, rosy with sunset, filled the pond to its flower-lined brim, and beside it—a Tupperware pitcher, and a neatly folded pile of Harley-Davidson beach towels.

"Oh, my loves, a footwashing," I said.

"No, Miss Angel," India said. "A baptism."

She nodded toward the front door, where four figures emerged, each in a black swimsuit that covered her cleavage and her midriff and every other part of her she had once shared with whoever would pay to touch it.

Mercedes, stately as a queen.

Jasmine, eyes lustrous, without a tear in sight.

Sherry, milky white. Pure.

And Desmond. Clad in black swim trunks and T-shirt and the cross Chief had given him, shed of the swagger and the fist bumps, but fully clothed in the shine of his latte skin.

From his black mama. And his white one.

The Sisters and their Brother knelt around the pond. Hank stood in it, shin deep, and invited each in her turn to join her. Each set herself on her knees in the water and bowed her head, while Hank poured from the pitcher, in the name of the Father. And of the Son. And of the Holy Spirit, whose presence whispered in the water and the light and the very air we breathed.

I listened with ears to hear as each of the Sisters touched us with her faith ... "I feel like my past been finally washed away ..." "I ain't jus' clean and sober—I'm clean and saved ..." "I'm free. That's all—I'm free."

But when Desmond came up sputtering from dunking his whole head into the water, I could hear him with my very soul.

"I didn't believe in no God when me and my first mama was on the street," he said. "And then I did, 'cause of Big Al, and it seem like, okay, you believe and all this good stuff happen to you. I asked Mr. Chief, though—"

Desmond turned, still standing in the water, covered in goose-flesh, and my heart sank. He was looking for Chief ...

Who was, indeed, there, parked in his wheelchair. With Kade at the helm.

"... 'cause I like to run everything by him, and he give me this cross to wear so when any *bad* stuff happen, I'd remember and still believe. Only, bad stuff did happen, real bad stuff, and I didn't never wear it 'cause it didn't stop more bad from goin' down. That's when I tol' Big Al I wasn't havin' no baptism." He paused for a second. Even my Desmond had to stop for a breath now and then. "They was always talkin' about Jesus dyin' for us and savin' us, and I didn't see no Jesus dyin' for *me* and savin' *my*—behind." His grin for me was brief, before he swallowed and worked that troublesome Adam's apple I loved so much. "Then today, I seen him. Not *him*—but I seen Big Al almost dyin' to save me, even though I steal her Oreos and don't tell her stuff, even though she already knows it, and it was like *seein'* Jesus. And I knew I had to get me some a that."

Just as she had done for each of the Sisters, India wrapped a towel around his shoulders and kissed one cheek, and then the other. That holy kiss that no one could give like India.

On the other side of them Kade stood behind Chief. The fading light erased the edges of the handsome man-features, softening his face into a little boy's. A little boy not sure he should join in. The little boy I didn't raise.

By my own choice. A choice that had made deceivers out of both of us.

Kade must have felt me watching because his eyes shifted from Desmond to me.

I'm sorry, they said.

Me, too, mine said. *Me, too.*

"Time to party!"

Mercedes gave Desmond's soggy Afro a smack. "We gon' have communion, boy."

"That's what I jus' said. Time to party."

The group moved to the porch, where India was already lighting the candles of the Easter Even vigil to follow. Sherry knelt beside my chair.

"I'll help you up there," she said. "You need to stop banging yourself up, girl."

I put my hand on her shoulder and pulled her toward me. "You heard how it happened," I said.

"Some loser with a rap sheet tried to mow you and Desmond down."

"It was Sultan, Sherry."

Panic shot through her eyes. "Sultan's dead."

"We don't know that anymore."

"*I* know it."

"How?" I said. "How is it that you know?"

"I told you before—just leave it alone."

"I can't anymore."

I tilted my chin toward the porch, where Desmond was hanging one lanky arm around Liz Doyle's neck and telling Stan the Man, "You can have bread, dude. Ain't nobody here cut outta the body a Christ."

Sherry's face paled, until I could almost see through her to the scene she was once more burying.

"Do what you have to do, Miss Angel," she said.

She got to her feet and went to join the others at the table. The fear had returned to her steps.

"Desmond says he's going to stay up all night for the vigil."

Chief eased his wheelchair over the tufts of grass and stopped beside me. I couldn't look at him.

"He'll be asleep the first hour, guaranteed," I said.

"Classic."

"Yeah."

I imagined him tilting his head, creasing the tiny lines, looking through me the way only this man I loved could do. But I couldn't make myself turn around and see it, and not be able to touch it.

"We're a pair to draw to," he said.

When I opened my eyes, he was so close his breath warmed my face. "If it comes to it, we can fight this out with our crutches."

"*What,* Chief?" I said. "What are we even doing?"

"You know what you're doing. You always do. I only know what I *want* to do."

"Then why don't you just do it?"

"Because I can't put you in that position with God."

Chief put two fingers on my chin and nudged my face toward the street. "Do you see that, down on the corner?"

All I saw at first was the skeleton of the school, now cast in black by the last of the sunset. As I looked, Garry Howard's form took shape. He was still standing at the curb.

"The good reverend is looking at the position he's in," Chief said. "I can't put you there."

"Garry Howard didn't go to God with his decision to accept

money from Troy Irwin. That's the position he's in." I turned back to Chief's breath. "I'm not there, and you can't take me there. I can't stop heeding the Nudges and listening to the whispers and paying attention to the pain. God won't let me."

"So is God going to let you be with a man who didn't get in the pond?"

"Would that be the God you told Desmond he should believe in?"

"The God I want to believe in."

I couldn't breathe. But I could say, "All we can do is ask him."

"How do we do that?"

I moved closer, close enough to make it safe to close my eyes. I felt Chief's hands in my hair and his breath on my mouth. And his kiss in my soul.

"Nudge?" Chief said into my lips.

"No," I said. "Just joy."

From the porch, Hank called out, "The Lord be with you."

I put my hands on Chief's, which were still holding my face. "And also with you," I said.

You would think as a prophet, I'd know what God was doing with me.

For that moment at least, I did.

... a little more ...

When a delightful concert comes to an end,

the orchestra might offer an encore.

When a fine meal comes to an end,

it's always nice to savor a bit of dessert.

When a great story comes to an end,

we think you may want to linger.

And so, we offer ...

AfterWords—just a little something more after you

have finished a David C Cook novel.

We invite you to stay awhile in the story.

Thanks for reading!

Turn the page for ...

- **Discussion Questions**
- **More about the Nudge**

Discussion Questions

The following are a few thoughts to spur discussion with fellow readers or simply to ponder on your own. Should your conversation lead to questions for *me,* I would love to hear from you at nancy@nancyrue.com.

- Before I start to write a novel, I always form the question I hope to answer in the course of the story. The question for *Unexpected Dismounts* was, to put it in Allison's terms: *Now that I've found Jesus and know what to do with him, how do I know what Jesus is doing with* **me?** After reading the book, what do you think is the answer to that question—not only for Allison, but for you?

- I also have a key word—a mustard seed, if you will—from which the story grows. The word this time was *feeling,* which seems sort of vague until you think about it in terms of Allison's having to feel something of what God feels in order to deepen her perceptions of what truly needs to be done. Do you think she got there? Do you ever get the sense that you and God are sharing an emotion?

- And then of course there's the scriptural basis, which was pretty much a no-brainer for this book:

> *Now that I, your Lord and Teacher, have washed your feet, you also should wash one another's feet. I have set*

you an example that you should do as I have done for you." (John 13:14–15)

◻ How do you see that applying to

- Allison

- Chief

- The Sacrament Sisters

- India

- Officer Kent

- Anyone else in the story

- Got any footwashing you need to do?

◻ The whole bathing of one another's feet in obedience to Jesus' instruction can be quite lovely on a Maundy Thursday evening. But when you go beyond the ritual and into the real dirt and grime of self-sacrifice, it's a whole other thing. When does the nitty-gritty of it get to Allison? Force her to make tough decisions? Did you ever doubt that she'd go through with it? How about you? Are you backing off from the dirty water and the bunions at all? I gotta tell you, Allison convicted *me* on a few things …

◻ This is a trilogy, which means there are still threads left to be tied up in book three, *Too Far to Say Far Enough*. Any thoughts on how Allison and Kade's relationship will develop? How Allison and Chief will work out the faith issues that stand between them? What Desmond will be like as he turns into a teenager? What will go down with Troy now that the whole town knows he's been a person of interest in a rape case? How the whole Sultan thing will be resolved? Will Allison return to the church? What's next for the Sacrament Sisters? I'd be fascinated to know your thoughts, so don't be shy about using that email address.

¤ Beyond just plot development, what thoughts linger now that you've finished reading *Unexpected Dismounts?* Have you felt the Nudge recently? Have you counted the cost of heeding it? Do you share the quite valid fears of characters like Ms. Willa, India, and Reverend Garry Howard? Zelda? Ophelia? Are there baby steps you could take to conquer those?

¤ And about those unexpected dismounts … which ones in your life have affected you the most? Is it time to get back on and ride?

The Nudge

The whole concept of being Nudged by God to do something you obviously didn't think up yourself has grown into more than a premise for a series of novels. Together with other Nudgees, I've formed a blog community called "The Nudge" (what else?), where we share the pokes and wild dreams and impossible projects we strongly suspect are coming from God. Please join us at www.tweenyouandme.typepad.com/the_nudge. You can also find me on Facebook (www.facebook.com/nnrue) and Twitter (@nnrue).

My Latest Nudge

If you would like to go deeper in discovering what your Nudges from God might mean for your journey, one or more of the following might be options for you:

- Skype session or conference call for your book club or women's group. Send me an email at nancy@nancyrue.com.
- Curriculum guides for six-week studies of *The Reluctant Prophet* and *Unexpected Dismounts* suitable for women's groups and adaptable for individual use. Download free of charge at www.nancyrue.com.
- I am available to lead women's retreats related to the novels. Find more details at www.nancyrue.com. Click on Events.
- Learn more about my books and other resources for teens at www.facebook.com/nnrueforteens.